# Praise for Iris Johansen's Eve Duncan Novels

## *Shadow Play*

"Johansen delivers a no-holds-barred mystery that maintains suspense throughout and boasts a cast of multifaceted characters." —*Publishers Weekly*

"Thrilling, emotional, and downright riveting certainly sum up this incredible tale!" —*RT Book Reviews*

"Eve Duncan novels by Johansen are so good that, supernatural or not, readers and fans remain completely engaged." —*Suspense Magazine*

## *Your Next Breath*

"A perfect storm of a thriller! Johansen never disappoints." —*RT Book Reviews* (4½ stars)

"Gripping . . . Iris Johansen's talent in character development, impeccable plotting, and remarkable depiction is nonpareil." —*Reader to Reader*

## *Silencing Eve*

"Johansen brings her tautly paced trilogy to a pulse-pounding conclusion." —*Booklist*

## *Hunting Eve*

"Building to a shocking conclusion, [this] thriller will have fans of Eve's exploits clamoring for the trilogy's final installment." —*Booklist*

"Gut-wrenching . . . Readers barely get a chance to breathe as the action moves from the peril Eve faces to the desperate lengths her friends and family are prepared to go to save her. Vintage Johansen!"
—*RT Book Reviews* (Top Pick, 4 stars)

### Taking Eve

"Johansen expertly ratchets up the suspense as the action builds to a riveting conclusion."
*Publishers Weekly*

"Keeping a long-running series both intriguing and suspenseful is no easy task, but superstar Johansen makes it look that way as she kicks off another trilogy. Johansen never misses!"  —*RT Book Reviews* (4 stars)

"A successful Johansen novel, filled with intriguing twists and characters and an overarching mystery that will keep fans coming back for Book 2."
—*Kirkus Reviews*

### Eve

"Johansen launches a trilogy that takes the reader on an action-packed journey filled with killers and heroes, leaving readers on tenterhooks."  —*Booklist*

"Gripping . . . Johansen deftly baits the hook for the next volume."  —*Publishers Weekly*

"The suspense and action will entertain all, even those new to the series."  —*Library Journal* (starred review)

"Read *Eve* and be hooked."          —*RT Book Reviews*

### Quinn

"The pulse-pounding pace will leave readers breathlessly anticipating the final installment."

          —*Publishers Weekly* (starred review)

"Awesome!"          —*RT Book Reviews*

"Suspenseful and entertaining . . . an integral read for fans."          —*Library Journal*

"Johansen's latest has myriad twists and turns . . . ideal."

          —*Booklist*

### Bonnie

"A stunning finale that will move series fans and newcomers alike."          —*Publishers Weekly* (starred review)

"Johansen conducts a nail-biting excursion through madness and physical endurance in this stunning conclusion to a very popular trilogy."          —*Booklist*

# ALSO BY IRIS JOHANSEN

# NO EASY TARGET

## IRIS JOHANSEN

St. Martin's Paperbacks

This is a work of fiction. All of the characters, organizations, and events portrayed in this novel are either products of the author's imagination or are used fictitiously.

NO EASY TARGET

Copyright © 2017 by IJ Development, Inc.
Excerpt from *Mind Game* copyright © 2017 by IJ Development, Inc.

For information address St. Martin's Press, 175 Fifth Avenue, New York, NY 10010.

ISBN: 978-1-250-07591-8

Our books may be purchased in bulk for promotional, educational, or business use. Please contact your local bookseller or the Macmillan Corporate and Premium Sales Department at 1-800-221-7945, ext. 5442, or by e-mail at MacmillanSpecialMarkets@macmillan.com.

Printed in the United States of America

St. Martin's Press hardcover edition / April 2017
St. Martin's Paperbacks edition / October 2017

St. Martin's Paperbacks are published by St. Martin's Press, 175 Fifth Avenue, New York, NY 10010.

10  9  8  7  6  5  4  3  2  1

# NO EASY TARGET

# CHAPTER ONE

San Diego Zoo

*Not mine!*

*Don't get angry.* Margaret Douglas tried to make the thought soothing. But there was little you could do to soothe a female tiger as bad-tempered as Zaran. Margaret had only just forged the link between them and it would take time and patience to influence her. Even now the Sumatran tigress was baring those sharp white teeth and glaring menacingly at her. She was probably not going to listen. *I'm just asking you to consider that the cub might be your own. Everyone here at the zoo appears to think so.*

*Stupid. Not mine.*

Margaret tried something else. *Let me try to help you remember when the cub was born. It might—*

*NOT MINE!*

The thought was immediately followed by a roar. The tigress's green eyes were blazing as she gathered the muscles in her powerful body and then bounded at top speed across the cage toward Margaret!

Zaran's lunge just missed Margaret as she dove out of the cage and slammed the gate behind her.

Margaret drew a deep breath as she got to her feet and stared back at the roaring tiger through the bars.

Close. Very close.

*Not polite, Zaran. I'm just trying to help.*

The tigress was still pawing through the bars at her. *Stupid!*

"What the hell are you doing?" One of the zookeepers was striding toward Margaret. "You volunteers are supposed to feed and water the animals, not get them all upset."

He evidently hadn't seen her in the cage, thank heavens. "The tigers are a little testy, aren't they?" She smiled. "I wasn't feeding her. I was just thinking about cleaning her cage. Maybe I'll wait for a while."

"You shouldn't be near her anyway. Why do you think she's not in the habitat? The vets are having problems with her. She's not been accepting her cub."

"Right. Sorry." She started to walk toward the road. "I'll go help out at the vets clinic instead."

She glanced back over her shoulder at the tigress. *But think about it, Zaran. I'll get back to you later.*

*Not mine!*

*We'll see. . . .*

Not exactly a successful session with the tigress, she thought ruefully as she paused to get a Coke at a refreshment stand. But no one else at the zoo had gotten any response at all and they might give up soon. She couldn't let that happen. It would have a lifetime of consequences for that cub. She would just have to let Zaran settle down and then go back later and try again.

Her phone was vibrating in her pocket and she vaguely remembered it also doing that when she'd been in the cage with the tigress. Not surprising that she hadn't paid any attention to it.

She pulled it out and checked it.

A text from Eve Duncan.

CALL ME.

She smiled as she dropped down on one of the green park benches at the side of the road. She hadn't talked to Eve in too long a time. Eve could be demanding, too, when it suited her, but she was one of Margaret's few friends. And she'd much rather try to soothe Eve than that tigress. She started to dial Eve's number at the lake cottage.

"No arguments, Margaret," Eve Duncan said firmly after making her wishes known. "I want you here at the lake cottage by the end of the week. I'm going to pre-pay an airline ticket to Atlanta for you, and Joe will pick you up at the airport. I'd do it, but I don't want to expose Michael to some of those germs floating around airports."

"And you can't bear to leave the baby yet," Margaret teased. "How old is he? Six months?"

"Six months going on six years," Eve said softly. "He's totally amazing, Margaret. You'll see when you get here. Yes, I'm besotted, but at least I'm trying to expose him to other people and experiences. That's why I'm demanding your presence. He should get to know my friend Margaret, who helped saved both my life and his big sister Cara's. How soon can you get here? What are you doing now?"

"I'm working at the San Diego Zoo. But it's mostly volunteer." She thought about it. "Four days' notice. But you don't have to buy me a ticket. I know a pilot for a movie company who has a studio in Atlanta whom I can hitch a ride—"

"No," Eve said immediately. "No hitching rides with anyone. Not safe. Joe lectured you about that the last time." She paused. "Is it that you don't have ID in your own name to get on a commercial plane?"

"Don't worry about it. This pilot is a good guy and he owes me for—"

"Hush, Margaret," Eve said resignedly. "Under what name should I buy this ticket? And don't give me any bull about it not being necessary. Someday I'm going to persuade you to tell me what's going on with you, but I owe you too much to force it right now. I just want you here to meet my son. What name?"

Eve wasn't going to be dissuaded. Oh, well, she really wanted to see Eve's baby. She'd find a way to reimburse her later for the airline ticket. "I've always liked the name Margaret Rawlins."

"You've got it," Eve said. "It will be at Delta Airlines in four days." She was silent an instant. "Everything okay with you, Margaret?"

"Everything's always okay with me. What could be wrong?"

"That's what I want to know. You're the closest thing to a Gypsy that I've ever met and you're always operating under the radar. Put those two things together and it usually spells trouble."

"Not for me. It's all in the attitude. I'll see you in a few days, Eve."

"Yeah, take care, Margaret." She hung up.

And I'll probably be bombarded with subtle and not-so-subtle questions when I reach the lake cottage, she thought as she hung up. No problem. She was used to fielding questions, and Eve would be so involved with that new baby and her career as a top forensic sculptor that she wouldn't press it too far.

Baby.

That reminded Margaret of Zaran and the brand-new tiger cub. She needed to find a solution on how to make the tigress accept the cub before she left for Atlanta. Which meant she should get working on it right now. If she couldn't work out the problem with a few suggestions to the vet about the way to handle it, she might have to pull an all-nighter on her own. Tigers were never easy. Females were twice as difficult when they were as unstable as Zaran.

So get moving so that she could finish her job before she left to go to see Eve and her son, Michael. She finished her Coke, got to her feet, and headed for the clinic. She could feel the happiness zinging through her at the thought of all the new things on the horizon. Babies and tiger cubs and friends she could love and trust. She wished she could explain to Eve that, in the end, nothing else was really important. All the fear and the running could be handled as long as she kept one truth in mind.

Life is good.

Summer Island
Caribbean

"Yes, I see him now, Officer Craig. He's near the exercise fields, talking to one of the techs." Dr. Devon Brady's narrowed gaze was fixed on the tall man in khakis and a black shirt, who was talking to Judy Wong beside the high white wooden fence. His back was to her, but she knew a great deal about body language, and she relaxed a little. "No sign of aggression that I can tell, but you were right to let me know he was on the island. I don't know how the hell he got this far without a security escort."

"I don't know, either," Craig said grimly. "He flew in early this morning and just slipped under the radar. Johnson was on duty at the airport terminal and said he seemed to be a nice guy and that the Gulfstream he was flying was pretty awesome. He didn't seem a threat to the clinic."

"That's not good enough," Devon said sternly. "He could be anyone from a rival researcher to a journalist. The Logan Institute doesn't want publicity about our work here. We're doing terrifically well and we want to keep it that way. How did he slip away from Johnson?"

"He doesn't know. Johnson turned his back for a minute and he was gone. We've been looking for him ever since."

Devon didn't like that, either. People who just flitted away from experienced security personnel could be either very clever or exceptionally well trained. This man had evaded the hunt of the island's very efficient security team for the past few hours, so he might be both. "Then you'd better have a few refresher training sessions with your men. And get some people down here right away."

"I'll come myself." He hung up the phone.

He knows his job is on the line, Devon thought. Craig was a good man, but this breach should never have happened. Just because they weren't dealing with biological agents or weapons on this island, everyone tended to let down their guard occasionally. They thought that just because the people here were working with very special dogs and documenting their unique, sometimes almost incredible abilities, there was no real threat. But industrial espionage was entirely possible considering the groundbreaking results they were getting working with the dogs these days.

And men like the one she was approaching now managed to take advantage of that carelessness. She studied that body language again.

No aggression, but something else . . .

Persuasion. He was bent toward Judy Wong and every line of his body was focused and aimed at her. He could not have been more intent or interested.

And Judy was responding. Oh, yes, she was definitely

responding to that persuasion. She was looking up at him and she was smiling, her cheeks flushed, and she appeared a little starstruck. No, more than a little.

Not good.

She increased her pace. "Judy, do you need me?" she called. "Do we have a problem?"

"No." Judy looked startled. "Everything is fine, Dr. Brady. I was just explaining to Mr. Lassiter what my job is with the dogs. He was interested in how I—"

"I'm sure he was," Devon said drily. "But suppose I explain it to—is it Mr. Lassiter? You need to get back to the morning exercises, Judy."

The man turned, and for the first time she saw his face. "John Lassiter. And you must be Dr. Brady, who is in charge of the clinic and research facility. Judy is a great fan of yours." He smiled. "Did I step on toes?" He turned back to Judy. "I didn't mean to get you in trouble. I was just so interested. Forgive me?"

"Sure." Judy grinned and turned back to the exercise field. "Anytime."

No doubt she would have forgiven him if he'd nailed her to a cross, Devon thought sourly. Lassiter wasn't movie-star handsome, but that was a fascinating face. Pale green eyes, high cheekbones, and wonderfully shaped lips, not more than thirty-something, but he had a few threads of silver in that dark hair. But it wasn't that face so much as the powerful charisma he exuded. She found herself being drawn as Judy had been.

"Please don't be hard on her," Lassiter said gently. "She's a nice girl. I'm sure you're lucky to have her."

"Yes, I am. And I don't appreciate your taking up her time with your questions. What are you doing on this island, Mr. Lassiter?"

He smiled. "Not trying to extract research secrets. I'm sure you do fascinating, humanitarian work here, but I have no interest in it. Actually, I'm here to try to locate a former employee of your clinic. I should prob-ably have gone to your office in the beginning, but I thought I'd amble around and see if I could find out a little on my own."

"We don't encourage 'ambling,'" she said coolly. "We work very hard here and strangers tend to be a dis-turbing influence."

"Oh, sorry, then I won't waste your time. Suppose we go to your office and I'll ask my questions and then get out of your hair." His smile remained, but Devon was aware of a subtle change in attitude. He had seen that she wasn't responding to that personal magnetism and had discarded it and gone on to the next stage of get-ting what he wanted. "I'm sure you've sent for security by now. But you don't really want them to get in our way when it would be so easy to end this by answering a few questions."

"I don't mind them getting in my way."

"But I do," he said softly. "So please accommodate me. Only a few questions."

There was just a hint of steel beneath that velvet softness, and she stiffened. "What questions? What employee?"

"Margaret Douglas."

She tried to keep her face expressionless. "I haven't seen Margaret in a couple years. I believe she's left the area. However, I don't know. She's never requested a ref-erence."

"And you haven't been in contact with her? Strange. Judy was telling me that you were good friends when she worked here."

"Once someone leaves a job, they often cut off rela-tionships. Why do you want to know where she is?"

"I may want to offer her a position." He tilted his head. "You see, we both have questions. We should really go up to your office at the clinic and discuss it."

She hesitated, gazing at him. Cool. Very cool. The threat was subtle, but she could sense its presence. He appeared to be as many-faceted as a glittering kaleidoscope. And who was to say that he wouldn't discover another way to find Margaret if Devon didn't satisfy him.

And the last thing Margaret needed was to have to deal with a threat like John Lassiter.

So maybe she should expose herself to the threat and try to find out more to tell Margaret when she warned her.

"Whatever," Devon said casually as she turned away. "I can give you an hour or so before my next appointment. But I can tell you now that I'm not going to prove very helpful to you."

"I appreciate your time, Dr. Brady." He fell into step with her and that smile had returned. "And you can never tell. I've found when it concerns Margaret Douglas, I always need to make it a practice of taking what I can get."

San Diego
Three Days Later

Margaret's phone rang as she was walking out the door to go for her shift at the zoo. She glanced at it casually and then stiffened warily.

Devon Brady.

It might be nothing, but she never liked to get a call from Summer Island. They were too close to what she considered ground zero, only several hundred miles from the place where all the nightmares had begun. And that made the threat not only to Margaret but to everyone on the island itself.

And this was Devon Brady. Margaret considered her a friend, but as head veterinarian at a cutting-edge experimental station that dealt not only with taking

gigantic steps in improving health but actually extending the life of the dogs in her care, Devon was far too
busy for casual chitchat.

Well, then don't waste her time.

She accessed the call. "Hi, Devon. How are things
down there? I've been thinking about going back to the
island for a month or two, if I'm still welcome. How are
the goldens doing? Still as much—"

"Don't come," Devon said curtly. "Don't come anywhere near here, Margaret. We had a visitor three
days ago."

"Visitor." Her hand tightened on her phone. "Who?"

"John Lassiter. Do you know him?"

Relief. "I've never heard of him. Maybe it will
be okay."

"He doesn't look okay to me," she said grimly. "He
looks like big-time trouble. He talked to a few of the
techs before I even knew he was on the island and managed to dazzle them a bit. Then he went on the offensive from the minute he sat down in my office. He's
sharp as a stiletto and he's used to getting his way. He
moves from strength to strength. Tough. Very tough. I
had a few problems fending him off."

Margaret had trouble believing that and it made her
nervous. She knew that Devon was a powerhouse of
both efficiency and skill. "What kind of questions?"

"All about you. He gave me some bull about wanting
to hire you for a job on his property in Texas. Where
you are now. Where you came from. Who you associ-
ated with while you were on the island. Whether you
had any off-island visitors. It went on and on." She
paused. "I didn't tell him anything and I got rid of him
as soon as I could. But that wasn't the end of it. He evidently doesn't like being frustrated. Because we had a
security break-in the next night."

"What?"

"Only the file cabinet containing your records. Not that there was much in them anyway. You made sure that they were pretty scanty before you left the island. But he must have wanted to know every single detail about Margaret Douglas." She paused. "One other thing. I think he managed to hack my phone. Which means that he has your phone number. And if he's as sharp as I think he is, he might be able to trace your phone location. I thought you should know."

"Yes, I should." She could feel her heart start to pound. Calm down. John Lassiter. As she'd told Devon, she didn't know the name. He didn't have to be connected to Stan Nicos, the monster who had tormented and almost broken her. "Thanks for calling me, Devon. I'm sorry you had to go through this."

"Don't be ridiculous," Devon said bluntly. "Besides your being the best tech I've ever had, or ever hope to have, I don't want you to end up in the same shape we found you when we stumbled over you on that beach. I didn't think you were going to make it."

"I wouldn't have if it hadn't been for you. I've told you how grateful I am."

"Not grateful enough to tell me who did that to you."

"It's my problem, Devon." That had been such a close call. One of many since she had escaped from Nicos. It seemed as if he had been on her heels forever. "I wasn't going to involve you or anyone at the clinic. You got me well again; you gave me a job. I wasn't going to repay you by heaping that kind of ugliness on you." She added drily, "But it seems I may have done it anyway. I was hoping that he'd give up the search. It's been over three years."

" 'He'?" Devon didn't wait for an answer that she knew wouldn't be forthcoming. "Look, if you don't want to talk to me about it, that's fine. But I'm going to give you the same advice I gave you two years ago when you came to us. Talk to the police. Or I'll do it for you."

"Not an option. But you might make sure that island security is doubled for a while. I don't believe they'll bother you again if they think they've found out everything you know, but don't take chances."

"You're the one who shouldn't take chances. Look, I'm sending you a photo of Lassiter that I managed to take before he took off after grilling me. We ran down the name that Gulfstream he was flying was registered under. It was a corporate registration in California. Still under Lassiter. And I notified our security chief, Craig, to run a check on him after he left my office that first day. I wanted to be able to give you the entire background before I called you. I'll let you know what he finds out."

"That's good." She had a sudden thought. "But I'm getting rid of this phone. I'll call you with a different number as soon as I buy a new one. How long ago did you find out you were hacked?"

"I just discovered it this afternoon, but I think it must have happened sometime after the break-in. It was very slick. Lassiter didn't want me to know that he'd managed to do it."

And that meant that this Lassiter had had more than twenty-four hours to trace her cell phone location. He could be listening now. "I'll call you," she said quickly. "Thanks, Devon." She hung up and drew a deep breath. She could feel her palms damp with sweat.

Close. Nicos hadn't been this close to her since Santo Domingo. How had he traced her to Summer Island? She'd thought she'd left everyone safe when she'd hopped that flight off the island. She hadn't even let Devon take her to that hospital in San Juan after she had found her. And she had been very careful not to leave any paperwork that might lead anyone to her since then.

It had happened. Nicos had evidently sent a particularly efficient bloodhound and tracked her down.

Stop worrying about how it happened. Accept it. Do what's necessary.

Her phone was pinging and she accessed the photo Devon had sent her.

John Lassiter.

He was half turned away, but he was gazing with a faint mocking smile at the camera, as if he'd known Devon was taking the photo.

As if he'd wanted her to take it.

And he appeared to be everything that Devon had said he was.

But she didn't recognize him, she realized with relief. It wasn't that he was traveling under a false name; he hadn't been on Nicos's island when she'd been there. The relief lasted for only the briefest moment.

That didn't mean Nicos might not have hired Lassiter after she had escaped from Vadaz Island. Since she had never set eyes on him, he had no other reason that she could see to go after her.

It had to be Stan Nicos. Nicos, with his fat wallet and hideous soul, had found a man as talented and corrupt as himself to hunt her down. Nicos, who controlled the major percentage of drugs and arms that made their way from South America to the rest of the world, wouldn't have found it that difficult. Just a small job in the scheme of his crime network, but he'd given the order to go and find her.

To bring her back to that house on the hill, as he'd told her he would.

*Blood on the black-and-white tiles of the guest house.*

*"Too late." Nicos met Margaret's eyes. "Remember this, Margaret."*

*His gun pointed execution-style at Rosa's head.*

*"Please, Margaret." Tears running down the young*

*girl's cheeks. "Make him stop. I'm begging you. I don't want to die. He'll listen to you."*

*Blood on the tiles. Blood on the tiles.*

Don't think of that day. It had taken her years to move beyond it and come to terms. No, that was a lie. She had never come to terms with anything connected to that day or Stan Nicos. It still haunted her dreams and it only took a chilling threat like this to bring the memories flooding back to her.

She swallowed hard. Okay, Lassiter represented a threat and she had to deal with it. It wasn't as if she hadn't had to run from Nicos before. But that had been during the early years, when she had been skipping from island to island in the Caribbean, just trying to stay one step ahead of him. Once she'd managed to come back to the United States, it had been merely a question of, as Eve had said, staying under the radar.

So that's what she had to do again. Just get out of here and lose herself as she'd done so many times before. Stay away from the friends she had made over these last years to protect them. After a while, maybe she could afford to make contact again.

So text Eve and tell her that she wouldn't be able to meet her Michael yet. If she didn't, Eve would start to worry, and that would mean that she would be likely to start a hunt of her own. But not with this phone. She just hoped Lassiter hadn't been able to tap her calls for the last two days.

Get moving. Time to get out of here.

She turned and headed for her closet across the room. She could be out of here and on the road within thirty minutes. She pulled out her backpack and started stuffing it with clothes from the paper grocery sacks on the floor. It took her only a few moments and then she headed for the bathroom. Toothbrush, comb, hairbrush, soap, washcloth. Anything else she could do without or pick up later. It was amazing what you could live without if you were forced to do it. She had found that out when she had lived those years in the woods. Sometimes it was even emancipating not to be dependent on—

She stopped.

She had caught sight of her face in the mirror as she turned to leave the bathroom. Good God, she was a mess. Her lips were tight and the blue eyes looking back at her were wide with strain. She looked pale, tense, and on edge.

No, be honest, she looked scared.

Nicos has made me look like this, she thought with self-disgust. Three years and he could still cause her to feel this fear. She wasn't that kid any longer; she was over twenty. He shouldn't still have this effect on her. Three years and he could cause her to run like a rabbit because he'd sent some creep after her who had even been able to intimidate Devon.

Okay, she would run because it was the smart thing to do. But she was no rabbit and she would not abandon the things she had to do before she had to leave. It shouldn't take that long. Her duties at the zoo could be done by someone else, except for that tiger cub. It had become clear that no one else could do that adjustment but her. She'd stop on the way out of town and spend enough time to try to reconcile the tigress to her cub.

She was already feeling better because of the decision, and the woman in the mirror was no longer looking like someone she wouldn't want to know.

She tilted her head and made a face at her reflection. Hey, you've had it too easy lately. We can get through this. Just stick with me, kid.

She opened the bathroom vanity drawer and took out the small wallet photo album and stuffed it in her pocket. You could do without most things, but memories were important and photos helped. Same for music. She took out her iPod and earphones and jammed them in her other pocket. Then she took the SIM card from her phone and smashed the phone against the porcelain bathroom sink until it was in pieces. She'd pick up her new phone at that shopping center near the zoo. She slipped on her backpack and headed for the door.

As usual, she had left nothing behind that meant anything to her, nothing that could show anyone who she was or where she would go next.

A broken phone, a few dishes in the cabinet, a couple paperback books.

Try to put that together and find me, Lassiter.

She didn't look back as she slammed the door behind her.

Lassiter isn't going to like this, Neal Cambry thought, as he looked around Margaret Douglas's one-room studio flat. He had orders to locate the woman and not let her get away. But she had clearly abandoned this place. Bite the bullet. Call Lassiter and let him know that Margaret Douglas was in the wind again. He reached for his phone.

"We have a problem," he said when Lassiter answered. "She's not here. I talked to her landlord and she slipped an envelope in his mailbox with this week's rent this morning. No forwarding address."

Lassiter was cursing. "Of course there's no forwarding address. She never leaves one. Did you search her apartment?"

"I'm there now. There's not much to search. It's pretty basic, a minimum studio apartment. I can't find any leads."

"Look harder. I'm on my way there from the airport now. I'll be there in fifteen minutes. Find something by the time I get there." He hung up.

Cambry flinched. When Lassiter gave an order, he expected it to be obeyed and the impossible to become possible. And he had only fifteen minutes to make that happen. Ordinarily, he looked upon working for Lassiter as a challenge; the money was excellent and his employer was usually not unreasonable. Besides, they were friends, and he owed him big-time. But *usually* wasn't in Lassiter's vocabulary where this woman was concerned. He was totally committed to finding her and nothing was allowed to get in his way. Lately, Cambry had actually found himself feeling sorry for Margaret Douglas.

But not sorry enough to pit himself against Lassiter unless it was absolutely necessary. They went back a long way and in Afghanistan he'd become fully aware of both his potential and ruthlessness. No way that Cambry would take his money and not turn in full value. That would be most unwise.

So find something that would make Lassiter believe he was earning that money.

Fifteen minutes.

"She smashed her phone." Cambry handed Lassiter the remains when he walked into the apartment. "She did a good job. It'll be hell checking her directory history."

"I managed to get a lot of info from the tap I put on it after Summer Island. I'll get my San Francisco office to put it on priority," Lassiter said. "What else?"

"Just a few paperbacks." He handed them to Lassiter. "Two mysteries and a how-to manual on how to set up a Wi-Fi system. She bought them at a used-book store in the Gaslamp Quarter." He hesitated. "That's how the entire apartment is set up. Everything cheap and second-hand. Her landlord said that she never had visitors and he had no idea where she worked. I asked if he'd made a copy of her driver's license, so we could at least get her photo, but she told him that she'd lost it and hadn't gotten her replacement."

"I have her photo now." Lassiter handed him a copy of a small faded photo. "I got it from one of the people she worked with on Summer Island. I suppose her landlord didn't even make her fill out a reference or credit application?"

"How did you know?" Cambry shook his head. "He said that he usually did that, but he kept putting it off. He said he knew that she would pay her rent." He met Lassiter's eyes. "He trusted her. He liked her. He said he was sorry to see her go. Kind of a surprise."

Not to Lassiter. It was the first time Cambry had been directly involved in the hunt, but this was old news to Lassiter. "She manages a great con wherever she goes. I ran into the same thing down in the Caribbean. I couldn't break through that protective wall she builds around herself." His lips tightened. "I was forced to take alternate steps."

"I won't ask you what they were," Cambry said with a grimace. "But any con she's working evidently isn't bringing her any money." He was looking down at the photo of the fair-haired girl in jeans, sandals, and blue chambray shirt. "This is Margaret Douglas? She's not much more than a kid. She looks like some fresh-faced college girl. She kind of . . . glows, doesn't she?"

That had been Lassiter's first thought, too, and he had tried to dismiss it immediately. He'd been having enough trouble keeping his perspective in the past months. He'd seen photos of Margaret before while he'd been on the hunt for her, but they'd all been scratchy, out of focus, and faded. He knew Margaret Douglas didn't like her photo taken. This one that he'd talked Judy Wong into giving him was . . . different. As Cambry had said, her blue eyes were shining with humor and she looked tanned and glowing, as if lit from within. Her smile was luminous. Even her pale brown hair was sun-streaked and seemed to glow. "It was taken three years ago."

"She doesn't look more than eighteen or nineteen. That means she was even younger when she was living with Stan Nicos."

"He has a reputation for liking them young. The son of a bitch has whores imported from bordellos in Bogotá who are much younger than that. And she must have been very satisfying. He kept her for nine months and he's been searching for her ever since she left him."

Cambry slowly shook his head. "If she was only a kid, maybe she had a reason to want to start a new life. Why else would she have been running all this time?"

"I don't know and I can't let it matter. He wants her back. That's what I have to concentrate on. She's the key, the only one I've found. That's what *you* have to concentrate on."

"I believe in new starts, Lassiter. You gave me one."

It wasn't the first time he'd said something like that. "Drop it, Cambry," he said. "The circumstances were different with you. In this life we have to pick and choose. And I can't afford to choose Margaret Douglas this time. Decisions always have repercussions. She'll have to live with the decision she made when she went to live with Nicos all those years ago. He probably dangled a few expensive baubles and she—"

" 'Expensive baubles'?" Cambry chuckled. "Look at this place. I've seen better apartments in the L.A. housing development where I grew up. She sure isn't into luxury."

"No?" Lassiter's lips twisted. "You should have seen the guesthouse where Nicos was putting her up before she decided to part company with him. It was very impressive." He looked around the flat. Cambry was right. It was clean but shabby and completely without personality. That very lack of comfort made him more frustrated. He had spent the last year trying to track down Margaret Douglas, but she had been like a ghost. She had carefully erased her presence wherever she had traveled. In a world that ran on bureaucracy and documents, he had been able to find only the flimsiest of paperwork pertaining to Douglas. A few photos. No fingerprints. He had traced her movements through five towns in the Caribbean, and it was only when he reached Summer Island that he'd found anything concrete to use to find her. "Okay, I admit she's clearly trying not to do anything that will draw Nicos's attention to her again."

"Then why not try something else?" Cambry said quietly. "I've never seen you like this before. I thought you'd give up when you couldn't locate Margaret Douglas after you checked out Santo Domingo and Curaçao. But you just went on and on, until it became an obsession. Why, Lassiter?"

"You know why."

"I thought I did when it started. Somehow I became lost along the way."

"Too bad. Because I can't afford to stop now. Time's running out and she's the only card I have left to play. Do you think I've been focusing solely on Margaret Douglas while I've been searching for her? I've contacted everyone I could, pulled every string, but I've come up zero. It *has* to be her." He looked him in the eye. "Do you want to back out?"

Cambry shook his head. "I wouldn't do that. I owe you too much. I just don't want anyone hurt who shouldn't be hurt."

"It will be up to her. I'll work with her, if she'll work with me."

"But you don't think she'll agree to work with you?"

After months of hunting and investigating everything about her, Lassiter knew that she wouldn't. "Maybe you can change her mind. I'll let you try, Cambry. She's been on the run for over three years. It's not likely she'll stop." He went to the window and looked down at the street. "And, as I said, time's running out."

"I know." Cambry sighed. "I might give it a whirl, but you'd have a better chance." He suddenly grinned. "And you were talking about cons? Who's better at it or has more experience than you? Besides, you seem to know her inside and out."

Inside and out, Lassiter thought wryly. Sometimes he thought that was true. After all the people he'd talked to about her, all the apartments and flats where he'd searched and tried to build a picture of the person who was Margaret Douglas. He knew her favorite pieces of music, he knew she liked comedy and adventure movies and shied away from anything sad. He knew she could drive a car but seldom did because she needed a license, and that required documents. He knew that she drew people to her but was wary about taking lovers.

And he knew a few other rather bizarre and interesting things about her that he had not shared with Cambry.

He knew all those things, but he'd never heard her voice and only recently had seen a decent photo of what she actually looked like.

"It won't work," he said. "I want it too much and I've waited too long. I'm past the point of persuasion where she's concerned." He shook his head. "And if she doesn't agree, then I'll use her anyway. I've gotten this close and I'm not letting her skip away into the sunset again." He turned and strode toward the door. "She's *mine*."

"Not if we've lost her again," Cambry said.

"I haven't lost her yet," Lassiter said over his shoulder.

"She was in this apartment only a few hours ago, before her friend Devon sent her flying away in panic. I have a few more places to search before I give up. I believe I found out more about her on Summer Island than she'd want me to know. . . ."

# CHAPTER TWO

San Diego Zoo
1:35 A.M.

Margaret watched the night security guard turn off his flashlight and get back in his vehicle after checking out the cages. He would be going to the habitat area next, she knew. She had at least three hours before he'd come back here on his rounds. She stepped out from the shadow of the enclosure she'd ducked into when she'd seen the security guard approaching.

Three hours should be enough. She'd been working for the last six after the zoo had closed for the evening.

And I've done the best I could, Margaret thought, gazing warily at Zaran, the beautiful, fierce tigress in the big cage.

Okay, now for the test.

Margaret drew a deep breath and then pressed the gate release on the door that separated Zaran's cage from that of the smaller cage occupied by her cub.

Zaran knew that the cub was there. Would she go to the cub or ignore him? She'd had a particularly difficult birth and they'd been separated for days. After that, the damage had been done; from the time they were reunited, she'd refused to accept him as her own. Once she'd even tried to maul him.

If Zaran chose to go to him, would she kill him?

There was nothing Margaret could do now if Zaran made that decision but go into the cage after her. She could only hope that the tigress had paid attention to what she'd told her over and over and would be able to get over that irrational antagonism.

The tigress was moving slowly into the cub's cage.

And Margaret quietly opened the gate to Zaran's cage and crawled into it. She should at least get in a closer position if she had to make an attempt to stop Zaran.

Zaran stopped just inside the cage, looking at the cub.

Margaret said quickly, *Yours.*

The tigress hesitated. *Not mine.*

Oh shit, Margaret thought.

*No, remember? We talked about it. Yours.*

Zaran just stared at the cub.

Dammit, Margaret thought in frustration. She had spent hours linked to Zaran, subtle persuasion alternating with less subtle domination. But it was difficult to dominate any tiger, much less one as stubborn as Zaran. The tigress was not only bad-tempered; she was obstinate as the devil.

Okay, be patient.

*I went over and over with you what happened that night the cub was born. It wasn't his fault they took him away from you.*

*Your fault?*

*No, not mine.* She'd better edge quickly away from that idea in case Zaran again decided she was the enemy. *But now you've got him back.*

Zaran stood there gazing at the cub without enthusiasm.

Margaret tensed, getting ready to follow Zaran into the cub's cage.

Keep calm. Spend a little more time.

Five minutes passed.

Ten minutes.

The tiger still didn't move away from the gate.

Then, abruptly, Zaran crossed the cage and plopped down beside the cub. But she still didn't touch it.

*Yours?* Margaret asked.

Impatience from Zaran. As if the question was stupid. *Mine.*

Margaret drew a deep breath of relief. So far, so good. Now just a little more time to monitor the situation.

An hour later, Zaran started to feed her cub.

Margaret's muscles relaxed and she slowly got to her feet. It would be all right now. Zaran had forgotten that first animosity and she would accept the cub. Now Margaret had to get out of this cage before Zaran decided she also had to be a protective mother to her offspring. It was possible that she would ignore Margaret's previous interaction with her if primitive instinct took over. Zaran hadn't shown signs of being particularly stable.

Margaret silently backed out of the cage and jumped to the ground. She swung the gate shut behind her.

"Don't move. Not a muscle. I don't want to hurt you." The barrel of a pistol was pressed into the middle of her back.

Oh shit.

Nicos.

Not Nicos's voice. But what the hell did it matter? It was probably the other one that Devon had called her about. She had a gun in her back.

She swung her left foot back and connected with his shin. Then she ducked sideways and started running. She heard him cursing as he ran after her. At least he hadn't shot her.

Yet.

If she could make it to the habitat, then she could hide until he—

He tackled her. She fell to the ground, striking her cheek on the cement.

Pain.

Dizzy.

She rolled over and socked him in the jaw. She followed it with a right hook to the stomach. Then she lifted her knee and struck with vicious force between his legs.

He grunted in pain at that last blow and his hands closed on her throat. "Be very still," he said through his teeth. "Or I'll go for the carotid and you'll be out for a long, long time. I'm tempted to do it anyway. You've annoyed the hell out of me, Margaret Douglas."

Tempted, but he hadn't done it, and if she wasn't unconscious, she might be able to find a way to escape from him. "Let me up. You weigh a ton. You're hurting me."

"And you nearly cracked my jaw," he said sarcastically. "Besides that more painful injury. You may be small, but you've been taught well. Nicos?"

Nicos. Use Nicos.

"Yes." There were some elements of truth to the word. Nicos had been instrumental in making sure that she could protect herself. She wasn't sure what Nicos had told him, but he might be a weapon she could invoke. "And you'd better be careful. He wouldn't like anyone to hurt me."

"Really?" He smiled down at her. "You just said the wrong thing, Margaret."

His hands moved, adjusted, wrenched.

Darkness.

Rocking.

She knew that slow, rocking rhythm.

A boat.

She was on a boat.

Keep her eyes closed until she knew what she was facing.

"You're awake." It was the last voice she'd heard before the darkness. "Stop pretending. Open your eyes. I'm getting a little bored with waiting, Margaret."

She slowly opened her eyes. Pale green eyes, lean tan face, high cheekbones. His dark hair had a few strands of gray at the temple. "Who are you?"

"I think you've guessed by now." He tilted his head. "I never intended that you not know who I am or I would have furnished your vet friend with a false ID. Who am I, Margaret?"

"John Lassiter." She moistened her lips. "And I thought I knew why you were looking for me, but I'm not sure now. You didn't like it when I told you Nicos wouldn't like you hurting me. You did it anyway. I'm confused."

"I'm a little confused myself." He took a knife from his pocket and cut the ropes binding her wrists. "But I'll just make adjustments and I suggest you do the same. It will be much less painful for you."

She reached up and rubbed her neck. "You knocked me out."

"I warned you. I've had a rough couple days. I don't make false threats. You managed to say just the wrong thing at the wrong time." He smiled faintly. "Oh, well, I had to find a way of getting you to this ship anyway. That way, I could just pretend you were drunk."

"How long was I out?"

"Two hours." He stood up. "We need to talk, but I'll let you recover a little first."

"No," she said fiercely. "You can't do this to me without an explanation. You can't do it to me at all. We'll talk now."

He stared down at her. "Have it your own way. I was actually trying to be considerate." He sat back down.

"Heaven forbid that I antagonize a woman who's crazy enough to crawl into a tiger's cage."

That surprised her enough to cause her anger to ebb a little. "You saw me with the tigers?"

"I was there watching for a while. I would have found it interesting if I hadn't been afraid that you'd get yourself killed and spoil all my plans."

The sheer coolness of that answer brought the anger back in full force. "Plans? I thought you were one of Nicos's men who had come to find me, but you aren't, are you? The wrong thing that I said was that Nicos would be angry if you hurt me." She was trying to put it all together. "That means that you don't like him and want to do anything you can to hurt him or make him angry."

"Don't like him?" Lassiter repeated, tilting his head as he thought about it. "You might say that. But, to be more accurate, I'd be pleased to send your old friend to the depths of hell and spend eternity stoking the flames."

"He's not my friend."

"That appears to be debatable. Nicos seems to think that he is. According to my information, he definitely wants to reconnect with you."

This might be even worse than she'd thought. "Is that what this is all about? You think that you can hurt him by hurting me?"

"It occurred to me, but it's not my style. I prefer going directly to the source. Stan Nicos is at the top of the heap of the world's scum. He's into drugs, arms smuggling, vice . . . you name it, he does it. You may have been his favorite toy, but you don't compare in scope, Margaret."

"Then why am I here?"

"Because, unfortunately, Nicos has built himself an impenetrable fortress on his island of Vadaz in the Caribbean. Which makes it difficult for me to get my hands on him or any of the information I need. I've been trying to use bribery, influence, or more violent and infinitely more satisfactory methods for the last eighteen months to find a way to get to the son of a bitch. No luck. I'd almost run out of patience." He smiled. "But then I heard about you."

"He doesn't care anything about me."

"Correction. He cares something for you. I don't know exactly in what way. But he's been searching for you since you left him three years ago. His orders to his men were to find you and that you weren't to be hurt."

"That would only last until he got his hands on me. He wants to hurt me himself."

"But he wants you. That's the key to everything. And if he wants you, I can use you to get to him."

"I won't go back to Nicos. I won't be your damn key." She struggled to sit up on the bed. "For all I know, you're as bad as he is. No, you're probably worse. You don't even know me and you're ready to turn me over to him." She could feel the heat in her cheeks and her eyes were blazing at him. "I won't be a key. I won't be a game piece. I won't be anything but a human being trying to live my life as best I can. Go send Nicos to hell without using me. When I left him, I swore I'd never let him take me back to that island. There's nothing you can do or say that would make me change my mind." She glared at him. "Do you think I'd let you do it because you've got some kind of vendetta going against him?"

"Evidently not. If I found out one thing from trying to find you, it was that you didn't want to be found. It was reasonable to assume Nicos was the one you were hiding from. But I'm afraid that all the hiding is over. I've got to bring you out in the open."

"There's no way on earth I'll let you do that."

"Look, I won't let him hurt you." He leaned forward, his face taut, intense. "I'll protect you, but you have to help me get to him."

"Do you think I'd believe you?" she asked shakily. "I've been to Vadaz Island. I know Nicos. I've seen him do things to people that— I've *tried* to stop him and I couldn't do it. I won't go back and have it start all over again."

He stared at her for a moment and then muttered a curse. "You *will* go back. Get used to the idea." He got to his feet again. "It will be your choice whether you cooperate or make it hard on yourself."

"You're not listening. I won't go. Nothing will make me go."

He shrugged. "I'm sorry you feel that way. It's no surprise to me, but I was hoping. Think about it." He turned away. "You'll find your backpack in the bathroom over there. Make yourself as comfortable as you can. The only thing I removed was that new phone you appear to have bought yesterday. I didn't want to tempt you. And we'll make sure that we don't leave any phones or weapons around that might also prove troublesome." He opened the door to reveal steps leading up to the deck. "Neal Cambry, one of my employees, is on the bridge. You'll be getting to know him in the next few days. I told him to get under way in the next thirty minutes."

" 'Under way'?" She sat up straighter. "Where are you taking me?"

"Down the coast to southern Mexico. Then we'll take a flight out of there to Vadaz Island in the Caribbean. We won't land on the island itself, just close enough so that I can deal with Nicos."

She stiffened. "No!"

"Yes. You'll go where I tell you to go." He started up the stairs to the deck. "Even if you don't cooperate, I'll try to make it as painless as possible. It might not be as bad as you think it will be. I might just be able dangle you in front of him."

"That's supposed to reassure me?"

"It's the best I can do. I don't want anyone to get hurt if I can prevent it. You have the freedom of the ship . . . within certain limits."

"Freedom shouldn't have limits. I won't go."

He didn't answer as he disappeared from view.

Tough. Very tough. That's what Devon had said, and she was right. Margaret couldn't remember meeting anyone harder or more ruthless. Nicos had been ugly and full of malice, but Lassiter appeared infinitely more dangerous. His determination seemed absolute. He might say he regretted doing this, but he wasn't going to waver. She had seen it in every line of his face and body. Stop shaking. She could find a way to get away from him. She just had to look the situation over and then make her move.

They were on a ship. They weren't supposed to get under way for another thirty minutes. How close were they to shore? She was a very good swimmer. That was how she'd escaped Nicos's island and later managed to swim to Summer Island from that fisherman's yacht all those years ago.

Okay, look the situation over, but she had a few minutes to rest and gather her strength. And try to gather any information she could about John Lassiter.

She looked around the bedroom. Good size. Fine polished teakwood. Probably a yacht, not a cruiser. Everything appeared top-of-the-line . . . and that meant money. So did the fact that Lassiter had been able to bribe answers about her from Nicos's men.

She got to her feet and steadied herself. She was still a little stiff from being tackled by Lassiter. She went to the door across the cabin. A hallway with two doors opening off it. More bedrooms? That meant even more expense. If Lassiter was Nicos's enemy, then he might have the funds to take him down. It must have frustrated him to find out that fear of Nicos had proved an even more powerful weapon than money when he had gone after him. She checked the drawers of the bedside table. Nothing. Should she go down that hall and search the other bedrooms?

No time. She had to find out if getting off this ship was possible before they put out to sea. She headed for the steps leading to the deck. She was still a little dizzy, but she could function.

She took a deep breath as the cool air hit her when she reached the deck. Her gaze flew to the bridge and she saw John Lassiter standing at the wheel with a tall, sandy-haired man. When Lassiter saw her, he inclined his head mockingly and said something to the man next to him.

Okay, her freedom of the ship evidently extended up here on the deck. She whirled to face the shore. Lights sparkled like a diamond chain along the bank. But those lights were a long way away from the ship, which would discourage most people. She could see why Lassiter had felt secure in untying her and giving her the run of the ship.

Too great a distance?

She would have to take a minute to decide. She had swum that far before, but she was tired and that was always a factor. If she passed up this opportunity, she might find another that was safer.

Or she might not.

Lassiter had seemed very determined and she didn't know if he—

"Hello." The sandy-haired man who had been talking to Lassiter was coming toward her. "I'm Neal Cambry." He smiled. "Don't worry. You're going to be fine. Just do what Lassiter tells you to do. You probably think he's been a bit rough on you, but he didn't really hurt you, did he?"

"Yes," she said bluntly. "And I don't intend to do anything that either one of you tells me to do. Why would you think I would?"

"That's what Lassiter said you'd say." He sighed. "Change your mind. It will go much better for you."

"No, it won't. And I won't change my mind. I'm not going back to Stan Nicos." She was feeling panic at the thought and tried to keep it from showing. "That's not an option."

Evidently, she hadn't entirely succeeded, because he said gently, "Look, you can work this out with Lassiter. Don't be stubborn. He doesn't want to hurt you. Talk to him. As long as he sees a way for him to get to Nicos, he'll make it as easy on you as he can."

"That's what he told me," she said bitterly. "I believe the word he used was *dangle*. It's a word that didn't impress me."

He grimaced. "At least, he's trying to be honest with you. Lassiter can coax the birds from the trees if he puts his mind to it. He's chosen not to do that with you."

She remembered that Devon had said something about how Lassiter had managed to mesmerize the people at Summer Island. She definitely had not seen that side of him. "No, he preferred knocking me out and kidnapping me."

"He would have used money, if he'd thought you'd take it," Cambry said quietly. "He said he couldn't take a chance that you'd bolt again. Time was running out."

"He was right. I wouldn't have taken it." Her gaze was on the lights on the shore again. It would be difficult, but she could make it. When she reached the shore, she could disappear and be safe. "And I have a right to do anything I want to do without him interfering." She turned away from him. "And I won't have you interfering, either, just because he pays you a fat check to do it.

Now will you stop talking to me and just leave me alone?"

He hesitated. "Sure." He turned and started back toward the bridge. "But think about what I said. Calm down and find a way to come to terms. Lassiter knows what a son of a bitch Nicos can be. He's just not letting himself think about it in connection with you. He doesn't believe he can afford it."

She turned back to face those sparkling lights. She could do it. She was healthy and strong. She knew that endurance and will were everything. She had only to set her mind and never give up.

She kicked off her shoes. "He can't afford it? Too bad. Because there's no way on earth I can afford to go back to Nicos." She started at a run toward the rail. "So screw both of you."

She heard him call out as she threw her legs over the railing and dove into the water.

Cold. Very cold. Breathtakingly cold.

Not good.

The waters off San Diego were often mild and warm. But not if the currents disturbed those temperatures. Then they could be cold . . . and treacherous.

She'd be better once she started to move.

She struck out for the shore.

Yes, that was better. It was chilly, but not too bad. It was the shock that had made the temperature appear dangerous.

"Margaret!" She heard someone dive off the ship behind her.

Lassiter. Cursing.

"What the hell? Do you have a death wish?" Lassiter said between his teeth. He was only a few yards behind her. "First those tigers and now this?"

"I'm probably a better swimmer than you are. I can make it to the shore. I've done longer swims. That's how

I got off Nicos's island. And if you try to stop me, I'll
fight you and we'll both probably drown. You wouldn't
want that after you went to all this trouble." She concentrated on shutting out the cold and taking long, easy
strokes. "You'll probably give up before I do. I have motivation, and you're just a bad guy trying to do a bad
thing." She looked at him over her shoulder. "But maybe
your friend will rescue you if he sees you drowning.
I won't."

"You might be a better swimmer than I am, but the
water's too cold tonight," he said quietly. "There's no
way you can make the shore."

"It's not that cold. Maybe a little under sixty degrees.
It just seemed that way at first. I'll make it." She forged
ahead in a breaststroke. "But I can't waste my breath
talking anymore."

"Have it your way."

"I will. I won't go to—"

Concentrate. Even strokes. Breathe deeply. Keep
moving. Keep the blood circulating. It wasn't cold
enough to give her hypothermia, but the temperature
was always a factor on a long swim.

She could hear Lassiter behind her, but he was no longer speaking. He was a very strong swimmer, she realized vaguely.

But so was she, and all she had to do was keep this
pace going.

The shore was much closer now.

Just keep her arms moving. She could make it.

Her body felt heavy, cold, but if she moved faster, that
would take care of that.

It wasn't really cold. It was just creeping up on her
because she was getting tired.

The lights were closer. . . .

Her arms were moving slower now.

Make them go faster to fight the cold.

She could do it.

She was almost there.

"That's enough," Lassiter said roughly. He had caught up with her and she saw his expression. Angry . . .

"Get away from me. I'm almost there."

"Yes, dammit, you are. I didn't think— But not close enough. You won't make it. You're probably already suffering from a mild form of hypothermia. Hell, probably so am I. But I'm stronger than you are. Your arms are going to give out and you'll drown."

"No. You're not stronger. I don't need you. I don't need anyone. I can do it. Get away from me."

"My God, I almost wish I could." His lips twisted. "But I didn't go to all this hassle to have you drown on me just because something in me wants to see you make it. Don't fight me, Margaret."

"Get . . . away . . . from . . . me." She tried to push him away.

"You keep ignoring warnings. This time, I really regret that you're doing it."

Her head snapped back as he struck her on the chin.

Pain.

That heavy, cold water.

Darkness.

She woke up on a bunk on the ship, naked, coughing, and shivering as Neal Cambry piled blankets on top of her.

"Keep still," he said. "I've got my orders. I'm to get you warm and I'm not to let you jump off the ship again. I intend to do just what Lassiter told me to do. He's not in great humor at the moment. He wasn't pleased that I let you go for a swim."

"Where . . . is . . . he?"

"Trying to warm up, too. You were both in pretty bad

shape." He supported her while she drank the hot tea he held to her lips. "You're very stubborn, you know."

"Could—have—made it."

"A matter of opinion," he said. "But I lean toward Lassiter's. I think you were going down for a long fall."

She shook her head.

He chuckled. "Okay, maybe not. Argue with him." He tossed a San Diego Zoo nightshirt on the bed beside her. "I found this in your backpack. Pretty flimsy, but I thought you'd be more comfortable." He headed for the steps leading to the deck. "I'll be right back. I'm going to make sure I complete that second order and get far enough to sea so that you won't be tempted to try to swim to shore again."

"We can't stay . . . out to sea forever," she called after him as she pulled the nightshirt over her head. "Sometime I'll get another chance."

"I'm sure you will." Lassiter was coming down the stairs. He was wearing a dark blue crew sweater and jeans and his hair was still wet. "I just hope you have better sense next time."

"Self-preservation is always sensible."

"Exactly." He sat down in the chair beside the bed, his gaze going to her zoo nightshirt. "That has elephants instead of tigers. Why?"

She frowned. "What difference does it make?"

"Curious. I only wanted to make sure you hadn't abandoned your allegiance."

"It was on a sale."

"Money can move mountains. Or tigers." He tilted his head. "You look like a drowned rat."

"I didn't drown. I wouldn't have drowned. I would have made it."

"I've heard that mantra before." He smiled faintly. "You almost had me believing it."

"It's only important that I believe it." She could hear the engine start and felt the ship's motion escalate. "You won't be able to keep me prisoner until you can turn me over to Nicos. There are all kinds of ways that I can get away. You can see how much trouble I am."

"Yes, I can. A great deal of trouble."

He didn't seem as angry this time. Or it could have been how exhausted she was. She could barely keep her eyes open. "Then wouldn't it be better just to forget about me?"

"You've made that extremely difficult to do."

"Surely I'm not worth it. You've probably already paid too much to try to find me."

"Considerable. Let's just say, to me you're a jewel beyond price."

"Bullshit. Nicos wouldn't think so. He has a price for everything. Why do you want to get to him anyway?"

"We'll discuss it tomorrow. You're about to go to sleep on me, and I'd find that very rude."

"I won't go to—" She yawned. "Well, maybe I would. It's all your fault. Everything is your fault. . . ."

"We've already established that fact." He tucked the blanket around her shoulders. "Tomorrow we establish what we intend to do about it."

"You can't keep me," she said drowsily. "And I could have made it. . . ."

"She's asleep?" Cambry asked as Lassiter came up on deck. "I think she'll be okay by tomorrow. She seems pretty resilient."

"That's an understatement," Lassiter said drily. "She's a combination of rubber and cast iron."

"She came close to making it to shore. Guts. Pure guts." Cambry smiled. "I admit I was rooting for her." He slanted a glance at Lassiter. "I think you were, too."

"Maybe. But then I would have made it an empty victory by capturing her again. I still need her. I still have to have her." He looked out at sea. "You know she's my way to Nicos. That's not going to change."

"But it's going to get harder for you. You saw what she's made of tonight. You're getting to know her. Rubber and cast iron. Not a bad combination."

"It can't change, Cambry," he repeated. "I can't let it change." He moved down the deck. It had been a rough night and these last hours had been filled with an incredible mixture of emotions. He'd expected the anger and frustration; he hadn't expected the admiration . . . and the curious sense of pride he'd felt in that sea while swimming behind Margaret.

Forget it. He should go to bed and stop thinking of Margaret's face in that last moment, when she was almost beyond exhaustion and pain. No surrender, even then.

*I'm almost there. I can make it. . . .*

When Margaret woke the next morning, she was sore in every muscle. She flinched as she struggled out of bed.

But she had slept well and deeply and she was thinking clearly, which hadn't been the case last night. Okay, it was a new day. She might be on her way to Nicos, but she wasn't there yet. Think positive. Shower and shampoo so that she would no longer look like a drowned rat. Then confront Lassiter and start asking questions.

She jumped out of bed and headed for the shower.

# CHAPTER THREE

She was still tying her hair up in a ponytail as she climbed the stairs to the deck forty minutes later. As she passed the galley, Cambry looked up from the stove, where he was frying bacon. "Breakfast in twenty minutes." He smiled. "You look ready for battle. I told Lassiter I thought you'd be resilient."

"He made sure I had to be. Where is he?"

"On deck." He tilted his head. "And I wouldn't attack if I were you. He could have been rougher on you. You put him through a lot more than I thought he'd take last night."

"You mean by defending myself from him? What a pity. He deserved anything that I could do to him."

"He could have stepped in sooner if he hadn't been wary about hurting you," he said quietly. "Lassiter was with the Special Forces in Afghanistan and he's one tough son of a bitch."

"That's what my friend Devon said." She met his eyes. "If what you say is true, then I honor his service to his country and I think it's sad that he's probably turned into a mercenary who is no better than Nicos."

"Ouch." He shrugged. "Okay, I'm through with defending him. We don't agree entirely on a lot of subjects anyway."

"Really?" Her eyes studied him with sudden alertness. Cambry was likable and had none of the quiet lethality that Lassiter projected. "Am I one of them? You're not as bad as he is. You might even be a good guy. You have to know that he shouldn't be doing this to me."

He chuckled. "Are you trying to seduce me into betraying my friend?"

" 'Seduce'?" She made a face. "Be real. Just look at me. I'm not equipped. But everyone has a bad side and a good side. I'm just trying to appeal to the side that will send me a thousand miles away from Nicos."

His smile faded as he looked at her. "You may be more equipped than you think. There are more ways to seduce than the usual accepted methods. I found that out in a Pakistani prison." He made a shooing motion. "Get out of here. I'm going to burn this bacon."

"No, we wouldn't want that." Lassiter was leaning on the doorjamb at the head of the stairs, looking down at her. "By all means, Margaret, come up on deck and stop disturbing the man."

She gazed at him, trying to read his expression. Not anger. Mockery? She had thought she was ready to face him, but now she wasn't sure. Sure or not, she had to do it.

She ran up the rest of the steps and pushed past him. She turned to face him as she reached the deck. "How much did you hear?"

"Pretty near all of it, I think." The smile was definitely mocking. "Don't waste your time. You won't be able to sway Cambry. We have our differences, but we go way back. And he's loyal to me."

"You never know." She plopped down on the deck and leaned back against the rail, lifting her face to the sun. "I thought it was worth a shot that he might have a conscience. He seemed kind of . . . nice," she said, then added, "for an accomplice of a criminal who doesn't know the meaning of the word."

"So you decided to make a try at bringing him over to the dark side." He dropped down beside her and crossed his jean-clad legs at the ankle. "Nothing too obvious, just a frank, girlish appeal that might stir memories of home and family." He leaned back against the rail. "Clever. Cambry's right: There are more ways than one to seduce." His gaze studied her face. "You look clean and glowing, as if you're drawing in that sun and making it yours. It arouses a certain emotional . . . response. I'm beginning to understand why Nicos is so determined to get you back."

"No, you don't," she said jerkily. "You don't understand anything about me. And I'm not the dark side. I could be, but I decided a long time ago that I wouldn't let anyone do that to me." She moistened her lips. "Evidently, you decided to go the other way."

"I just decided that there are some things that are worth embracing the dark side for. Sometimes it's the only way to go."

"Bullshit."

He was silent, and then he chuckled. "That's Cambry's response, too. I'd better keep the two of you apart. I want no united front."

"Because we're right."

He shrugged. "I disagree. But we won't argue. Instead, I'll let you try to seduce me."

She inhaled sharply, her eyes widening. "How do you mean that?"

He smiled. "No jumping to conclusions for you. You really don't realize your potential. I would have thought Nicos would have taught you." He got to his feet and reached down to pull her to her feet. "But, as it happens, you're right. I don't understand you, and I'm beginning to believe I can't do what I need to do unless I do."

"You don't have to understand me. You just have to let me go."

His lips turned up. "But Cambry says that if I get to know you, it will make it harder for me to turn you over to Nicos. One thing may lead to another. Don't you want to try?"

"No. Why do you?"

He laughed. "Maybe I have a tiny bit of conscience that's urging me to leave the dark side? Or maybe it's going to be a boring few days until we get to southern Mexico? I like the idea of playing Q and A with you. I thought I knew a good deal about you, but you showed me a new page last night. You intrigue me. Exploring that bizarre mind of yours would be amusing."

"What if I don't want it explored?"

"But then the seduction would be null and void. I wouldn't get to know you and all that softening influence Cambry was predicting goes down the drain."

He was still grasping her wrist and she wanted to pull away. She forced herself not to do it. Ignore that heat and magnetism. She didn't want him to realize he had any physical effect on her. "Shouldn't it go two ways?" she asked. "Are you going to let me ask you questions?"

"Within limits."

"But I'm not supposed to have any limits?"

He smiled. "No, you're the one seducing me."

And that seemed a good time to jerk her wrist away from him. "Not fair."

"I never said any of this was fair." His smile faded. "Only necessary, Margaret." He turned away. "Time to go down for breakfast. Do what you like. I'm probably better off if I don't get to know anything more about you than I do now."

She watched him stroll back down the deck. She

might be better off, too. What he was offering had an element of intimacy that she should avoid. He was complicated and dangerous and there was a sexual magnetism that she couldn't ignore. Add them all together and she might be biting off more than she could handle.

So she should meekly bow her head and let him send her back to Nicos?

Doing what he'd asked and spending time with him might provide an opportunity to get hold of a weapon or phone. It might be a way to persuade him that she wouldn't be coerced into doing this.

She could handle him.

She hoped.

"Well, I'm not going to let you just interrogate me." She ran after him. "Do you play chess?"

"Moderately well."

"Good. Then I'll probably beat you and that will make me feel better. While we're playing, I'll answer a question now and then . . . if I feel like it." She mocked him. "If it amuses me."

He nodded. "If not, I'll try to find something else that will amuse you." He opened the door for her. "It shouldn't be too difficult to—"

"But I want you to answer a question or two right now to show good faith. Is John Lassiter your real name?"

"Yes."

"Do you own this ship or are you leasing it?"

His lips curved. "Mine. Is that important?"

"It shows that you have money. I thought you probably did. I don't like it. Money is power."

"I thought so, too. It hasn't proved to be very helpful lately."

"How did you get it? Are you a criminal, like Nicos?"

"I'd rather you didn't compare me to him on any level."

"Are you?"

He shook his head. "Though some of my competitors claim I am. I own a computer company in Silicon Valley." He added, "And, in the interest of total honesty, I should mention that as a boy growing up, I was far from law-abiding." He held up his hand as she opened her mouth to speak. "You said a couple questions to show good faith. You've had them, Margaret. I'm going to be very sparing with those answers unless you decide to agree to what I need. I know the value of information and I believe you're smart enough to use anything I give you as a weapon."

"But you said that if I—"

"And I will, but it will be at my pace, not yours." He gestured for her to precede him. "Breakfast."

"You're better than moderately good," Margaret said as she gazed down at the chessboard. "I should have known you'd lie to me."

"Yes, you should. When have I ever shown myself to be trustworthy in our brief acquaintance?" He looked at her with a smile. "Consider your circumstances. Not encouraging. But it was only a small lie. I'm too impatient to really be good at this game. You're far better at it than I am."

"Impatient." She made a face. "Yes, I can see that you are. If you weren't so impatient, you wouldn't have decided that I was your only way to get Nicos. You would have taken the time to study him and not hurt innocent people."

His smile faded. "You're not hurt."

"Yet." She looked up at him. "And I won't be hurt. But the risk is there. You shouldn't expose me to that risk."

"Why do all of our conversations come back to—" He shook his head. "Never mind. It's just annoying. But you have a perfect right to voice your displeasure."

"Yes, I do." Her gaze narrowed on his face. "I thought that I'd get a few jabs at you to make up for your prying into my privacy. But we've gone all day and you haven't asked me anything. Why not?"

"Perhaps I'm not as curious about you as I thought?"

She thought about it. "Or maybe you're protecting yourself from me. Maybe Cambry was right and you don't want to see anything in me but what you want to see. Why else would you back off?"

"How very perceptive."

"It makes sense." She leaned back against the rail. "So ask me whatever you want." She grinned at him. "I dare you."

"That's a dangerous challenge." He met her eyes. "It could get you into trouble."

She felt suddenly breathless. Her heart was beating hard. Spending these hours with him had lulled her into a false sense of security. He had been so easygoing and amusing that she had felt totally confident and at home with him. Now that was gone and she was vividly aware of everything about him. And none of it was in the least easygoing.

He smiled as he read and deciphered that response. "Now who's backing out?" He cleared the chessboard and started setting up the pieces again.

"Let's talk about tigers."

She hadn't expected him to head in that direction. She wasn't ready for it. "That's right, you said you saw me with the tigers." She tried to sound offhand. "I work with all kinds of animals at the zoo. I do everything from cleaning cages to acting as a kind of a tech assistant. The tigers are just part of the job."

"Is it also part of your job to creep into their cages in the dead of night when no one else is around?"

"Sometimes it helps to be able to have private time with them," she said warily. "They can be . . . sensitive."

"And your superiors at the zoo approve of your crawling into tigers' cages?"

She didn't answer directly. "There are times when it's necessary. There are injuries and illness, even tooth removal, and the vets have to—"

"But not a humble tech and not alone," he said softly. "That's why you had to do it in the middle of the night. What were you up to, Margaret?"

She stared at him with exasperation. She had hoped not to get into this. "I'm a tech, but I'm not humble. And I wasn't doing anything to hurt Zaran or the cub."

"I misspoke. You're definitely not humble. Zaran?"

"The tigress. They were having problems getting her to accept her cub. She had trouble at birth and she didn't see him for three days. When they were introduced, she totally rejected him. She thought he wasn't hers and refused to feed him. She even tried to attack him once. I had to convince her that she was wrong."

"And your method was to throw them together and then crawl into the tigress's cage yourself? I really don't believe that would meet with the vet's approval."

"Perhaps not. It seemed the thing to do at the time."

"Why?"

"Does it matter?"

"Yes, I find it does."

"I had to be ready to try to save the cub if Zaran decided that she didn't believe me when I told her that the cub was hers." She stiffened, waiting for the response. . . . Laughter? Bewilderment? Ridicule? She had heard them all.

She hadn't heard this one.

"Interesting," he said quietly. "I thought it might be something like that. But, of course, the chance you took was completely irrational."

Her eyes widened. "You thought that it—" She stopped and said carefully, "Would you care to explain?"

"Yes." He smiled. "Though you're interfering with my Q-and-A time. I couldn't have tracked you down if I hadn't talked in depth to the people with whom you interacted. And the jobs you took always were connected with caring for animals. I heard a few amazing and often unbelievable stories about your skill and bonding with them. You tried to be careful and discreet, but a few of your employers still thought you were some kind of witch doctor. That you actually knew what an animal was thinking, that you could communicate with them. I found it completely absurd, of course. But it was hard to dismiss." He tilted his head. "And then I found my way to Summer Island and I thought, maybe not absurd at all."

"Why?"

"Because it was the perfect place for you, an experimental research facility that was only interested in extending the life span and intelligence of dogs. You fit right in during the time you were there. You felt free to meld with those dogs you began to love. The vets and techs noticed you were different, of course, but they were receptive, not critical, and you were very content. At least everyone thought you were." His brows lifted. "Was it true?"

"It's true," she said curtly. "But Devon never told you any of that stuff about me."

"No, she was very loyal and discreet. But I had a few hours with your fellow techs, and they weren't as close-mouthed. They admired and liked you, but when you don't understand something, you tend to want to discuss it. I was glad to furnish a sounding board."

"I imagine you were. Why? My life at Summer Island had nothing to do with Stan Nicos."

"I had to know everything about you. I knew you were going to be difficult." He shrugged. "Though I admit I was a bit stunned when I found out that you might have a mental connection with certain animals. I thought it was only dogs, until I witnessed your session with those tigers. Any other kind of bonding?"

She might as well answer him. She could see that he wasn't going to let her avoid the subject. "Yes," she said reluctantly. "Some are easier than others." Her gaze suddenly flew down the deck to Cambry. "Does he know?"

"No, for some reason I didn't feel I wanted to share it. I wanted it to be between us."

"It's not between us. And I can't share it. It's mine alone. That's the way it is. And you're taking this entirely too receptively. Why?"

"I traveled all over the Middle East while I was in the service. I've seen everything from snake charmers to Buddhist monks training their animals to do amazing feats. But I don't believe I've ever run across someone like you, Margaret."

"Lucky you."

"Not so lucky." He looked out at the sea. "And you're not all that lucky, either. It had to be difficult for you to cope with a gift like that."

"Why?" She made a face. "Because everyone thinks you're either lying or crazy? I learned that very young. My mother died when I was born and my father let DEFACS take care of me until I was four. But then he petitioned to get me back because of the welfare checks. He was neither understanding nor forgiving of having a kid who told the next-door neighbors she knew their dog was sick because he told her so and that they should take him to the vet. He beat me every time I said something that made him uncomfortable or that he couldn't accept. I learned very fast, Lassiter."

"Bastard," he said roughly. "Wasn't there anyone you could go to for help?"

"Not at the time. Later. But it was okay. I got along fine."

"Yeah, sure. When did you even realize you could communicate with animals?"

"I always knew. I thought everyone could do it. Of course, the people in the orphanage just thought I was a little wacko. There was a marmalade cat named Tamby who lived in the alley in back of the orphanage and visited every day for scraps. And then there were birds, who weren't nearly as interesting, but they saw all kinds of wonderful things when they were flying that they just took for granted. I spent a lot of time listening and watching them." She shrugged. "But they got pretty bored with me. I guess three-year-olds who were locked up in an orphanage didn't have much to offer. But none of the personnel at the orphanage seemed to think much about it. I guess kids who were as alone as we were often had imaginary friends."

"I suppose that's definitely a possibility," he said quietly.

"Anyway, it wasn't until I had to go to my father that I knew I could be punished for it. And, once I understood, most of the time I could avoid it. And then when I was eight, I ran away from home to escape from him and lived in the woods for a while."

"What?"

"You heard me. I was safer there than anywhere else. Like I said, I got along fine."

"I don't believe that."

"You should. I was better off there than I would have been at home with my father or in a child services facility."

"Why? The woods? Give me a break. The entire idea is bizarre. If I didn't realize that your recent background is just as bizarre, I'd have trouble believing it."

"Then don't believe it."

"But I *do* believe it. And for some reason, it drives me crazy. You were a child." He shook his head. "It had to have been hell for you. Some kids are even scared of the dark, much less being alone in the forest."

"It wasn't hell for me. At first, I didn't like being alone, but then I realized I wasn't alone at all and I—" She stopped. She didn't like being on the defensive and she didn't really like remembering that night she'd run away from home. She certainly didn't want to share it. "Let's talk about something else."

"No, I want to know how you felt." His eyes were suddenly holding her own. "Tell me."

"Why? You know too much about me right now. You don't have to know about that girl back in Dodson, Indiana. I'm not her any longer. There's nothing from that time that you can use to manipulate me."

"Maybe not. I still want to know." His face was taut, strained, intense. "*Tell me.*"

But if she told him, she felt she'd give him something of herself that belonged only to her. That night of rejection and rebirth had been painful, and yet it had formed the person she had become. He wouldn't be able to understand. No one could understand. That's why she never talked about it. To talk about it would bring back the memories, would bring back that night. . . .

Dodson, Indiana
12:40 AM
Thirteen Years Ago

*It was going to rain. She could smell it in the air.*

*I shouldn't have picked tonight, Margaret thought as she ran down the highway toward the cornfield she could see in the distance. Beyond that cornfield was the forest, but she might not be able to reach it. Her father had been drunk, but she wasn't sure that he had passed out yet. She should have waited. She had no shelter built in those woods. And if it rained hard, there would be mud and she'd leave footprints.*

*She couldn't wait. Her back still stung from the whip her father had used on her earlier in the evening. The drinking was getting worse and so were the beatings. She tried to stay out of his way, but it was getting harder all the time. Lately, it had seemed as if it was no longer punishment but pleasure he was looking for. When he had knocked her against the wall yesterday, she had seen that pleasure when he saw the blood running down her face.*

*And she knew he'd want that pleasure again.*

*She had known she'd have to be prepared, that it was going to get worse, but she had thought she'd have a little more time.*

*No more time.*

*He wouldn't let her get away. He would keep coming after her because of that joy he felt in hurting her. If she hid, he would try to hunt her down.*

*She knew about hunting; she could see it all around her when she joined with animals. When an animal knew it was being hunted, it didn't wait; it fled. It seemed to be pure instinct. But it was confusing for Margaret, because when an animal was hunted, it was usually for food, not for pleasure.*

*But she had known that she had to leave that night.*

*Because her instinct had told her she might not have another chance.*

*Headlights on the road behind her!*

*There were only two houses on the road where she lived, and their occupants had to get up early to go to work and weren't likely to be out after midnight.*

*And she recognized the sound of the seven-year-old Chevy truck her father drove.*

*Run!*

She tightened the shoulder strap of the book bag she'd used to pack her belongings and started to run.

"Margaret!"

He'd seen her!

He'd stepped on the accelerator and he would catch up with her in seconds.

No! She ran faster down the road.

"Margaret, you come back here. You little freak." His voice was slurred, but it was angry and full of menace. "I'll beat you senseless when I catch you."

And he would do it.

No! She wouldn't let him. Never again.

She jumped over the ditch and ran toward the cornfield.

He was cursing as he pulled over to the side of the road. "Margaret!" He took out his flashlight and shined the beam on her running figure. "Come back here and get in this car!"

She was almost to the cornfield.

"I'm going to get out and come after you!"

Threats and fear and him always there waiting for her. She couldn't stand it any longer. She wouldn't stand it. She suddenly turned around and faced him. Both the beam of his flashlight and the headlights were on her, blinding her to the darkness of his car only yards away. "You won't get out of the truck," she shouted at him. "You're too drunk and I'm not worth it to you unless I'm easy prey. You'd only fall down and probably break your stupid head open. Come ahead. I'll lose myself in this cornfield and you'll never find me. I'm not going to be easy for you ever again."

His voice was harsh with rage. "I'm going to kill you, freak."

Freak, again. He always called her that when no one but she could hear him. It had started the first time he *had realized that she could actually bond with animals and he had treated it as something loathsome. "No, you won't. I won't let you. Maybe I am a freak, but I'm natural and I'm clean. You're the real freak. You're twisted in a sick and ugly way."*

*"I'll show you ugly. I'll get you back and you'll—"*

*"No, you won't. You won't do anything to me. You'll never see me again. . . ."*

*She turned and ran into the cornfield.*

*Tall stalks of corn on either side of her. The rustle of the dry leaves as she ran through them.*

*She heard her father cursing and then the car door slam. He was coming after her. She had probably made him so angry by her defiance that he'd been driven to chase after her. It hadn't been a smart thing to do.*

*But she'd had to do it. She hadn't been able to just disappear after all that had gone before. She'd had to tell him what he was and defend herself at last.*

*She heard him crashing through the cornfield behind her.*

*She was smaller, but faster, and he was drunk.*

*It was starting to rain.*

*Even better.*

*He would be slipping and sliding and maybe get discouraged. He might just rely on DEFACS to find and bring her back. She wouldn't let that happen. Never again.*

*She ran faster. She couldn't see the forest beyond the cornfield ahead of her, but she knew it was there. She had spent many hours in that forest while she was hiding out from her father.*

*It was raining hard now and even though the stalks of corn were partially protecting her, she was getting soaked to the skin. That was okay; he would be getting this wet, too.*

*"Margaret!"*

*He sounded far behind her as well as frustrated and furious.*

*And she was getting closer to the forest every minute.*

*It was silly to think it was calling to her. There was no sound but the rain and an occasional roll of thunder. Maybe she was the one calling. . . .*

*And she might have been answered. She could no longer hear her father crashing through the tall stalks behind her. He was not shouting her name. . . .*

*Safe?*

*Not yet. Not until she got out of this cornfield and into the woods.*

*She increased her pace, listening for any sound behind her.*

*Nothing.*

*Only the rain falling on the leaves and the earth.*

*And then she was out of the cornfield, and in the next few minutes she had entered the trees.*

*Shelter.*

*Dimness.*

*So many familiar scents . . .*

*She dropped down beneath an oak tree to catch her breath and look out at the cornfield to make sure that she hadn't been fooled by that lack of sound.*

*Nothing. No movement. No sound but the falling rain.*

*He had given up for the time being. Probably until tomorrow, when he'd call DEFACS and tell them she was lost and he needed their help to find her.*

*She leaned back against the trunk with a sigh of relief. It would be all right here for a little while. She could rest before she started out again. But she'd have to be far away from here by morning and keep traveling until she felt safe.*

*Safe?*

*She looked away from the cornfield and back into the depths of the woods.*

*It looked . . . different at night.*

*Dense and mysterious and threatening.*

*She could feel herself tense. Silly. She had been here so many times. She had even tried to make friends with some of the animals who lived in these woods.*

*But she didn't know everything about this place, and animals could be as different from one another as people. Maybe, after all, there was something to fear here. . . .*

*There is something to fear everywhere, she told herself impatiently. If there were bad things here, she'd find out and avoid them. Just as she'd learned to avoid her father. But it couldn't be as bad as what she'd faced in that three-room house only a few miles from here.*

*See, she was already feeling better. The dimness and mystery of the forest were not so threatening after all. If she kept thinking like that, she'd be fine. She closed her eyes and forced herself to relax.*

*The rain on the leaves of the oak tree above her.*

*The scents . . .*

*Could she hear the sounds of the animals sheltering here? If she reached out, could she join with any of them?*

*She put out a tentative probe. "I'm here. I'm no threat. I'm just alone and I need to be part of all this. I'm not wanted out there. But neither are you. Maybe we can help one another?"*

*A stirring. Raccoon?*

*Yes, definitely a male raccoon. No real interest in her.*

*But there was another stirring near the stream to the north.*

*She put out another probe in that direction. "No threat. It would be nice not to be alone."*

*"Yes. To be alone is not good." A pause. "No threat."*

*It was a doe. Margaret could sense the freedom, the*

*wildness, the singing speed held in restraint. What would it be like to be joined to all that beauty?*

*"Later?"*

*"Later."*

*Margaret felt a rush of sheer exhilaration. This was different from the cautious approaches she'd made to domestic and farm animals in the past. This bonding was pure and clean and as wildly natural as the forest itself. Because now she was part of the forest, and, if she studied and was careful, she could become one with the animals who inhabited it. She had the sudden wild impulse to rush out giddily and start right now to do that.*

*Not yet. There was time for all of that later. She mustn't intrude, any more than she'd want to be intruded upon. It was enough to be here, to be one of them, to have a chance to be free and not alone any longer.*

*To have a home at last.*

"You're not answering me," Lassiter said. "How did you feel that night?"

His words jarred her back to the present. "You wouldn't understand." She shrugged. "And I have no intention of trying to explain myself."

He smiled. "You'll tell me someday."

"No, I won't." She hurried on to divert him from that very personal question by giving him a more general answer. "It took me quite a while to learn how to adjust, but I did it. Nature is a great teacher. Animals understand survival and they accept what you are without question. On the other hand, when you're not 'normal,' people feel uneasy around you. It can be . . . lonely."

"Can it?" He was holding her gaze, and she suddenly felt as if he was surrounding her with warmth. Strange, when she had rarely seen him anything but wary and edgy. "You were only a kid. Someone should have been there for you."

She laughed and shook her head. "That's life, Lassiter. You take what you get. I'm sure you know that. I've been lucky in a lot of ways."

"Someone should have been there for you," he repeated. He slowly reached out and gently touched the hair at her temple with an almost caressing hand.

She inhaled sharply as she felt the warmth of his fingers through the pulse point beneath that strand. She could feel her heartbeat escalate as she looked up at him, and it bewildered her. It wasn't sexual, was it?

No, it was something else, something that she didn't think she had ever felt before. That touch was so gentle, so exquisitely caressing, that she felt safe and infinitely . . . treasured. And his intent gaze was giving her that same sensation of—

No, it was too weird and she shouldn't be feeling like this.

She tore her gaze away and jumped to her feet. "And now that we've covered that particular question, I think that I'll take a break and go talk to Cambry for a while. You caught me by surprise and I don't like to feel this vulnerable."

He was silent, still looking at her. She could see a multitude of expressions crossing his face, but she couldn't decipher any of them. "Neither do I." He was suddenly standing and looking down at her with a reckless smile. "But it's worse for me, because I appear to also be finding you're becoming addictive. I've been hunting you, searching for every detail about you for too long. Yet it's evidently not enough. I want to know more, get closer, go deeper. And that's the worst thing that I could do." He took out his phone. "So let's try to slow it down, shall we?"

She was staring at his phone. "What are you going to do?"

"I'm going to call Juan Salva." He was punching in the number. "You remember Salva? He works very closely with Nicos. He remembers you. I paid him very well to tell me all about any of Nicos's weaker links."

She moistened her lips. "Yes, I remember him." She could see him now as she'd seen him that night. High forehead, brown hair tied back to reveal his finely molded features, faint mocking smile.

*Blood flowing across those black-and-white tiles.*

"I thought you would." He'd made the connection and spoke into the phone, "Lassiter. I have Margaret Douglas, Salva. Let Nicos know that we might be able to deal in a couple weeks. I'll get back to you." He hung up the phone. "Done."

Done, she thought numbly.

It had only been a phone call to Vadaz Island, but she felt as if Nicos were close enough to touch her. Memories were flooding back to her. Yes, she remembered Salva. He had been there in the room when Nicos had fired the shot and Rosa had crumpled to the floor. He had even smiled when Nicos had done it.

"Stop looking like that." Lassiter was suddenly beside her, his eyes glittering fiercely, his hands closing on her shoulders. "I told you I was going to do it."

"Yes, you told me." She pulled away from him. "And for some reason, you wanted to hurt me now. I'm a little confused and I can't figure it out. It's not as if I did anything to hurt you. I'm the one who you put through the wringer, and you tore my privacy to shreds." She lifted a shaking hand to her hair. "But you must have had a reason, and I'll work it out. But I wish you hadn't called him. It will take me a little while to get over it so that I can—"

"Look, all you have to do is what I need you to do."
His hands were so tight on her shoulders they were
almost painful, and his eyes were blazing down at her.
"I'll make sure that Nicos doesn't hurt you. But you have
to know that I'm going to do this. I *have* to do this."

"I knew. You told me. You didn't have to show me
anything." She pulled away from his grasp and started to
back away from him. "Were you just trying to scare me?
Well, you did it. Does it make you feel bigger, stronger?"

"I didn't want to scare you," he said roughly. "That
wasn't it."

"No?" She turned and moved quickly away from him.
"Then I don't know why you did it. And I can't stand
here and try to figure it out." She was almost running
now. "So I'll let you call Salva back and discuss how
you're going to—"

*Blood.*

*Black-and-white tiles.*

*Rosa.*

She was running past Cambry, then down the stairs
to the cabin.

She slammed the door behind her.

She leaned back against it and closed her eyes.

Fear. Cold fear.

And hurt. Hurt because Lassiter had done this to her.
She shouldn't be hurt. It was stupid. She knew that he
had a purpose and nothing was going to stand in his
way. Yet she'd been lulled by that smile and charm for
most of the day.

And that last gentle touch that had magically soothed
and made her feel . . . treasured. Made her feel that no
matter what had gone before, all the pain would be gone
now. And then he'd struck when she was most vulnerable, followed by the shock of his moving so quickly to
toss her back in time to Salva and Nicos and . . .

*Black-and-white tiles.*

*Blood.*

*The gun.*

Dammit, the tears were running down her cheeks. Weak. She couldn't be this weak. Get control.

"Margaret."

Lassiter on the other side of the door.

She didn't answer.

"Margaret, I'm coming in. Is that okay?"

"No." She quickly wiped her cheeks on the back of her hands. "But I can't stop you, can I? You showed me how helpless I am. Do what you like." She moved away from the door. "But I don't want you here, Lassiter."

Silence. "Then I won't come in right now. But I'll have to do it later. I won't be able to take it if I don't."

The sound of his footsteps going back up the stairs.

She didn't have any idea what he meant and she didn't care. She hadn't expected that he'd pay any attention to her words. The fact that he'd given her this time to recover both her composure and her independence filled her with a deep sense of relief. She needed this period to prepare herself to face him again. She didn't know why he had given her that grace period, but she would take it.

And try to block out that memory of the blood on those black-and-white tiles.

And the hurt when Lassiter had hurled her back to that day three years ago.

She'd be all right. She'd be fine. She just needed a little time to heal. . . .

# CHAPTER FOUR

There was someone in the cabin.

Someone there in the darkness.

The realization jarred Margaret from deep sleep to instant consciousness. She jerked upright in bed.

"It's all right," Lassiter said quietly from his chair on the far side of the cabin. "Don't be afraid. It's only me."

"Only you?" She could see his shadowy form in the darkness. "There's no 'only' about you, Lassiter." She started to reach over to turn on the lamp on the nightstand, but then stopped. She didn't want to see him right now, didn't want to feel the impact of the intensity and power that emanated from him. "And I'm not afraid."

"You could have fooled me," he said quietly. "I've been sitting here for the last twenty minutes and you were moaning and whimpering for at least fifteen of them. I was just going to wake you. I couldn't take it. Nightmares, Margaret?"

Vulnerable again. "So?" She pulled the bedcover higher over her arms. "Everyone has nightmares. Don't you, Lassiter?"

"Oh, yes." He leaned back in the chair. "But I'm finding I don't like the idea that I may be responsible for yours. It bothers me."

"Guilt? Don't flatter yourself. I wouldn't let you have that kind of effect on me. I learned a long time ago that no one could hurt me if I didn't let them. It was the shock. I should have been expecting something like that from you and I didn't. I had to come to terms— I had to go—"

"Be quiet," he said roughly. "I *did* hurt you. I could see it. Maybe I even meant to do it. Why else did you run down here like an animal in pain? Why wouldn't you eat the supper Cambry brought you?"

"I wasn't hungry. And I didn't want to be around you, Lassiter."

"And you were hurting enough that you curled up in that bed and tried to go away from it any way you could. But it followed you, didn't it?"

Yes, it had followed her. She had been afraid that it would. "Everyone has nightmares," she repeated. "Why are you here? I don't want to talk to you. Our last conversation didn't turn out so well for me."

"Tell me about it. It turned out shit for me. And I can't leave it like that. May I turn on that light?"

"No. Why would you want to?"

"I have no idea. It's probably a mistake. You have some weird effect on me. That's what got me into trouble up on deck."

"You weren't in trouble. You just saw that I was in trouble. Or would be, at your earliest convenience. Isn't that why you called Salva and—"

"Be quiet." He was across the room in seconds. The lamp was suddenly lit and glowing softly.

That's the only softness in the room, she thought. Everything about Lassiter was razor sharp, green eyes glittering, muscles filled with leashed tension. She tensed, instinctively responding to it.

"That's better," he said curtly as he sat down on the bed beside her. "Now stop talking around me and talk to me."

He wasn't touching her, but she could feel the tingling warmth he was emitting. It was . . . disturbing. "What am I supposed to say?"

"Anything you want to say. Curse me, tell me what a son of a bitch I am. Whatever comes to mind," he said harshly. "Just don't look at me like you did on deck. It . . . was not good."

She gazed at him in bewilderment. "How did you expect me to look?"

"I didn't expect anything. I wasn't thinking. I was just feeling."

"That's two of us. And it was all your fault, so I can't see—"

"I know that," he said through his teeth. "I'm trying to say that I'm sorry."

Her eyes widened. "Well, you're not doing a very good job, are you? Is this some kind of trick?"

"No, to both questions." He shook his head. "Somehow I got myself tangled and I can't get out. It has something to do with all those months when I felt as if I was practically living with you. Hell, it might have ruined everything. That call to Salva was my last attempt to play the game the way I planned it."

"What are you talking about? It didn't seem like a last attempt to me."

"You were beating me," he said simply. "I wasn't seeing you as a tool to get Nicos any longer. I had to do something to get back on course." His lips twisted. "I had no idea that it would prove so traumatic for both of us."

"Beating you?" she said. "I was the one who took the beating."

He nodded. "But that may turn out to your advantage."

"What?"

"I'm finding that I can't use force to get you to go to Nicos. I came here tonight to tell you that. Even if you won't agree to help me voluntarily, I can't hand you over to him."

She stared at him, stunned. "Then you'll let me go?"

He shook his head. "Not yet." He shrugged. "Hope springs eternal. You may still agree to bait the trap. You'll go with me to Nicos's island and you can make your choice then."

"I've already made my choice."

"People change their minds." He smiled. "Just like tigers."

"But you won't be able change mine." Her gaze narrowed on his face. "Is this just a ploy of some sort? Are you lying to me?"

"Look at me." He reached out and took her chin in his hands. "Am I lying to you, Margaret?"

Pale green eyes intent on hers. His hands warm against her skin. She could feel her heart begin to pound. She couldn't look away from him. "I . . . don't think you're lying. But Devon said you're good at getting people to do what you want. Maybe I couldn't tell."

"I haven't been able to get you to do anything I want yet."

"But that's different; you haven't really been trying anything but arguments and force." She moistened her lips. "But I did feel something different today when we were playing chess on deck. And I can feel it right now."

"Can you? You shouldn't be telling me this, you know." He took his hands away and ruefully shook his head. "Margaret, I'd say you were as open and defenseless as a baby if you hadn't just negotiated me into a corner that may prove very dangerous for me."

"I haven't negotiated anything." She paused. "You really mean it? You won't make me go back to him?"

"I won't make you," he said as he got to his feet. "But

then you've been telling me all along that I couldn't do that anyway. So what's different?"

"It's different because I thought maybe you *could* do it," she said frankly. "You're very intelligent, very strong. And you managed to track me down. That means you know me well. I knew I could get away from most people, but I wasn't sure about you."

He nodded. "If you'd gotten away from me, I would have found you. Because I do know you well. I've dedicated a year of my life to you. The reason I didn't ask you many questions this afternoon was because I already know the answers."

"And that makes me very uneasy," she said flatly.

"It shouldn't. You've won, haven't you? Once we get to Nicos's island, it will be your choice whether you want to help me." He headed for the door. "I'll tell Cambry. He'll be very relieved. He was looking at me reprovingly all evening. He likes you. This was difficult for him."

"It wasn't easy for me," she said drily. She was talking in the past tense, she realized. It just proved how convincing and soothing Lassiter had been during these last minutes. He had effortlessly lifted the burden of panic and depression she had been feeling and given her hope. It seemed almost too good to be true.

And it might be.

She looked at him standing there at the door, cool, strong, the passion and emotion now gone from his face. So much intimidating power and competence . . . "Do you promise that what you've said is true? That I'll have that choice? That you'll not lie to me?"

"You have my promise that I won't lie to you." He smiled. "You have my promise that I won't force you to do anything." His smile deepened. "But I also promise you that I'll use every means I have to get you to see things my way. You can hardly blame me for that."

"Since you intend to drag me across Mexico and then the Caribbean while you do it, I can see why I would have a few reasons to blame you."

He chuckled. "But it's on a minor scale compared to kidnapping you."

She found her lips twitching. "It depends on how you look at it."

"That's what I'm trying to tell you. My goal in life is to make you look at it my way." He opened the door. "I'll go up to the galley and make you a sandwich and a cup of tea. Maybe you won't have any more bad dreams with something in your stomach."

"I told you that I'm not hungry."

"You will be. I make a great club sandwich. Besides, you've lost a pound or two since you've been on the boat. You really shouldn't have taken that midnight swim. Burned up a hell of a lot of calories." His eyes were shimmering with mischief as he opened the door. "I feel bound to correct your mistake in judgment. I'll be back in fifteen minutes."

The door closed behind him.

She stared bemusedly at the door. He had changed again in the space of a heartbeat. Her mind was whirling and she didn't know what to think . . . or what to feel. On the surface, it appeared that everything was better and going her way. But just the fact that Lassiter had told her she had won made her suspicious. She might have won a battle, but Lassiter would not even think of suggesting she had won the war. He had even laid out his battle strategy for her.

It would be okay. It wasn't her nature to dwell on what Lassiter might pull out of his magic bag of tricks to try to convince her that she should go back to Nicos's island. All she had to do was stick to her determination and everything would be fine. She'd believed Lassiter when he'd made her that promise.

So do as she always did. Lassiter was apparently going to exert himself to be both pleasant and amusing, so enjoy the moment.

And try to find something of value to take with her when she had to leave again.

Vadaz Island

"Margaret Douglas." Stan Nicos leaned forward in his office chair, his dark eyes suddenly bright with excitement. "You're positive, Salva? You have her?"

*Yes.* Juan Salva had known that Nicos's response would be this intense, and he felt a corresponding excitement himself. He had been right to take the chance on Lassiter. "Not exactly. But I will soon."

"Not exactly?" The excitement turned to anger and Nicos's voice lowered threateningly. "What are you doing? You came in here and said that I'd have her. Now you're waffling? Don't play games with me."

Salva said quickly, "Would I do that? I'm not a fool. I know how much you want her."

"But you haven't been able to find her in the last three years. You've completely failed me, Salva." Nicos smiled maliciously. "If you hadn't been useful to me in other ways, I might have been tempted to replace you. That little Greek girl you just brought me from the house in Bogotá is proving to be interesting. You may be an inadequate fool in many ways, but you know my tastes, and as a pimp, you're superb."

Salva kept his face expressionless. "I thought she'd please you." Arrogant son of a bitch. A pimp? He was the one who kept Nicos's syndicate running on greased wheels and he received no respect from him. "And I know that I haven't been totally successful in finding

Margaret Douglas, but you don't know how clever she's been about hiding from us."

"I don't know or care," Nicos said coldly. "You should have expected that when she managed to get off the island. It should never have been permitted. Do I have to do everything? I almost had her broken. In another few days, she would have been kneeling at my feet. You were there. You saw it."

"Yes, I saw it. That's why I never thought she'd have the nerve to try to leave you." Time to change the subject and veer away from that failure. "But we can put that behind us now. I'm certain within a few weeks you'll have her back. That's why I made the deal."

"Deal?"

"Lassiter." He paused. "He contacted me about six months ago and said that he'd be willing to make an exchange if you'd meet his terms."

"Lassiter?" Nicos threw back his head and laughed. "My how the mighty have fallen. It must have made him choke to have to come to me." He frowned. "But he didn't come to me. He came to you. And it was six months ago. Why didn't I hear about it?"

"He said he was on her trail. He didn't actually have her at the time." He smiled. "But he just called me and said that he does have her now."

"You believe him? It could be a trick."

"I believe him. We both know that if anyone could find her, it would be Lassiter. He has both the experience and motivation." He paused. "And when he came to me, I took the precaution of sending him certain photos to spur his enthusiasm. I hope that's what you would have done, Nicos?"

Nicos nodded. "Yes, that's what I would have done."

"It evidently worked. She's practically in your hands."

Nicos scowled. "Which she should have been three

years ago." Then his face cleared as a thought occurred to him. "But we may get her back just in time. Providing you haven't fumbled this deal with Lassiter."

Nicos wouldn't have even had the deal if I hadn't seen the advantages and negotiated, Salva thought sourly. Everything about Nicos, from his words to the way he looked to his lack of tact, breathed of arrogance. His tall, powerful body, his heavy, dark features and shining brown eyes. And that ugly tongue that Salva often wanted to cut out. Not yet. "You're thinking about Montego Bay? Yes, just in time. Don't worry, he'll be getting back to me."

"I can't wait for weeks. I have to have her on the twenty-third," Nicos said. "And I'll need to have a few days to get her back to the place I had her when she left me."

Salva felt confident enough to jab. "On her knees?" he said softly. "You said you hadn't quite got her to that point." Then when he saw Nicos start to frown, he added quickly, "But I'm sure that you'll get there soon. And I'll just send Lassiter another photo to hurry him along."

"Do that." Nicos got to his feet. "And while you're at it, start thinking of a way for me not to have Lassiter receive anything in return. It's been far too entertaining having him scurrying around for the last year and a half for me to give it up."

"We've lost four men to him," Salva reminded him. "And if you're not going to go through with the exchange, we'll lose more."

"Then they won't be men I want to have working for me anyway. I'll just replace them." Nicos turned toward the French doors. "As I discussed doing with you, but you've earned a reprieve. You may even get a bonus if you bring me Margaret Douglas by the deadline I gave you."

"I'll get right to work on it. Anything else?"

"No, not right now. I'm playing with the new toy you brought me today. I have her down in the pool." He glanced at Salva over his shoulder. "She's never had two men at once. Firsts are always exciting. You're welcome to join us."

Salva shook his head. "Twelve is too young for me. But if you like, I'll send Ricardo down. He might enjoy it."

"It's only important that I enjoy it," Nicos said. "Your loss, Salva. Yes, send Ricardo."

The door closed behind him.

Salva made the call to Ricardo and then sat down at Nicos's desk and pulled up the Colombian file. He scrolled down, chose a photo, and marked it for Lassiter. He'd send it when he got back to his own office. But he was in no hurry to leave Nicos's luxurious digs. He sat back and ran his hands caressingly over the fine leather on the arms of the chair.

This is where he belonged, surrounded by all the fine things that Nicos possessed. He'd have them someday when he managed to get rid of that son of a bitch and take over the syndicate himself. He was on his way. He just had to be careful how he balanced what he gave Nicos and what he took for himself.

And Margaret Douglas was going to be a part of that balance. . . .

He heard the Greek girl screaming, sobbing, down by the pool. That will please Nicos, he thought as he got to his feet. But it was just noise to Salva, and disturbed the dreams of power and glory to come. He'd go back to own quarters and go over the details of the shipment they were planning from Montego Bay. The more he insinuated himself into the business itself, the more power he took away from Nicos.

Let Nicos have his little girls and his vicious torture games. Salva would give him all he wanted to distract him from what he was losing to Salva every day.

He would even give him Margaret Douglas, who was in a class by herself to Nicos.

As he left Nicos's house, he realized the Greek girl had stopped screaming.

Careless fools. He hoped that didn't mean what he thought it did.

Or he might have the bother of going back to Bogotá to get Nicos another girl.

"Why was it so important that you got that tigress to feed her cub?" Lassiter suddenly asked as he looked up from the chessboard. "Couldn't they have bottle-fed him or something?"

"They could have, but it wouldn't have been as healthy for him. Any more than bottle-feeding is considered as healthy for a human baby."

His gaze narrowed on her face. "But you were willing to risk your neck to make that difference?"

"It wasn't only the fact that it was healthier. There were other elements that made it—" She looked up at him. "Why are you so curious about those tigers? That's the third question you've asked about them since we came on deck this morning."

"I have a curious nature." He smiled. "And I figure it's sort of a way to learn about you as well as your striped friends. Cause and effect." He went back to the question. "Why did you think it was important enough to risk your neck?"

Margaret shrugged. "Tigers generally live between fifteen and twenty-five years, and that cub would have had to spend his life without being a member of a family if Zaran hadn't accepted him. It's bad enough having to live in a controlled habitat when they should be in the wild. I didn't want him to be alone."

"You don't approve of the zoo's arrangements for your friends?"

"It's as good as it can be. They try to use habitats more than cages. And considering the poachers out there, it may be the only way to save the species. They're really the savages, not the tigers." Her lips tightened. "But it doesn't stop me from being sad and trying to help as much as I can to put their lives right."

"As you did on Summer Island?"

"That was different." She smiled. "Everyone there wants to do whatever they can to save and help those dogs. Do you know that they have the ability to heal themselves and others just by touch? We're trying to find out why it's so predominate in these particular dogs. They're kept together because the talent seems to be shared if they touch one another. Isn't that fantastic? It's a wonderful place."

"Then why did you leave?"

"Things happened." She shrugged. "And it was time I left there anyway. I'd been there too long."

"Because you were afraid that Nicos would find you?"

"You found me, didn't you?" She looked up at him. "My turn. I've asked you this before. Why do you want me to go back to Nikos? What am I the key to?"

"He has something I want." He smiled. "And I have something he wants."

"You don't have me." She pursued it. "What does he have that you want? Tell me."

He slowly shook his head. "It's not the right time. You've left me with fewer weapons than when I started out. I learned when I was just a kid that if I want to manipulate and have my own way, every single part of a scheme has to flow at just the right tempo. Then I go for high impact. Bad timing can screw up everything."

"You might as well tell me. You're not going to get your way anyway."

He laughed. "I'll never know if I just give in to you, will I?"

She gave it up and went for something he'd said that had caught her attention. "Just a kid? Why would a kid be thinking of manipulations and schemes and bad timing?"

"I'm sure a lot of children are more manipulative than they're thought to be."

"Why were you?" She thought of something else. "You said that growing up you were far from law-abiding. What did you do?"

"Why do you want to know?"

She wasn't sure herself. "You don't tell me very much. Maybe I'm just curious. It can't hurt you to tell me, can it? Do you think that I'll go call your parole officer or something?"

He threw back his head and laughed. "No, I'm not afraid of that, Margaret. You insult me. I was always too good to get arrested."

"Too good at what?"

"A few things. I grew up on the streets of Atlantic City under the kind guardianship of my uncle Bruce, who was a con man and gambler and several other less-than-legal occupations. Naturally, he thought a fine, upstanding young boy like me would be an asset, so he took me under his wing."

Her eyes widened. "That was a terrible thing for him to do."

He nodded. "In retrospect. But at the time, it was interesting and challenging. My uncle presented it as sort of a game and told me not to think of depressing things like morals or right and wrong. I also had a real flair for computers and I learned how to make them do whatever I wanted, whatever dear Uncle Bruce wanted. As a hacker, I was quite extraordinary." He added sardonically, "He was very proud." He saw her expression and shook his head. "You're looking at me as if I were that tiger cub you were so soppy about. I had a much better childhood than you did. No one beat me or sent me to camp out in the woods."

"Was your uncle kind to you?"

"Kindness didn't enter into it. It was all teacher and student. I did what was required and I was repaid with food and clothes and a fairly stimulating life."

"And that was enough?"

"Of course." He smiled crookedly. "Until I got busted."

"Busted? You told me you were never arrested."

"I wasn't. But I should have been. When I was seventeen, I hacked into the CIA data banks just out of curiosity to see if I could do it. But they didn't appreciate that I wasn't trying to do anything particularly criminal." He shrugged. "Hey, I admit I might have yielded to temptation if I'd seen anything that was irresistible. But I was mainly doing it to see if I could."

"But they caught you."

"The firewalls on my computer weren't nearly as impenetrable as they are now. I've never been that cocky again. I could have ended up in a federal jail for a long, long time."

"Why didn't you?"

"I was paid a visit by a CIA agent, Sean Patrick, who was kinder and more generous than I deserved him to be. They had a complete dossier on me by that time. He told me that he thought that my work in getting into the data banks was brilliant and should be encouraged. Too bad I was going to spend the next twenty years in prison. Then he offered me a deal. I was to spend the next four years in the army and was not to do anything illegal that my uncle Bruce had taught me to do or that I had been innovative enough to think up myself. At the end of that time, I was to be at the service of the CIA for at least another three years."

"And you took the deal."

"After trying every way I could to talk my way out of it. But Patrick was not to be conned, even by an expert like me. So three weeks later, I found myself reporting for service." He grimaced. "And not to a cozy niche babying computers. Patrick had arranged that I was going to go through basic training and, if I qualified, directly to Special Forces. I thought the bastard was trying to get me killed."

"Cambry told me that you served in Afghanistan, so obviously that didn't happen. Did you work for the CIA for those three years afterward?"

"Oh, yes. But I decided I wasn't cut out for it. It gave me too much latitude."

"I would have thought that would have been a plus for you."

He shook his head. "It was too appealing. As Patrick said, some people have to have at least a hint of boundaries or they try to take it all." He smiled. "So I spent a year or so developing some computer software that would keep me on the straight and narrow. I opened up my own company and started on the way to becoming the next Steve Jobs."

"I'd say that was in keeping with trying to take it all," she said drily.

"But I wouldn't end up in prison if something went wrong . . . maybe." He tilted head and said mockingly, "So there it is. I've bared my soul to you. Curiosity satisfied?"

"I guess it is." She suddenly frowned. "No. What happened to your uncle?"

"He disappeared when the CIA found out what I'd

done. I never heard from him again." He shook his head as he saw her expression. "There you go again. I didn't expect anything else, Margaret. After I started training, he would have just gotten in my way if he'd tried to lure me back into the fold."

She didn't answer.

"It's the truth, dammit. You have the most idealistic viewpoint, considering that there's not been anything remotely idealistic in your life."

"I'm not idealistic, but I try to be optimistic. There's no way that my father and I could have ever been close. But your uncle and you might have—I don't know. At least he didn't physically hurt you. It could have been different. I just hate the waste. If I'd been there, I think I would have tried to change things."

"Like Zaran and her cub?"

"It worked with them. If I hadn't been optimistic, I would never have tried." Her gaze narrowed on his face. "What you told me was kind of personal. I didn't expect that you'd— Why did you answer me?"

"Maybe because I know the fact that I know so much about you bothers you." He smiled. "Or maybe it was just the right time. You decide."

She wasn't about to decide. After what he'd told her, it was entirely possible that he'd make a move to con her in some way.

She instantly rejected it. She wanted to believe he'd done it to put the two of them on equal footing. But then, as she'd told him, she was an optimist.

She pushed the chessboard away from her. "I'm tired of this game." She wasn't speaking only of chess. "I think I'll go put on my suit and go for a swim." She grinned. "I guess you won't object, since there's no land in sight."

"But there might be sharks. I wouldn't think you'd be bonding with them."

"Not very often. They don't respond very well. The

urge to eat is too strong." She looked out at the horizon. "When do we get to that port in southern Mexico?"

"Tomorrow morning. If you survive the sharks."

She chuckled. "I'll survive them." She was striding down the deck. "And I'll survive you, Lassiter. Want to come along?"

"I'll pass. I'll keep an eye on you from the bridge with my rifle handy. I'm not going to lose you to Jaws."

"I liked that movie."

"I know you did. I'm sure you were rooting for the shark, but you always like a good adventure movie."

"I wasn't rooting for the shark. But he was just reacting according to his prime motivation, and those poor people didn't really have a chance in his world. It's kind of an underdog situation that—" She stopped as a thought occurred to her and turned to face him. "You told me that you knew most of the answers about me. Who told you that one?"

He was silent and then said, "I believe it was a Sandy Webber, whom you worked for in a veterinary hospital in Curaçao. She was sorry to lose you. She liked you very much."

"I liked her, too." Sandy had probably been easy for Lassiter to probe. She was bouncy and kind and energetic and had probably not even known she should be wary of him. The man she'd been with since Lassiter had come to her cabin last night would never have set off any alarms. That charisma and humor was in full force. "And she liked *Jaws,* too."

He had caught the hesitation. "She was your friend. She didn't tell me anything that personal. I just had to know who Margaret Douglas was."

"Yeah, sure. You know how I feel about that. And it's not very fair, since I didn't get a chance to interrogate everyone in the universe about you." She turned and went down the steps leading to her cabin. It wasn't a big thing and it probably wasn't important, but it had bothered her. She could see Lassiter smiling, coaxing Sandy, and gazing at her with that curious, intent look that he'd focused on her just this morning.

And all the doors had opened for him. With Sandy, with Judy Wong, with who knew how many other people he had tapped to find out about her.

Intimacy.

She should feel invaded, as she had when she'd first found out that he'd been shadowing her. It was a tribute to Lassiter's skill, warmth, and easy charisma that she felt instead this intimacy, closeness, and lack of threat.

Which might be the biggest threat of all.

Forget it. She'd decided to trust Lassiter's promise. And as long as she recognized the threat, it was nullified.

Maybe.

If not, she'd handle it when she had to. Right now, the sun was shining and the sea was blue and inviting, and she wanted to enjoy both before they reached Mexico tomorrow morning. You could never tell what that tomorrow would bring, so you had to seize today and hold on tight.

She turned and started to go through her backpack for her swimsuit.

"She doesn't look like much of a kid in that bikini, does she?" Cambry murmured as he watched Margaret swimming next to the ship and then turn over and start to backstroke. "It's the first time I've thought of her as a . . ." His voice trailed off.

"As a sex object?" Lassiter asked, finishing the sentence for him. "Back off, Cambry. I don't want that kind of conflict raising its head. We have enough problems with her."

"Yeah?" Cambry shot him a mischievous glance. "And what are you thinking as you look down at her undulating like a mermaid?"

"That I hope a shark doesn't come on the horizon and make me take a shot that will cause her to read me the riot act."

And that the sea beneath her looks like a damn bed, Lassiter thought. And that she's all golden, from that yellow bikini she is *not* wearing to her shimmering skin and wet hair, which the sea had corded into tan-and-gold strands around her face.

Cambry was wrong: It hadn't taken a bikini for Lassiter to be fully aware that Margaret was a woman and not a "kid." In spite of the almost childlike honesty and simplicity that she exhibited on occasion, her sexuality was undeniable.

And it was damn difficult to ignore so that he wouldn't scare her off while he was treading delicate ground.

In fact, it wouldn't be ignored at this particular moment. Lust. Pure lust.

"I'll go get her a towel." He spun around and headed for the cabins. "Keep an eye on her."

"Oh, I will." Cambry chuckled. "Since it's absolutely clear that it's no longer comfortable for you to do it."

# CHAPTER FIVE

"You've been swimming for three hours," Lassiter called. He was standing at the rail, holding a large orange beach towel. "It's time to come in. I'm tired of mounting a shark patrol."

She reluctantly started to swim back to the ship. "I saw you with that rifle. You would have been careful not to shoot a dolphin or a—"

"Nothing that wasn't attacking you with big sharp teeth." He reached down and pulled her out of the water and onto the deck. "But I was wondering if you were ever coming out." He wrapped the huge orange towel around her. "I thought you were going for a dip, not a marathon."

"I like the sea." She felt relaxed and warm and mellow. Most of the tension she had been feeling before had faded away in those few hours. She started drying her hair with the corner of her towel. "And I was pretty much alone out there. Actually, I was hoping for company. Maybe a school of dolphins . . ."

"Friends from the deep?"

"Maybe. You can't be sure of dolphins, though I've

never had trouble with them. But they're always interesting. Killer whales are different, but they—"

"You've worked with them?" He pulled the towel, which had slipped to her waist, back over her shoulders. "I've never run across any mention of that."

"Good." She grinned at him. "That means that I still have some places that are still my own. That was at an experimental project in Seattle."

"I didn't get to your U.S. experience until San Diego. I concentrated on the Caribbean."

"But you would have turned your attention to the United States when you found out that I'd moved on to San Diego?"

"Of course. One bit of information leads to another."

"There's one thing that's been worrying me about your 'bits of information.'" She stopped drying her hair to look up at him. "You traced Devon's phone and found out where I was. The way technology is today, I'm sure that you were able to tap my phone conversations and call history after you located me. What did you find out?"

He was silent a moment. "I found out where you worked from a call you made to the office to check your schedule."

"And what else?"

He tilted his head and gazed at her thoughtfully. "This is important to you, which might be bad for me. I'm tempted to lie to you." He shrugged. "But I promised I wouldn't lie. You had a conversation with an Eve Duncan. You'd talked to her before, about eight months ago. You also spoke to a Kendra Michaels about the same time. I haven't gone beyond that time frame."

"And you won't," she said quietly. "You leave Eve and Kendra alone. You've delved enough into my past. I made a new life when I got to the United States, and I won't let anyone be hurt by what I left behind."

"It's a big mistake to let me know you're vulnerable

in that area, Margaret," he said quietly. "If I hadn't decided to go in a different direction with you, then I could have used it. More than likely I would have done just that."

"Oh, I'll warn Eve and Kendra," she said. "And they're strong enough to take care of themselves. But I wanted to tell you that it has to stop or I won't be able to trust you." Her lips curved in the ghost of a smile. "And whatever game you're playing now involves my trusting you, maybe even liking you. Isn't that right?"

He nodded slowly. "That's right, Margaret." He smiled. "And I can accept leaving your friends entirely out of whatever we're doing together." He firmly tucked the towel around her for the third time. "And now it's time for you to go down and shower and change. I'll help Cambry with supper and make it absolutely mouthwatering to increase my likability factor."

"It's not going to work, you know."

"You can never tell. We'll just have to see, won't we? Now go shower and get dressed. If you can manage to get down there without dropping the damn towel again."

"I'm almost dry anyway. I don't need it." She started to take the towel off. "What's the big fuss about any  " She broke off as she met his eyes. Her chest felt suddenly tight and she inhaled sharply. But that caused her nipples to brush against the damp material. She felt heat when there should have been only coolness. "Oh. That."

"That," he repeated. "You've got to be the least self-aware person on the planet, Margaret. I admit, it stuns me."

"About sex?" She moistened her lips. "I don't think about it all the time, but I'm definitely aware. I guess I just didn't expect you to be thinking about it. After all, I'm not some kind of sex kitten or anything like that. And your mind hasn't been on anything but getting me to Nicos."

"It wasn't my mind that was involved. I'm damn sexual, Margaret," he said drily. "And I was doing pretty well until I brought the tension down and you decided to take off your clothes."

"Not all of them."

"Enough."

"Okay, I won't do it again." She frowned. "But it shouldn't entirely lie on my shoulders. You really should have better control. Like I said, I'm no—"

"Margaret," he said slowly and precisely. "I'm going to say this once and not again. I look at you and I see warmth and heat and I want to stretch out my hand and touch you. All the time, anytime. It's been that way since that first night, when you jumped off the boat. Maybe it's just one of my idiosyncrasies. And you may not be what is popularly known as a sex symbol, but whatever you are is someone I want to drag into bed to indulge in every erotic variation ever invented. So don't talk to me about control."

She realized her mouth was open and she closed it and swallowed. "Okay, I won't. It just surprised me. But I guess everyone has someone who appeals to them in some way that's not . . . usual."

He stared at her, then shook his head and gave her a faint smile. "I don't know about everyone. I only know about me. And if you mean by 'not usual' that I'm a little twisted, I don't believe that's the case. And you're insulting yourself and me."

"I didn't mean to do that. I'm stumbling a little. I know I'm not bad looking." She grinned. "And you're not crazy. You're just a little peculiar. And I'm sure you don't ordinarily pick women like me to take to bed. It must be all those months that you've been on my track that sort of influenced you or something." She turned to leave. "And I promise I won't be going around half-naked from now on."

"Too bad." When she looked back at him, she saw he was smiling. "Just joking." Then his smile faded and he said, "I never meant this conversation to take place. I've been purposely avoiding it. But you just kept pushing, Margaret."

"It . . . I didn't know I was pushing. It happened."

"It was the one subject I didn't want to 'happen.'" His expression was grave. "Because I knew it might make you feel awkward or even afraid. And now I have to deal with it. I fully intend to find a way to persuade you to help me get Nicos, but it won't be by getting you into bed and screwing you until we're both out of our minds." He drew a deep breath. "Damn, that sounds good. But I won't let it happen. Don't worry about it."

"I'm not going to worry about it. I have something to say about all this, Lassiter."

"Yes. I only wanted you to know you don't have to be afraid. I won't use sex." He met her eyes. "I was there when you had those nightmares about Nicos and Juan. I could see the fear. I don't know what you went through when you were living with Nicos, but I've heard stories about him and his 'girls.' I want you to know you won't have to go through that again." He turned on his heel. "Supper will be in an hour. You'd better get hopping."

She watched him walk away before she turned back toward the steps. She wasn't sure how she felt about the last few minutes. Her emotions were in turmoil. Well, why not, she thought ruefully. It wasn't every day she was told she was some kind of femme fatale and then totally rejected. And, after what had gone before, when she had gotten an insight into Lassiter's background and what made him tick, the combination had been enough to put her mind in the same chaos as her emotions. He had told her that he'd been raised to con and manipulate, and yet the very fact that he'd been honest with her about it had offered a protection against him that she might not otherwise have had.

She watched him go up on the bridge to where Cambry stood at the wheel. Cambry smiled and said something that made Lassiter smile in return. They were close, friends more than employer and employee. Cambry had said he owed him. Why? She had a sudden urgent desire to know, to put together more of the pieces of the man who was John Lassiter.

And maybe Lassiter had known that giving her a taste would make her want to do that. He had studied her, knew so much about her.

Back off.

If she began to know him, she would start to identify, even with a man as different from her as Lassiter. It was her nature and had gotten her into trouble in the past.

*Rosa.*

*Blood on the black-and-white tiles.*

The sudden onslaught of memory came out of nowhere.

A warning? It couldn't be stronger.

Yes, she must smother the curiosity, try to avoid him, and be very careful not to start empathizing with Lassiter.

If it wasn't too late already. . . .

The sun was going down on the horizon in a blaze of pink, scarlet, and purple. The sea was no longer brilliant turquoise blue, but a deep cobalt.

"Nice, huh?" Cambry had come to stand beside her at the rail. "How's that for an understatement?"

"Excellent." She smiled at him. "And so was that spaghetti you made for supper."

"I thought that we should have something substantial for our last night at sea. There may not be an opportunity for my fine cuisine after we get to port tomorrow morning."

"Who knows?"

His brows rose. "That wasn't particularly argumentative."

"I'm sure Lassiter told you that he wasn't going to force me to go to Nicos."

"Yep, I was glad he made the decision." He chuckled. "Or you made the decision. But you do know he's not giving up? Lassiter never gives up."

"Neither do I. And I can tolerate a trip across Mexico if he believes positioning me close to Nicos will make his little pipe dream suddenly become a reality."

His smiled faded. "You're trusting him."

"Shouldn't I?" She turned to face him. "Is he lying to me?"

"No." He looked out at the sea. "But he wants this more than I've ever known him to want anything. He'll do almost anything to get it."

"Get what?" she asked. "Why is he—" She broke off. Probing—it was what she'd told herself she wouldn't do. "Never mind." She turned back to face the sunset. "Where is Lassiter, anyway? I haven't seen him since supper."

"Downstairs on the computer. He's been working to hack into a site that showed promise, but he's not had any luck so far."

"What site? And I thought hacking was a past—" She stopped again. Wherever she turned, she ran into this constant need to know the details that surrounded Lassiter. Dangerous. Extremely dangerous. "I think I'll go for a stroll." She turned and moved down the deck. "Or maybe you'd like to give me a lesson and let me take a turn at that wheel?"

He chuckled. "Somehow I think we'd end up back in San Diego."

"It's possible. But you should at least try—"

"I heard that." Lassiter had come up on deck and was smiling at her. "And I don't believe we'll take a chance on you. It would be too much temptation."

"Like you and that CIA job?"

"Exactly."

She hadn't meant to mention anything personal; it had just come out. Unfortunately, that happened too often with her.

"Did you get through?" Cambry asked him.

Lassiter shook his head. "I'll go back to it later. I needed some air." He looked out at the sunset. "And I needed that. It's why I bought the damn ship. I'm not going to let Nicos take it away from me." He leaned his elbows on the rail. "Your hair is all streaked with pink and purple in this light, Margaret. You look like an alien from outer space."

She laughed. "And your skin is all dark red and leathery-looking. Not an alien. Maybe Geronimo or Sitting Bull."

"I'm out of this." Cambry held up his hands. "You two are getting a little too insulting, and you haven't even started on me yet."

"I wasn't insulting," Lassiter said solemnly, though there was definitely a twinkle in his eyes. "Aliens are different. I like different. And Margaret is certainly that, as everyone will—"

His cell phone rang.

It startled Margaret. She had seen Lassiter on the phone a few times since she'd been on the ship, but she'd never seen him take an incoming call.

And his response was also startled.

And wary.

He moved a few steps away and took out his phone. His shoulders were abruptly tense as he gazed down at the screen. "Excuse me. I seem to have a text." He turned half away from her and pressed the access button.

But not far enough away from Margaret so that she couldn't see his face when he read the text. He jerked back as if he'd been struck; a muscle jerked in his cheek.

Pain.

Sheer unadulterated agony.

Even in the light of the setting sun she could tell he was a shade paler.

Cambry stepped forward. "Lassiter?"

"Nothing. Reinforcement," Lassiter said unevenly. "I should have been expecting it." He thrust the phone at Cambry. "Juan Salva chose well."

He turned and strode down the deck to the bridge.

Cambry looked down at the message and inhaled sharply. "Oh shit." He strode after Lassiter and joined him on the bridge.

Margaret gazed after them in bewilderment.

Dear God, Lassiter's expression. The pain, all mockery gone, just that agony that was tearing him apart.

That was tearing her apart.

No, back away.

It was probably nothing she could help.

Nothing that wouldn't bring her back to the nightmare that had haunted her all these years.

It was his problem, not hers. Everyone had problems, and she couldn't let herself try to solve this one.

Not this one.

She tried to turn and gaze out at the sunset instead of at Lassiter.

She couldn't move.

She watched Lassiter half-shrug and then take his phone back and turn away from Neal Cambry. The shocked rawness was gone from his expression, but the pain was still there.

It isn't easy to hide an emotion that strong, she thought. She knew from experience that you had to burrow your feelings down to some deep place far away and then let them heal.

"Sorry." Cambry was coming back toward her. "Not a great text."

"I'd have to be blind not to be able to see that."

"No questions?"

"Not my business."

"No?" He tilted his head. "Then why does your expression remind me a little of Lassiter's?"

"I have no idea." She still couldn't take her gaze off Lassiter. "He probably needs you. You're his friend, aren't you? Why don't you go back to him?"

"Because I wouldn't be welcome. Lassiter has trouble sharing. Probably because he's been alone so much in his life."

As Margaret had been alone.

Don't compare. Don't identify.

Don't keep looking at him.

Don't wonder what would cause a man as tough as Lassiter to look as if he were being burned alive.

Tough. Cling to that word, that concept. He didn't need her. No matter what she thought, he was strong enough to stand alone.

"What are you thinking?" Cambry asked curiously.

She finally managed to turn away from Lassiter to look back at the sunset. "Every day is a new day. I'm thinking you should forget about past experiences and go up there and try to help him," she said jerkily.

He shook his head. "If he needs me, he knows where I am." He hesitated. "Stay away from him right now, Margaret. He might not be very civilized for a little while."

"Don't worry, I have no reason to go anywhere near him."

Not where the pain was, not where she might forget, not where she might make his agony her own.

She heard Cambry walk away from her, but her gaze never left the flame-streaked clouds of the horizon.

Don't look at him.

Let him be nothing to you.

Oh God, don't *feel* his pain.

The sun was down and it was almost dark when Margaret left the rail and strode up to the bridge.

"Lassiter." She held his gaze as she climbed up the three steps and came to face him. "I want to see that text."

"No, you don't." He was suddenly wary. "Has Cambry been talking?"

"No, you have him well trained. He wouldn't violate your friendship." She added jerkily, "And I made sure I didn't ask him to do it. I was hoping to avoid this. Do you think I want it?"

"You're angry." He was looking at her appraisingly. "And I don't know what the hell you're talking about."

"Yes, I'm angry," she said fiercely. "You're *strong, dammit. You shouldn't be hurting like this. I shouldn't have to deal with it. I stayed down there fighting it for almost a half hour and it didn't do any good. I knew it wasn't going to do any good." She gazed up at him, her hands closing into fists. "Most of the time it doesn't. Not when the pain is so bad. But I thought this time, when it could hurt me, too, that I had a chance."

"Go away, Margaret," he said wearily. "I'm not up to figuring out what you're talking about right now."

"I'm not going anywhere," she said through clenched teeth. "You've seen to that. I have to stay until this over." She was shaking. "You want to dangle me in front of Nicos? Go ahead. It might work. If I don't think it will, I'll think of something else."

"What are you talking about?" His eyes were narrowed on her face. "My God, you're shaking as if you have malaria. What's happening to you?"

"I'm just telling you that you've won. Show me that text."

He slowly held out the phone.

Margaret looked down at the screen. Not a written text. A photo of a man with a shock of gray hair chained to a wall. Whip strokes all over his legs and torso. His shirt pulled aside to display burn marks all over his chest. She stared at it for a moment, trying to overcome the waves of horror. "He looks like he's a walking skeleton. Starvation as well as torture?"

"Yes."

"How long?"

"Eighteen months."

"You care about him?"

He didn't answer.

"Tell me," she said through her teeth. "I have to *hear* it. Though I already know."

"Yes."

"Nicos?"

"Who else?"

"No one." She couldn't look at the photo any longer. It was tearing her apart. She handed the phone back to him. "That's all I can take right now. I'll ask you more questions when I'm able to function. Later." She turned and headed toward the steps leading down to the deck. "You'll get what you want. But it's not going to be all your way, Lassiter. I won't be a puppet. Not Nicos's, not yours."

"Margaret," he called after her. "What the hell happened here?"

"I lost. You won."

"How?" he asked roughly.

She didn't answer. "You would have won a long time

ago if you'd learned as much about me as you thought
you had." She jerked open the door and started to run
downstairs to her cabin. Escape. Sanctuary. "You found
out a lot, you guessed a lot more, but you never took that
step farther down the road. You should have done that,
Lassiter. . . ."

3:35 A.M.

Lassiter's knock on her door was soft but firm. "May we
talk now? I don't believe either one of us has been sleeping. I thought I'd give you time to calm down a bit, but
I have to know."

"Come in." She turned on the bedside lamp. "You're
right: I wasn't sleeping. We might as well start."

"Start what?"

"Nicos. What he's doing to you. What he's doing to
that poor man." She was managing to keep her voice
steady. It was more than she would have been able to
do two hours ago. "How we're going to stop it."

He stood there in the doorway, staring at her. "That's
what you said up on deck. Or something like it." His lips
tightened. "Along with some other things that made no
sense to me at all. I can't grasp this complete turnaround.
After you went down, I talked to Cambry to see if I
could get a clue what happened with you. He said that
when he talked to you earlier, you were still as determined as ever. What changed?"

She sat up in bed, tossed the cover aside, and tucked
her legs beneath her nightshirt. "Nothing changed.
Everything's as it's always been. You just didn't realize
it. And I didn't have any idea that Juan Salva would
do something to trigger it."

"Don't tell me that," he said harshly. "Something
*changed*. Stop the double-talk and tell me what it was.

It's been driving me crazy trying to figure it out. You said I screwed up. You said something about me not taking a step farther after I found out everything about you."

Her lips curved in a ghost of a smile. "That would bother you. You'd hate to think the failure was yours. All that searching, all your hard work, and you missed the most important thing that would have given you everything." She shrugged. "But don't feel bad; it's not too late."

"What did I miss?" he asked through clenched teeth. "I have to know what the hell set you off and made you act as if you were—" He stopped. "Tell me."

"Sure." She smiled without mirth. "It's my so-called gift that allows me to join, meld with animals. It comes with a side effect. Quite a reasonable and natural one when you come to think of it." She met his eyes. "I'm very empathetic. I identify not only with an animal with whom I'm trying to join but sometimes with people. Almost certainly if there's high emotion or intense mental pain involved. I can't avoid it. I can't dismiss it. It becomes a part of me. I have to accept it and then hope I can find a way to stop the pain." She paused. "*Your* pain, Lassiter."

"That's crazy," he said roughly. "Why should you be caught up with what I'm feeling? I can handle it myself. I don't need anyone else. Hell, after everything I've done to you, there's no way you can even give a damn what happens to me."

"That's why I wasn't worried. At first, I was uneasy, even afraid, and definitely on edge around you. I knew that would keep me from identifying with you. But things have changed lately. I wasn't afraid any longer. I . . . trusted you." She moistened her lips. "But I would still have been all right if Salva hadn't sent you that photo earlier. It was too powerful. It blew you out of the water. It blew *me* out of the water."

"I could see that." He was silent. "I still don't see how it could do that to you. How does it work, Margaret?"

"I explained it to you as well as I could. At times I feel what other people are feeling. Not all the time, not every person. There has to be a certain amount of—I have to feel at ease with them. I have to be able to identify with their emotions. Look, it's not as if I read their minds or anything like that. I just sometimes feel what they're feeling if it's particularly intense."

"And how long have you known you could do this?"

She shrugged. "Much later than when I realized I was bonding with animals. I was maybe nine or ten. I wasn't around very many people, so it didn't really show itself. Like I said, this isn't really like that; it's just a kind of side effect."

"Evidently not a comfortable one," he said grimly. "Not for me, either. It's not as if I couldn't solve my own problems, Margaret."

"And you're resenting it. It hurts your pride. Too bad. You shouldn't have started all this if you didn't want to accept everything that went along with it. If it makes you feel better, usually I can't tell what the hell you're thinking. That's why it came as such a shock when your damn feelings reached out and grabbed me. No *way* did I want that to happen. Didn't you wonder why I didn't dig harder into why you were going after Nicos? I tried not to ask questions. I didn't *want* to know if there was a good reason why you had done all this. I wanted to focus only on the thought that you'd invaded my space and threatened me with a horror I'd left behind me. And yes, you're tough. That's what I kept telling myself when I was trying to convince myself that I had to ignore what was tearing you apart. You're tough; you could handle it." She wearily reached up to brush the hair back from her forehead. "It didn't make any difference. It's something ingrained in me. No, probably a part of my rather peculiar DNA. As long as I can sense that pain, I can't close my eyes to it. It rips me to pieces. It won't leave me alone. I have to try to stop it." She straightened on the bed and met his eyes. "And I'm surprised that you're worried about how and why when I've told you what's most important to you. I'll do whatever you want to keep Nicos from causing any more pain."

He was silent a moment. "I'm surprised myself. I guess I was still in shock from the way you attacked me up on the bridge. You looked as if I'd crucified you. But you were definitely on the offensive."

"I had to get it done quickly and get away from you. Crucified? Yes, that's a good description." She gestured to the chair beside the bed. "We should talk. I have to know everything now. You might as well sit down, instead of standing there glaring at me. None of this is my fault. And, for once, none of this particular portion of the mess is your fault, either. It's just the way it has to be."

"Then why do I feel guilty?"

"That's your problem. It might have something to do with kidnapping me outside that tiger's cage."

He dropped down in the chair and studied her expression. "I've never seen you look like this. Hard . . ."

"Not really. I'm just trying to get through this and hold it all together. I won't let myself be changed by anything you do to me or that Nicos does."

He smiled crookedly. "I'd appreciate it if you wouldn't group us together."

"I can see why, considering what he's doing to that man in the photo." She shuddered as she remembered that brutalized body. "A friend?"

He nodded. "Sean Patrick." He was silent and then said, "More than a friend."

"Patrick . . ." she repeated. Then she remembered. "He was the CIA agent who kept you out of prison when you were a teenager."

"And was my mentor in those years when I was with the CIA. He even dropped in on me occasionally when I was doing my stretch in the Special Forces. From the day he came into my life, there wasn't a time that I didn't feel that he was there for me."

When Margaret thought back on that conversation, she could see how Patrick had dropped in and out of Lassiter's life, forming it, changing it. She had been so absorbed with Lassiter's background that she hadn't dwelt on that impact. "Sort of a father figure . . ."

"God no." He grimaced. "Wrong, Margaret. Get off that track. First, my lovable uncle Bruce and now Patrick? I assure you that Patrick would be insulted. He was only in his thirties when he saved my ass with the CIA during that hacking brouhaha. We just liked each other and kind of hung out together when we got the chance."

She blended the emotion he had felt on deck with that description and translated: "Your best friend."

"If you need to put a label on it. He's a great guy and I owe him. After I grew up a little, I realized what he was doing for me. I know how I would have turned out if he hadn't been around." He leaned back in the chair. "When I quit the CIA and opened my computer business, I thought I might be able to pay him back a little. I persuaded him to resign, too, and I made him vice president and executive director of international sales. He laughed at the title; he called it pompous. But he took the job." He paused. "I think he'd gotten kind of used to looking out for me. Crazy, huh? It's not as if I was that seventeen-year-old kid any longer."

But Margaret could see why the closeness had developed between them. She did not know Sean Patrick, but he must have been the kind of man who had been able to overcome Lassiter's wariness of trusting anyone. "Maybe not so crazy."

"Anyway, I tried to give him a percentage of the

business, but he wouldn't take it. I wanted him in charge of the Silicon Valley office, but he refused that, too. He said that he'd been globetrotting too long to be stuck in an office."

She could see where this was going. "International," she repeated. "Nicos?"

"We were doing very well. Besides the office in Silicon Valley, two factories in Bangkok, three in Vancouver. We were planning on opening a new factory in Colombia. So Patrick went down to Bogotá to check out the area. It was located in a small seaport, and it turned out that Nicos had decided that he wanted to use it for running his contraband. He started using strong-arm tactics to keep us from getting a business license. He burned down a warehouse. Then he murdered one of Patrick's construction engineers. Patrick went after Nicos and there was a confrontation. Patrick barely got away without being killed. I was on my way down there by that time and I told Patrick to back off and let me handle it. Nicos had paid off the local *policía* and I couldn't get any help there. So I knew I'd have to do something else to keep Nicos from going after Patrick and his crew. I warned Nicos to back off and then started to research. I thought I'd found a way to hurt him enough that he'd rethink the situation."

She could feel his pain start and she ignored it. She had to get to the end. "How did you hurt him?"

"Money is important to everyone. Particularly to scum like him. I hacked into one of his Grand Cayman bank accounts and eliminated it as if it had never existed."

She knew the rage that would have ignited in Nicos. "And then what happened?"

"He went after Patrick and the construction crew immediately after he'd been told he'd lost some 3.5 million dollars. I'd told Patrick to pull everyone out of the construction camp and get out of Colombia before I went after Nicos. I'd timed it to give them plenty of leeway." The pain was growing within him and she had to try to block it now. "But they were still at the private airport near Bogotá. They couldn't get out because of weather, some freak tropical storm that prevented takeoff for over six hours." He stopped and she knew he was having trouble going on. "A storm. Everything would have gone off like clockwork. They would have been safe. Son of a bitch. A *storm*." He went on quickly, jerkily: "Nicos killed two men, took Patrick and another man prisoner. That was eighteen months ago."

"You couldn't get him out." It was a statement, not a question. "Why?"

"Patrick and the other prisoner just disappeared." His lips twisted. "There are stories that Nicos has a stockade in Colombia that he uses as his own private concentration camp. I've got a security team made up of my Special Forces buddies I worked with in Afghanistan that I sent all over the jungles down there, but they came up with zilch. I even called in the CIA and asked them to try to find out something, anything. After all, Patrick had worked for them for years. But they told me that I could only expect limited help. It seems Nicos has been considered an asset lately because he's been persuaded to back off supplying arms to the Taliban in Afghanistan." He paused. "I even contacted Nicos and offered to ransom Patrick and Ben Karick, that other prisoner."

"He wouldn't do that," Margaret said. "You beat him when you stole that money from him. He's an egomaniac. The revenge would mean more to him. Besides, he likes to cause pain. Any way that he can."

"I found that out," he said. "He texted me a photo of Ben Karick the next day. He had a machete in his chest. He said he was saving Patrick for something long-term and special."

Margaret remembered the burn wounds, the scars

from the whip on that emaciated body. It made her feel sick. "And he's been doing it." She swallowed hard. "How many photos, Lassiter?"

"Twenty-two. He tries not to send too many." He added bitterly, "I suppose he thinks I might get jaded and they'll lose effect. That hasn't happened so far."

She inhaled sharply at the bolt of pain she felt issuing from him. "How long can he last?"

"I don't *know*," he said hoarsely. "Until Nicos gets bored and kills him? Until he picks up a bug or gets pneumonia? You saw what kind of shape he's in."

"Or until you find a way to locate that camp and get him out," she added. "Or until you strike a deal to get to Nicos and make him release Patrick." She tapped her chest. "That was plan A, right?"

He shook his head. "It wasn't plan A; it was the last resort. I was down to desperation measures," he said quietly. "But I wasn't desperate enough to trade you or to leave you with Nicos. I told you the truth. I would never have done that. I just had to have a card to play."

"Whether I wanted to do it or not."

"I have to save him."

"I know." She could *feel* the frantic desperation that had driven him, that was still driving him. "And now you have your card to play. I hope you play it well, Lassiter. Because it's a beautiful world out there and I don't intend to leave it anytime soon." She lay back down and drew the covers over her again. "And don't think you're in charge of how this is going to play out."

"You don't trust me?"

"Actually, I do trust you. Or I wouldn't be in this predicament. I don't believe you'd want me to be hurt, and that's why the empathy is so strong. It's only that I probably know Nicos better than you do and I won't be shut out. I want this over as soon as we can do it. For my own sake as well as your friend Patrick's." She punched the pillow to make it more comfortable before she settled her head on it. "Now go away and let me sleep a few hours. I need it."

"I guess you do." He got to his feet and moved toward the nightstand. He paused to look down at her as he reached out to turn off the lamp. "I meant it: Nothing is going to hurt you, Margaret." His hand moved to brush her hair back with a whisper touch. "I have to take what you're giving me. I wish I didn't. And I'm sorry that it happened this way. It's not how I wanted it to go. Who would have known that you'd be—"

"Weird? A freak? Hard to find the word, isn't it?"

"Not at all." He bent and brushed his lips across her forehead. "I was thinking of sensitive." He smiled as he drew back. "Or perhaps very special."

"Are you conning me, Lassiter?"

"I'll save that for another time, when you're not so fragile." He turned off the light. "And it will be done only with humor, not an attempt at manipulation, I promise." She could hear him move across the room toward the door. "Good night, Margaret. Sleep well."

She heard the door close behind him.

She stared into the darkness. Disturbance, as usual. Always disturbance with Lassiter. Only this time there was also this closeness she had never wanted. Even his hand on her hair had felt terribly intimate. She had wanted it to remain, to keep giving her that sense of being treasured. It was the way she had felt when he had touched her like that on the deck before he had pushed her away and called Juan Salva.

"Desperation," he had called it, "a last resort."

And she realized why he had called Salva. He might not have had her empathy, but he'd realized he was softening, and that couldn't be allowed to happen. At that point, he might not have been certain how far he'd have to go or what he'd have to do to get to Nicos.

He had no doubt meant it when he'd said that he wouldn't have sacrificed her to Nicos. But everything was always changing in this world. Except Nicos. Nicos never changed. Evil that dark always stayed the same.

Nicos.

*Black-and-white tiles* . . .

She closed her eyes tightly.

Go to sleep. She'd made her decision.

Don't think of what waits for you on Vadaz Island.

# CHAPTER SIX

Port Tendalos
Mexico

"It doesn't look like much of a seaport," Margaret said as she gazed at the sleepy little Mexican town, which possessed only a handful of piers and a strip of weather-beaten shops on the sandy beach. From where she stood at the rail of the ship it resembled one of the many Caribbean islands where she'd lived after she'd run from Nicos. "More like a fishing village."

"That's exactly what I wanted," Lassiter said. "Nicos has contacts all over Mexico and Central America. I've no desire for him to know where I am or what I'm doing at any given time. I've used this village before. There's a small private airport about three miles from the beach, beyond that dune. I have a Cessna waiting for us in a hangar there. I'll have Cambry drop us off and take the ship to an inlet about a hundred miles north to anchor and hide it. We'll pick him up there."

"You can fly that plane?" Then she remembered. "That's right, Devon said something about a Gulf-stream."

He nodded. "I learned while I was in the Special Forces. It comes in handy."

"I imagine it does." Her gaze remained on the sandy

beach. A peaceful seaside scene, a sleepy town. She didn't feel either peaceful or sleepy. All she could think of was that this town was the first step toward Nicos. "You had it all planned."

"It shouldn't be a surprise to you," he said curtly. "I wasn't in the least secretive about it. If you'd asked, I would have told you anything you wanted to know."

"At the time I was either avoiding thinking about this place or planning how to escape so that I'd never have to see it. I guess I should be grateful now that you've been careful about not alerting Nicos or Salva."

"Don't be ridiculous. I'd be a fool to expect gratitude from you." He turned away from the port, his gaze raking her face. "You've got circles beneath your eyes that look like bruises. No sleep at all?"

"A little. But I had a lot on my mind."

He stiffened. "Nicos?"

She shook her head. "I try not to think of him. I'll do that when I have to do it. No, I remembered what Cambry told me about your working on the computer before you came up on deck yesterday evening." She smiled faintly. "He was being discreet and wouldn't tell me exactly what you were doing, but I gathered it was important to you and not going well. Don't you think I should know now?"

He nodded. "I've been trying to get a clue to where that camp is where they're holding Patrick. It wouldn't be totally self-maintained; there would have to be supply records, maybe salary, transportation, something. . . . Perhaps even names and backgrounds of the guards who are holding him. If I can trace any items back to the source, I might be able to get my hands on someone who knows where he's being held."

"But you've not been able to do it yet?"

"I managed to access one of Nicos's main files from

the cloud." His hands clenched on the rail. "I'm betting that it's the right one. Everything points to it. But I couldn't break in or decode it. Whoever Nicos hired to create it must have been supertalented, genius caliber. The firewall is megatight. But I'm close. I know I'm close."

"That must be frustrating for you. You were able to break into CIA data banks when you were seventeen and you can't get into Nicos's files?"

"I'll get there," he said grimly. "I'll just work until I can find the password Nicos buried in that file."

"By all means, that would simplify everything, wouldn't it? If you were able to go around Nicos to find that camp, you wouldn't be forced to confront him." She made a wry face. "Or should I say, I wouldn't be forced to confront him? Because that's how it would end up."

"No, it wouldn't." His eyes were glittering in his taut face. "I told you that I wouldn't let that happen."

"I know you'll try not to let me have to face him."

"*Try?* You're not listening to me."

"Yes, I am. You don't have to get angry or upset. I just know Nicos."

"I *feel* angry and upset. If that empathy thing really worked, you'd know that. You're not believing what I say. And you're too damn calm. You should feel the same way."

She was feeling all those emotions, but she couldn't let them free. Control. She had to be controlled and keep a tight rein on what she was thinking, remembering. "You don't want me to be upset. It would be counterproductive. You're usually so cool and composed yourself. I wouldn't have thought I'd have to remind you of that."

"I haven't been cool and composed since the night I saw you climb into that tiger cage. It was a harbinger of things to come."

"For me, too." She suddenly chuckled. "But you fooled me, Lassiter. I always seemed to be the one treading water."

"'Treading water'?" He smiled grudgingly. "That's entirely too reminiscent. You always seemed to be in the water, literally and figuratively."

Memories were flooding back to her. So short a time with him to have so many memories.

"That's the first time I've seen you smile since you came on deck this morning," he said quietly, his gaze on her face. "You told me you had an optimistic nature. Be optimistic now. I promise I'll make it right for you and for Patrick."

"I'm working on it." She forced herself to keep her smile in place. "I'm having trouble with shock right now. I thought I wouldn't have to deal with Nicos again."

"And what were you going to do? Keep running? Moving from place to place. Changing your name and job every few months until you were a little gray-haired senior citizen?"

"I don't know. Maybe. I didn't think much about anything but staying out of Nicos's way. Perhaps that would have changed in a year or so."

"You won't have to worry about staying out of his way after we get Patrick away from him. It will no longer be an issue."

Her eyes swung quickly to look at him. It was clear what he meant. "People have tried to take Nicos out before. His protection is impregnable. You haven't even been able to get on his island."

"Because I had to be careful as long as Patrick was being held by him. Once I get Patrick away from him, I'll bring him down." His voice was cold. "I've had a plan in place for months. Six hours after I take Patrick from whatever hellhole they've stuck him in, Nicos and his men will be history."

Six hours. Nothing would have convinced her more surely of Lassiter's intentions and planning than his precision in the exact timing for destroying Nicos and his men.

"You're not saying anything," Lassiter said. "It's the only way, Margaret. He'll just keep coming after you. Though I imagine I'll be first on his list after I take his favorite toy away from him." He paused. "I've learned you instinctively lean toward life in everything around you. But this is different. Nicos isn't even human. He couldn't be and do what he's doing to Patrick."

"You think I don't know that? You're right: I hate death. I applaud life. But both exist in nature and have to be accepted." She shook her head. "That sounds sickeningly noble, doesn't it? I'm not at all philosophic where Nicos is concerned. There was a time I thought I'd kill him myself. There's not a chance I'd condemn anyone for doing what I wasn't able to do."

"It was that bad for you?" His lean face had hardened; his pale eyes glittered. "Then I may make it take a little longer than I planned to put Nicos down."

"No. Don't use me as an excuse. You have plenty with your friend Patrick. But death should be clean even if the victim is filthy." She turned back to the shore. "Isn't it time we got moving? The longer we stay here, the more on edge I get."

"In a couple minutes." He reached down and picked up a canvas tote that he'd set on the deck when he'd come up from the cabin. "I need to give you this first."

"What is it?" She rifled through it. "A shirt? A bandanna. Sunglasses. I guess I can use them. The shirt is too big for me, though, and I've got—" She broke off as she saw a gray graphite case gleaming at the bottom of the tote. "A phone?" She pulled it out to look at it. "Very fancy. But you could have just returned the one you took from me."

"It was a basic burner. I had an extra phone. There may come a time when you need all the bells and whistles."

She looked down at the phone. "Well, it's clear you don't believe I'm going to call any of my friends or the FBI if you've upgraded me to satellite."

"No, I think we're beyond that." He smiled faintly. "Friends were the only threat. I was never afraid you'd call on government agencies. They ask too many questions." His smile faded. "There's one question I'd like to ask. No, that I *have* to ask."

She gazed at him warily.

"You told me how well you knew Nicos. Much better than I did, you said." He looked her in the eye. "If you knew him that well, did you have any knowledge of that camp where Nicos keeps those prisoners he wants to give special attention? Maybe he said something and you didn't know what it meant at the time. Maybe you blocked it out and didn't want to know."

She stared at him in disbelief. "My God, Lassiter."

"I had to ask it," he said hoarsely. "I owe it to Patrick."

"No, you did not. Do you think that I wouldn't have said something the minute you told me about Patrick and that camp?"

"I don't know what your life was like with Nicos. It had to have been hell. I know how afraid you still are. There's no way I'd blame you. I'd understand if you were struggling to come—"

"You don't understand anything about me." She was fighting the hurt and anger. "And I don't understand you. Every time I think I do, you come up with some bullshit like this. No, I knew nothing about that camp. And it goes to show that we know nothing about each other. We're still strangers." She turned away from him. "Maybe we'll always be strangers."

"Wait. Does this mean that we're back to square one?"

"Why?" she asked over her shoulder. "Do you want your phone back? You think because you're being an ass that I'll just back away? I wish I could. But it doesn't work that way, Lassiter. Not with me. If I walked away, I'd never forget that photo you showed me. I'd never forget the pain. Now it's not only your pain; it's Sean Patrick's, too. He's the one who's important to me right now." She strode down the deck toward Cambry. "Now get me the hell off this ship."

"Definitely not like the company jet," Cambry said as he ran toward the Cessna from the brush surrounding the small inlet. "You told me to beat it up a little, but it offends me that I have to ride in such a heap of junk." He jumped into the backseat and slammed the door. "I have my status to maintain." He grinned at Margaret. "Hi, how are you doing? You were a little miffed when I last saw you."

Lassiter gave him a glance. "Cambry."

"*Miffed* is an understatement." She smiled back at Cambry. No matter how she felt about Lassiter, she found it hard to be angry with Cambry. "*Outraged* is more like it." She glanced at Lassiter as he started taxiing down the field. "And I'm working my way through it. It may take a long time."

"It's already taken a long time," Lassiter murmured. "At least from my perspective."

"But you were at fault. It's natural for the guilty to try to slide out from beneath the blame." She turned around to say to Cambry, "I noticed all the scratches and dents. Why did you have to beat up a perfectly good Cessna?"

"When Lassiter sent me down to make preparations,

he said he wanted it to look older and not attract attention. I risked a fine and my freedom when I painted another ID number on the plane, but that wasn't enough for him." He looked down at the map on his computer screen. "It shouldn't take that long to reach Cancún if we go direct. What do you want to do?"

"I'm not in that big a hurry right now," Lassiter said. "I want to have another try at hacking into that file of Nicos's. Find me a halfway point where we can overnight."

"That's a surprise," Cambry said as he started to plot a course. "Since you've been pushing at warp speed to find a way to get to Nicos for the last year."

"There are more ways than one to get to Nicos."

"Hey, that sounds familiar. Isn't that what I tried to suggest to you? You didn't think that it would be soon enough to—"

"Find that place to overnight," Lassiter said curtly. "I need the time to work."

Because if he can find out the information from that computer file, he might not have to use me to get to Nicos, Margaret thought. She might not believe she knew that much about the way he thought, but she knew he didn't want to have to do that. "You haven't been able to do it yet. You said that it was megatight," she said. "You have to be prepared that you won't find that—"

"I can *do* it." He didn't look at her. "I'm good. Hell, Patrick used to say I was a damn genius at getting through firewalls. As far as the password is concerned, everyone chooses what's easiest for them to remember. If I can tap Nicos's memories and experiences, then I'll be able to run thousands of possibilities until I find the right one. I just need more time."

"How much more time?"

"Three, four days. A week at the most."

But how much time does Sean Patrick have? she wondered. And she realized Lassiter was probably wondering the same thing. He must desperately want to barge past all the barriers to get to his friend, she thought. "What will you do if the time you're allowing yourself isn't enough?" she asked.

"A week is plenty of time. It shouldn't even take that long. It will be enough."

"What if it isn't? I'm certain you have another plan, too." She smiled faintly. "One that concerns me. You had a long time to work it out while you were hunting me."

"It won't be necessary."

"I have a right to know. After all, I might have to veto it."

He was silent. "An offer to exchange you for Patrick. A meeting set up that is *not* on Vadaz Island and with the guarantee that he'll bring Patrick to the site of the exchange."

"He won't keep his promises."

"I know. But if he wants you enough to show up himself, I'd get the opportunity to grab him and force him to give the order to release Patrick. I'll bring in the Special Forces team I told you about to stage an ambush." He paused. "But I'll make sure that he doesn't get a chance to get his hands on you at the same time."

"He'll bring enough men with him to make any of that very difficult."

"It's only to be expected. But it's not as if I won't be prepared. My security team is waiting for word from me in Cancún right now." He glanced at her. "It's not as if I haven't had experience at this kind of thing, Margaret. All I have to do is stage the ambush, get my hands on Nicos, and then get you out of there."

"Piece of cake."

"No, but I can do it. I have the men and the weapons and the experience."

She didn't doubt he had all of those priceless advantages because of his years in the Special Forces and the CIA, and she had found him to be much more clever than Nicos. But it didn't stop her from going cold at the thought of having to face Nicos again.

"You're afraid." Lassiter's gaze was on her face. He muttered a curse. "Of course you are. You'd be nuts if you weren't. Don't think about it. It's not going to happen."

Maybe not this time. Maybe not this way. But she had a terrible feeling that there wasn't going to be any path she could take that would let her avoid being there with Nicos again. "I have to think about it. I've kept myself from thinking about Nicos for the last three years, but you've changed all that. I don't have Special Forces or weapons or experience, but I have a mind and I have determination and I *know* that son of a bitch Nicos."

He glanced warily at her. "Does that mean you're issuing that veto you mentioned?"

"No, it means that I hope to hell that you find that password, because I'm scared. But I'm not going to panic, and I'm not going to discount any plan unless I can work out something else to do."

His lips twisted. "That appears reasonable. But you know I didn't agree with your veto power."

She didn't answer. There wasn't anything more to say. She would do what she had to do.

"Is this discussion finished?" Cambry asked politely. "I'm getting tired of being the invisible man. There's too much temptation to interject my opinion and, though that would be invaluable, I doubt if I'd be appreciated." Before they could reply, he went on: "I've found a small town that should meet your criteria, Lassiter. San Chapo. It's about three hours from here, close to the Guatemalan border. No formal airport, but a tarmac strip and a couple of hangars available for rent. It's very small, a couple of played-out silver mines, but mostly farm country. But there're a couple restaurants and one motel on the edge of town. Do you want me to try my extremely spotty Spanish and attempt to get us rooms?"

"I'll do it," Margaret said. "I spent a year in Guatemala and I picked up enough Spanish to function pretty well." She took out her phone. "Give me the number."

"Gladly." He handed her his computer. "Morales Motel. Let's hope they have cell access. This information is pretty scanty."

"There aren't many places in the world that don't have cell towers nearby these days. Besides, I have satellite, compliments of Lassiter." She quickly punched in the number. Three rings and the call was answered by a woman who sounded very young, perhaps even a teenager. A conversation of four minutes and the reservations were made. She hung up and handed Cambry back his computer. "Three rooms, smoking. Evidently, they don't have nonsmoking rooms at the Morales Motel. I made the reservations under the name Rawlins. Hopefully, no one knows the name I've been using. You wouldn't want Lassiter to show up on any computer banks if hotels or rental-car companies are being monitored."

"Very efficient," Lassiter said. "Even to sheltering us beneath one of your false identities. You don't take any chances."

"Isn't that what you'd do?" She met his eyes. "You told me how sophisticated Nicos's computer guru turned out to be. I've found out how easy it is for someone to trace a name when there are zillions of linked computer networks out there that can trigger one another. I hate those network links. That's why I had to change my name so frequently."

He nodded slowly. "Yes, that's exactly what I'd do."

"And I bet you have a wallet full of phony ID in your pocket right now."

He smiled. "Only a few quality cards. They come in handy."

"You know all about computers. When you were hunting me, did you ever find out where I'd gone by tracking me through those links?"

"Only once in the early days. You were very careful most of the time. It was almost all legwork. Very frustrating."

"Good." She leaned back in her seat. "By the way, it wouldn't be Nicos who would set up links with other organizations and hire computer experts to safeguard records. It would be Juan Salva. I guess you know that."

"I know that he's smarter than Nicos, but he doesn't have the power to topple him. I knew when he was taking my bribe to give me information that I couldn't count on him."

She nodded. "He's . . . terrible. But not like Nicos. He . . . uses people and he doesn't—"

*Salva smiling as Nicos raised the gun.*

Don't think of it. She'd start to shake again.

She closed her eyes. "I'm going to rest now. Cambry said we had three hours. . . ."

The Morales Motel was at least thirty years old, with peeling yellow paint and a red tile roof. It was a single-story building that wrapped in a U shape. The pretty dark-haired girl at the desk was a teenager, as Margaret had thought, not over sixteen, with the single name Nita on her ID badge. She handed them their keys and pointed casually down the side of the building to indicate their rooms. Then she went back to talking on the phone to someone named Rico.

But once they had reached their rooms, they found them to be moderately clean, and there were soap and towels in the adjoining bathrooms.

"It's okay," Cambry said as he came from next door

into Margaret's room. "And okay for a tiny town like this is excellent. I chose well."

"Yes, you did," Margaret said as she unzipped her backpack. "I need to take a shower. Should I do it now, or are we going to try out that restaurant that's across the street first?"

"I vote for the shower. How about trying the restaurant in about an hour?" Cambry headed back toward the door. "But we're on our own. Lassiter told me he was starting back to work on that computer file. He said to drop off a sandwich and a thermos of coffee when we come back."

"Okay." She should have expected it. Lassiter was nothing if not driven. "Then I'll see you in an hour."

A few minutes later, she was under the cold spray in the shower. No hot water. But the cold water felt good after the warm, stuffy motel room. Though she would probably have been better off with a hot shower. She didn't need to be jarred awake before she went to that bed, whose comfort was marginal at best. She'd had only minimal sleep last night and only dozed on the plane.

*Sadness.*

The emotion hit her with full force.

*Hunger.*

*Death.*

*Sadness.*

*Sadness.*

*Sadness.*

Her hands went out to grab hold of the plastic shower curtain as the emotions cascaded over her, drowning her in the pain of loss.

*Not loss. Not yet.*

*Soon.*

Where was it coming from? She couldn't tell; she was only getting jagged wisps of sensation. She couldn't even tell if it was animal or human.

*Sadness.*

*Loss.*

*Sadness.*

Then it was gone.

She waited for it to come back.

Nothing.

What had happened? That reaching out had been in-credibly strong.

But it hadn't been a reaching out; it had been a cry of desolation. Last night with Lassiter, she had felt terrible pain; this was different. But it had been almost as in-tense.

She got out of the shower, dried off, and sat down on the bed.

*Okay, I'm here. I may not be what you want, but I'm here. Maybe I can help.*

Nothing.

Only that poignant sadness that still lingered in Mar-garet's mind.

She waited another fifteen minutes.

Nothing.

Maybe that contact had only happened because the feeling had been so intense. Perhaps the origin of that cry was too far to be within normal range.

*If you change your mind. I'll be around for a while.*

She couldn't force a contact. Perhaps the fact that she had heard it had only been a freak of nature.

She got to her feet and started to dress.

But her father had called Margaret a freak, too.

And it wouldn't hurt to do a little checking.

"What are you doing in here?" Cambry had poked his head into the office, where Margaret was standing at the desk, going through the registration book. "I thought something had happened to you and I was going to have to answer to Lassiter again."

"I was just seeing who is registered in the other motel rooms." She turned back to Nita, the young receptionist. The girl was looking at her with a wary and bewildered look. "I'm finished now, Nita," she said in Spanish. "I don't think there is any trouble. Just a few businessmen. No families."

The girl was frowning. "I don't think I should have let you look in the book. My uncle wouldn't like it."

"But you have a good heart," Margaret said gently. "You wouldn't want anything to happen to a baby. We had to be sure." She smiled warmly. "And now we are and you don't have to even tell your uncle." She reached over and pressed Nita's hand. "Your Rico is a lucky boy."

Nita giggled. "He's not mine. He's only someone from school." She reached for her phone again. "I'm glad there's no trouble. . . ."

"I only caught a few words of that," Cambry said as they left the office. "Trouble. And a baby. Would you care to translate?"

There was no way Margaret was going to describe what had happened in that motel room. She had been relieved that Lassiter hadn't shared her background with Cambry before, and this would be even more weird and difficult to explain. "I told that nice little receptionist that I'd thought I'd heard a baby crying for a long time somewhere in one of the rooms in the motel. I said that I was afraid someone had left a baby alone in a room and I wanted to be sure that it was safe. But there don't appear to be any families registered. I might have been mistaken."

"You must have been. These walls are paper-thin and I didn't hear anything." He was gazing at her curiously. "Can we go to the restaurant now?"

She nodded. "In a couple of minutes." She took out a Post-it she had stuffed in her pocket. "There are only four other people registered in the motel right now.

I have their room numbers." She was moving quickly down the walkway, looking at the brass numbers on the doors. "I want to make certain it was only my imagination." She stopped in front of a door. "Room twenty-six. That's the first one."

"You're going to knock and ask questions?"

"No, I only want to listen."

She stood there, close to the door.

*I'm here. Do you need me?*

Nothing.

She moved on down the sidewalk to the next door on her list.

Nothing.

At the third door, Cambry said. "Look, if you want to start knocking on these doors, I'll take the flack if anyone gives you grief about interference or privacy. After all, a baby is a baby."

But I don't even know if it *is* a baby, or if it's an animal of some sort, she thought ruefully. That cry had been too faint and remote to identify. But she knew that babies in peril arouse instant sympathy, so she had used that knowledge when she had gone to the office to explore possibilities. Threatened animals don't arouse the same urgency. It had worked with Nita, the receptionist. And it had triggered the same warmth and sympathy in Cambry. She had told Nita she had a good heart, and so did Cambry. She smiled. "I don't need to talk to anyone. I just want to listen and make sure that I was mistaken about what I heard." She moved down the walk toward the last door on her list. "You're right about those thin walls. You should have heard it, if I did."

"Yeah." He was watching her with narrowed eyes as she stood before that final door. "Ghosts? Poltergeists?"

She chuckled. "No way. Might have been the pipes in my shower."

Nothing here, either.

*Dammit, I didn't think you'd be this close, but I don't have anything else to work on. Help me.*

"Are we done?" Cambry asked. "Or are you trying to starve me?"

"We're done." She started to cross the motel parking lot toward the diner across the road. "Thanks for being patient."

"No problem. Toward the end, it was even becoming intriguing. I've never felt as if I was communing with a door before."

And Cambry was no fool. He might not know what was going on, but he suspected it wasn't what she had told him. She wasn't going to explain, but she could address the suspicion. "It's over." She smiled. "No more doors."

"Except this one." He opened the glass door of the diner. "And I refuse to stand in front of it. That red booth over in the corner looks as if it has my name on it. If you promise not to do anything bizarre that will delay my meal any longer, I'll let you share it. Let's hope the food is passable."

# CHAPTER SEVEN

The diner's food was passable if you didn't mind grease and burgers mixed with jalapeños and really good soft tortillas. And the coffee was strong, black, and aromatic, and the waiter kept it coming. They were able to buy two thermal travel mugs at the cashier's stand and filled them to the brim with that coffee for Lassiter.

Cambry handed Margaret the bag with the sandwich and coffee as they were crossing the parking lot back to the motel. "You give Lassiter his food. You have a better chance of getting him to eat it. Sometimes he doesn't pay attention to me."

"He's a grown man. No one should have to persuade him to do what's good for him."

"Right. But he's going to be working all night and he often forgets to eat." He made a face. "I sound like a nanny. How humiliating."

"Yes, you do." She looked at him. "Why? I know you work for him, but it's more than that, isn't it?"

"I told you: I owe him." He smiled. "I was in Afghanistan with him and I got mixed up with drugs." His smile ebbed. "When I got out of the service, I was pretty messed up. He got me off them. He stayed with me for six months before he had to report to train for the CIA. He was there for me, watching me, holding me when I had the shakes, yelling at me. . . ." He met her eyes. "Being a nanny. Which was a hell of lot harder for him than it is for me right now. You can see his temperament is light-years away from that particular vocation."

"Definitely," she said drily.

"And that I have to do what I can to repay him?"

"Yes." She shook her head. "But not by pawning off the nanny duty on me. Not cool, Cambry."

"He tends to ignore my sage advice. You, on the other hand, are obviously pissed off at him, probably with good reason. Sheer guilt will force him to pay attention to you. Get him to eat the sandwich and drink at least one cup of coffee."

"No, there's no way I want to do this."

"There's no way I wanted to stroll around the motel and hover like a gargoyle outside those doors." He paused. "Or watch you at the restaurant tonight going off into space and missing a few lines of my fascinating conversation. It wasn't me that you were listening to or for at that table this evening." He nodded at the paper bag. "But if you'll deliver that food and assure that it's eaten, I won't ask questions you clearly don't want to answer. And I won't even discuss it with Lassiter and possibly distract him from what's important for him to do tonight."

He was very sharp. She hadn't been aware that her inattention had been so obvious at the restaurant. He had even used the word *listening*. He had guessed that she was doing the same silent monitoring as she had done outside those doors. Not that it had done any good. There had been no contact there, either. "That sounds a little like blackmail."

"Perish the thought. It's only an exchange that will benefit both you and Lassiter."

"No, it's not."

"Go ahead," he wheedled. "Fifteen minutes and you can go get a good night's sleep."

She could refuse. She could explain. But both options would lead to complications and explanations, and she was too tired to become involved in either. She certainly didn't want Lassiter made aware of that strange moment she'd experienced. He already knew too much about that melding that she considered belonged only to her. Just do what Cambry wanted and get it over with. Her hand tightened on the bag and she moved toward Lassiter's door. "Fifteen minutes. Good night, Cambry."

"Thank you, Margaret." He turned toward his room. "We must sit down and have a chat soon. I'm sure it would prove interesting." He looked over his shoulder as he unlocked his door. "I didn't tell you how glad I am that you're going to help Lassiter. No, not really glad. I'm worried about you. But Lassiter will keep you safe. You're much better off working with him than fighting him."

"I don't know if I am or not. But it was my choice."

"He told me." He added gravely, "I want you to know that I'll do everything I can to help you."

He meant it. She found herself smiling. "As long as it doesn't get in the way of your keeping Lassiter well and happy." She knocked on Lassiter's door. "I warn you this is only going to work once with me, Cambry."

"That's what I thought." He was laughing as he went into his own room and closed the door.

And Lassiter wasn't answering her knock.

She knocked harder. "Open the door, Lassiter. I want to get to bed."

He opened the door. He was dressed in dark jeans and a navy blue T-shirt, which made his green eyes look blue. "That's not something you want to shout outside a door at a motel." He smiled. "It could be misconstrued or regarded as an invitation."

There was something different about him, something there hadn't been a few hours ago when they had checked into the motel. His eyes were glittering and vibrantly alive. The muscles of his body seemed more lithe and exuded explosive energy. She couldn't stop looking at him.

So different . . .

Then what he had said hit home. "I didn't shout." She thrust the bag at him and walked past him into the room. "Here's your food. And if you'd answered the door, I wouldn't have had to pound on it."

"Sorry, I was busy."

He didn't look sorry. He looked . . . exhilarated.

She glanced at the computer on the table across the room. "You broke through the firewall?"

"About fifteen minutes ago."

Relief rushed through her. "What about finding the password?"

"Not yet. That may be harder." His smile lit his face. "Or maybe not. I'll run a brute-force attack and maybe I'll get lucky."

"What on earth is a brute-force attack?"

"It's when I gather everything I know about Nicos down to the last detail and let the computer run probable suggestions for passwords. It could work. I'm feeling like everything's going my way tonight."

She could tell that from his entire demeanor. That glowing triumph, the sheer aliveness that he was casting out was contagious. She wanted to reach out and touch him, bask in it.

She stepped back instead. "Then I know you want to get back to work on it." She sat down on the edge of the bed. "Go ahead and eat that sandwich and I'll get out of here."

His brows rose. "You said you wanted to get to bed. I didn't think you'd waste any time after you dropped off the food." His eyes were suddenly twinkling with mischief. "But I'll be glad to supply the bed, although I don't guarantee you'd get much rest."

Tingling heat.

Don't let him see the disturbance.

"I'm perched on the corner of it right now. That's all I need. I promised Cambry that I'd see that you had something to eat. He appears to believe that you'll fade away if he doesn't make sure that you ingest a sufficient amount of proteins." She added wryly, "Though that sandwich has more grease and bun than meat. It doesn't taste bad if you don't mind the jalapeños."

"I like hot." He took out the sandwich and unwrapped it. "When I was in India with the CIA, I became used to dishes that would clear anyone's sinuses for a solid week." He dropped down on the one chair in the room. "But I'm surprised you were so obliging to Cambry. What did he do to convince you?"

She didn't answer directly. "He can be persuasive."

"I know. But you were still irritated at me when I saw you last." He corrected himself immediately, "No, outraged. *Irritated* is almost as weak as *miffed*."

"That's not funny."

"I know." He took a swallow of coffee. "But nothing seems that bad to me right now." He took a bite of his sandwich before he said, "Though I realize that I should kneel at your feet and beg forgiveness."

"You're joking again."

"Heaven forbid." He met her gaze over the rim of his coffee mug. "I can't help it. I know that you have a right to be angry. I'm truly sorry I felt I had to do that. But I'm so damn happy that everything has a chance of working out."

She could see that happiness shining out of him.

Since the moment she had met him, he had been closed in, not permitting her to see more than a shadow of his character. On the surface she had seen only grimness or mockery mixed occasionally with curiosity and charisma. All very fascinating but worn like a mask to hide what was beneath. She felt warmed, drawn to this John Lassiter. "Needless to say, I'm pretty happy myself." She smiled. "And the outrage may fade in time to a miff if you come up with the password."

"I'll do it." He drank another sip of coffee. "I just have to isolate the things that are the most important to Nicos." His smile was suddenly gone. "You might help me with that," he said quietly. "You told me that you knew him well. I've been running background checks on him from the time I realized he was going to be a nightmare, but you may know . . . details."

Details. She felt as if she'd been struck in the stomach. From relief and happiness back to Nicos. "I suppose I do . . ." she said shakily. "Though I've been trying to forget them for the last three years."

"It might help." His gaze was raking her face. "Hell, you're scared to death. Forget it. I don't need you. I'll work it out for myself."

"No, give me a few minutes." She moistened her lips. "I'm a little upset at the moment. I thought generalizations would do, but details are—"

*Blood.*

*Black-and-white tiles.*

*Rosa begging on her knees.*

"I'll work it out for myself," he repeated.

She shook her head. "I can help. A few minutes . . . Tell me what you know about Nicos. I'll see if I can add to it."

Lassiter didn't speak for a moment, his gaze on her face. "He's in his early forties, born in Kingston, Jamaica. His father was Erik Nicos, a drug kingpin on the island, as well as the owner of several bordellos. Nicos's mother was Azara Lua, a prostitute in one of the bordellos. She was made the madam of the place when she gave birth to Erik Nicos's son. She raised Stan Nicos until he was ten and then his father decided he wanted a son and heir for the family business, so he took the boy away from his mother. He was very pleased with young Stan, who was even more brutal and bloodthirsty than he was. The drug business thrived, but his son was ambitious and wanted to branch out into running arms to the rebels in Colombia and the Taliban in the Middle East. They had a conflict of interests that ended in his father being found in a ditch in a swamp with his throat cut. Then Nicos was free to rise to his full potential. He continued with the drugs but often used them to bargain with arms suppliers and sweeten the pot with the buyers. He did so well that he bought himself Vadaz Island and surrounded himself with an army of goons like himself. But he was smart enough to make that island impregnable to anyone attempting to infiltrate or attack it. And he believes he's made himself so secure on and off the island that no one can touch him." His lips tightened. "Other than that, he's a vicious cobra who has a penchant for torture, which he enjoys even more than the money I offered him for Patrick."

"It's not only Patrick," she said. "Patrick is only a means to an end. He wants to torture you. You're the one who beat him. Of course he wouldn't give up someone you wanted. And he stretched out the torture to make certain that it wouldn't end too soon. Not for either of you."

His lips twisted bitterly. "You do know him."

She nodded jerkily. "I know him well enough to realize that he'll never give Patrick to you. He may pretend he'll do an exchange, but in the end he'll kill him. You'd better find that password."

"That's what this is about. Can you remember anything that Nicos might lean toward using as—" He stopped as he saw she was shaking her head.

"Let it go for now. I'll work on it tonight and I'll ask you again in the morning if I don't have a breakthrough." He grimaced. "I'm sure that I've kept you from getting any decent amount of sleep again. You might come up with something."

"I'll try; it's not that I don't want to—" She stopped. How could she explain the memories that kept blocking anything not connected to that nightmare she had lived?

Don't explain it. Try to overcome it.

She got to her feet. "Then I'd better go to bed and try for a nap at least." She headed for the door. "Which is better than you'll be getting while you're—"

Lassiter's phone rang.

She instinctively went rigid as she recalled the night on deck when he'd received that other call.

It didn't have to be Juan Salva.

It didn't have to be another horrible photo of torture and pain.

Hell, it could be Cambry calling to check to see if Lassiter had eaten that damn sandwich.

But she could see by Lassiter's expression that it wasn't Cambry.

He nodded at her as he answered the phone and put it on speaker. "I said I'd be in touch with you, Salva."

"Yes, but it appears that Nicos has time constraints and is too impatient to wait for you to get around to making a deal. You'll have to do it now. He has to have her right away."

Margaret flinched as she heard Juan's familiar smooth, mocking voice. She could almost see his face before her.

"He'll have to be patient," Lassiter said. "I need at

least a week to get her to you. After three years, a few
more days won't be that long."

"It's too long for Nicos. He has a schedule to keep.
He needs her in four days. July twenty-third. And he
wants her here ahead of time for a little schooling. So
two days at the longest."

"I said he'll have to wait," Lassiter said harshly.

"Not possible. You're hesitating." He paused. "Could
it be that you don't have her after all? That would be a
blow to me, and a reason to take action for Nicos."

"I have her. But it will be my decision when to turn
her over."

"Wrong. You saw the latest photo? The next one will
be somewhat different if you don't supply Margaret on
time." He paused. "Nicos just came into the office. He
wants to talk to you, Lassiter. I believe he thinks reinforcement is necessary."

"Did you lie to Salva, Lassiter?" It was Nicos's voice.
Margaret's stomach clenched at the sound of it. The
same. He sounded exactly the same. "I hope you didn't.
I've been enjoying our little talks and texts so much
during these last months. But if I find you've lied to me
or if you fail to give me Margaret in the next few days,
then I'll have to do without that occasional burst of stim-
ulation. I need her by the twenty-third. If she's not on the
island by the twenty-first, then I'll give your friend
Patrick a final twenty-four hours of extreme torture and
send you a photo with him minus body parts, including
his head."

"You're bluffing. What are a few days more? We can
arrange an exchange that will—"

"We might have discussed an exchange if I didn't
have a pressing need for Margaret. All you'll get right
now is more time for Patrick. If that's valuable enough
for you to give her to me, then he'll live for another week

or month." He paused. "But I'm concerned that we're not certain that you're not lying. I have plans to make. I believe I need to talk to Margaret. Is she there with you?"

"I won't let you—"

"I'm here Nicos." She hadn't known she was going to speak until the words came out. She had been standing here as horror after horror raced through her. As she had listened to him, she had felt dizzy, as if she couldn't catch her breath, chilled to the bone. She wanted to hide. But there was no hiding from him now. "Lassiter didn't lie. He tracked me, and took me down just as you would have done."

"How good it is to hear your voice," Nicos said softly. "You've been a very bad girl. But I've missed you, Margaret."

"I'm sure you have." She had to keep her voice steady. "I haven't missed you, Nicos."

"That's because I hadn't completed your training. I can make you miss me. I can make you feel anything I want you to feel."

"No, you can't. That would spoil everything for you."

"It might be worth it. Or perhaps I can work around it." He laughed. "I'm going to get the opportunity. Please tell Lassiter that I meant what I said. Patrick dies if you aren't on the island by day after tomorrow. I'll need you at Montego Bay two days after that."

"You're on speaker. I don't need to tell him."

"Then I'll say good-bye, Lassiter," Nicos said. "Our association has proved to be of enormous benefit to me. I never dreamed that just taking Patrick would cause you to bring me such a wonderful prize as Margaret. Enjoy her for the time you have with her. But please don't damage her. I regard that as my privilege." He hung up.

Lassiter was cursing as he turned to her. "You didn't

have to talk to him. I could see what it was doing to you."

"You're wrong. I had to do it," she said numbly. "I couldn't do anything else or he might have thought you were trying to fool him. I've seen him blow up when he thought that was happening. He doesn't think; he just strikes out." She swallowed hard to ease the tightness of her throat. "He would have struck out at Patrick. One telephone call and Patrick would have been dead. I had to do what he wanted."

"Is that how it worked with the two of you?" His eyes were blazing in his taut face. "To keep the peace, you gave in to everything he wanted of you? How could you take it?"

"Sometimes I couldn't. But I tried; it was safer for everyone." She had to get out of here. It was bad enough that Nicos's words, Nicos's voice seemed to linger, echo in the air. She could feel Lassiter's frustration and rage and it was hurting almost as much as Nicos's venom. "I'm going now. I have to leave." She turned toward the door. Escape. Run away. "I'll see you in the morning."

"No, stay." His voice was hoarse. "I'm not going to let you run out of here and then have to remember the look on your face all night. Everything seems to have gone wrong, but I'll make it right. I'll find that password. I'm not going to let you go back to him."

"I know you don't want to do it." She didn't look at him as she opened the door. "I know that."

"But you believe I'll do it anyway. My God, after listening to that son of a bitch talk to you like that? I'll find that damn password."

"I hope you do."

He was suddenly in front of her, his hands grasping her shoulders. "Listen, I put you in this position. You're right: I tracked you and then took you down. But I had no idea it would turn out like this. I thought I could use you to stall, set up an exchange, and then get my hands on Nicos."

"Yes, you told me."

"I don't know why the hell Nicos got it into his head that he wouldn't negotiate. Salva said there would be no problem with an exchange. It seemed as if an ambush would work."

She still didn't look at him. "It probably would have worked if Nicos hadn't had that date in mind. After that, there was no chance." She had to say one more thing before she broke free of his hold and got out of here. "He meant it, you know. He'll do exactly what he said he'd do to Patrick if I'm not there day after tomorrow. There won't be any question. You won't be able to bargain or bribe or procrastinate. Patrick will die that day."

"Look at me." His hands tightened on her shoulders as she lifted her eyes to his face. "Why the hell did you tell me that? Do you *want* me to send you back to him?"

"I don't want Patrick to die. You had to know." She tore away from him and called back over her shoulder, "Find that password. You told me you needed three or four days, maybe a week. Well, you don't have that any longer. You have two days. But if you don't find it, you'd better start thinking about what's going to come next. Because that's what I'll be thinking about tonight."

She slammed the door behind her and ran down the walk to her room. Her hand was shaking as she unlocked the door and threw it open.

Two minutes later, she had thrown off her clothes and crawled beneath the coverlet on the bed like a wounded animal. Nothing new. Nicos had always made her feel wounded and helpless.

No, not at first, not until he'd found the key to punish and take away her independence. It had been a long time after she had run away that she had regained that freedom. And that sense of oppression had come flooding back to her in a smothering tide as she'd spoken to Nicos tonight.

Fight it. She couldn't let it happen again. He didn't have the weapon that had broken her any longer. She didn't have to let him win.

But he had another weapon in Sean Patrick and he was using it against Lassiter. She couldn't turn her back when she had seen that photo that had torn her emotions apart. She could see it before her now and the memory was as fresh and painful as when she had first seen it.

All right, try not to remember it yet. Right now, lie here and concentrate on healing from that hideous encounter with Nicos. When she was just a little calmer, she would force herself to go over things she knew about Nicos that might help locate the password. See, she was getting better. She had almost stopped shaking.

Then she would pray that Lassiter's work tonight would be successful, that the password would magically appear on his screen. It wasn't impossible. Prayers were sometimes answered.

But Rosa's prayers had not been answered. Neither had Margaret's when she had been on Vadaz Island.

Then don't count on prayers. Think about what alternatives might succeed if they didn't find the password.

And she started to shake again.

*Sadness.*

*Desolation.*

*Fear.*

The emotions as well as the words were all surrounding her. She thought at first it was that strange calling she'd heard earlier in the evening.

It was not. It was her own emotions that she had to fight so desperately tonight.

*Sadness.*

*Desolation.*

*Fear . . .*

5:15 A.M.

Margaret turned off the shower but stayed there a minute trying to gather the effort to get out and start what had to be done. She would have welcomed the calling that had come to her yesterday while she standing here in this spot, just to have another reason to delay.

No cry.

No calling.

And she had to stop being a coward and face what she'd decided had to be faced. She got out of the shower and grabbed a towel. Maybe all this worry was for nothing. Maybe when she went to Lassiter, she'd find those prayers had been answered.

But when he answered the door to her knock fifteen minutes later, her hopes plummeted. He had a dark stubble on his face and his eyes were strained.

"You're too early. I'll get it. Come back in a couple hours."

It was the answer she'd dreaded. "Did that brute-force thing work? Are you close?"

He didn't answer her. "I'll get it."

It hadn't worked. "And what if you don't do it in time? You can't risk it. I've been thinking all night, trying to put together some clue that would help you find that password." She shook her head. "But bad things were going on all around me and I didn't pay attention to anything but how to keep it from getting worse." She paused. "But I'm not stupid. If I concentrate, I should be able to notice something, find something that would give you what you need."

He stiffened. "What the hell are you saying?"

"I'm saying I'm not going to go away and let you frantically keep searching for that password if I can find a way to make it easier. Stand aside and let me come in. I need to sit down. It's been another long night."

He didn't move. "Margaret, I promised you that—"

"I know." She pushed him aside. "And I'm certain you promised yourself that you wouldn't let your friend Patrick be butchered and killed. Which promise is the most important for you to honor?" She sat down on his chair in front of the computer. The entire area was strewn with papers scrawled with notes, and the computer screen had multiple lists of numbers and words. A testament to Lassiter's driving, relentless search. "He's hurt and helpless. I'm not helpless, Lassiter. I'm scared, but I can get over it. I just have to remember that things aren't the same as they were the last time." She gestured toward the bed. "Now sit down and let's talk and decide what's the best way to do this."

"You're talking about going to Nicos."

"It's the only thing to do now," she said simply. "We both know it. You just won't admit it."

"You're damn right I won't. I could see what he was doing to you last night. You were white as a sheet and you could barely talk."

"But I did talk to him and it got better once I got over the first shock." She met his eyes. "You're feeling guilty and you don't want me to have to face Nicos. I don't want that, either. But I can't stand the thought of a man dying because I was too afraid to fight a monster like Nicos. He's haunted me for years and I can't let him kill someone else because I didn't find a way to stop it."

" 'Someone else'?" Lassiter's eyes were narrowed on her face. "What are you talking about?"

She held up her hand. "I can't deal with that right now. I only wanted you to know that it's not only for Patrick that I have to do this."

"I *can't* let you go. He'll rape you, probably torture you, and possibly kill you. I couldn't live with any of that."

"Yes, you could. To save a life." Her lips curved in a

mirthless smile. "But none of that happened before, so it may not happen this time. If we're smart, if we plan it right. I didn't have anyone to help me three years ago. We have a chance now." She leaned forward. "Listen, you need to buy time to work on that password. I can give it to you. And I know Nicos's house; I might be able to find something in his office that will help."

"And get caught and maybe get your throat cut."

"I repeat, I'm not stupid," she said. "I know the island well enough to have escaped from it before. It's well guarded, but I might be able to get a message to you. I'll have to think about it. But Nicos will be watching me, so you won't be able to get me off the island once I'm there."

"So I'm just supposed to leave you there?"

"No, there may be another way," she said. "Let Nicos take me off the island."

"What?"

"Montego Bay. July twenty-third."

"That's supposed to mean something? The twenty-third is the day Nicos is demanding you show up at the island."

"No, he wants me there two days before. Because he has something planned on July twenty-third for me." She shook her head. "And that's the reason he won't negotiate with you."

"And what does he have planned?"

"It has to be a shipment. Either explosives or drugs that are being delivered to Montego Bay Airport on the twenty-third."

"And he needs you there for that?"

"Oh, yes," she said bitterly. "He always likes an insurance policy. Why do you think that he's been searching for me for the last three years? He must have been overjoyed when he found out from Salva that he would have me on hand just in time for the Montego Bay shipment."

" 'Insurance policy'? What kind of insurance policy?"

"The dogs. Couldn't you guess? The drugs or explosives are always very carefully hidden in freight or luggage, but the illicit-substance dogs they have trained these days are supersharp and can zero in on almost any hidden contraband." She added sarcastically, "It makes it very difficult for poor Nicos. That's why he values me so highly."

"I believed it might be for another reason. And what did you do for 'poor' Nicos?"

"He'd find a reason and a way to get me to customs when the shipment was unloaded. Usually, I'd have to be there fifteen or twenty minutes before the shipment showed up to be able to meld with the dogs. It's not easy to convince an animal as highly trained and experienced as those airport dogs that what they're smelling isn't what they're smelling. Sometimes all I could do was make them confused. Which also usually worked."

He was silent. "And how did he know that you'd be able to do that? I'm certain you didn't tell him."

"Are you?"

"Yes, I'm gradually learning about you, Margaret. Though you've not been helping me. How did he know?"

"Someone . . . close to me told him. Then he made me show him."

"And then he forced you to go with him to the airports and give him his 'insurance.' "

"Oh, yes, he was very pleased with me. He said I had the true magic and was obviously meant to serve him. I think he might have even believed it." She shrugged. "He grew up in Jamaica with Azara Lua, a mother who took him to voodoo rituals from the time he was a toddler. She was a prostitute and I think she might have brainwashed him to keep her hold on his father. He told me once she was a priestess but had no really strong magic. Not like I did. I didn't care if he thought I was some kind of mystical priestess, voodoo or otherwise. I played on it to survive and keep him away from me."

"And it worked?"

"I'm here, aren't I?"

"Yes, you are. But that doesn't mean you can survive him if you go back."

"I'll survive him." She drew a deep breath. "And I'll give you the time you need to work on the password. Two days until you have to deliver me. At least two more days after that before I have to go to Montego Bay. But if you can't get me away from him by then, I don't know how long it will be before I'll get another chance."

"I'd get you away if I had to blow up the damn airport," he said roughly. "But I won't let you go back there when I know how he'll be treating you."

"I told you: I'll survive—" She stopped, gazing at him as she realized what he meant. "You're worried that he's going to rape me? I don't believe that he will. I managed to instill the thought that my magic might not work if he had carnal relations with me. He'd already heard all kinds of stories about virgins being the most powerful priestesses. He might have changed his mind, but I don't think so."

"And you're willing to take the chance. I'm not willing for you to take it, Margaret."

"Why are you so upset about this? It's not as if I was a virgin. I just didn't want him touching me. Yes, it would have been rape, but I know about rape. When I was twelve, I ran into two hunters while I was living in the woods, men who wanted to have a little fun. It took me a long while to get over it, but then I realized that they couldn't touch or change anything that I was inside unless I let them. And I wasn't going to let them take one bit of joy from my life." She added curtly, "And Nicos wouldn't have been able to hurt me, either. Not that way."

"My God."

She felt uneasy about the way he was looking at her, and she said quickly, "But as I said, I think I managed to handle that, so don't worry about me taking care of myself. I'll walk a fine line and do what I have to do. I'll leave the rest to you, with all your Special Forces and your CIA and fancy computers and . . ." She got to her feet. "Now I'll leave and go see if Cambry is awake. You didn't tell me what time we're flying out of here. I'll tell Cambry to be ready at eight."

"You think this is settled? It's not settled, Margaret."

"Yes, it is." She looked him directly in the eye. "When I was lying there in bed last night, I realized that I was partly to blame for the situation that Patrick is in now."

"Bullshit."

"No, if I'd done something to resolve that nightmare with Nicos three years ago instead of running away, you and Patrick might not even have had to deal with him. I didn't choose to do that and I share some of the blame. So unless you can tell me you have that password, I have to do this. With or without you, Lassiter." She went to the door. "Don't let it be without you. I'm still pretty scared."

"You couldn't prove it by what I just heard. You're not to blame for any of this, dammit. I dragged you into it."

She shook her head as she swung the door closed behind her. "There are always choices, Lassiter. I could give you excuses, but I chose to be a victim three years ago. Which had ramifications all down the line. I can't make that same choice again."

# CHAPTER EIGHT

"I called Lassiter," Cambry said when he knocked on her door at 7:30, carrying a bag of bagels and coffee. "He said for us to go ahead and take a taxi to the hangar and get the plane ready for takeoff. He said he'd had a new idea that he wanted to explore, and that he'd be with us as soon as he can."

He's still working on the password, she thought. She hoped that the new idea had promise. Heaven knows, they needed new and promising. "Whatever." She walked ahead of Cambry to the ancient rust-encrusted black taxicab parked in front of the office. "I checked out for all of us. Lassiter may be disturbed by maid service wanting to clean the rooms."

"Not likely. They don't appear to be that motivated here." After they had settled in the taxi, he added, "Lassiter told me about the phone call. You didn't mention it."

"I would have eventually. I'm still having trouble dealing with it." She leaned back on the seat as the taxi driver pulled away from the motel. She took the coffee cup Cambry handed her. "But then, so is Lassiter."

"I noticed." He added quietly, "This isn't the way he had it planned. He won't let you do it, Margaret."

"He doesn't have a choice. I know he's caught in the middle, but he has to go with the lesser evil. He cares about his friend, who will certainly die if he doesn't let me go to Nicos. If we work it right, I have a good chance of living and giving him a way to save Patrick." She turned to look at him. "Do you know Sean Patrick, Cambry?"

He nodded. "For the last eight years. He's a good guy. One of the best."

"I thought he might be. It seems as if everything that's happened has happened because of him. I just feel as if I need to know him. He's gone through so much. Lassiter has gone through so much for him. I know Lassiter believes that he's worth it."

"He is worth it," Cambry said. "And Patrick would be doing the same thing for Lassiter if the situation was reversed." He paused. "But that doesn't mean that you have to—"

*Sadness.*

*Sadness.*

*Sadness.*

*Loss.*

*Soon.*

*Sadness.*

Her hand clutched her coffee cup as the cry suddenly struck her. Strong. So strong that it took her breath away.

*Sadness!*

And close.

"Margaret?" Cambry was looking at her, puzzled.

*Soon.*

"I'm okay," she said absently.

*Where?*

No answer.

*Show me!*

No answer.

*I can't help you unless you show me.*
*Trying.*

"You're not okay," Cambry said as he reached for his phone. "I'm calling Lassiter."

"Do what you want. Just leave me alone."

And then she saw it.

She leaned forward and said to the taxi driver in Spanish, "There's a mine near here, isn't there? Probably only a couple miles? I need to go there."

He shook his head. *"Sí, pero está cerrado ahora."*

"I don't care if it's closed down right now. I need to go there," she repeated fiercely. "Now."

He shrugged. "No use. *Está cerrado.* And very bad road."

She looked him in the eye. "Now."

He scowled. "As you wish. But I charge you more." He made a left turn onto a bumpy dirt road. "And if I get a flat, you buy me a new tire."

"Just get me to that mine."

"May I ask where we're going?" Cambry asked. "I caught something about a mine. Second question: Why the hell?"

"Yes, it's a mine. Second answer: I don't know."

"You're acting weird, like you did last night. What's going on? And don't tell me this time that you heard some baby crying."

"I never told you that was what I heard. I said it was a possibility. I didn't know. It was just easier to get things done."

"But you know now?"

"Yes, I know."

A wire fence about twelve feet in height loomed just ahead.

"Pull over!" She jumped out of the taxi even before it had come to a full stop and ran toward the gate. It was ajar, as she'd guessed it would be. The wide timber-reinforced opening of the mine was twenty or thirty yards from the gate. She darted toward it.

*Where?*

No answer. Then a rush of overwhelming grief.

*Sadness.*

*Don't tell me that. And don't give up. You've gotten this far. Show me where.*

Hesitance. Then a picture, clear and detailed.

"Oh shit," she murmured. She turned to Cambry, who had run up behind her. "Deep. And lots of timber and debris. Find me a shovel."

"Where is she?" Lassiter strode toward the main tunnel entrance, where Cambry was standing. "And what the hell is she doing here? That roof looks like it's going to collapse any minute."

"I checked. It's sounder than it looks," Cambry said as he wiped the sweat from his face. "But the roof up ahead did collapse, probably fairly recently. At least that's what Margaret thinks." He grimaced. "That's what she told me before she crawled under that pile of timber up there."

"What?"

"I tried to stop her. But she had me shoveling debris away from a hole up there and she was under that pile before I knew it. She told me that I should stay near the opening we'd cleared and watch out for any sign of another cave-in."

"For God's sake, how long has she been down there?" Lassiter moved quickly toward the timbers. "Cambry, I may strangle you." He knelt down and peered down into the darkness. He couldn't tell how deep the hole was or how fragile the balance of the rocks and timbers.

And he could hear nothing. Had Margaret already been knocked unconscious by one of those displaced timbers after she'd crawled down there? He took out his flashlight and shined the beam into the darkness. "Margaret," he called. "Lassiter. Stay where you are. I'm coming down."

"No. It's going to be difficult enough getting back up there. If you want to help, get me a board or something that I can use for a stretcher."

"Are you hurt?"

"No, but she is. Find me something to bring her up."

"She?" Not the time to ask questions. "Never mind. Hold on. I'll find what you need. I'll take the door off the security booth at the gate. . . ."

Yes, he'll find what I need, Margaret thought with relief as she turned back to Juno. She'd been glad to hear Lassiter's voice. Cambry had been helpful and done everything she'd asked him to do, but Lassiter exuded confidence. Not that she wasn't confident; everything had gone as well as it could, considering the problems she was having with Juno.

*No problems. Just sadness.*

She quickly sent a message back. *Sadness is always a problem.*

More sadness. *Loss.*

*I know that's what you're afraid of, but we might be able to fix it.* She couldn't make promises. *But you have to keep fighting, or we won't have a chance.*

*Tired.*

*I don't want to hear it. You're strong. I can feel your heartbeat and it's strong, too. You were meant to live. You have to live.*

*Sadness . . .*

Margaret cuddled closer and held Juno tight. *No more sadness. Do you hear me? Trust me. It will never be the same. But it can be good. We'll make it good together. . . .*

*   *   *

"Be careful," Margaret called up to Lassiter. "I've tied Juno on that door with strips of my shirt, but you can't slant that stretcher too much, or they'll break with the weight of her body."

"We'll be careful." He was cautiously lowering himself down the timbers. "I can see the door now. I've threaded the rope through the hole I punched through the glass window. I'll support the frame and have Cambry pull the rope. It will—" He stopped. "Juno. I believe it's time I asked just what kind of animal Juno is. From this angle, she appears to be of substantial size."

"She's a golden retriever. She's probably only a little over a hundred pounds. Maybe less now. She hasn't eaten for days."

"And she's not likely to eat us?"

"Don't be silly. She wouldn't do that. Not now."

"That's comforting." He swung down a couple more feet. "You wouldn't have been able to give me those assurances about that tigress you were cosseting when we first met."

"Juno is nothing like Zaran. Well, maybe a few similarities, but even those are for completely different reasons." She positioned Juno more securely. "And *cosseting* is the wrong word, too."

"At the moment, I don't give a damn. I just want to get you and this Juno out of this hole before the mine collapses." He jumped the last few feet, landed beside her, and studied the dog strapped to the door. "Beautiful. If I'm not mistaken, she's pure white beneath all that mud. What breed is she?"

"I told you: golden retriever. English cream variety."

"Beautiful," he repeated. "But she's very quiet. You said she was hurt?"

"Left rear leg. I think it's only sprained. Plus, she's not eaten in days. She's lucky there was a trickle of water that came in from an underground stream, or she'd be dead by now. We have to get her to a vet." She went to the other side of the stretcher to help brace it. "Yank the rope to let Cambry know we're ready."

"I can do this without you."

"No, you can't. Why should you? I'm strong enough to help." She made a face. "And I just got finished telling Juno that she has to be strong. I can't wimp out."

His lips quirked. "No, I guess you have to set a good example for the dog. What was I thinking?" He yanked on the rope to signal Cambry. "Let's get your Juno taken care of. We do have a few more things on the agenda."

"It's not going to hold us up too long. This is important to me." She braced her side of the door as the makeshift stretcher started to move upward. "I'll be responsible."

"I imagine you say that a lot," he said as he braced himself and began to climb on the next foothold to take more of the weight. "I'm not arguing with you. It's a relief to be able to do something to save even this dog. I haven't been very successful in the rescue department lately."

"We haven't saved her yet. She has problems." She looked down at Juno.

*You stay alive. Do your job. I can do only so much.*

No answer.

"But we *will* save her." The words were for Juno as well as for Lassiter. "I just hope the vet clinic in this town has a good staff."

San Chapo Veterinary Clinic was small and had only one veterinarian. But that was Dr. Hector Nalez, who was caring and knowledgeable and already knew Juno.

"Hello, girl. What's been happening to you?" he murmured as he knelt down beside her. "I've been wondering how you've been making it." He glanced up at Margaret. "How did you get hold of Juno? Did they give her to you?"

She shook her head. " 'They'? I don't know anything about her. I found her hurt and buried beneath the rubble in a deserted mine. She was alone."

"Yes, she is." He gently stroked Juno's neck. "Poor girl. Alone." He straightened. "Well, let's get her cleaned up and make sure there's nothing worse than that sprained leg. We'll deal with the rest of her problems later."

He set to work immediately, checking her over and setting the sprained leg. Then he gave her a nutrition shot and started fluids as his tech began to clean her up.

He turned to Margaret. "We'll have to start her on light, gradual feedings to begin with. That shot should help, but she's not in good shape. Did you know that she's going to have pups?"

She nodded. "Is she going to lose them?"

"I don't know. She's severely malnourished. But I've seen cases like this where the unborn pups managed to survive by taking enough nourishment from the mother. She might have saved her pups by giving them what they needed at her own expense. But I'm not detecting movement. We probably won't know until it's closer to her time. But we have to make sure that we keep pumping nutrients into her. I'll write you a prescription and you can—"

"You said that you knew her. You took care of her?"

He nodded. "From the time that she was a puppy. Great dog. Adored that little girl. It was wonderful to see them together."

"Little girl," Margaret said. The name that had been in the back of Juno's mind all the time they had been linked. "Celia . . ."

"You know the family?"

"Sort of. Juno belonged to Celia?"

He nodded. "Her parents gave Juno to Celia for Christmas when she was about eight years old. She loved that dog. They were inseparable. A few months ago, she told her parents that she thought Juno would be happier if she had her own puppies, and so they arranged to breed her." He shrugged. "I'm glad she had her for those two years. A dog can enrich life. Juno certainly enriched Celia's."

"Only two years?"

"That's all Celia had." He glanced at Juno in the anteroom with the tech. "She was in a car accident when she was ten and was in the hospital for three weeks before she died. Her parents even got permission to take Juno to the hospital. They thought she might help to give Celia a reason to live. They were trying everything they knew to keep her alive."

"But it didn't work," Margaret said sadly. "Sometimes there's nothing you can do."

*Sadness.*

*Loss.*

*Pain.*

"How did Juno get down in that mine?"

He shrugged. "I have no idea. I only know that after Celia died, her parents couldn't stand to even look at Juno any longer. The dog was mourning and they had to coax her to eat. And she was such a painful reminder of their daughter that they found it unbearable. A month after Celia's funeral, they gave her to a young couple who were moving to Brownsville, Texas." He added, "If I had to guess, I'd say that probably Juno ran away from them on the trip up there and came back here to everything she knew."

Even though the most important person in her world was no longer here for her. "That would be my guess, too," Margaret said. "And who knows why she wandered into that mine. As you said, she's mourning." She looked at Juno. "So Celia's parents wouldn't want Juno back, and Juno ran away from two virtual strangers. If that couple didn't go to the trouble of looking for her, then they didn't really want her, either."

He nodded. "Though we could try to contact them and—"

"No, Juno knows that nobody wants her. We can't throw her back to them."

"She knows?"

"You're a good doctor. You know that dogs sense things."

*Sadness.*

*Loss.*

"Is it okay if I go in to see her?" Margaret asked.

"I don't see why not." He smiled. "After all, you probably saved her life."

"She saved it herself. Maybe she didn't want to do it, but there's always instinct." She went into the anteroom, where Juno was lying on a mat on the floor. She was clean now and her white coat gleamed under the strong lights. Lassiter was right: She was beautiful. Her huge dark eyes appeared to glow against that shiny white coat. But she didn't lift her head when Margaret came into the room.

*You're going to be better now. The doctor said that you have to eat, though. You were probably not eating well even before this happened. It has to stop. You have to save the pups.*

Juno still didn't look at her. *Loss.*

*Sadness.*

*Not better.*

*Not wanted.*

Margaret knelt down beside her. *You are wanted. I want you. And there will be others who want you. The pups will want you.*

*Gone.*

*I know she's gone. Or maybe she's not. Maybe she'll always be with you. Love has a habit of staying around even if you can't see or smell or hear it. But you can't know unless you stop feeling sorry for yourself.*

*Sadness.*

*Yes, and it won't go away; it will always be part of you. But it can still be good. And it's time to think of the pups now. You thought of them when you were down in the mine, or you wouldn't have called out to me. But you're not finished yet. Celia wanted you to have these pups. She thought they'd bring joy to both of you.*

*Gone.*

*I've already told you that you don't know that. But you do know what she wanted you to do. You're not alone. I'm here to help you.*

*But you're not her.*

*I know I'm not. But we can get through this together. You may even get to like me. Then, after the pups come, we'll take another look to decide what you need to do. What she'd want you to do.*

*Confusion. Pain. Sorrow.*

*Juno?*

She lifted her head at last and looked at Margaret. *Maybe . . .*

*Not maybe. Trust me. Just do as I say and we'll be fine. First, you eat. Then, when you're better, exercise. Then we'll go on from there. Okay?*

Silence.

*Okay? You'll do as I say? We stay together? It's what she would want.*

Silence. *Yes. We stay together.* A pause. *But you're not her.*

A tentative victory at best. But it was a victory.

Though she wasn't certain Lassiter would consider it a triumph in any meaning of the word.

\*   \*   \*

"How's she doing?" Lassiter rose to his feet as Margaret came into the waiting room. "Was the leg broken?"

"No, just a sprain." She looked at her watch. "It's almost one. I suppose you're eager to get going. I didn't mean to delay you. Where's Cambry?"

"I sent him to gas up the plane and get ready for takeoff." He tilted his head. "Are you ready to go?"

"Almost. I have to get some prescriptions and nutrition supplements for Juno and then thank the doctor for his help. He's a very good doctor. And he's taken care of Juno since she was a few months old."

"I gathered that when you brought the dog in and he welcomed her so enthusiastically. So he must know the owners. Is he going to return Juno to them?"

"Not exactly."

He gazed at her warily. "And what does that mean?"

"Completely wrong," she said bluntly. "We're taking Juno with us."

He stiffened. "I beg your pardon."

"I told you that Juno has problems. Her owner was a ten-year-old child who died only a couple months ago. Juno is in mourning for her. Her parents are finding it too painful to keep her dog." She paused. "And she's going to have pups probably in the next few weeks. We have to keep her eating and healthy."

"I'll say she has problems." He shook his head. "You're supposed to be a grief therapist, nutrition specialist, and a possible midwife? May I point out that this isn't a good time for you to be involved with any of that?"

"There's never a good time. It's life, Lassiter. I can't afford to let her be boarded, even by a nice man like Dr. Nalez. She might give up and slip away. I'll be responsible for her." She frowned. "Though I'll have to work it out. There will be times when I won't be able to care for her. I can't take her on the island. Nicos would use her as a weapon. I'll have to—"

"Margaret, this isn't smart."

"I know. But I have to do it." She turned and went to the reception desk. "I'll get her prescriptions. You'd better call Cambry and prepare him for the fact that he's going to share the rear seat."

"Margaret."

She glanced over her shoulder. "I know that you could refuse to take her, but you won't do it. You might think that Juno's intrusion is just adding chaos to chaos, and you'd be right. But I can't not take care of her right now. And when you think of it, she may be an opportunity for us to think of something besides Nicos. I don't know about you, but I need a distraction."

"I know you do." His frown disappeared and he smiled. "The optimistic approach again. Frankly, I don't know how you manage to keep that banner flying nonstop."

"It's not nonstop." She smiled back at him. "But it's the way I ordinarily think. And when I can't find a reason, I look for a distraction."

"Evidently you found it," he said drily. He took out his phone. "I'll call and tell Cambry another challenge is on the horizon and then call a taxi. Get Juno ready to go and out here in the next fifteen minutes."

She nodded. "She'll be ready. I've told her she has to do what I say."

"Let's hope she pays more attention than that tigress you were schooling. You don't have all night to work with Juno, as you did with the tigress and her cub."

"She'll pay attention. Like most retrievers, she's very sweet natured." She had a thought. "But she's stubborn. It was really hard to get through to her. Every time I told her that she should do what I said, she told me, 'You're

not her.' She meant her friend Celia. It was almost like
a mantra. No one appears to mean anything to Juno but
that little girl."

"Sad."

"Don't you start. I'm trying to jar her out of it." She
started speaking to the receptionist. She was vaguely
aware of Lassiter, who was talking on the phone in the
background. By the time she'd gotten the prescription
and gone to the back to fetch Juno, he had finished and
was waiting outside for the taxi.

Dr. Nalez gave her a leash for the dog and walked
with her out of the clinic. "You're sure this is what you
want to do?" he asked. "It won't be easy dealing with
her right now. I can try to find her a good home."

"I'm sure. I think she needs me. I don't believe anyone else will do right now." She shook his hand. "Thank
you for taking care of her. We'll get along fine."

*But you're not her.*

She looked down at Juno, who was standing quietly
but whose thought was crystal clear.

"Just fine," she repeated. "Thank you again." She
turned to Lassiter, who had opened the door of the taxi
for her. "You ride up front. I'll ride in back with Juno."

"Compromises, already," he murmured. He slammed
the door shut behind her and the retriever and then got
in the passenger seat. "I hope she appreciates all this."

"She doesn't, but that doesn't matter. She needs me."
She put a gentle hand on Juno's back. Soft. Silky. Warm.
She stroked her gently.

*Nice . . . But you're not her.*

She kept her hand on Juno's body.

*Nice is good enough for now. . . .*

"I couldn't believe this when Lassiter told me," Cambry said, looking down at Juno as they were walking
toward the Cessna while Lassiter settled up for the

hangar rental. "Or maybe I could. It's just bizarre." He knelt down and rubbed Juno's ears. "How are you? You're quite the beauty, you know."

"She knows. People have been telling her that since she was born."

*Still . . . nice.*

Evidently, Cambry had made a hit. Probably because he was making the effort and he was a big, strong man who had no resemblance to Juno's Celia. No comparisons.

So take advantage of it.

"Cambry, this is Juno. I hope you're going to be very good friends."

Cambry looked warily up at Margaret. "I'm not sure I like the sound of that."

"You'll fall in love with her. Look how she's staring up at you. She has a very affectionate nature. She already likes you."

"Because I'm scratching her ears." But he kept scratching them. "Lassiter said she'd be your responsibility."

"And she will be, but I may need a little help." She suddenly grinned. "Juno may need a nanny."

Twenty minutes later, they were in the air, with Juno lying a little uncomfortably in the seat next to Cambry. But Cambry had settled her sprained back leg so that it wouldn't be stressed. Every now and then he would reach out and readjust it or simply pet her.

"Are you finessing this situation to suit yourself?" Lassiter asked Margaret as she turned back from watching Cambry with the dog. "I believe Cambry is being hijacked."

"He won't mind. He just has to get used to her. Dogs are all love. Particularly golden retrievers. Juno will give more than she takes."

"Are you planning a permanent arrangement?"

She shook her head. "She's just in need. It's a healing time. He'll help her heal."

"Not you?"

"I'll be there for her. But right now she's pulling back from me. She keeps saying that I'm not her. She means Celia. At first, I couldn't figure it out. Then I remembered what Dr. Nalez said about Juno and her Celia being so very close." She paused. "I think perhaps that Celia might have been a little like me."

"What do you mean?"

"I believe . . . that they could read each other. Maybe Celia couldn't read any other animals, but the love was so strong between them that she could bond with Juno."

"Oh for God's sake." He was silent, thinking about it. "But wouldn't that make Juno more likely to bond with you?"

She made a face. "If it didn't confuse her. She recognized that I was more like Celia than any other person she'd ever been around but that I wasn't her. That's why she keeps saying it. It's a reminder that would constantly hurt, that she won't accept."

"But she'll accept other people?"

"She can't help herself. I told you: She's all love. It's been a while since she lost her Celia. She just has to be shown the world is still a good place. She'll accept me, too, in time. When she's ready."

"And in the meantime, Cambry is your stand-in?"

"I couldn't be with Juno all the time anyway." She moistened her lips. "I told you that. Not on Nicos's island." She glanced at him. "Unless you were able to figure out that password? Cambry said you were going to join us later because you had an idea about going in a new direction about that."

"*Now* you're interested?" He shook his head. "You

didn't give me much time to figure out anything before Cambry phoned me to rescue Juno."

"I had to get her out of there. I didn't stop him because I thought you might have more experience than Cambry."

"It appears we all have our places in your agenda," he said sardonically.

"I had to save her," she said soberly. "Just as we have to save Patrick. It's all life. I'm sorry I didn't give you time to work this morning."

"I had time, just not enough. But I was able to shoot off a couple orders to my think tank in Silicon Valley before you yanked me out of that motel. They should be working on it now."

"Working on what? What was this new direction?"

"Same goal—information. New path. It was taking too long to find that password. Even if I let you go to Vadaz Island to buy time and try to locate that password in Nicos's office computer, it could be an involved process and might take too long." He looked at her. "And you could get caught because you ran out of time."

"I'd be careful. I wouldn't get—"

"It's too complicated," he said, interrupting her. "And too dangerous for you. It's better to simplify."

"What do you mean?"

"We're not going to search for the password. We're going to go after the computer wizard who created that file for Nicos. Who would know better than he what that password is?"

"No one." Her mind was moving from possibility to possibility. "If we can find him."

"Would Nicos have opted to keep him on the island in case he needed him?"

"He never kept outside techs on the island while I was there. He only used them infrequently and made sure they were intimidated enough so that there would be no question of betrayal. But that might have changed if Juan Salva had his way. Nicos was arrogant and thought no one would ever cross him. Salva was always more cautious."

"We'll have to see if it did change. I'm hoping that it didn't. Then all I'd have to do is find out who this computer guru is and zero in on him. That's why I texted the Silicon office to tap into all our resources and try to find a computer genius somewhere out there who is corrupt enough to work for Nicos."

"Would you have done it?" she asked suddenly. "I mean, when you were a boy? You said you had a very twisted sense of right and wrong. After all, you hacked into the CIA."

"I wasn't that twisted. The challenge might have tempted me, but I would have walked away from Stan Nicos." He added, "Like you're going to be able to do when I get the name of Nicos's pet computer guru. I'll make a dozen calls myself and I'll put pressure on Silicon. Once I get a name and address, we're on our way."

"That will be good."

"But you don't believe it will happen."

"I'm afraid to believe it." She smiled with an effort. "We both know that I have to show up on the island tomorrow or we face the fact that Patrick will be killed. I'm even becoming accustomed to the idea."

"Not if I can find that computer expert."

"Good luck to you. But you said time was against my finding that password in Nicos's office. Time's against you, too, Lassiter."

He swore under his breath.

"I feel like swearing, too," she said. "But as I said, I'm beginning to be accustomed to the idea of confronting Nicos again. I'm not as afraid as I was. That's a good thing."

"I don't see anything good about it."

"I do." She glanced back at Cambry and Juno. "Everything okay with you two?"

"Peachy," Cambry said. "I just gave her those nutrition pills and she went to sleep. I think she believes I'm boring or just another slave."

"She's comfortable with you. Hey, she's pregnant and she's had a rough couple weeks. It's good that she's sleeping."

"Yeah." He gently stroked Juno's throat. "I guess that's right. And no one ever said I was all that stimulating. Do you know, she reminds me of those French mountain dogs. She doesn't look like a retriever."

"It's that thick white coat. She's definitely a retriever." Margaret glanced back at Lassiter. "She should have another feeding soon. We're supposed to keep them small today, until she becomes used to eating again. When are we going to land?"

"Another hour or so." His lips twisted. "I'm sorry I didn't consult you with the travel plans. I didn't realize we had food-schedule priorities. We'll land south of Cancún at a private airport that I had Nick Mandell, the head of my security team, check out. He'll leave a rental car beside the hangar and we'll drive it to a beach property several miles away. It has a beach house and it's very secluded and should give me the privacy I need to work. Any objections?"

"No, I like the sound of it," she said quietly. "I can use privacy and seclusion in the next twenty-four hours. But I thought Cancún was a big tourist mecca."

"You haven't been there? I suspected that you'd hit most of the Latin towns while you were skipping around the Caribbean."

She shook her head. "Cancún is big into drugs. I wouldn't have risked going to any city where Nicos had contacts after I got away from him." She added, "And

when I first came down here from the States, my first
stop was Guatemala. I liked it there, so I stayed awhile."

"First stop," he repeated. "And how old were you
when you traveled all the way from the States to Central America?"

"A little younger than you were when you were trying to bilk the CIA." She grinned. "I was sixteen. I
thought of it as a great adventure, too. And I guess it was
technically illegal. I didn't have any papers."

"You started that young?"

"It was a great adventure," she repeated. "And I didn't
feel all that young. I'd been running from my father and
DEFACS for years and I saw it as a chance to get far,
far away."

"I'd say that Guatemala fits that description." He was
silent. "But I'd bet that something happened to make
you take a radical step like going alone to a foreign
country."

"I never said I was alone."

"No, you didn't, did you?" he said curtly. "It just appeared to be your modus operandi since the moment I
began hunting you. And the United States is a big country. Why did you feel you had to find somewhere else
to hide? And who was with you?"

She tilted her head. "Why do you want to know?"

"It's always annoyed me that I know only bits and
pieces about you. It's like opening a book in the middle
and not knowing the beginning."

"Or the end?"

"Not the end. You'll have plenty of years to write that.
It will probably be an epic. I just want to catch up."

And for some reason, it was important to him, she
could see. Just as it had been important for her to know
about his background, the way he thought and felt. She
had fought that desire to know him, to let herself open
to him, but now there was no reason why she should do

it any longer. They were too close, with an intimacy that had been born of what she was and what he needed from her.

So give him what he wanted. Not everything. She had to keep the walls high if she was going to survive going back to Nicos.

"When I was thirteen, I met a couple who lived on a farm near Markville, Kentucky. Jason and Marcia Nixon. We . . . liked each other. They accepted me. They took me in and sent me back to school. I helped out on their farm and they told everyone I was their niece, whose parents had been killed in a car accident." She cleared her throat. "It was good. And pretty soon I realized that I loved them. I wasn't used to that. I hadn't been around people very much since I'd run away. But there it was, and I didn't know what to do about it. I thought I might even stay with them if I wasn't in the way. But they didn't treat me as if I were a burden. I think they might have loved me, too. It looked as if it was going—" She drew a deep breath. "But DEFACS traced me to the school where I was enrolled. One day my father showed up at the farm and was shouting and threatening the Nixons with a lawsuit."

"And what did you do?"

"I picked up a frying pan and hit him over the head. Then, before he could regain consciousness, I packed a bag and took off."

"Frying pan," Lassiter repeated. "Excellent decision. Except for the running away. Wouldn't the Nixons have fought for you?"

"It was my place to fight for them. I didn't want to cause them trouble. And my father would have given them nothing but problems. It was time to move on."

"Guatemala?"

"Not then. I headed south and ended up in New Orleans. I got a job at a petting zoo and worked there for six months. Then I met a girl, Rosa Gonzalez, who worked behind the refreshment stand there. She was a little older than I was, but we struck up a friendship. She was fun and made me laugh. She lived in Guatemala City and she said her father had a speedboat that he used to transport 'clients' back and forth from New Orleans to Guatemala."

"Clients without proper documents, I assume?"

She nodded. "I didn't care about that. I'd been traveling without documents myself since the time I ran away from home. The only time I got into trouble was when the Nixons falsified my birth certificate to get me into that school near their home. Anyway, Rosa was going back home at the end of the summer and asked me if I wanted to go with her."

"And you saw a great adventure looming."

"And a way to get below the radar if my father was still looking for me. There wasn't much chance that he wouldn't be. It seemed a perfect solution."

"And was it a great adventure?"

"At first. Rosa was kind to me, and so was her mother. I grew to love them both. I had a good time that year."

"Only at first?"

She shrugged. "Sometimes perfect solutions don't turn out so perfect. Things happen."

"What things?"

Time to back away. "You've had the beginning, Lassiter. Be satisfied."

"I want more."

"And I don't want to give it. Maybe when I get back from Vadaz Island, I'll be ready."

He stiffened. "You're not going to—" He stopped. "You're trying to distract me."

"Yes." She leaned back in the seat. "And it worked really well. You're beset with guilt these days. Of course, you should be, considering how you started with me."

She tilted her head. "I'll make a bargain. You find either the password or the name of our computer whiz before you have to turn me over to Nicos and I'll tell you how the perfect solution turned sour."

He flinched. "That hurt."

"Yes, it did. It's meant to spur you on."

It wasn't the truth; she knew that he didn't need anything to drive him any harder. "Maybe I'm getting tired of having you know everything about me. I'll make you work for it from now on."

And keep the pain at bay as long as she could.

*Black-and-white tiles.*

*Rosa . . .*

# CHAPTER NINE

The sand was warm beneath Margaret's bare feet as she walked toward the front door of the small beach house. She'd taken her shoes off the minute she'd hopped out of the Toyota. She'd seen the blue sea lapping up to the beach as they'd driven up to the house and felt the sunlight strong and pure as it touched her face.

She *needed* this. It might be the last time she could relax and enjoy these natural wonders until she got off Vadaz Island. There would be only tension there, and Nicos had managed to taint even the beauty of the island with his ugliness.

"You look like you did that afternoon on the ship when you took your swim." Lassiter grinned and glanced at her bare feet as he unlocked the door. "All golden and ready to face the sharks."

"They never came. You scared them away with your big bad gun." She glanced back at Cambry, who had chosen to feed Juno beside the car and was now walking slowly toward them to accommodate the dog's sprain.

Cambry grimaced as he saw her looking at him. "Don't say it."

"I was just thinking you'd found your true vocation," she called back to him as she entered the house.

Just one large living area with a kitchenette, a long spice-colored couch, a round oak dining table, and five chairs. There were three doors opening off the central room that presumably led to bedrooms or baths. Nothing luxurious. But there were also huge, wide French doors opening to the beach. That was luxury enough for Margaret.

"You like it?" Lassiter asked, his gaze on her face as she wandered toward the French doors. "I can see you do. I'll tell Nick Mandell that he did well."

"When do I meet this Mandell?" she asked as she threw open the doors to let in the sunlight. "He's clearly a man who knows what's important."

"In more ways than one," Lassiter said. "He's the most lethal man I know with a Remington 700 rifle. He can pick off a target at over a thousand yards. He was invaluable to our team in Afghanistan." He threw his backpack on the couch and grabbed his computer equipment bag. "As for when you'll meet him, it depends on how soon we locate Nicos's computer expert and I squeeze the information out of him. We'll be moving fast then."

"Yes, I guess we will." She lifted her face to the sunlight. It felt so good. . . . "You got a text right after you landed. Your people in Silicon Valley? Were they able to give you any help?"

"Too much help. Too many names. I told them to refine and narrow down the list. I'll be working on it myself now that we've landed. One of those rooms is supposed to be an office where I can set up." He paused. "You seem very subdued. Are you okay?"

She turned to look at him. "Fine."

He frowned. "Is there anything I can do for you?"

"You're doing it." She nodded at the computer bag.

"I've taken care of myself all my life, Lassiter. What makes you think I need anyone else now?"

"How the hell do I know? Maybe because I feel as if it's time someone stepped in and gave you a hand. As far as I can see, that's not been happening." He shook his head. "And I don't like it that you're so damn quiet."

"You'll forget all about it once you start working. Most of the time, you have your priorities straight." She went outside and started to walk down toward the sea. "I'm fine, Lassiter."

She could feel his gaze on her back until she reached the surf. Then she closed him out as she rolled up the legs of her khaki pants and started wading through the water. Warm sand and cool water and blue sky. It was all soothing and healing and promising that life was good now, no matter what happened tomorrow.

So block the thought of Nicos out for this brief period. Build her walls and make her preparations.

And let life weave around her, through her, reminding her that she had something to finish that should have been finished three years ago. . . .

The sun was going down in a blaze of glory over the horizon when Margaret heard Cambry behind her, coming down from the house.

"Hey, I brought you a cup of coffee and a sandwich," he said. "I gave up on you coming back to the house for a decent supper. It seemed as if you were communing with nature, and heaven forbid I interfere with that."

She looked over her shoulder and saw him standing a few yards behind her, carrying a thermos and the sandwich. Beside him was Juno, who was sitting looking at her with head cocked.

"Thanks." She took the thermos. "It was nice of you to bother. It was too beautiful out here to go inside."

"No problem. I didn't have anything else to do. Lassiter hasn't stuck his head out of that office since we got here. Actually, it was Juno's fault. I was having trouble with her. She saw you out here and wanted to come down to you."

"She did?"

"And don't blame me for not letting her rest that leg. She was being a pain in the ass." His hand went down to stroke the dog's head. "She's pregnant. I figured maybe she was having problems with the pups or something. What do you think?"

She looked at the retriever.

*Pups, Juno?*

The retriever moved a step nearer to Margaret.

*No, you.*

That was a surprise.

*Why?*

The answer came in a confused barrage of concepts and words.

*Hurting. You're not her. But you're hurting. Need me.*

Margaret felt a rush of warmth and affection as she gazed at the retriever. Pure love. The need to heal. The need to give whatever was required . . . forever.

And she couldn't refuse what Juno wanted to give. Because fulfilling that need might also heal the dog.

*Yes, I do need you. Will you stay with me for a little while?*

Juno limped forward and dropped down beside Margaret.

"Have I lost a dog?" Cambry asked ruefully.

"No." Her hand reached out to gently touch Juno. "She should stay with you. She just needs a little time with me right now." And Margaret needed time with her. No excuses. No guilt. No need to be strong. No fear. Just love. "Come back in an hour or so and take her back to the house with you. Then you can give Juno her meds and settle her down for the night."

"Whatever you say. It wasn't the pups, I take it?"

"No, it was something else." She stroked the dog's head. "She'll be fine soon."

"Okay, I'll be back in an hour."

She heard him walking away, but she was looking back at the setting sun again.

*Beautiful*.

No answer from Juno, but the retriever reached out and put her chin on Margaret's lap.

Comfort. Love. Togetherness.

No other answer was needed.

2:35 A.M.

"You should be in bed," Lassiter said roughly. "Cambry said you were communing with nature, but I don't think so. What's wrong with you?"

"Nothing now. I'm feeling . . . good about this." She turned to look at him. The moonlight was bright enough to see the tension in his body language and the tautness of his face. "And I guess you could call it 'communing with nature,' but for me it seems more like letting it flow into me and take everything else away. That can be pretty great, Lassiter."

"I imagine it could," he said thickly.

"But that's been over for hours. I've only been out here waiting for you."

He stiffened. "I'm not going to be able to tell you what you want to know. I've pared down the names on that list to three and we have the last known addresses for all of them."

"What are the names?"

"George Bildwan, Simon Zwecker, Carl Montgomery. I've put both Silicon and Mandell's men on them to tap sources and start the hunt. But it's going to take time.

Some of these experts work for the highest bidders and are constantly moving."

"It will go faster when you get personally involved. And I'll be able to help."

"The hell you will."

She ignored that remark. "I've thought of a way to get a message to you. I've always been allowed to swim in the cove on Vadaz Island. I don't expect that to change. Of course, there's always a guard with a rifle watching, but as long as I don't attempt an escape, I should be able to plant a message on the rocks on the south end of the cove. There are sentries all around that area, but you can send someone in scuba equipment to get it."

"You have it all planned. Providing you can find either the password or the name of the computer expert who created it. Providing you don't get caught and butchered if Nicos shows up at the wrong moment. Providing that guard who's watching you doesn't get suspicious and decide to shoot you."

"I told you, I'm feeling good about it now. Almost mellow. None of that is going to happen." She got to her feet. "If it does, then I'll find a way to work with it. I'm not afraid any longer."

He grabbed her shoulders. "Well, I am."

"I know. But sometime tonight or tomorrow, you're going to get a call from Salva or Nicos, and I'm going to have to go to the island."

"And I'm supposed to let you go?"

"You know you are." She looked him in the eye. "I'm *going* to go, Lassiter. My job. My choice. Your job is to find a way to get Patrick away from that camp or at least get a plan together that will do it." She smiled. "And then you're to get me away from Nicos at Montego Bay Airport. I'll be very annoyed with you if you fail to do that."

"I can imagine you would be." His hands were

kneading her shoulders. "I'll offer him anything he wants, dammit."

"No, you won't. He'd enjoy it too much and refuse you anyway. You'll have to take me. And you'll send Cambry to deliver me to him. Nicos hates you. He might decide you're too tempting a target not to swoop up. Purely from a selfish viewpoint, I have to point out that then I'd be lost, with no one to help get me away from him."

" 'Purely from a selfish viewpoint'?"

She gazed at him and shook her head. "You're thinking that I'm some kind of sacrificial lamb? No such thing. If I didn't have to behave in accordance with who I am, I wouldn't be forced to do this. That's true of everyone who has to be what they are. I'm just a little . . . different."

"I've noticed."

She smiled. "I guess you have. But this time who I am is telling me that it's time I righted wrongs and put the nightmare behind me. Purely selfish, Lassiter."

"Yeah, sure. Well, it sounds like something else to me. And I don't know if I can—"

His cell phone rang.

He went rigid. "That's the text. I don't believe there's much doubt who would be texting me at this hour of the morning."

The pain was starting, Margaret realized. He hadn't even answered yet and the pain was there.

He punched the access button.

He jerked back as if struck. "Shit."

So much pain. She couldn't *stand* it.

She had to stand it. She had to stop it.

She stepped closer and looked down at the photo in the text.

Patrick. Of course it was Patrick. He was hanging from the branch of a tree by his arms, which looked as if they'd been pulled out of the sockets, his feet not touching the ground. His face was twisted in unbearable agony.

Below the photo was her name, Margaret, and the time and place for the meeting: 12:30 P.M., Puerto Morelos.

*Pain.*

Her own pain, Lassiter's pain. Oh my God, and Patrick's pain. She bent double as the waves of agony poured over her, drowning her.

"Margaret!" Lassiter was there, holding her, his hand pressing her face into his shoulder. "For God's sake. Stop shaking."

"Sorry." She could barely get the words out. "Too . . . close now. I know you shouldn't have to deal with . . . all this pain. You have so much pain. He has so much pain." She couldn't stop the shuddering that was tearing her apart. "Shouldn't have to know what I'm feeling. It's not right. I'll try to—"

"Shut up," he said gruffly. "I wasn't sure that I understood all that empathy business you told me about. But I understand now." He held her tighter. "Dear God, I understand. What the hell can I do to stop it?"

"It will be better . . . soon. Too . . . close." Her arms slid around him, trying to stop his pain, which was now her pain. "Sometimes . . . it's like an avalanche that picks up everything in its . . . path," she whispered. She could barely get the words out. "But . . . we have to . . . stop . . . him from doing that to Patrick. You have to . . . call Nicos now. You have to tell him that you'll have me at Puerto Morelos on time. But only if he sends you a photo of Patrick in thirty minutes that shows he's been taken down . . . from that tree. And you want another photo of him right before delivery to make sure he hasn't cheated you."

He stiffened against her. "I *can't* do that."

"Do you want to look at that photo again?" Her voice

was suddenly fierce. "I don't want to see it ever again. I'd make the call myself, but he can't know that I have any feeling for you or for Patrick. He has to think I'm just a bargaining chip. He'd use it against me. He's done it before." She pushed away from him and looked into his eyes. "But I'll have to do it anyway if you don't. I have to stop the pain." She dropped down on the sand and linked her arms around her knees, rocking back and forth. "Now *call* him."

He stood staring at her.

She had to brace herself. This pain he was going through was almost worse than that first blast when he'd opened the text.

Then he muttered a curse and began to place the call. "Nicos, you bastard, take him down," he said roughly when Nicos picked up. "She'll be there tomorrow on time. What the hell do I care? But not unless you stop playing your games with Patrick. Take him down. I want a photo in the next thirty minutes showing that you've done it. Another at eleven tomorrow morning, right before the delivery." He met Margaret's eyes. "I'll be glad to get rid of her. She's caused me nothing but trouble. When this is all over, I'll expect you to be ready to negotiate for Patrick. I'm already putting together a package I don't think you can refuse." He disconnected and asked her roughly, "Satisfied? I believe he was."

"We'll know in thirty minutes." She was glad she hadn't had to hear Nicos's voice this time. "And you sounded . . . sincere."

"You mean like a son of a bitch." He dropped down beside her. "A prick of the highest order."

"It's the only kind of person Nicos understands." She reached out and touched his arm. "It was the right thing to do."

"The hell it was. There was no right thing to do."

Pain, again.

She got on her knees, then moved over him and sank into his arms. "It was right. You'll see. But I know it hurts, too."

He went still. "What are you doing?"

"Contact helps. Hold me, Lassiter."

He hesitated and then his arms closed around her. "This isn't a good idea."

"Yes, it is." She lay there, feeling his warmth, feeling a little of the pain ebbing away. "Too close to pain. Too close to death. This is life, Lassiter."

"More than that," he said thickly.

"Just hold me."

"I'm holding you, dammit. Now stop shaking."

"Better. See? Not so much. You're better, too."

Warmth. Opening. Easing.

Pain still there, but not as sharp.

Minutes passed.

Pain fading, but something else . . .

He was still stiff; she could feel the tension.

"Do you want to have sex? That could help, too."

He went rigid. "What?"

"Sex. It's renewing. It's one of the greatest forces of life and reminds us that—"

"No." He pushed her aside and sat up. "I knew this wasn't a good idea. What the *hell* are you doing?"

"If you don't want me that way, then I understand. I just thought—"

"You just thought after I'd turned you over to Nicos only minutes before, that you'd offer to screw me because it would be good for me?"

He was angry. She'd obviously made a mistake.

"I thought it might be good for me, too."

"Don't *say* that."

She nodded. "If that's what you want."

"That's not what I want. It's nowhere near what I want at the moment."

"Then why don't you—" She could tell by his expression that would be a mistake, too. "I'll sit here and wait until you get the text and then I'll go to bed. Would that be all right?"

"No, but it's better than the other offers you've made tonight. At least it's not self-destructive."

She shook her head. "I don't regret any of them."

"I know you don't, and that makes it worse for me. I'm supposed to reach out and take because it's offered? Or maybe you're like one of those gladiators going into the coliseum who want a last night of debauchery before they face the beasts."

Her mouth fell open, and then she had to smile. "I don't believe there were women gladiators, and I don't think sex with you could be described as debauchery." Her smile faded. "But Nicos and Salva are definitely beasts."

"You're smiling?" Lassiter was silent and then shook his head. "You see, I can't understand what you—" His phone rang and he went rigid. "Text."

He got to his feet and accessed the message.

Pain. But not the pain he'd experienced before.

"I won't show you this photo because I don't know how it would affect you," he said as he hung up. "You scared me before. Patrick is lying on the ground. He's off that damn tree. But he still doesn't look good."

"But Nicos paid attention to you. Patrick might not have lasted if Nicos hadn't taken him down." She got to her feet. "Now I'll go back to the house. Good night, Lassiter."

"Wait." He took her hand as she was passing him. "I didn't mean to—" He stopped. "As usual, you shocked the hell out of me and I said all the wrong things." He reached out and cupped her face in his two hands. "You're completely extraordinary and I never know what to expect. But whatever you do and say, it's good."

He touched her lips with his forefinger. "It's the rest of the world that hasn't managed to catch up yet. Including me. I'm way behind, Margaret."

She was experiencing that golden sensation of being treasured that she'd known before when he'd touched her. She wanted it to go on and on. "No, you're not. It's only a bad time for you. And I'm not a gladiator or some kind of sacrifice. I'm just me. We'll both get through this." She smiled up at him. "But maybe not with the sex. It seemed to upset you too much."

He grimaced. "Oh, you could say that. In several different and unique ways."

"I'm glad you're not angry any longer." She backed away from him and started to walk back to the house. "I'll see you in the morning, Lassiter."

And he would be as upset in the morning as he was right now, she knew. It had been an hour of tumult and incredible pain and she had tried to distract both of them until it passed. For the most part, it had worked.

Yet she'd face the same challenge tomorrow.

But she was exhausted and felt limp from the emotional roller coaster she'd ridden tonight.

And she'd also have to face Nicos tomorrow.

Juno was sitting, waiting, at the French doors.

*Hurting. Need me. You're not her. But need me.*

*No, I'm not her.* She stroked Juno's head. *Tonight I'm not sure who I am. Maybe I do need you. I'm going to bed. Want to come and keep me company?"*


8:45 A.M.


Lassiter was still working on the Nicos file when he heard the car start in the driveway.

What in the hell . . .

He pushed his chair away from the desk and ran out

of the house, only to see the gray Toyota rental car heading down the driveway toward the road with Cambry behind the wheel.

And Margaret in the passenger seat beside him.

"Son of a bitch!" He reached for his phone and called Margaret.

No answer.

He dialed Cambry.

No answer. He received a text in return.

I TRIED TO TALK HER OUT OF IT. BUT SHE MIGHT BE RIGHT. NOTE ON DOOR.

He turned and strode back to the front door. There was a handwritten note tacked to it.

*I told you last night it would be too much of a temptation for Nicos if you showed up to hand me over. He hates you and he sometimes acts purely on impulse. By the time you get transport to follow us and drive down to Puerto Morelos, I'll already be with Nicos.*

*I'll try to find out which of the computer experts is the one in Nicos's pocket. I'll put the info in a waterproof bag I took from the kitchen cabinet and place it on the third rock in the boulder formation in the south cove I told you about. I hope it will be at least the day before he takes me to Montego Bay. I drew a map of the cove area and left it on the kitchen bar. I'll have to give Cambry my phone when I leave him to go to Nicos. They'll search everything I have with me before they let me on the island. If you can, arrange to find a way to send the phone back to me by the person who picks up my message.*

*That's all, I guess. I know you'll be angry. But
I promise I'll keep Cambry safe. Please take care
of Juno until Cambry can get back to you.*

**Margaret.**

"Shit!" His hand crumpled the paper and he threw it
to the ground. He tried to call her.

No answer.

And there wouldn't be an answer, he knew. She had
made up her mind, made her plans, and would carry
them out. Alone. Just as she'd done all her life.

Alone.

She hadn't even let him go with her to give her what
little support he could. She probably hadn't trusted him
to go through with handing her over to Nicos. God
knows, he hadn't been sure what he would have done at
that last minute.

So she had made it easy for him. If you could call
easy being racked with guilt and feeling as if he were
writhing on that same tree branch as Patrick had been.

And she was right: There was no way he could get
there to Puerto Morelos in time.

So stop standing here and do what you can to make
sure that Margaret's action has not been taken in vain.

He phoned Mandell in Cancún. "I need you to come
down here with the entire team. We'll use this beach
house as command central. I want you to bring me down
an LX-40. Have Norris rent a seaplane to have immediately available."

"Seaplane?"

"You heard me. You and I have a job to do. And then
there are those three computer experts that we have to
find and question in the next twenty-four hours. After
that, we go after Patrick."

"There's some connection with those computer geeks?" Mandell asked. "I thought that you were arranging an exchange of some sort for Patrick."

"It didn't work out," he said curtly. "And yes, there's a connection. Get down here and let's find them." He disconnected and went back into the house.

Juno was sitting outside Margaret's bedroom door.

*Take care of Juno.*

Okay, do what she'd asked. God knows there wasn't much else she'd left him to do.

He went toward the dog. "Come on, let's get you some breakfast and your meds. She won't be back for a while."

Juno didn't move. She stared up at him with those huge dark eyes.

"But she *will* be back. I'll get her back. Don't give me trouble, okay?"

Juno slowly got up and came toward him.

At least Juno trusts me, he thought as he went to the kitchen bar to get her bowl and food. She *should* believe me.

Because I'm going to move heaven and earth to get Margaret off that damn island.

"Stop here," Margaret said when Cambry reached the end of the dock. She sat there gazing at the sleek white yacht anchored off the long pier. She could feel the muscles of her stomach clench. Her heart was beating hard.

In a moment she would see Nicos.

Three years.

Black-and-white tiles.

"Margaret?" Cambry said. "You can still change your mind. I'll turn this car around and get you out of here."

"No, I can't." She moistened her lips. "He probably has someone with a gun trained on us right now. I just wanted to catch my breath for a minute." She swallowed. "Here's what you do. I get out and walk down that pier until I reach his yacht. You stay until you see him take me. Then you turn and get the hell out of here. No matter what happens, what you see, you don't stop. You don't try to come back for me."

"I can't promise that I—"

"If you don't, you'll ruin everything." She met his eyes. "And Patrick will die. Do as I say, Cambry." She tried to smile as she opened the passenger door. "Juno needs someone to take care of her. I can take care of myself."

"I'm beginning to think this wasn't such—"

She didn't hear the rest as she slammed the car door behind her.

She started to walk down the long pier.

She could see someone standing by the gangplank now. Dark gray jeans, white tunic shirt, swarthy skin, sleekly barbered black hair.

She inhaled sharply. Don't get sick. Don't stop. You have to go all the way.

Stan Nicos. He was standing there, smiling at her with smug triumph. He didn't say a word as he watched her walk toward him.

Of course, it was one of the ways he showed her how he could dominate her. He made her come to him as if he were some kind of royalty. But she couldn't let him play that game now. If she let him dominate her, then she'd be helpless to do anything but be a prisoner on the island.

First, get Cambry safely on his way back to Lassiter.

She stopped when she was several yards from the gangplank. "Here I am," she called defiantly to Nicos. "But it wasn't you who brought me here. You had to turn loose that son of a bitch Lassiter on me. You would never have caught me otherwise, Nicos."

"I would have caught you. It was just more convenient to have Lassiter at my beck and call." He looked beyond her shoulder at the gray Toyota on the dock. "But that's not Lassiter behind the wheel, is it?"

"It's Neal Cambry," she said curtly. "He's had a gun pointed at my back all the time I walked down this pier."

"And where's Lassiter?"

"He said he was through with me. I hadn't been able to get him what he wanted, so he turned me over to Cambry for delivery."

Nicos smiled. "He thought that he had a true ace in the hole in you, Margaret. I'm sure he was disappointed." He came down the gangplank. "And I see your Neal Cambry is taking off and leaving you to my gentle care."

Good. Cambry was doing as she asked. "I didn't expect anything else. Lassiter told him that he was done with me and he wasn't to waste any more time on me than necessary." She looked him in the eye. "Lassiter's a monster, just like you."

"That's not polite, Margaret," Nicos said. "I thought I'd taught you better manners. I guess I'll have to start all over again." His hand lashed out and connected to her cheek with a force that sent her down to the deck of the pier. "But I'm looking forward to it. I even have your old suite ready for you." He stood over her. "Memories, Margaret?"

She shook her head to clear it of dizziness. She had to get to her feet. Cambry might have seen her fall and she couldn't trust him not to stop and come back for her if he thought she was hurt. She got to her knees and then struggled to stand. "Why should I have memories? I blocked those months out of my mind. I blocked *you* out of my mind. Anything we do together is a fresh start." She raised her hand to her burning cheek. "And if I show up at Montego Bay looking as if I was someone's punching bag, it's going to raise red flags. Not that I care, but I'd think you would."

His smile ebbed a trifle. "I might be able to wait until after Montego Bay. It might be all the sweeter."

"I'm not that same girl you knew three years ago, Nicos. I know I have to do what you want me to do, but you'll have to allow me some measure of freedom."

"I allowed you freedom before and you ran away from me. That won't happen again."

"Then have me watched. I don't care. I just can't be a prisoner anymore. I'll do anything you say." She paused. "I'm three years older, Nicos. I'm more powerful now. You always said I had more power than your mother. I can do things that you couldn't dream I could do."

His eyes narrowed on her face. "What things?"

She shook her head. "I won't be a prisoner. We work together."

"Perhaps. I don't like the idea. Maybe if you make it worth my while . . ." He took her arm and pushed her toward the gangplank. "But you'll have to convince me. I had it all my own way before."

"You don't have Rosa now. You made a mistake."

His hand tightened on her arm with bruising force. "That was your fault."

She had thought that perhaps he was right, and it had tormented her for a long time. "You made a mistake," she repeated. "You don't have any weapons. Make a deal with me."

He scowled. "I'll consider it." He pushed her up the gangplank. "But now you have to reacquaint yourself with Juan Salva. He's been looking forward to having you back with us. He's such a fine businessman and it upset him as much as it did me that we lost several shipments when you weren't here to take care of the dogs."

"I'll be wherever you want me to be from now on, if we can make a deal. If we can't, someday at the most inconvenient time, those airport dogs are going to let their handlers know they've discovered a bonanza."

He scowled. "I don't appreciate threats. I said I'd consider it." He gestured to Salva, who was sitting in a deck chair with his laptop computer. "Come and greet our Margaret. She's coming home again. . . ."

Cambry had to park far down the driveway when he arrived back at the beach house. There were three cars and one truck that he knew belonged to Mandell already there ahead of him.

Evidently, Lassiter was in full battle mode.

Mandell and two other men were standing around a map laid out on the kitchen bar. Mandell looked up from the map and nodded as Cambry walked into the room. "Cambry." Then he looked back down at the map again and was totally absorbed. Mandell's concentration was always absolute when he was on a job, Cambry knew. In his early thirties, Mandell was of Spanish descent with dark hair, olive complexion, brown eyes, and a quiet intensity that could sometimes be intimidating. But it wasn't Mandell he was worried about today.

Lassiter was standing gazing out the French doors at the surf and turned to look at him. "I received that second photo of Patrick an hour ago." He asked curtly, "It's done?"

Cambry nodded. "I know you're pissed off. But she was right about it being a risk for you to get near him, if you weren't ready to take him out."

"Yes, I'm pissed off," he said coldly. "And if you ever do anything like that again, I'll not only fire you; I'll break your neck. Who was there besides Nicos?"

"I don't know. Margaret wouldn't let me get out of the car. She walked down the pier by herself."

"That's no surprise."

"Nicos was the only one who came down the gangplank. I started to drive off after he began talking to her." He said quickly, "That's what she told me I should do. She said if I didn't, Patrick would die."

He stiffened. "You're sounding very defensive. Why?"

He hesitated. "He hit her . . . hard. She fell down on the pier."

Lassiter began to swear. "And you didn't do anything?"

"No. She got up right away." He paused. "I think she might have been expecting it. That was probably why she gave me exact instructions and warned me about risking Patrick." He shook his head. "And why she made me take her instead of letting you do it. You wouldn't have been as easy for her to handle. I almost turned around and went back myself. But she said it was the right thing to do."

Lassiter was silent.

"Lassiter?"

"The right thing according to Margaret. Maybe the right thing for Patrick. Apparently not the right thing to keep Margaret alive and unhurt." His eyes went back to the surf crashing against the beach. But Cambry didn't think he was seeing it. "But how the hell can I blame you when Margaret set it all up herself? She made sure I wouldn't be there for her. She made sure you wouldn't take any action."

"So what can I do? I felt so damn helpless."

"Join the club." His gaze shifted back to Cambry. "We make sure it doesn't happen again. We do our job, we find Patrick, and we get Margaret away from Nicos."

"And then?"

"Then I find the son of a bitch and I kill him . . . slowly."

# CHAPTER TEN

Vadaz Island

Those rolling, verdant hills and gentle surf are just as beautiful as I remembered them, Margaret thought as her hands tightened on the rail of the ship.

Dear God, how she had prayed never to set eyes on them again.

"Almost home, Margaret," Nicos murmured as he came to stand beside her. "Does it bring back memories? I told you that you'd never get away from me."

"But I did get away." She didn't look at him. He was right: Memories were flooding back to her, and she was trying desperately to push them away. He would enjoy it too much. "You would never have found me if you hadn't brought in that bastard Lassiter."

"He was only a means to an end. You didn't have a chance. Not from the moment I had my men take you and sweet Rosa from her home in Guatemala City. I knew you were going to belong to me. Do you remember her face when she woke up from that sedative we gave both of you? So bewildered, so innocent, so frightened. But not you, Margaret. You were only wary and looking for a way out. I knew then that I'd have to find a way to give you very special handling."

She didn't speak. She looked straight ahead.

Nicos shrugged. "Not as satisfactory a response as I'd like from you. But there are so many more memories that can be stirred, and I'm certain those will be more pleasing to me." He turned away. "We should be docking soon. Do you remember what I was doing to Rosa when we docked that first day?"

She didn't answer. She heard him laugh as he strolled back to sit down beside Salva.

Block it out. Don't remember. He wanted her to remember, because he knew it would hurt her.

But the memory came, and she couldn't stop it from attacking her.

*Rosa screamed!*

*"Stop it." Margaret flew across the deck and tore at Nicos's shoulder to get him off her. "Why are you doing this? Neither of us has hurt you. Do you want money? I'll find a way to get it for you. Just leave her alone."*

*Nicos turned and punched her viciously in the stomach. "You don't touch me unless I want you to touch me."*

*Pain.*

*But she managed to stagger back and still stay on her feet.*

*Rosa was sobbing. "Margaret, he hurt me. Why are we here? I don't understand."*

*"It's okay, Rosa." It wasn't the truth. Nothing had been okay since the moment she'd awakened in the middle of the night as those men had run into her bedroom and plunged that needle in her arm. But Rosa was frightened enough. And there had to be something Margaret could do to stop this. She turned to Nicos. "This is kidnapping. Why? We've never even seen you before. Why are we here?"*

*"Because I wanted you here." He slapped her and*

*she fell back against the railing and had to grab it to keep from falling. "Not your pretty friend here. She'll be entertaining, but I only thought there was a possibility she might become necessary when I heard you were very close." He slapped her again. "Because it's been brought to my attention that you have a skill that I might be able to use, Margaret."*

*"I don't know what you're talking about."*

*"Oh, you'll learn. I'll make it very clear to you."*

*"You said you didn't really want Rosa. Let her go."*

*"No tears." He was gazing at her appraisingly. "I hurt you. I struck you three times. You bent double when I hit you in the stomach. Your face is already starting to swell. But you're not giving up. You didn't let it stop you. Tough. It may take extraordinary measures. . . ."*

*"Let her go." Her voice was shaking. "I don't know what you want from me, but it doesn't have to involve her."*

*"I think it might. I'll have to experiment and find out." He nodded at his two men, who had been standing across the deck. "Hold her. I want her to see how helpless she is to keep me from doing anything I want with either of them." He turned back to Rosa. "Are you ready for me, my pretty little whore?"*

Black-and-white tiles.

Margaret stood inside the French doors of the guesthouse and gazed down at the gleaming floors that stretched a good twenty feet to where they ended at the two arched bedroom doors.

She drew a deep breath and turned away so that Salva and Nicos wouldn't see her shock and pain. She had probably shown them too much already on the yacht earlier today. How many nightmares had she had about these floors and the atrocity that had happened here? "Nothing much has changed, has it? You're very predictable, Nicos. What do you expect me to do? Faint? Or have hysterics? I told you, I'm not the same person I was three years ago." She turned and let him see her face. "I'll stay here if you like, but I'd prefer a change of scene."

He was obviously disappointed. "Really? I suppose we could add a little color to the place."

Blood on the tiles.

Salva laughed. "Very good, Nicos. Excellent suggestion. That should bring back memories." He turned to Margaret. "It certainly does for me. It was a singularly different experience. Usually, Nicos and I don't agree on what's enjoyable, but he showed great imagination that night."

"I don't need your approval, Salva," Nicos said.

Margaret saw the flicker of expression cross Salva's face. The conflict had increased between them in these three years. Could she use it?

"Of course you don't," Salva said. He looked at Margaret. "I was only commenting on one of your better manipulations. She's telling us she's changed. It could be true. But I might be able to re-create the circumstances and mood of that night and it could send her spiraling back to where you want her."

Don't let him see the terror that thought sends through you. Don't change expressions. "Salva, I hoped we could work together. Stop trying to turn back the clock. It's not going to work."

"No?" he said softly. "You were terribly upset that night. Nicos enjoyed it. All I have to do is supply him with a young girl who—"

"It wouldn't work," she said, interrupting him. Evil. Salva was so terribly evil. Perhaps more evil than Nicos, because he was smarter and more innovative. "Rosa meant something to me. I've learned my lesson. I wouldn't let myself care about anyone else." She stared him in the eye. "You both taught me to close out emotion. You do it so well yourselves."

"That could be true." He gazed thoughtfully at her. "We might still experiment, Nicos." He turned away. "I have work to do setting up the Montego shipment. If you need me, I'll be in my office." He smiled at her over his shoulder. "Good to have you back, Margaret. You're going to make my job much easier."

He strolled out of the guesthouse.

Nicos was gazing after him. "Salva has a habit of getting above himself, but he might be right about—"

"He's a fool." She had to distract him. "I'm not that person anymore. Do you want me to stay here in this guesthouse or not?"

He nodded. "It's still a good idea. I like to think of you here in this place. Weeping. Begging me . . ."

"And are you going to allow me my freedom?"

He hesitated. "Maybe. Within limits. But I won't make the mistake of underestimating you. You'll have guards all around you. I'll assign Ricardo to watch you. You remember Ricardo?"

"Yes, he's a bastard. I don't care. Just tell him to keep his hands off me." She added, "Unless you want me to turn him against you."

"What?"

"I might be able to do it. I've gone way past animals now, Nicos."

He stiffened. "Spells?"

"Didn't your mother cast a spell on your father that made him do what she wanted? You told me she might have done that. I've been experimenting."

"And you could be bullshitting me."

"Yes." She grabbed her backpack and headed for the bedroom. "But you don't want to take the chance, do you? Keep everyone away from me as you did before and you'll never know how powerful I've become. I'm going to go for a swim now. There's something about this place that makes me feel very dirty."

She slammed the bedroom door behind her and leaned back against it.

She felt sick. Her heart was practically jumping from her chest. So many memories. So much evil. If she'd stayed in that room a minute longer, Nicos would have seen how upset she was. It had been terribly difficult to keep control of herself and remain without expression. Particularly when they'd been talking about that night three years ago.

Rosa . . .

Memories were flooding back to her, as they'd wanted them to do. Because they knew that remembering would make her weak and pliable. As she'd been when Nicos had only had to pull the strings and she would do what he wished.

But she wasn't weak; this time she'd shown them strength. And she had to continue to do that until she was off this island. Until Patrick was safe.

She pushed herself away from the door and looked around. Everything was the same; luxurious, gleaming, the bed huge and dressed in a magnificent red velvet coverlet and pillows.

Red.

*Blood running in rivulets on the tiles.*

Block it. She had a task to perform.

*Rosa . . .*

Block it. She couldn't think about her, either. Not now.

I'm sorry, Rosa. They have to pay, and I can't focus if I remember you.

She sat down in the cream-colored brocade chair near the bed and tried to concentrate. What had she learned in the past hours that she could use?

Things were basically the same as when she'd escaped

three years ago. Nicos was a degenerate killer who was as arrogant as she remembered. He appeared not to have lost any of his superstitions and he had learned how valuable she could be to him. Absence had, if not made his heart grow fonder, shown him that he was definitely better off with her than without her. No wonder the search had never ceased.

Juan Salva? He had broken off in the middle of baiting her to go attend to Nicos's business. He might be as horrible and vindictive as Nicos, but his ambitions had grown and Margaret could sense the recklessness that was beginning to grow within him. He would be taking as much of Nicos's business into his hands as possible. He'd probably been subtly using bribes and threats to bring Nicos's men under his direct orders.

Which meant that she'd been right when she'd told Lassiter that it was Salva who would have been the one who'd set up any computer network for Nicos.

And it was Salva who should have immediate access to the name of the computer expert who'd created the file that would lead them to Patrick.

Okay, then find a way to get to Salva that won't be suspicious and discover how to find either computer or phone access to that name.

Not now. It was too soon. She'd just arrived back on the island. Give it a little time.

Go take that swim. Come back and eat supper. Then maybe pay a visit to Salva.

She was getting tense again at the very thought. If he thought it would advance his ambitions, Salva would get rid of her; he'd even convince Nicos to replay that horror of three years ago.

Fear.

Smother it. She was going to do this. The fear had gone on too long.

\* \* \*

The cove is the same, she thought as she walked toward the surf pounding against the sandy shore. Beauty, sunlight, and a gentle breeze that soothed. Three years ago, she had welcomed that beauty because of the dark ugliness to which she had to return every single day.

To which she'd have to return today.

But today she'd not be helpless; today she could take action.

Set a precedent.

She carelessly dropped her backpack on the beach, close to the surf. It was too soon to expect Lassiter to have arranged to send someone with her phone, but she would do everything exactly as she'd repeat it tomorrow.

Ricardo would notice and be more lulled into accepting what she would be doing.

Then she waded into water. It was warm, but she felt chilled. It was almost sundown, but that probably wasn't the reason. It could be that Ricardo Basanez was sitting on that dune watching her as if she were going to be his next meal. Or it could be that there was no way she could predict what Nicos was going to do. Or wondering if she would be up to the task when he finally exploded with his usual venom. Because it always came; the question was when.

Just swim. Look like she was enjoying herself. Not too far from shore, or she'd have Ricardo coming down and dragging her out of the surf. She kept swimming for the next twenty minutes and then leisurely headed for the third rock formation in the group of boulders.

Set the precedent.

She stayed in full view of Ricardo as she pulled herself out of the water onto a flat rock and lazily wrung out her hair. Then she tilted back her head as if enjoying the last long rays of the sun.

And that's when she saw it.

It was small, not more than three inches, and wrapped in a dark green waterproof package.

She was so shocked, she found her herself staring down at it before jerking her gaze away.

Good God, how had Lassiter managed to get this to her so soon?

She knew how he'd done it. He'd started the minute that he'd seen she'd left the beach house and mustered every bit of effort and manpower he had at his disposal. Who knew better than Margaret what a powerhouse he could be when he was driven?

She drew a deep breath. She wasn't chilled any longer. She felt glowing with warmth and vitality. Incredible how the sight of that small package could chase the cold and fear away.

Because it told her that even in the house of the enemy, she wasn't alone.

How to get that package into the backpack she'd left on shore? It was small enough for her to palm and not be seen if she waited until the light faded a little more. She'd left the backpack unzipped, as she would have done tomorrow, when she might have actually expected to retrieve the phone. Okay, the only moment of danger for Ricardo to notice anything wrong would be when she ran out of the water and grabbed the towel out of her backpack. There was no place to hide the phone in this bikini.

She could do this. If Lassiter could get this phone to her, then she could get it safely back to the house.

Think. What would distract Ricardo?

Ten minutes later, it was dim enough to start swimming back to shore. It took only two minutes to reach the point where she could stand. She could feel Ricardo's eyes on her as she stood up and started to walk toward the shore.

She stopped short as her bikini bra began to slip

down, baring her breasts. She frantically reached around
to the fastening in the back with the hand holding the
phone as it slipped even farther. Holding the bra in place,
she ran for the backpack, grabbed the towel and wrapped
it around her upper body while slipping the phone into
the backpack in the process.

She saw Ricardo laughing as she started to try to re-
fasten the bikini top. "Do you need help?" he called.
"Nicos told me to watch you closely. If you're having
trouble, I think I should get even closer, don't you?"

No suspicion, she realized with relief. For once, Ricardo's lechery had been her friend. "Nicos also told you
not to touch me." She finished drying with the towel and
tossed it into her backpack and zipped it closed. "I had
enough bother with that damn hook; I don't want to have
you thinking it was some kind of invitation." She got to
her feet, grabbed her backpack, and started to stride
back toward the house.

She didn't look back, but she heard Ricardo laugh
again.

I did it, Lassiter.

Yet, that wasn't quite true. She was again feeling that
sense of having someone here for her. Of not being alone
to face what was to come. It was as if he were beside
her, out of sight, but still . . . there.

No, *we* did it, Lassiter.


Lassiter surfaced near the seaplane in the cove at the far
end of the island. He took the rope Mandell threw him
and went hand over hand until he reached the door. Then
Mandell pulled him into the plane.

"Long swim." Mandell handed him a towel. "Did you
have to land this far out? Maybe a little overkill?"

"No. We don't take chances," Lassiter said curtly.
"Not with this one."

"You said she probably wouldn't be able to make the pickup before tomorrow. Why the hurry?"

"I wanted it there for her. She's running her own show, but I'm not going to let her do without anything she needs . . . when she needs it."

"Not exactly your way of handling an operation. You like to be in control," Mandell said. "No wonder you're a little tense."

"You could say that." But Lassiter couldn't even imagine how Margaret was feeling now. Not only tension but the isolation. "Let's get out of here." He began stripping off his scuba gear. "Keep on the water for the next five minutes or so before you take off. I don't want any noise that would let Nicos's men know we've been here."

Mandell nodded as he started toward the cockpit. "You know, I could have done this drop-off, Lassiter. Once you supplied us with that map of Vadaz Island, I'd have had no problem. There was no reason for you to have to do it."

"There was a reason." He trusted Mandell, but there was no way that he'd have let anyone else complete that mission. He had to *know* Margaret was as safe as he could make her. *Know* that she had the tool that would make a dangerous task less perilous. "Don't worry, once we get Patrick back, your knowledge of Nicos's island will come in very handy. Just not this time."

Not this woman. Not Margaret.

"But we'll be heading for Santo Domingo, in the Dominican Republic, after we take off from here, and you may get some action there. I've tracked down George Bildwan to that city, and we have a contact who may be able to locate his current address." He started pulling on his clothes. "I've ordered the Gulfstream flown into the airport there and we'll trade off this plane for it. We'll need its speed from now on. We may be bouncing from island to island until we locate the man we need. Thank God almost everyplace in the Caribbean is only a few hours distant from the next."

Margaret was barely aware of the black-and-white tiles of the guest cottage as she crossed them hurriedly to get to her bedroom.

She slammed the door and threw the backpack on the bed.

Then she took a deep breath, unzipped the backpack, pulled out the towel she'd used at the beach, and then the small waterproof package.

Definitely not *her* phone. Now to find what Lassiter had sent her and why.

She sat down on the bed and carefully unwrapped the object. Sleek stainless steel, it appeared to be a device of some sort.

But it was also wrapped in a waterproof sleeve that contained a brief message.

*LX-40. It's one of my designs and not out on the market yet. Press activate and it will record all history and contacts on any mobile phone carried by anyone within fifteen feet of the device. Depending on quantity, it will take from eight to fifteen minutes. I've set it to transmit info to my phone the moment you turn device off. At the same time, it will erase all trace of the recording and the LX-40 will appear to be just a smart phone, in case you're caught with it.*

*I tried to make it as safe for you as possible, Margaret. I won't try to contact you again unless you call and tell me you weren't able to transfer the info. Otherwise, urgent you phone me from Montego Bay. If you can't do it, I'll find a way to get you out regardless.*

As safe as possible. Yes, he's done that, she thought as she let the paper drop on the bed. She should have known Lassiter would have some super-duper technology that would make stealing information both slick and speedy. Not only was he a computer magnate, but he had all that CIA experience.

She didn't care where he'd gotten the technology; she was just glad that he'd given it to her. It would make finding out what was necessary incredibly simpler.

Perhaps.

Eight to fifteen minutes. She'd have to aim for fifteen minutes to be safe. That meant engaging Nicos or Salva in a conversation that would not make them suspicious if she had to stretch it out.

Nicos or Salva? Which one?

She'd already mentally made the choice. Every instinct said Salva would be her best chance of getting to Nicos's computer expert. But he might also be the most difficult choice. He didn't have Nicos's total lack of respect for women. He regarded them as tools that could be used but that could also cut and lacerate. Anyone who could possibly hurt him or stem his ambitions would be looked upon with suspicion.

She gazed down at the small phone. If Salva discovered her with this device, he wouldn't let her make explanations. He would kill her and make explanations to Nicos later.

Then trust Lassiter. He wouldn't have given her a piece of equipment unless it was absolutely without flaw. Salva wouldn't be searching her to see if she was carrying a weapon or phone. That had already been done. All she had to do was stay close to Salva for fifteen minutes and let that LX-40 do its work.

Tonight? Or wait until tomorrow?

Lord, she was exhausted. It had been another nightmare day.

But Sean Patrick had probably suffered an even more nightmare day. And his nightmares might kill him if they couldn't stop them. If she delayed even one more night to get that information Lassiter needed, it might be Patrick's last.

So it was going to be tonight.

She stood up and headed for the shower. Take a hot shower and eat a little of the meal that Nicos's servants always left outside the front door of the guesthouse. Then take a trip across the courtyard to Salva's living quarters to have a fifteen-minute chat with him.

And hope she'd made the right choice.

Santo Domingo
Dominican Republic
10:40 P.M.

"Yes, I found Bildwan. But he isn't the right man," Mandell said flatly as he met Lassiter outside the small apartment building on Aguilera Street. They had split up earlier in the night to check out two separate prospects they'd been furnished by the Silicon Valley Office. "This man is a fairly good computer geek but nothing on the scale that you said you found on Nicos's file. Hell, I accessed his personal computer and even I managed to get through his firewalls. You know I'm not that good."

"You're not that bad, either," Lassiter said. But it had taken Lassiter days to get through that firewall developed for Nicos, and Mandell had been in Bildwan's apartment for only a little over an hour. "Did you question him?"

"Not seriously. He fell apart after the first ten minutes. He doesn't know anything, Lassiter." He shrugged. "Trust me, wrong guy."

Lassiter did trust him. Mandell was savvy and would not have been fooled. He should have known that he wouldn't get lucky the first time. It would have been too easy. "You made sure he wouldn't talk about our visit to anyone?"

Mandell looked pained. "Lassiter."

"Sorry. The next few days are going to be rough. We can't afford any leaks."

"There won't be any. Who's our next person of interest?"

"I don't know. On the way to the airport, I'll call Cambry and see if he's received any more updates about addresses on Montgomery or Zwecker." He got into the driver's seat of the rental car. "Right now, I'll take whatever we can get."

Vadaz Island
11:05 P.M.

The lights were still burning in Salva's office across the courtyard.

Margaret stood outside the guesthouse, gazing at Salva's quarters, trying to brace herself to start across the courtyard. She had the LX-40 phone recorder in the pocket of her khakis; all she had to do was press the button before she entered Salva's office.

Fifteen minutes.

It wasn't that long a time. The only thing she had to do was find a logical reason why she had come to him, and then stretch that conversation out for fifteen minutes.

Only? She thought she had figured out somewhere to start, but heaven knows where it would take her. Well, it wouldn't take her anywhere if she didn't stop standing here and cross that courtyard.

Don't think. Don't dread it. Just move.

A moment later, she was standing in front of the door of Salva's office. She hesitated one last moment, then punched the button on the recorder and knocked on the door.

It wasn't opened immediately and her nerves were immediately on edge. Then the door swung open and Salva stood there looking at her with a sardonic smile. "Hello, Margaret. What a surprise. I was about to go to bed. If you were planning on joining me, I'm afraid that I'll have to disappoint you. Nicos still believes that nonsense about keeping you pure as the driven snow, and I'm not ready to go against him yet."

"Don't flatter yourself," she said curtly. "I'm not one of those poor girls you bring to Nicos. I know that's a one-way street. I'm only trying to survive, and I realize how bad my situation may turn out to be. I may need your help before this is over. May I come in?"

He stood gazing at her for a moment. "You think I might help you? How bizarre. And why now? Why not wait until tomorrow?"

"Because I know I won't sleep unless I talk to you and let you know I may be valuable to you." She added grimly, "You've never given a damn about me. You just stood by and watched as Nicos put Rosa and me through hell. But I don't have anyone else to turn to, so you're my only option. I'll do anything I can to help you, providing you can keep me alive."

"Interesting." He stepped aside. "I suppose I can take the time to listen to you. Come in and sit down."

At least three minutes must have passed since he opened the door, she thought as she moved toward the chair in front of his desk.

Twelve more minutes.

Stall.

She looked around the office. The only thing that interested her was the gold clock with the ivory face on the desk. Yes, three minutes. "This is very nice. Quite luxurious. I've never been in here before."

"Why should you? You had no business here." He sat down behind the desk. "Three years ago, you were Nicos's special servant and I had no part in what he did with you." He smiled. "Until the end. Then he wanted an audience. I admit I didn't even have to pretend. I really enjoyed it."

"Obviously. You were eager to replay that night before you left the guesthouse this afternoon."

"Because you always annoyed me a little. You had sharp eyes and I always felt as if you saw too much. I wasn't all that surprised when you escaped from the island. If you hadn't been useful, I would have put a few roadblocks in front of Nicos's men who were searching for you." He smiled. "But I didn't have to do that. You were very clever about keeping ahead of them. And, as it turned out, it was good that it was Lassiter who found you. It amused Nicos much more that he could find another way to hurt him."

"I don't care about Lassiter. I don't care about Nicos. All I want to do is be safe when Nicos has one of his explosions, like the night when he killed Rosa. You might have stopped Nicos that night, but you didn't do it. When he decides he wants another 'audience,' I want you to be in my corner."

"And why should I do that?" He tilted his head. "The only amusement you gave me was watching you try to keep Nicos from tormenting you and your friend. You went to some fascinating lengths, a regular Scheherazade, to make Nicos believe your lies."

"I was young and desperate. I'd handle it differently now."

"Would you? But Nicos is extremely hard to handle unless you're an expert."

"Like you?"

He shrugged. "I've had a good deal of practice."

Ten minutes.

"That's very clear," she said quietly. "Why do you think I'm here?"

"You still haven't told me why you're here. What can you offer me that would make me bother trying to interfere with Nicos when he's in a mood?"

"The same thing that Nicos finds valuable in me. The dogs. I'm able to control the minds of those substance-containment dogs at the airports. I can influence them or merely confuse them. Either way, it works. I can make the shipments a hundred percent safer. I'm certain that you've found that out since I've been gone. Even Nicos realizes that I was worth keeping."

"I don't argue that you have value. But that again is a value that belongs to Nicos. He wants you on your knees, and eventually you'll be there."

Three more minutes.

"If he doesn't kill me first." She added quickly, "Which could be very bad for you, Salva. We both know that someday you're going to take over Nicos's syndicate. I believe that's going to happen sooner than I thought." She paused. "You have the hunger. I can almost smell it."

He threw back his head and laughed. "Are you trying to convince me that voodoo bullshit you hand out to Nicos is sending out vibes? Anyone can see that I'm more intelligent and far better able to run this business than Nicos. Of course it will all belong to me."

"Then you need to keep me alive so that I can perform the same service for you as I do for him." She met his eyes. "And, since you *are* more intelligent, I'm sure that you'll treat me with the respect and cooperation you'd show to any important asset."

"Oh, you think so?" He got up from his desk and came around to stand before her. "You believe you understand me, Margaret? You don't have any idea who I am. Respect and cooperation? If you have enough power, you don't have to give either of those to anyone around you. I've watched Nicos all these years and it's the only thing we agree about."

He was too close to her. And his eyes were narrowed on her face. Was he becoming suspicious?

She wanted to jump to her feet and run out of the office.

One more minute.

Stay one more minute.

"You're saying that I can't count on you to help me?"

"I didn't say that. If my plans fall into place before Nicos becomes difficult for you, you might have a place with me." He reached out and touched her throat. "But don't expect more of me than you would of Nicos. Less. He calls me his pimp because I know the type of girl that appeals to him and I never disappoint. He likes the weak and the breakable. Like that little girl he has at his house now. Like Rosa." His hand moved down to the hollow of her throat. "He doesn't know how much more exciting it is to mold the strong into whatever you wish her to be. One of the reasons I kept away from you three years ago was that I knew I'd be tempted. Nicos almost broke you that night. If I'd been doing it, there would not have been an almost." His thumb moved into the hollow. "You're pulse is leaping. Are you afraid of me, Margaret?"

"No. Yes. Why shouldn't I be?" She brushed his hands away and got to her feet. "This wasn't the result I wanted or expected." She backed away from him. She had her fifteen minutes. Get out of here. Run back to the guesthouse. "You're just another Nicos for me to fight." She had reached the door. "But I could be much more if you'd change your mind. Let me know. . . ."

She slammed the door behind her and ran toward the guesthouse. The next moment, she was inside and running across the black-and-white tiles toward her bedroom. So much more evil had been in this room that night than she had imagined. Salva had not only been a bystander; he had wanted to take over and participate.

With her as the key victim, not Rosa.

She closed the bedroom door and went into the bathroom and splashed water on her face and throat. In that moment when he'd touched her, she had felt as weak and dominated as he'd wanted her to feel.

But I wasn't dominated, she told herself. She'd gotten what she needed from Salva. She wasn't weak, and she certainly was not breakable.

Unlike Rosa.

It could have been that comparison that had frightened her so much when he'd touched her. Rosa had been breakable and they'd broken her. Margaret hadn't been able to help her.

But she could help Sean Patrick.

She took the phone recorder out of her pocket. It was still running. If she turned it off, it would automatically transmit to Lassiter.

Not yet.

She had to make sure that she'd gotten what she needed from Salva.

Otherwise, she'd have to go through the same nightmare process with Nicos tomorrow. She reversed the recorder while she tried to remember the exact names of the three computer experts that Lassiter had given her. George Bildwan, Carl Montgomery, Simon Zwecker.

Okay, scroll through Salva's call history and see if any of those names were listed. Or any other name with any notations concerning computers after them.

She started to scroll, not too fast, in case she might miss something. She was already ten minutes into Salva's list and there were no names she recognized.

So many names . . . Some were just initials. When

you dealt with drug dealers, sometimes you didn't want them accidentally identified. She hoped to heaven that computer guru wasn't listed under only initials. All of this might be for nothing if—

Simon Zwecker!

That had been one of the names Lassiter had mentioned.

And Salva had called him two months ago.

Don't get too excited. He might not be the only expert Salva had hired. Keep going through the history and see if any of the other names pop up.

But her hands were trembling as she carefully went through the rest of the history. None of the other names on Lassiter's list appeared anywhere in the history. But Simon Zwecker's name appeared several times over the previous months. And the communication between them had evidently started over two years ago. During that initial period, there was a spurt of daily calls that indicated intense activity.

So it had to be Simon Zwecker.

And Lassiter had to know it was him right now. Would he be able to trace him from this phone interchange? He'd had no problem when he'd tapped her phone. He'd been clever enough to create this small jewel of a device. So trust him. She'd done her part.

Now let him do his.

She pressed the turn-off button that would transmit the recording to Lassiter's phone.

Santo Domingo
11:50 P.M.

Lassiter heard the soft ping of his text alert as he was striding with Mandell toward his Gulfstream on the tarmac.

Cambry?

He'd phoned him in the car and he'd said he'd check with the office in Silicon Valley and get back to him. But that had been only minutes before and he had—

Not Cambry.

No ID.

Just the designation of the device the message was transmitting from.

LX-40.

"Holy shit." He stopped on the tarmac and stared down at the text. "My God. Margaret."

Mandell was gazing at him, puzzled. "What is it?"

"I don't know." He moved quickly to the plane and ran up the steps. "You get the plane in the air. I need to go through this list and see if she managed to get us what we need." He headed for the cockpit. "Though it would be a miracle if she was able to pull it off this soon."

"It *would* be a miracle," Mandell said drily. "You just dropped off that LX-40 late this afternoon. You weren't even expecting her to pick it up until tomorrow."

"Margaret thrives on doing the unexpected," Lassiter said. "And if she actually had that LX-40 in her hands, then she'd do anything in her power to get us what we need. She's nothing if not determined." He dropped down in the copilot's seat and began to scroll through the list. "This is Salva's call history. She told me once that he'd be the one to set up Nicos's computer system. . . ."

"And she thought Salva would be easier?" Mandell asked as he did the preflight check.

"That wouldn't have anything to do with it. She knew he wouldn't be easy. He's smarter than Nicos. She just knew he'd be the most likely one to tap."

"Well then, you'd better see if she was right." Mandell was taxiing down the runway after he got the okay from the tower. "I thought your taking that Olympic-distance swim to leave that recorder for

Margaret Douglas was a bit extreme, certainly a long shot. But she may be proving me wrong. If we manage to get her away from Nicos, I'll be interested in meeting her."

"When, not if," Lassiter said sharply. "We pick her up in Montego Bay in two days."

"We may be in the middle of a Colombian jungle in two days, going after Patrick, if we can follow up on her information." He glanced at Lassiter as he took off. "You always told me that was first priority."

"We pick her up," Lassiter repeated as he continued to scroll through the history. "I'll work it out."

*I don't know when I'll get away if you can't do it at Montego Bay.*

And he would have to do it. Because if they found a way to grab Patrick, then Nicos would be looking for reasons why it had happened. Leaks, bribery, or anything different that would have signaled a change or weakening in his security.

And Margaret would be the one different element.

"Well, we won't discuss priorities until we're sure that your Margaret's given us a name that will take us to Patrick," Mandell said. "I saw a few of those photos Nicos sent you and I don't think the decision will be—"

"We're sure," Lassiter said, interrupting him. He looked up from the text. "We have a name. Simon Zwecker. The last address we had for him was in Trinidad. Cambry's checking on any updates, but we're not waiting. Now let's go get him."

# CHAPTER ELEVEN

Vadaz Island
2:40 A.M.

*Blood!*
 *Black-and-white tiles!*

Margaret jerked upright in bed, panting, her face wet with perspiration.

*Rosa.*

No, it was only a nightmare. It would have been really bizarre if she hadn't had a dream about that night, after everything that had happened today.

And the fact that she was back in this house, where the nightmare had started.

She looked at the arched door across the room. Beyond that door was that gleaming tile floor that had haunted her for years. The memory that had been a constant torment and that had sent her running and hiding like a child afraid of the dark.

It was dark now in this bedroom. It would be darker in that room where Rosa had died, because evil still lived there. Margaret didn't want to think of that room. She wanted to lie back and cover her head and pray for sleep.

Like the young girl she'd been three years ago. But she wasn't that girl any longer. She'd come here to stop

Nicos and Salva from ever being able to send her on the run again. She had to keep them from performing those atrocities they'd done to Patrick and Rosa on anyone else.

Yet she wanted only to go and hide again.

I've given you what you needed, Lassiter. I don't know if I can help you anymore. Dear Lord, I'm afraid.

*Black-and-white tiles.*

They were waiting for her.

And if she didn't go to them, she might be afraid for the rest of her life.

And Nicos and Salva would win.

She tossed the bedcovers aside and swung her legs to the floor.

Take it slow.

There was nothing in that room beyond the door but memories.

And it was time that she faced those memories so that she could be strong, not weak.

She moved toward the door.

Just as she'd done that night three years ago.

She'd heard Rosa and Nicos come in from the courtyard and Rosa was crying.

That wasn't strange. Rosa was always afraid those days and tears came easily to her.

But Nicos didn't usually bring her back to the guesthouse to "school" her, as he called it. He made her stay at his mansion across the courtyard except when it amused him to shock Margaret by showing her the terrible things he was doing to Rosa. She'd only been able to count on him letting her see Rosa when he brought Margaret back from picking up one of the airport shipments. A "gift," he called it.

But he hadn't let her see Rosa that day when they'd returned from picking up the shipment at Santo Domingo. He'd sent Margaret back to the guesthouse and gone with Salva to his office. He'd been so angry. . . .

And Margaret had been sick with dread when she'd heard him bring Rosa to the guesthouse. She'd been shaking as she opened the door and seen Nicos standing in the center of the room.

*Rosa was kneeling at his feet. Her blouse was torn off her shoulders and there were whip marks on her back. Her lower lip was swollen where Nicos had struck her.*

*"Just in time." Nicos looked across the room at Margaret. "I wanted to make sure you saw what you did to your little friend. Sit down there against the wall. I haven't finished with her yet."*

*"I didn't do anything to her. I did everything you wanted me to do. Now don't hurt her." She took a step into the room. "Or, if you're angry with me, whip me instead."*

*"Sit down." His eyes were glittering in his flushed face. "That dog almost tipped his handler off. You didn't get to him in time."*

*"He was difficult. But he didn't give the signal that there were drugs in that suitcase. You were still able to pick it up."*

*"It was too close." The whip came down on Rosa's shoulders, cutting into the flesh.*

*She screamed.*

*"Shut up, bitch. You speak when I tell you to speak." The whip came down again.*

*"Stop it." Margaret couldn't stand it. She was across the room, tearing at the whip. "It won't be close the next time. I'll find a way to—"*

*"You know you don't stop me from doing whatever I want to her. She belongs to me." His hand lashed out and knocked Margaret to the floor. "Just as you do.*

*I told you that as long as you do what I wish, Rosa won't be hurt too badly. But you're becoming a little too defiant. I think you need a lesson."*

"Don't hurt her." She lifted a shaking hand to brush back her hair as she sat up. "I'll do what you want. Why don't you just punish me? I'm used to it. Rosa wouldn't ever do anything to make you angry."

"No, I wouldn't." Rosa was gazing pleadingly up at Nicos. "She's right. I'll do anything for you. Just tell me."

"But that doesn't make your friend Margaret as obedient as I'd like. So it was fortunate I found the key to making her as humble as I do you." His face was flushed with excitement as he looked down at Margaret. "But there comes a time when you have to give the final lesson. I didn't like you tearing that whip away from me. You have to learn there are consequences." He took out his phone and hit the number buttons. "Salva, come over to the guesthouse. It's time I taught Margaret that the patience I've shown her has limits. I want you to be here to watch." He hung up. "Now come here, Margaret. I want you to be close to your dear friend Rosa."

She didn't move. "What are you going to do?"

"Come closer. Don't you want to give Rosa an affectionate embrace. You're such good friends."

She slowly got up and crossed to where Rosa was kneeling on the floor. "What are you going to do?"

"Hold her. Tell her how much you care about her. After all, she must know all you've gone through for her."

"She knows." She knelt beside Rosa and pushed the hair away from her eyes. She said softly, "Hey, it's going to be okay." She hoped she was telling the truth, but she was terribly afraid. "He's only angry with me. But nothing really bad happened. If I do what he says, it will be all right." She stroked Rosa's cheek. "Try not to be afraid."

"I can't . . . help it." *The tears were running down her cheeks.* "I'm . . . sorry, Margaret. How did this happen? I know it was all my fault. But it shouldn't have happened. I never knew what—"

"Shh, just don't be scared. I'll try to—"

"Enough." *Nicos was pulling Margaret away.* "That was very touching, but I really don't want Rosa to be too comforted at the moment. And I certainly don't want you lying to her. It's not going to be all right. You had a job to do and you didn't do it. You'll learn I won't tolerate that again."

"I did do my job. Some dogs react differently, just as people do. But the end result was the same. He appeared jumpy and restless, but he didn't signal anything was actually wrong with the shipment." *She had to convince him. She had seen that expression on his face before, but never around Rosa. There was a wildness, a cruelty to the set of his mouth, an eagerness about his entire demeanor. He'd had that same look when he'd killed one of his men who he'd suspected betrayed him.* "But I'll work on it anyway. Perhaps if you let me go to the airport a day or two earlier, so that the dogs become accustomed to—"

"And tip customs off that you may be casing the area?"

"Maybe you could find a reason. Get me a temp job at one of the—"

"Here I am." *Salva had opened the courtyard door.* "I do hope you're going to make this entertaining, Nicos. I have work to do." *He glanced at Rosa's huddled figure kneeling on the floor as he came into the room.* "This doesn't look promising. I've seen it before."

"Did you hear that, Margaret?" *Nicos asked.* "Salva wishes entertainment. Shall we give it to him?" *He drew out his 9mm Beretta.* "I believe we have to give him something different tonight."

"No!" Keep calm. He might be only trying to frighten you. "What good would that do? Things have been going well until today. I'll keep on doing what you want. Just don't hurt her."

"What about it, Salva?" Nicos said, not looking at him. "Shall I listen to her?"

"Entirely up to you, as usual. But if you don't mind, I'm a little bored. I believe I'll go back to my office."

"No, don't do that." Nicos took a step closer to Rosa and pressed the gun to her temple. "I assure you that things are going to perk up at any minute."

"No!" Rosa was sobbing. "I don't want to die. I'll do anything." She gazed frantically at Margaret. "Make him stop. He'll listen to you. Tell him not to do it. I'm begging you. Do whatever he wants, but don't let him kill me."

"You heard her," Margaret said as she took a step closer. "She'll do anything. I'll do anything. Just don't kill her because you think I made a mistake." Her voice was shaking. She could see that she wasn't getting through to him. If anything, his expression was wilder than before. It reminded her of her father's face on the night she had run away. The night she had known that she had to run or be killed. Only she couldn't run and leave Rosa. "Isn't what you've done to her enough?" She swallowed. "Do you want me to beg you? Okay, I'm begging you. Please, don't kill her."

"Yes, please. Margaret won't do it again," Rosa said frantically. "Do anything else you want with me, but don't kill me."

"Too late." Nicos met Margaret's eyes. "She has to pay for her mistake. Or rather, you do." He smiled. "Remember this, Margaret."

He pressed the trigger.

Margaret screamed.

Blood on the black-and-white tiles.

*Rosa's blood.*
*Rosa lying on the tiles with her skull half blown off.*
*Blood everywhere.*
*Nicos eagerly drinking in Margaret's expression.*
*Salva smiling in the background.*
*Blood on the black-and-white tiles . . .*

Blood . . .

Margaret found that she'd sunk to those tiles and was leaning huddled against the wall in the darkness as memory after memory flowed over her. She was shaking, shuddering, as she had that night.

So much evil.

She had felt so helpless to save Rosa. Nicos had saddled her with the blame, and she had been so numb that she had accepted it rather than face thinking or analyzing. She'd been so traumatized that it had been over a year after she'd escaped from Nicos before she'd even been able to think of that night. It was a long time after that she'd been able to be objective enough to realize that she'd not been at fault for that savage act. She'd thought that somehow she should have been smarter, been able to find some way out for both of them. The one time that she'd persuaded Rosa to try to escape from the island, they'd been caught and Rosa had been beaten unmercifully. After that, Margaret had kept an eye out for another opportunity, but it had never come.

And then it was too late.

Too late. That was what Nicos had said that night before he'd put a bullet in Rosa's head.

I'm sorry, Rosa. I don't know if someone else could have helped you more than I did. I think I tried as much as I was able at the time. And I'm sorry that I was afraid and ran away from that night as well as from Nicos.

She closed her eyes as she felt the tears run down her cheeks. She could see Rosa, smiling, gentle, full of fun, the way she'd been when Margaret had first met her at that petting zoo in New Orleans. So different from the slave Nicos had made of her toward the end.

It was so evil. They mustn't be allowed to do that ever again to anyone else.

Not ever. No matter what she had to do to stop it.

I promise you I'll never run away again, Rosa.

Port of Spain
Trinidad
4:35 A.M.

The small, cream-colored house had a terra-cotta tile roof. It was half a block from the ocean and surrounded by an ornamental wrought-iron fence.

"Not bad," Mandell murmured. "The houses this close to the beach sell for a pretty penny in Trinidad. Nicos must be paying him well."

"Then Zwecker is in his pocket and not being threatened or intimidated," Lassiter said grimly. "I'm glad. We don't have to feel in the least hesitant about doing anything we have to do to get the information I need." He looked at the cobalt blue front door. "You go in the front door and disarm any alarms. I'll take the back door and hit the bedroom."

Mandell nodded as he opened the ornamental front gate. "No problem." He glided down the walk.

Lassiter went around to the backyard, climbed over the fence, and in another moment was at the back door. He was about to take care of the lock when the door swung open.

"What kept you?" Mandell whispered. "For a computer expert, Zwecker leaves much to be desired in the alarm department. Do you want this to be a dual assault?"

"No, find his office and start looking through his notes and computer files." He was moving silently down the hall. "I'll go after Zwecker." He silently opened the door to his right. A bathroom. He opened the next door down the hall.

Bedroom. A bed, empty, with covers rumpled, pushed hastily aside, one on the floor—

Not good.

Lassiter dove down and forward into the room, then rolled to the side against the man standing behind the door.

A knife descended toward him.

He reached up and grasped the man's wrist and twisted it. The knife dropped to the floor.

Obscenities.

He swung his legs in an arc that hit the man's knees and brought him down. Then he was straddling him, his hands on his throat. "Zwecker?"

"Let me go." He was tearing at Lassiter's hands, grasping his throat. "Do you know who you're dealing with? I have friends who will like nothing better than to cut your throat. I have protection."

"I don't doubt you had it," Lassiter said grimly. "Past tense. But you've lost any protection you might have had the moment we found out you worked for Nicos. That made you vulnerable. Nicos won't like the idea of anyone being able to tap someone who knows his secrets."

"I don't know anyone named Nicos."

Lassiter's hands tightened on Zwecker's throat until his eyes bulged. "I don't have time for this bullshit." He loosened his grip and let Zwecker take a deep breath. "Would you like to go over that again?"

"Maybe I do work for him." Then he spat, "But he won't care that you've found out about me as long as he can rid himself of you. And he'll do that. I'm important to him. He knows I'd never betray him. I've been working with Salva for the past three years and he trusts me. Now let me go."

"What's all the uproar?" Mandell stood in the doorway. He reached over and turned on the wall switch, lighting the room. "You didn't handle this at all smoothly, Lassiter. You should have left it to me. I take it that's Zwecker?" He took out his phone and checked the photo Cambry had texted them. "Fortyish, skinny, Vandyke beard, receding brown hair. Yes, at least you got that right."

"I'm glad you approve." Lassiter got off Zwecker and pulled him to his feet. "Did you find the office?"

"Across from the living room. But I didn't have a chance to try to get into his computer before I heard you causing a ruckus."

"Then we'd better go do it now." He said curtly to Zwecker, "Get some clothes on. We're going to go to your office, and by the time we leave it, I'm going to know everything that you know about Nicos's operation."

"I don't know anything," he said quickly. "Why should I? I'm only a tech expert. I set up Nicos's system, but I don't have any information about what he enters into his files."

"You might make someone who didn't realize how good you are believe that," Lassiter said. "But I know a little something about computers, and I looked at how many calls Salva made to you. They must have had you do constant adjustments to make that file work efficiently for them. And I'm wondering if they didn't have you set up other files concerning other Nicos enterprises."

"I don't know anything," Zwecker said stubbornly. "I just set it up."

"No, you didn't. You created that file and made it yours. And it's so complicated that I'd bet you wouldn't have been able to resist putting in a command to slip out a copy into your personal computer. You're going to tell me every detail of what's on that file. Do you understand?"

Zwecker shook his head. "Why? Nicos will kill you as soon as he finds out that you came and threatened me."

"He's not going to find out. He's a dead man. Now get your bony ass in gear. We're going to go to your office and start work." He reached down and picked up the knife Zwecker had dropped. "And if you're cooperative, I may not cut off any of your fingers. That would make it so difficult to operate a keyboard, wouldn't it?"

Zwecker's eyes widened, and for the first time he appeared uncertain. "You wouldn't do that."

"No? I've spent eighteen months trying to find a man whose location has probably been at your fingertips for that entire time." Lassiter's voice was soft but icy cold. "I won't go into what Nicos has been doing to him during that time. You might even already know. You said he trusts you." He stared Zwecker in the eye. "Look at me. Then tell me I won't do anything I have to do to make sure that I find out what I have to know."

When Zwecker finally pulled his gaze away, he was pale. "I'm just a tech." He moistened his lips. "And Nicos would kill me if I told you anything."

"And I'll kill you if you don't. I'm the devil you know. I'd advise you not to be concerned about Nicos. Worry about me." He glanced at Mandell. "My friend Mandell here and I will take turns questioning you. We'll start on the little programs and build up to others. I have an idea we may find a few interesting nuggets that you've squirreled away in your own computer. But I'm not going to waste my time. If you don't cooperate, I'll start on the index finger of your left hand. I don't want to interfere with your dexterity by disabling your right hand in case you become more sensible. You might be able to access your own data quicker than I can. I'll break that index finger first. Then if you don't begin to answer, I'll show you the knife again. Is all that clear?"

"Yes," he said hoarsely, his eyes now wide with fear. "But I'm just a tech."

"Don't say that again. I know exactly what you are. And now you know what I am." He turned to Mandell. "Get him started by having him give us his own password to bypass his firewall. I'll go make a pot of coffee. I figure we can afford giving him until noon before we have to get on the move."

"I can't let you have my personal password," Zwecker said quickly. "What good would that do you? You're after Nicos."

"Ah, maybe I struck a nerve? Interesting . . ."

Trinidad
10:35 A.M.

"The password for Nicos's file is Bakulu," Mandell said as Lassiter walked into the office an hour later. "It's some kind of monster voodoo god who ruins lives and causes pain. The file is a nice healthy one. And Zwecker evidently has his own copy of this file, as he does several other of Nicos's directories. He was just about to break it down for me."

"Good." He glanced at Zwecker. "You didn't exactly earn that trust that you said Nicos gave you." He made a clicking sound with his tongue. "I'm certain Nicos wasn't aware you have your own copies, was he?"

"It was just a protective measure, a backup," Zwecker said sourly. "In case there was a loss of power or something of that nature."

"And you think Salva would approve of that backup?"

He dropped down in a chair, his gaze on the screen. "Somehow I doubt it."

"I wasn't intending to—" He shrugged. "It was only smart to take out insurance in case Nicos decided that I wasn't reliable. He's a little erratic."

"Tell me about it." The heading at the top of the file was NALSARA. Lassiter's gaze was going down the subheadings. He could feel the excitement grip him. "NALSARA. What do you know about this, Zwecker?"

"It's the name of a camp, an installation in northern Columbia. I assumed it was some kind of drug-related storage facility. You see that it has employees, transportation, and supplies listed. It's deep in the rain forest and the supplies have to be trucked in from the coast. The forest is so thick and impenetrable that there's no place to land a plane or helicopter anywhere nearby. Here are the dates of deliveries and receipts for salaries. Salva is very efficient."

"And how many people are at this facility?"

Zwecker pointed to the employees list. "Twenty-two on staff who are paid bimonthly."

"You're sweating. You're hand is shaking." His eyes narrowed on Zwecker's face. "You're lying or not telling me everything. Why?"

"I'm telling you what—"

"I think it's time we start on that index finger, Mandell."

"Wait." Zwecker hesitated. "There may be other people down there. The food-supply orders indicate that there may be."

Lassiter went still. "How many?"

"How should I know? I could be wrong. I just found it curious."

"How many more?"

"At least six."

That meant five more of Nicos's enemies he'd kept prisoner who might have been suffering as much as Patrick had.

"Six," he repeated.

"I thought it was nine, but the food order went down a couple months ago," Zwecker said impatiently. "What difference does it make? It probably doesn't mean anything. I just thought it was curious."

"And you wanted to explore every aspect of Nicos's little kingdom in the jungle," Mandell said. "Were you thinking about blackmail?"

"Maybe." He scowled. "If I could do it without getting myself killed. Nicos wanted that camp to be kept very confidential. He had to have a reason."

"You said drug storage? Truth?"

He hesitated. "No, I've set up other files for him that concerned drugs and arms. He was more careful with this one."

Lassiter leaned forward. "And you think you may have guessed why," he said softly. "Haven't you, Zwecker?"

Zwecker didn't speak for a moment. "Powerful men have different needs than other people. Nicos might have wanted a place to— What do I know? I'm just guessing."

"And what are you guessing?"

"Salva had me add this heading a few months ago." He pointed at the bottom of the document. "EXIT. A substantial amount of money was allotted at that time."

"About the time that the food-supply orders reflected a drop of three," Lassiter said. "They had three deaths and had to arrange to make the bodies permanently vanish. Nicos wouldn't have wanted any evidence connecting them to him if the camp was discovered. I'm sure the corpses were gruesome in the extreme." He shook his head. "And you 'guessed' what was going on and you didn't do anything about it."

"I had to protect myself." He moistened his lips. "I didn't actually know anything."

"Oh, I think you did," Lassiter said softly. "Those guesses were a little too accurate. You've been studying this file for a long time and you had plans for it. Let's see, I don't think you have the nerve to try to blackmail Nicos. What's another option?"

Zwecker shook his head.

Lassiter thought about it. "I don't know about the other prisoners, but if they have as much potential as Patrick, then that detention camp could be a pot of gold. Nicos didn't care how much money those prisoners were worth. He had his own agenda. But it would be enough to dazzle someone on the outside. Did you know how much money I offered to ransom Patrick?"

"No. How could I know that?" he asked quickly.

"Monitoring. Hacking." He paused. "Or maybe someone who had been told how much the merchandise they were holding was worth leaked it to you. Maybe to emphasize to you how carefully it had to be guarded."

"You're only making wild guesses. I'm cooperating. Let me go. I've told you all I know."

"You've told me enough so that you were hoping I'd not dig any deeper. I'm digging deeper. I think you've been planning this scheme for quite a while. But you had to be sure of your facts and knew you might need an accomplice. It wouldn't be anyone close to Nicos. . . ." His finger went down the screen to the STAFF heading. "Twenty-two. Monsters every one. You knew what they were doing to those prisoners. Which one were you going to share the booty with, Zwecker?"

He was silent.

"I'll give you thirty seconds." He took out the knife.

"I believe I'll skip breaking the finger first. You're annoying me."

"No!" Zwecker was breathing hard, his gaze fixed compulsively on the knife. "Don't be a hard-ass. What I did wasn't all that bad. I needed help. Some of those prisoners could be ransomed. At least three would bring in a fortune. If I couldn't blackmail Nicos, I could go in another direction. Hell, it would even be the humanitarian thing to do."

"I'm touched. Which guard did you make a deal with?"

He hesitated and then brought up a photo on the screen. The man was in his early forties, with craggy features, a broken nose, blue eyes, and a white-blond crew cut. "Lars Brukman. He's in charge of the Nalsara Detention Camp and is a favorite of Nicos. He's been down there for over four years and gets the highest pay. He's a former mercenary and he's tough enough to run the camp efficiently. But he's tired of being stuck down there in the jungle and he liked the idea of the ransom." He smiled tentatively. "We would have let you buy back Sean Patrick. We'd even talked about it. Maybe we could still make a deal?"

"Lars Brukman was also probably in charge of the torture they did on Patrick. What do you think?"

His smiled vanished. "Then what are you planning on doing with me?"

"I'm sending you back to Cancún under guard and letting you live . . . for now." He got to his feet and moved toward the door. "I don't know for how long. It depends on how many details you can give me about that camp and Lars Brukman. Where do you meet when you contact Brukman?"

"We either text or phone most of the time. When one of us wants to meet in person, I go down to Colombia. When Brukman's not at the camp, he stays at a hotel on the coast at Puerto Ponce. It's about sixty miles from the camp. We usually met at the bar off the lobby."

"Then call him and tell him that you need to see him this evening. Tell him that you think you've negotiated a deal that will make you both rich. Set it up for eight tonight."

He frowned. "Why can't we make that the truth? Couldn't we discuss an arrangement that would—"

Lassiter was across the room in seconds and knocked Zwecker crashing off his chair onto the floor. His voice was fierce as he glared down at him. "Listen, I'm within a heartbeat of breaking your neck. Eighteen months that you knew this was going on and what they were doing with those prisoners. Make the damn call."

"I'll take care of it," Mandell said quietly. "You're a bit upset. He's got to be alive to make the call."

Mandell was right. Lassiter was on the edge of violence and he had to control it. Zwecker and his cohort Brukman were as filthy as Nicos, and the knowledge of the torture and deaths they'd so casually accepted and the lives they'd played with during these months had made him go ballistic. Margaret was risking her life while those scum were calculating how to sell those people in Nicos's death camp for the most money. He nodded jerkily. "And I'll call Cambry and tell him to get the rest of the team down there to Puerto Ponce by tonight." He turned and strode from the room and out onto the veranda.

He stood looking out at the sea for a moment before he made the call to Cambry. Things were beginning to flow together and he should be happier. But it had gone on too long and his nerves were raw. There was still too much to do in too short a time. He had to be at that airport in Montego Bay by tomorrow evening or Margaret might be killed. He had to pull Patrick out of that camp before he went to Montego Bay or the first thing Nicos would do after Margaret escaped would be to order Patrick killed.

*"So what's wrong, kid?"* Lassiter had a sudden memory of Patrick, his eyes twinkling, sitting in that hotel room in Atlantic City all those years ago. *"Too much for you? Hell, you're only seventeen and you can do all kinds of hocus pocus to dazzle my buddies at the CIA and con the entire world. But you can't straighten up and find a way to get through a few years in the army?"* He added teasingly, *"Need a little help? Maybe we can work it out together."*

*"I don't need help from anyone."*

*"No, you don't. All you've got to do is start thinking and get your priorities in order. So go ahead and do it."*

And Lassiter had done it. All through those years he and Patrick had been together and moved from stage to stage in their friendship, they'd never found a mountain they couldn't climb.

But now he had to climb this one alone.

Okay, then start thinking and planning and get your priorities in order. Then find a way to do it all.

Move!


Vadaz Island


"Good morning, Margaret," Nicos said. "As I recall, you never used to sleep this late. I'm glad you're feeling so at home."

Margaret's eyes flew open and she saw Nicos standing above her bed, looking down at her. She jerked upright in bed, her heart pounding.

"Or is it that you had a bad night? I see you have circles beneath those pretty blue eyes. Memories? Did you hear Rosa calling to you from that room next door?"

"You know I did. It's what you wanted, isn't it? What are you doing here?"

"I felt the need to see you helpless." He smiled. "When you're awake, you're always very strong. Because of the power inside you. Just like my mother. I have to catch you unaware to feel my control over you." He reached out and touched her shoulder. "Do you know how much I wanted to make you the whore I made Rosa? It would have been the supreme pleasure."

She jerked away from him. "But you decided against it. What's a whore compared to the money I can bring to you? You were always too smart."

"But Salva says that's all bullshit, that it shouldn't make a difference. That none of that voodoo shit means anything. That my mother was just a whore and not a voodoo priestess."

"And what do you think?"

"He didn't see what I saw at those voodoo meetings. He didn't feel the power sing through him. Yes, my mother was a whore, but she also had the power. Not enough. My father eventually broke free of her and killed her. I watched him do it. She begged me to stop him."

"But you didn't do it."

He shrugged. "I was through with her. And she didn't have the power. What a waste. I thought it might be that she'd had so many men in her body that it had drained her of the only thing that should have been important in her life."

"And you decided that you wouldn't take a chance on having that happen to my power," she said bitterly. "It's just as well. I don't know what would happen if you used me as you did Rosa. She became . . . nothing. Not the same person."

"I don't know, either. But Salva is beginning to sway

me to his way of thinking. I believe he might want to participate. I just thought that I should let you know what you might anticipate in the future." He met her eyes. "Maybe the not-too-distant future. I've begun to have fantasies about you kneeling on those black-and-white tiles."

"You're not that self-destructive." She kept her voice steady with an effort. "And you have plenty of women you use for that kind of ugly fantasy."

He laughed. "Very true. We'll see how long I can make do with substitutes." He turned and headed for the door. "By the way, I thought I'd tell you that we'll be leaving for Montego Bay late this afternoon."

She stiffened. "Why? The airport delivery isn't until tomorrow evening."

"The last time, you'll recall, you had a small problem with the dogs." He looked over his shoulder with a malicious smile. "Which brought all kinds of problems down on you and poor Rosa. I decided I'd let you have a bit more time for those dogs to become more accustomed to you."

She frowned. "You want me to go visit Montego customs today?"

"No, I've found out the handler's home address. We'll pay a visit this evening and give you your chance to become best friends."

"You've never done that before." Her gaze was searching his face. "You're worried about this shipment. It's important to you. What is it?"

"That's none of your concern. Or maybe it is. It might be important that you realize that I'll be very upset if this delivery doesn't go smoothly. The shipment is a very powerful and sophisticated bomb that was built in Mexico City and that I'm going to fly down to Caracas. There's a terrorist group there that's having a bit of trouble at the U.S. embassy." He stopped at the door. "So it *will* go smoothly, or I'll let Salva convince me that you're worth only one thing to me. Do you understand?"

Death. Destruction. Rape. Not empty threats, and now she knew why Nicos had come to her this morning. "I've always understood you, Nicos."

"But it's never bad to be very clear." The door closed behind him.

She sat there trying to recover from that barrage of poison Nicos had thrown at her. So clever. He had used Rosa and that night and mixed it with a not-so-subtle threat to Margaret. He had attacked her at her most vulnerable to make her feel weak.

And for a little while, it had worked. But now the strength and determination of last night were flooding back to her.

It's not going to happen, Rosa. We won't let it go on.

She threw the covers aside and headed for the bathroom. She glanced at the mirror and saw the circles Nicos had spoken about. Yes, she'd had a bad night. It had been filled with memories and sorrow and regret. But it had also been a night to build strength.

Screw you, Nicos.

She headed for the shower. It might be a good thing they were leaving a day early for Montego. Lassiter had asked her to phone him when she arrived there, and she might be able to give him advance details on how many men Nicos was going to deploy at the airport. The more time to prepare, the better.

While she was still here, she'd take another swim and see if there had been anything else placed on that rock. She doubted that there would be anything, but she wouldn't take a chance. She'd already slit the pocket of her khaki jacket and slid both the phone and a makeshift dagger into the lining. They were her only weapons, but she'd try to make the most of them.

Perhaps not the only weapons.

What about the dogs?

Nicos was giving her extra time with them because he wanted her to bond with the dogs to keep that damn bomb safe.

Oh, yes, she'd definitely have to think about a unique way to bond with them. . . .

# CHAPTER TWELVE

Hotel Reyes
Puerto Ponce, Columbia
7:45 P.M.

Lars Brukman.

Lassiter recognized the man who had come into the bar from the photo Zwecker had brought up on the computer. Same close crew cut, same broken nose and craggy features. He was frowning as he gazed around the bar looking for Zwecker.

Time to move.

Lassiter put his drink down and stepped away from the bar. "Brukman."

Brukman froze. "Lassiter?" He was immediately wary. "Where's Zwecker? You weren't supposed to be here."

"You recognized me?" He took another step closer. "Nicos, I suppose?"

Brukman nodded. "He wanted to make sure that I knew who'd be coming after Sean Patrick." He met his eyes. "Zwecker said that you'd be willing to deal with us for him. But you're not supposed to be here. Zwecker and I have to talk money."

"Do you want to know what I offered Nicos?"

"That could be a start," he said cautiously. "Nicos mentioned the first negotiations, but I'm sure you went higher. But we'd have to have more so that we could lose ourselves from Nicos—"

"But you might think the offer I'll make you is so good that you'll take it without question. Let's have a drink and talk about it."

He hesitated. "After I call Zwecker and ask him why you're here."

"Suit yourself. But what I saw in that last photo of Patrick made me think that you won't have any merchandise I'll be willing to offer for soon. I won't pay for a dead man, Brukman."

"He still has time." He grimaced. "But it's a good thing you've come now. I told Nicos that he couldn't take that kind of punishment, but he insisted."

"And you complied," Lassiter said without expression. "But, of course, he pays the bills. I understand your position."

Brukman nodded. "But you're smart to deal with us. Nicos isn't ever going to let him go."

"I know that." He took one more step. "So make your call to Zwecker so that we can start negotiations."

Brukman reached for his phone.

And Lassiter clamped his palm down on Brukman's hand and pressed the needle with the knockout tranquilizer hidden there into his wrist.

"What . . ." Brukman reached for his gun. "You son of a bitch, what did—"

His knees buckled and Lassiter caught him before he fell unconscious.

"Drunk?" Mandell appeared immediately at Lassiter's side. "Maybe we should take him out to the car so that he can get some air?"

"Good idea." None of the few customers in the bar appeared to be noticing what had occurred. The bartender had been liberally tipped to turn his back. "He never could hold his liquor."

Three minutes later, they'd deposited Brukman in the passenger seat of the van they'd rented.

"Will you need me here any longer?" Mandell asked. "I'd really enjoy having a discussion with Brukman. Zwecker was much too easy."

Lassiter nodded. "I want you there when he wakes up, but follow in your own car. You'll have to leave right away." Lassiter started the van. "You'll need to get out to that detention camp and position yourself. I'm estimating you'll have about two hours before I bring Brukman to the party."

"That's not long. His record was pretty impressive while he was a mercenary. He could hold out."

"If he does, I'll hang him up on the branches of a tree and see how long *he* lasts. I'll try to find the same type of tree he used on Patrick."

Mandell gave a low whistle. "That might do it."

Lassiter started to drive in the direction of the nearby rain forest. "That's what I figured," he said over his shoulder.

Brukman regained consciousness twenty minutes later. By that time, they'd traveled to the rim of the rain forest and Lassiter and Mandell had tied him securely to a palm tree.

"You son of a bitch." Brukman was struggling futilely to get out of the ropes. "I'm going to kill you. I'm going to chop you into pieces. You think that Patrick was hurting? You'll scream until you—"

"You're being boring," Lassiter said. "And you're being stupid enough to remind me of all the things I have against you. It's a big list, and I was only recently given a face to go along with it. But I'm beginning to put the two together. Did you know I was sent twenty-four photos of your work on Patrick over the last eighteen months?"

"I don't care." His eyes were blazing in his white face. "If you want him back, you'll have to deal with me. Money, Lassiter."

"And I'd pay it if I hadn't seen those photos. There has to be accountability. Added to the fact that there's every chance you'd take my money and not follow through." He gestured to Mandell. "But I'm being rude. Permit me to introduce you to my friend Nick Mandell. Considering your mercenary background, you've probably heard of him. He's possibly the best sniper in the world today. He's something of a legend in those circles."

"Please. In any circle." Mandell smiled. "How many times do I have to tell you I'm a man with no limits, Lassiter?"

"I've heard of him," Brukman said impatiently. "Do you think I'm going to be intimidated by some has-been shooter?"

Mandell looked pained. "Now that hurt." He glanced at Lassiter. "I either get out of here and go set up at the camp or I kill him now."

"Get going."

"Right." Mandell glanced over his shoulder at Brukman as he headed for his car. "I'll see *you* later."

Brukman glared at Lassiter. "What was that about?"

"I just wanted you to know what you're up against. I'm sure that Nicos gave you my credentials and those of everyone who works for me. He'd want you to be prepared." He took a step closer. "So I'm going to tell you how it's going to go down. You're going to take me to that detention camp and tell your men that Nicos has made a deal to turn Patrick over to me. You're going to be very plausible. Then your men are going to load Patrick into my van and we're both going to leave quietly and without incident."

"You're dreaming. You're going to walk into my camp and then expect to get out alive? Didn't Zwecker tell you that if something ever happened to me that my lieutenant, Herb Stockton, would take over? He'll have questions. And even if you have a gun and I don't, what's going to stop me from—"

"Shouting out and bringing down firepower on both me and Patrick?" He leaned forward and said coldly, "Because the moment I lift my hand, you'll be a dead man. That's the reason you met my friend Mandell, even though he was in something of a hurry after I gave you that knockout injection. He's going to your camp to get ready for us. If there are any trees or rocks anywhere overlooking that camp, he'll find just the right place. As I said, Mandell was the best sniper I'd ever seen when I was in the Special Forces. He's a natural. And he's been missing it. He'll be able to take down you and at least two others before anyone realizes what's happening."

"You're bluffing."

"You could take that risk. But you should know there will also be five other of my men in the woods surrounding the camp. Not as uniquely talented as Mandell, but all equally qualified to blow you all to kingdom come. And yes, I know about Stockton. That's why you're going to have to be very plausible. It shouldn't be too much of a problem. Zwecker said that you keep Stockton firmly under your thumb."

"You're the one who's at risk. How do you expect to get Patrick out of the area? There are checkpoints on every road leading from the camp to Bogotá. They wouldn't ask questions; they'd just blow you away."

"All the roads leading north. Only one checkpoint on the one road leading south. And that's where there's a helicopter pad that Nicos uses when he comes down here to supervise your work personally. I imagine he's been down here to see you while you've had Patrick here. He likes to observe. It's really rough country and it's unlikely that anyone would be coming by ground

from that direction." He paused. "And so Mandell ordered his men to take out that checkpoint. Mandell's
men are all excellent and it will be done quietly and efficiently. Ten minutes later, a helicopter will be arriving.
The pilot will wait there until I show up with Patrick."
He smiled. "And then we'll be off to the private airport
outside Bogotá where I have my Gulfstream waiting."

"And you think it will work? Too many things could
go wrong." Brukman said through his teeth, "You're
*crazy.*"

"Yeah, I'm certainly a little off balance. It's been a
long hunt and stress can do that to you. So don't push it."

"Pay the money."

"Not one penny. But I'll still deal with you. After we
get Patrick safely out of that camp and I'm through with
you, I'll put you on a plane out of Bogotá to the desti-
nation of your choice. After that, you're on your own.
You'd better run hard and fast. Because we both know
that Nicos will be after you the minute he finds out you
helped me. And so will I."

"And that's supposed to be a deal?" Brukman asked
scornfully.

"It's all you'll get from me. A running start. You'll
probably get lucky, because I intend to take Nicos out.
Then you'll only have to worry about me. But do worry,
Brukman, because you're definitely on my list. I just
have to give you a lower priority at the moment."

"I could go to Nicos and tell him that you forced—"

"And you think that would save you?" He shook his
head. "No, you don't. He wouldn't care. Betrayal is an
automatic death sentence with him. You have to know
him better than that."

He was silent. "And what's to keep you from killing
me the minute we leave the camp?"

"Nothing. Except for the fact that I want to keep Nicos from knowing that I've taken Patrick from you for

the next twenty-four hours. I need a safety net to get Patrick to a secure medical facility. You might get a text or a phone call from Nicos or Salva and I'd want you to give the appropriate answers. That guarantees that you're alive until then." He paused. "That's twenty-four hours longer than I want to give you. So take that plane ticket, Brukman."

"The hell I will." His eyes were blazing into Lassiter's. "That's all bullshit."

"Yes, the hell you will," he murmured. "I'm so glad you refused. Did I mention that I was with both the Special Forces and the CIA? As you know, they make sure we have very good training in your particular speciality. I'd bet that I might be as good as you when I have motivation. I *do* have motivation now. Mandell was saying that you're tough and might be difficult. I don't doubt it. But you're also practical and greedy, or you wouldn't have made the deal with Zwecker. I think you'll opt for a way to live and fight another day. So you'll take some token punishment and then cave. Because I have two hours to convince you that I've offered you the deal of a lifetime. Your life. Two hours should be plenty of time. . . ."

Hyatt Hotel
Montego Bay, Jamaica
10:40 P.M.

"Ah, ready and eager to go," Nicos said mockingly as Margaret threw open the door to her room at his knock. "I approve, Margaret. You're starting out as I'd like you to continue."

"I'm not eager," she said as she passed the guard in the hall. "I just want this over. Where's Salva?"

"He's closeted with a few of the local distributors and

decided that he wasn't needed to escort you. I agreed. I wanted this time alone with you." He added sardonically, "I want to watch you while you do your magic."

"You've seen me work with the dogs at airports before."

"But you told me that your magic was stronger now."

"You won't be able to tell a difference from what I do tonight." She didn't want to be alone with Nicos. This morning had been a little too much for her to cope with. "Why don't you send one of the guards with me?"

"Because I don't choose to do that. And everything you do and are is because I choose for it to be so. I thought I made that plain." He punched the button for the elevator. "Here's what's going to happen tonight. We're going to the house of Julio Ramirez. He owns and trains two German shepherds who are considered the finest substance-detector dogs in Jamaica. Julio Ramirez and his son, Alfredo, work together as a team at the airport, and you'll have to deal with both dogs when that shipment comes in."

"There's usually only one dog at customs."

"Not this time." They were off the elevator and crossing the lobby to the waiting car in the driveway. "There have been a few suspect shipments in the last couple months. I didn't have you to smooth things over. The local DEA requested that the security be pumped up to maximum."

"And yet you still arranged for the shipment to come through Montego."

"It was easier to transport out of Jamaica. I was considering changing it, but then I heard I was going to have you returned to me." He added mockingly, "I can't tell you how grateful I am to Lassiter. You can see how much I trust you, Margaret."

"But you're still taking me out to Ramirez's house to make sure I don't screw up."

"Merely a safety measure. And, as I said, I want to watch you perform your magic." He nodded to his driver. "Let's go, Nardo."

Twenty minutes later, they were parked down the street from a good-size property that consisted of a house, garage, and a rolling field that had several empty pens and dog-training apparatus. The house was dark except for a single porch light.

"Empty pens," Margaret said. "They keep the dogs inside."

Nicos frowned. "Is that a problem?"

"No, it just means I'll have to get out of the car so that I'll have a clear line to the dogs." That was a lie, but it would get her out of the close confines of this backseat with Nicos. The ride out here had been over-poweringly intimate, like being in the same straw basket with a cobra. She had felt his eyes on her for the entire trip. She opened the door and jumped out. "I'm going over there to that ditch by the fence and sit down. This may take an hour or two. If you want to watch me, do nothing but stare at that house. You're welcome to go over there with me, but you'd be much more comfortable in the car."

He slowly got out and followed her. He frowned. "It's muddy."

She settled herself gingerly on the edge of the ditch. "You ordered me to do this, Nicos. I have to do it my way."

"I'm wondering if it's a little too much your way."

She ignored him and turned her gaze to the house.

Focus.

Ignore him.

*Where are you?*

No answer.

But she could detect a stirring. One of the dogs had heard her.

*What do they call you?*

Bewilderment at the intrusion.

*They call me Margaret. What do they call you?"*

No answer.

And then . . .

*Taro.*

It had started. Now to reach the other dog . . .

She was vaguely aware that Nicos was no longer beside her. It didn't matter. She was too absorbed to let him bother her anyway. The other dog's name was Pedro and he was the less dominant of the two. She would have to balance both the emotions and the competitiveness of the two. It could take quite a while. But she would start the way she meant to finish.

*You do fine work. Smart. Both of you are so smart. You do your duty and that's wonderful. But there may be something you need to do better. Let's think about it together. . . .*

"It's about time," Nicos said sourly as Margaret climbed back into the car. "I thought you were going to be out there all night."

"You gave me orders. I had to obey you." She slammed the door shut. "I told you that you'd be bored."

"You were right." He nodded at the driver. "And I couldn't see that you were doing anything. I'm beginning to believe Salva may be right about your powers all being bullshit."

He couldn't be allowed to go in that direction. He was too volatile right now. "One dog is a tan-and-black German shepherd whose name is Pedro. But you were wrong; the other dog isn't a German shepherd; he's a black Lab and his name is Taro. The Lab is dominant, but the German shepherd is much more highly strung. Pedro, the shepherd, will be harder to handle and could be more easily confused. But now they both know me and recognize that I'm more dominant than either one of them. Tomorrow they'll do whatever I tell them to do."

He was silent for a moment. "You found out all of that tonight?"

She nodded. "You were right to give me the extra time with them. I would have had better control before if you'd seen that I'd had that opportunity."

"Of course I was right." He paused. "I'm going to check and make sure that there's a Lab instead of two German shepherds."

"Go ahead. I'd be stupid to try to fool you on something so easy to verify." She leaned wearily back on the seat. It had been a tiring couple hours reprogramming the dogs and she still couldn't be sure that she'd done enough.

And the night's work was still not done. She had to call Lassiter when she got back to the hotel and tell him she was here in Montego. Lord, she hoped he'd been able to do something with Salva's call directory. "And you'll see tomorrow if I managed to do what I said I'd done."

"Yes, I will."

He reached out and put his hand on her knee.

She went rigid.

It doesn't matter if he touches my body, she thought. No one could hurt her if she didn't let them. Her body was nothing. It was what was inside that counted. And no one could destroy that but herself.

But sometimes, at moments like this, it seemed as if it mattered.

"You don't like that, do you?" His voice was mocking as his hand moved up to her inner thigh. "Too bad. I can do anything I like with you. You're nothing and I'm everything."

She had to go carefully. He was closer than he'd ever been to dragging her down into those depths where he'd taken Rosa. "I know," she said without expression. "And, no, I don't like it. But you wouldn't care about that. It's all about suffering to you. So do whatever you want with me. But you should realize that it disturbs me and it interferes with my concentration. It keeps me from focusing on what I have to do tomorrow. Perhaps that would be better for me in the long run, because it would give me an excuse if I mess up my part in the airport delivery."

Nicos stared at her for a long moment. She could see that he was trying to stifle the anger. Then his hand fell away from her. "No excuses, Margaret. Not tomorrow." He smiled mockingly. "We'll have to wait a little longer."

"Whatever." She looked away from him so that he wouldn't see her relief. It had been terribly close. This entire night had been another nightmare to get through. Just being in the close confines of the car with Nicos had been suffocating. And, from what he'd said, it wasn't going to end. After tomorrow he'd feel free to—

What was she thinking? Tomorrow she had a chance to escape from Nicos. It wasn't as if she was alone. She had told Lassiter that she might not be able to get away from Nicos if he didn't help her here in Jamaica. He'd told her to call him when she arrived in Montego. He would have a plan. She wasn't alone.

But Lassiter would probably now be frantically working to free Sean Patrick, who had been the reason and the impetus that had brought them together. How could she expect him to drop that hunt to help her when she knew that Patrick had a chance to be saved?

She might be alone after all.

"Sleep well, Margaret." Nicos watched her unlock her door with that faint smile that was tinged with malice. "You have to be alert and ready to face the day. I wouldn't want you to disappoint me."

"I won't." She slipped inside the room and closed the

door behind her. She stood there savoring the moment of privacy. She wasn't permitted to lock the door, but just being able to shut herself away from Nicos and Salva was a merciful relief.

And after the tension of being with Nicos tonight, she'd take whatever reprieve she could get. Okay, it was over. Try to forget Nicos and make the call that Lassiter had asked her to do when she arrived in Montego.

She took her phone from the lining of her khaki jacket and started to place the call. She stopped before she'd completed entering the number.

No, not yet.

Allow another ten minutes to pass.

She wanted to make sure Nicos and Salva were settled in their rooms and would not come and interrupt her.

She sat down in the chair beside the bed and waited.

The ten minutes passed very slowly.

Then she called Lassiter.

No answer.

No message. The phone just kept on ringing.

She waited for ten rings before she hung up.

What the hell was wrong? What has happened to Lassiter, she thought in a panic. He had asked her to call. He wouldn't ignore her.

Calm down. It could be nothing.

And, if there was a problem, she would handle the problem herself. It was what she had done all her life. He had offered to help her, but that didn't mean help would come. She could hope, but she'd have to assume she'd be alone in this.

She tried to call him again.

Fifteen rings this time.

No answer.

She hung up and put the phone on vibrate. It was all she could do. He would know that she'd called and she'd just have to wait until he called her back.

Go to bed. Try to sleep. Wait for him to call.

But what in the hell was Lassiter doing that he hadn't answered that call?

Nalsara Detention Camp
1:45 A.M.

"There it is." Brukman gestured to the wire fence of the camp at the corner of the trail. "Not that it's going to do you any good. There's a good chance you won't get out of here alive."

"I thought we'd discussed that." Lassiter parked the vehicle in front of the gate. "That's your job, Brukman." He met his eyes. "And you'll do it, won't you? I believe that you realize now that I don't bluff about anything."

"Yes, you son of a bitch." He was glaring at him. "But worry, Lassiter, because I don't know if it's not worth risking a bullet just to take you out."

"I won't worry. You have a well-developed sense of self-preservation or you wouldn't have gotten this far." He opened the car door. "Now let's do it. Mandell already has you in the crosshairs. He'd like nothing better than to press that trigger." A camouflage-garbed man carrying an AK-47 was coming toward the gate. "Step forward and be counted, Brukman."

"It's me, Jorge." Brukman jumped out of the car and opened the gate. "I was just settled in at the hotel and I got a call from Nikos that I had to come back to this hellhole. He's made a deal for Sean Patrick."

"Who's this?" The guard was looking at Lassiter. "He looks familiar."

"Lassiter. You saw his photo on the wall of the mess tent." He nodded at Lassiter. "He finally came through with the money." He added sourly, "I hope Patrick is still alive after Nikos got me out of bed to come after him."

"I didn't hear anything different from Stockton when he did the evening check." Jorge turned and headed for a building to the right of the gate. "Patrick was in bad shape, but he was still breathing. He's chained up on the wall outside the detention building. I'll go get him for you."

"We'll go with you," Lassiter said. In that last photo, Patrick had appeared as broken and twisted as a rag doll torn apart by an animal. He didn't want this muscle-bound Neanderthal damaging him any more than he was already. "Coming, Brukman?"

"I don't have a choice, do I?" he murmured. His gaze was wandering over the trees surrounding the camp. "But I'm wondering if I fell for an elaborate con."

"You didn't. Mandell is there, watching you. He'll meet us after we get Patrick away from here." He was moving quickly after the guard. Suddenly, he felt the phone in his pocket vibrate as a call came in. There was no way he could take that call right now, even if it was Mandell. Later. "If you don't do something stupid that will get you killed. It's not the—"

He stopped short, his gaze on the concrete wall of a long building ahead of them. Even in the dimness he could see that there were three prisoners chained to giant rings hammered into that wall. The prisoner who occupied the center position . . .

*Patrick*.

He was chained upright, in a sitting position, his arms lifted and wrists chained to the wall. Lassiter had known what was happening to him, but the actual sight of him still came as a shock. His formerly gray-streaked hair now was almost white; emaciated, broken, tortured—he looked like a death-camp survivor. And that was exactly what he is, Lassiter thought.

"He's out cold," the guard said cheerfully as he unlocked the manacles. "But he's not dead yet, Brukman."

"Yet," Brukman repeated. "And he's your responsibility once we release him, Lassiter. You waited too long to make a deal." He turned to Jorge. "Go wake up Stockton and tell him to get his ass out here. I want him to witness that I'm turning over Patrick to Lassiter alive, as agreed."

"And get a stretcher," Lassiter called after him. "I see at least one compound fracture in his left leg. I'm not going to risk carrying him myself and doing more damage."

"A little late," Brukman said sarcastically as Jorge disappeared. "Though he might live. Patrick is a tough bird. He's survived whatever we threw at him."

"This isn't the time to remind me of that." Lassiter fell to his knees beside Patrick. "I'm trying to remember that I made a deal. It's becoming more blurred every minute." He touched the pulse in Patrick's throat. Not strong. Probably in shock as well as suffering from malnutrition and whatever infections his body was trying to fight. His skin felt burning hot. "I want him out of here. When you talk to this Stockton, make it fast."

"Lassiter . . ." Patrick's eyes were open, staring up at him. His voice was only a breath of sound. "Knew . . . you'd come. . . ."

"Shh . . ." His hand closed on Patrick's. Hot. So damn hot. "We're getting you out of here. Just hold on."

"Others . . ." His eyes were closing again. "Get . . . the others out. . . ."

Lassiter hand tightened. "Not this time. Things are a little dicey right now, Patrick. I have to get you out first."

"Get . . . them out. No one leaves here . . . alive. Promise me."

"I promise. But not now. I can't do—"

But Patrick was unconscious again.

It was just as well. He didn't need to argue with him when Patrick was this fragile. Just the sight of him had scared Lassiter. His gaze went to the man chained to the wall next to Patrick. He was younger and not as emaciated, but he was still in bad condition. Patrick had shared this torture with the other prisoners and it was natural he would want them saved, too.

"No," Brukman said, as if he'd read his thoughts. "I'm not going to help you to—"

"I'm not asking." His gaze went beyond Brukman to the guard, Jorge, returning with a portable stretcher under his arm. There was a small, stocky man with tousled black hair beside him. "Stockton?"

Brukman nodded as he turned and spoke to the man. "Stockton, Jorge told you what Nicos did? Look, I want you to witness I turned him over to Lassiter alive. Just in case this bastard Lassiter lets him die and complains to Nicos later. Okay?"

Stockton shrugged. "You got me out of bed for that?" He scowled. "Okay, he's alive. I'll be glad to get rid of him. He's caused us twice as much trouble as any other prisoner. Nicos just wouldn't leave him alone."

Brukman nodded. "Not that he won't concentrate on someone else soon. I'm surprised he agreed to let Patrick go."

That last sentence was far too provocative, Lassiter thought. The last thing he wanted was for Stockton to start thinking and analyzing. "You wouldn't if I told you the amount of the ransom Nicos demanded." He turned to Jorge, took the stretcher from him, and laid it on the ground. "I'll lift him on the stretcher myself. You help me carry him to the van."

Jorge nodded.

Lassiter carefully gathered Patrick in his arms and transferred him from the ground to the canvas of the stretcher.

So light, practically weightless in his arms. Patrick was over six feet and yet he was almost a skeleton.

Lassiter could feel his throat tighten as he straightened Patrick on the stretcher. "You go ahead and open the back of the van, Brukman."

"Always willing to be helpful," Brukman murmured as he moved toward the gate. "I know you want to keep both your friend and us in full view until you have him safe. But you should trust us, Lassiter. We've done everything Nicos asked us to do." He opened the gate and then slid open the rear door of the van. "There we are. Now I'll just stand here until you get Patrick situated," he said, then repeated as his gaze went to the trees, "in full view."

"Yes, that's exactly what I want. I don't want any double crosses from Nicos at the last minute." Lassiter and Jorge placed the stretcher in the van and slid the door shut. "Now we can get out of here."

"Does that mean I can go back to bed?" Stockton asked sardonically. "Not that I needed to get up anyway. Total waste of my time." He glanced at Brukman. "When will you come back to camp? Do you have to go with him?"

"Only as far as the airport to see that Lassiter gets Patrick on the plane and out of here. But then I'm going to go back to the hotel and get a good night's sleep." He grimaced. "Providing I don't get another call from Nicos to disturb it. I'll be back here at the camp day after tomorrow. If there are any problems, give me a call." He got into the passenger seat of the van. "But don't expect me back unless it's important. I'm getting sick of the stench of this place."

"Tell me about it. I don't get to run away to a fancy hotel a couple times a week like you do." He turned and walked back toward the bunkhouse. "I think maybe we may have to negotiate that when you get back. . . ."

Lassiter watched him for only an instant. "Very good, Brukman," he murmured as he jumped into the driver's seat and started the van. "Smooth. Now no one will expect you for two days and you'll be able to be out of Colombia and on your way before Nicos suspects you're gone." He turned on his headlights as he rounded the curve in the road. "I wasn't entirely sure if you'd actually go through with it."

"Why not? You made it plain that I'd be dead meat if I didn't." His lips twisted. "I wanted you dead, but I wanted to live more. And I told Stockton the truth: I'm tired of the stench and living like a prisoner myself. Maybe I'll lose myself and find another Nicos somewhere who will appreciate a man of my talents."

"I'm sure you will. Though it might be difficult to find another man like Nicos unless I decide to send you to hell."

Brukman stiffened and then relaxed. "You made a deal. I think you'll keep to it. I wouldn't, but you're . . . different."

"You mean stupid?"

"Maybe. I don't know. I think you're looking forward to going after me and hunting me down."

"Am I?"

"Yes." He was suddenly glaring at him. "And I don't like all the money you cheated me out of. I was looking forward to getting that ransom. I might decide to get back on a plane and go after you someday and not wait for you to come after me."

"By all means. That would save me both time and money," Lassiter said. "Bring it on, Brukman. I didn't have enough back in that rain forest."

Brukman met his eyes and then glanced away. "I might just do—"

The van screeched to a stop.

The headlights had picked up Mandell, who was standing in the middle of the road ahead of them.

Mandell ran down the road and climbed into the rear

of the van. "Slick." He threw his gun case on the floor beside him. "But disappointing. I didn't get any action." He frowned as he looked down at Patrick. "He doesn't look good. How is he doing?"

"Exactly the way he looks," Lassiter said grimly. "I was hoping to get him to Bogotá, but I can't risk transporting him more than a few more miles in this condition. He'd never make it on that hellhole of a road to the helicopter pad. It's too far and too rough. He could die before he got there."

"Shit."

"We have to get him a doctor right away and somewhere safe to heal. He's burning up with fever." He glanced at Brukman. "By the way, Brukman thought your presence in those trees might just be a huge con, Mandell."

"And he still didn't give me a chance to take my shot?" Mandell shook his head. "My unlucky day."

"Where are the other men?" Lassiter asked.

"I told them to scatter and wait for orders when you pulled out with Patrick." He was still looking down at Patrick. "There's that old monastery that was on Zwecker's map. San Gabriel's. It's about thirty miles from here. It looked like it was off the beaten trail and might be safe for a little while. We could see what kind of help we could get for Patrick there. He'd at least have a bed where we could start him on some antibiotics."

Lassiter nodded. "We'll do it. And get on the phone right now and get him the best medical team you can bring down here from Bogotá. Send the helicopter back there to pick them up. I want them here in hours, not days." He glanced back at Patrick and felt his stomach clench. He looked as if he was barely breathing. "And that might still be too long."

"He's tough. Give him a chance and he'll make it."

Mandell glanced at Brukman. "What do you want me to do with him?"

Lassiter shook his head. "Not anything satisfying. We'll have to take him with us to the monastery. We have to monitor any calls between him and Nicos. I don't believe he's fool enough to initiate a call to him after he was involved in Patrick's escape, but I can't take the chance."

Mandell shrugged as he looked at Patrick. "I've always liked Patrick. Perhaps Brukman will try to get away from us. I'll be prepared."

"No," Brukman said. "Don't get your hopes up. That won't happen. Not this time."

"Maybe you'll change your mind." Mandell leaned back against the front seat. "When I was scoping out the detention camp, I saw a few prisoners who looked almost in as bad shape as Patrick, Lassiter. Brukman's work, too?"

"Probably. I'm sure he didn't reserve his expertise for Patrick."

"Then if he doesn't change his mind, maybe you should."

"Drop it. We have other things to worry about right now." He glanced at Brukman. "However, you should know, Brukman, that if Patrick dies, all deals are null and void." He said to Mandell, "Get on that phone. We've got to get that doctor down here quick."

"Right away." He started dialing. "Anything else?"

"Yes, you know there's still Margaret's situation. But I'll make any adjustments necessary."

But he remembered he'd gotten a call while he was in the detention camp and it hadn't been from Mandell. He took out his own phone and looked at the call history.

He stiffened.

Margaret.

Twice.

From Montego Bay.

It was the middle of the night. She wasn't supposed to be there until later today.

But everything else was moving at warp speed. It shouldn't have surprised him that Margaret, who had thrown Patrick's rescue into high gear, would now find her situation escalating, too.

But he couldn't call her until he got Patrick settled and safe. He could only hope that she'd be all right until he was able to get in touch with her.

Brukman's malicious gaze was on his face. "Trouble? What a pity."

"Everything else is fine," Lassiter said. He hoped it wasn't a lie. "Keep quiet, Brukman. You're walking on very thin ice."

# CHAPTER THIRTEEN

San Gabriel's Monastery was a weathered cream-stucco building with many arches, a gray tiled roof, and a large courtyard with a simple fountain.

When Lassiter drove into the courtyard thirty minutes later, the huge oak doors opened and a huge man in a gray robe stood looking warily at them. He was carrying a lantern and his expression was not welcoming. "I am Father Dominic. We have nothing of value here but the word of God."

"We're not here to rob you." Lassiter jumped out of the van. "I know that showing up here in the middle of the night is suspect. But we need your help. I'll reimburse you. My friend is very ill. If you have a bed and shelter, that's all we'll need. I've already arranged for a doctor." He slid open the door of the van. "See for yourself, Father."

Father Dominic came forward and gazed in at Patrick. He quickly crossed himself. "He's from the devil's camp. How did you get him free?"

"You knew about the camp?"

"There are stories about it in the villages." He shook his head. "He's dying. You're too late."

"He won't die," Lassiter said. "Not if you help us."

Mandell was suddenly beside him. "Patrick may not have much time for either arguments or persuasion. Do you need me, Lassiter?"

Lassiter could sense both his tension and his readiness. "Easy, Mandell," he said quietly.

Father Dominic's gaze went from Mandell's face to the rifle in his hands. "You're a violent man. Do you threaten us?"

"I don't want to do it. But we need help for our friend," Mandell said. "We hope you will give it."

"And if not, you will take it." He turned to Lassiter. "But you don't need this violent one this time. We will help you try to save this poor soul." He motioned and two monks hurried forward from the shadows beside the door. "Perhaps God will be merciful." He glanced at Mandell. "To your friend and to you, my son."

He turned and disappeared back through the arched doorway of the monastery.


Montego Bay
5:05 A.M.


Her phone was vibrating.

Margaret could feel the movement through her pillowcase, which she'd slid the phone into last night after she'd failed to make contact with Lassiter.

She grabbed at the phone. "Lassiter?"

"What are you doing in Montego Bay?"

"Nicos. He decided I needed time to bond more with the dogs, so he brought me in early. He's worried about this shipment." She glanced at the clock. Five in the morning. Not much chance of the guard in the hall hearing her, but she wouldn't take the chance. "Wait a minute. I'm going into the bathroom and turning on the shower. It won't seem that unusual at this hour and it will drown the sound of voices." She ran into the bath and turned on the shower. Then she sat down on the commode. "Anyway, you told me to call you as soon as I got into Montego. I'm here. I couldn't reach you last night. You got Salva's call directory?"

"More than that." He paused. "I've got Patrick, Margaret."

She closed her eyes as relief streamed through her. "Oh, thank God." She couldn't believe it. "When?"

"Last night. About the time you called me."

"How is he?"

"Not good. High fever, shock, broken bones, God knows what kind of infections. I could see he was fading fast. I had to bring him to a monastery in the middle of this damn rain forest just to keep him alive. The abbot, Father Dominic, took him in and tried to do as much as he could for him. We've just managed to fly Dr. Armando here from Bogotá and he's working on him now. I wanted to get Patrick the hell out of here, but the doctor doesn't want him moved again."

"But he's going to live?"

"Not sure. He has a fair chance. If he doesn't take a turn for the worse."

"But will Nicos be able to find him there?"

"Not if we can get Patrick out of here fairly soon. Nicos hasn't found out yet that he's gone from the detention camp."

"Why not? How could—"

"Margaret, listen. I'll answer all your questions, but not now. There's no time. There are too many things I have to know about you. Tell me about Nicos's setup at customs at Montego Airport. It will take me about four hours to get from Bogotá to Montego Bay, and I have to know what to expect when I get there."

Margaret drew a deep breath. She knew he was right,

but she was bewildered and scared. Okay, focus on what was important. Patrick was no longer in Nicos's hands and might have a good chance of staying alive. And Lassiter was alive and well and could be coming to help her.

"Margaret."

"Give me a minute. You just blew me away." She swallowed. "Here's the way it usually goes down at the airports. There are always a lot of people at customs. Nicos generally picks a time of day when both the security and airline personnel are very busy. I usually have to stand behind the barriers until the man who checks the luggage through picks it up and takes it to security to have it examined. Raoul Garon will be doing it this time. He's in his forties, thinning dark hair, a little on the heavy side. He'll be dressed in a dark suit and will appear to be an ordinary businessman. Nicos will have a guard standing with me beyond the barrier to keep an eye on me." She took a breath. "But this time he'll have two more men, one outside the door and one standing beside Nicos's car at the curb. Nicos isn't going to let this shipment get away from him even if he has to use force. It's too important to him. There will be two dogs at security and I'll be expected to divert them or just make them ignore that particular piece of luggage."

"Nicos will be in the car? What about Salva?"

"Salva will wait at the hotel until the luggage is delivered to him and then arrange for immediate distribution. As I said, it's an important shipment."

"Then we can use that." Lassiter paused. "If we stage it right. But I don't like those extra guards. We may have to go another way. . . ."

"What other way?"

"Let me think about it. I believe I might have an idea. How much control do you have over those dogs?"

"Enough. More than I usually have. I made sure of that last night." She was silent. "We don't have to do this today, Lassiter. You have your hands full with Patrick. If I can get Nicos the shipment with no real problems, I might be all right."

Silence. " 'Might'? That sounded very tentative. How much trouble are you having with him, Margaret?"

"He's . . . becoming difficult. Salva is influencing him. But I'll be able to handle him if I have to do it."

He cursed low and vehemently. "You *don't* have to do it. You're out of there tonight."

"Not if it means that you lose what you've gained. I can—"

"Be quiet, Margaret. I won't lose Patrick and I won't lose you. I wouldn't have 'gained' anything if you hadn't gotten me that lead to Zwecker. When Nicos finds out that he's lost Patrick, you don't know what the hell he'll do to you. There's every chance he'll suspect you were involved in getting Zwecker's name for me. From the beginning, you warned me that you wouldn't be able to be extricated safely if we didn't do it in Montego. Well, we're doing it. I'll call you back in twenty minutes, once I get the details worked out." He cut the connection.

*He's going to get a plan together in twenty minutes?* she thought as she hung up. She had thrown several dangerous escalations in Nicos's arrangements at him and Lassiter was already working to overcome them. The knowledge was giving her both a feeling of tentative confidence and the beginning of excitement. She sat there a moment and let the tension flow out of her.

They could do this. They'd just take one step at a time.

It wasn't as if she hadn't escaped from Nicos before. She could do it again. And the odds were on her side this time, because she had Lassiter.

Not really. No one would ever be able to say that

Lassiter belonged to them. But for today, Lassiter would be the wind beneath her wings. She'd always loved that song because it was the essence of togetherness. She was finding that thought very comforting in these days when she felt so alone.

So take advantage of that twenty minutes Lassiter had given her to jump in the shower while she did some planning of her own.

## San Gabriel's Monastery

"How is he?" Lassiter turned and saw Cambry hurrying down the hall of the abbey toward him. "I got here as soon as I could. That road from the helicopter pad was as rough as a roller coaster. Is Patrick any better?"

"He's stable right now. Dr. Armando said that's as good as can be expected," Lassiter said. "I'm glad you got here before I left. That's going to be in about ten minutes. I was hoping to get out of here sooner, but I have to stop in the room where they're holding Brukman and do some reinforcement before I leave. I was just going in to check on Patrick again." He turned away. "You can come with me, if you like."

Cambry nodded as he followed him through the arched doorway. "You're heading for Montego Bay?"

"As fast as I can get there." He was crossing the large room toward Patrick's bed. "Right now, it doesn't seem fast enough. I've called ahead to Montego and gotten as much in place as I could, but it's still going to be close." He glanced at Cambry. "You know what you're supposed to do? No questions?"

"Lots of questions, but I'll work them out for myself. Shall I go down the list? I'm to stay here and coordinate with the doctor and make lifesaving decisions. I'm to make certain Mandell's team is alert and doesn't make mistakes. If there's a possibility of Nicos's goons coming near the monastery, I'm to get Patrick away without getting him killed or killing him myself." He grimaced. "Piece of cake."

"One other thing: Mandell is leaving three of his best men to guard the monastery and they'll be under your direct orders. One man, Dietrich, is assigned to watch Brukman and monitor any calls he might receive. He'll let you know when a call comes through and you'll make certain Brukman tells Nicos nothing."

"Of course I will. It's just another beautiful day in paradise."

Lassiter smiled grimly. "That's what we're aiming for. Right now, it looks as if there might be a few storms on the horizon. We've got to get through them." He shook his head. "And I know I'm overloading you. But I need Mandell in Montego. With any luck, I should be back not too long after midnight."

"I'll be glad to see you. I can handle the rest, but I don't like the idea of being in sole charge of Patrick. I do much better with Juno. She's pregnant but not on the verge of dying if I do something wrong." He suddenly snapped his fingers. "I left her in the jeep with my driver. I was only going to run in for a minute. But if you're going to leave right away, I need to go get her." He was already trotting back toward the arched doorway. "I'll be right back. . . ."

Lassiter shook his head as Cambry vanished from view. He'd insisted on bringing Juno and at least that would make Margaret feel more at ease. There was no doubt that Cambry would handle everything here with efficiency in spite of any qualms he had.

But, dammit, he didn't want to leave Patrick while he was this sick and vulnerable. He took a step closer to the bed and covered Patrick's hand with his own. It was still hot. Too hot. The doctor had said that it would take time to get that fever down and that it was a great threat.

"You're . . . frowning." Lassiter's gaze flew up to Patrick's face. His eyes were open. "Don't you . . . know that you shouldn't make a . . . man in my state . . . worry?"

"Then you should try to heal a little faster. I did everything right and you're still in this hospital bed."

"Complaints. Complaints. I'll . . . work on it." His eyes were closing. "Now get out of here and let . . . me sleep."

"In a minute. I just wanted you to know I have to go away for the day. Cambry will be with you. You'll be safe. . . . I promise."

"You're . . . going to go . . . get them? You did promise. . . ."

He was talking about the other prisoners in the detention camp. "Not yet. There's someone . . . else."

"Who?"

"Margaret. You don't know her. But she knows you." His hand tightened on Patrick's. "I'll tell you about her later. I have to go now. I'll expect a dynamite report on you from Cambry when I call to check."

"Pressure. Pressure." Cambry was walking with Juno toward the bed. "Hi, Patrick. You're looking lousy. I hear I'm supposed to work miracles while Lassiter is gone. You'd better cooperate." In spite of the flip words, the tone was gentle. "And it wouldn't hurt if you'd put a word in with all these monks and the doctor about Juno. I had to fight to get them to let her in. I guess they've never heard how hospitals permit dogs to help heal patients. I bet she's cleaner and more germ-free than I am." He made a face. "I guess I shouldn't admit that." He dropped down in the chair next to Patrick's bed. "Get out of here, Lassiter. Juno and I have everything well in hand."

"Yes, get . . . out, Lassiter. Tired . . . of . . . you." Patrick's eyes were closing again. "In . . . the way. I'll be—" He broke off as he looked down at his hand on the bed.

Juno had placed her chin on Patrick's hand and was staring at him with those huge dark eyes as if she was trying to tell him something.

"Hey . . . What . . . do you want?" Patrick asked.

"Juno," Cambry called softly.

Juno didn't move. She just stayed there, touching Patrick, looking at him.

Then Patrick put his hand on Juno's head. The retriever stayed still, accepting, her eyes still on Patrick's face. The next moment, Patrick was asleep.

And Juno dropped down to lie beside the bed.

"I wonder how often Juno did that while she was visiting her Celia in the hospital," Cambry said softly. "I believe we're okay here, Lassiter."

"I do, too." He headed for the door. "And now I have to make sure we're going to be okay in Montego. I'll call you once we're headed back."

7:30 P.M.
Montego Bay Airport
Jamaica

"The flight's on time," Nicos said as Margaret got out of the car at customs. "But it will take another twenty minutes or so for Raoul to get off the plane and the baggage to be sent down here to customs. You go inside and look eager and excited at your daddy's arrival." He added, "I've already sent Ricardo inside to keep you company. He's always delighted to keep his eye on you."

"Which is going to make it hard for me to appear eager about anything," she said. "I'll see you when it's over." She slammed the car door and stepped around José, Nicos's guard, who was standing beside the driver's seat. Then she was hurrying toward the glass doors that led to customs.

Ricardo chuckled as he opened the door for her and then moved to one side to let her enter. Then he leaned back against the wall, watching her.

She walked several yards away from him toward the barrier and tried to ignore him.

It was busy.

It was noisy.

But no sign of Lassiter.

Crowds of men and women gathered in front of the long tables where security was examining the luggage.

And the black Lab and the German shepherd were being led by their handlers up and down the hall as the passengers got in the lines in front of the custom tables.

She focused on them. *Are you ready for me?*

Pedro was immediately tense. *Don't like it. Not used to this.*

Taro was scornful. *It's right. She told you. Is that the man beside you? Is he the one who will want to hurt you?*

Just the way she'd thought they'd each react. *Yes. But Pedro can do his duty with the man checking in at the customs table if he's more comfortable. I just need lots of noise and disruption."*

Pedro was relieved. *What I'm supposed to do.*

*Except more. No politeness. I'll tell you when.*

And it was going to be soon. She could see Raoul coming into the hall carrying his Vuitton black leather case. He appeared totally at ease as he came toward the custom's table and stopped under the green line for frequent travelers.

But where was Lassiter?

Ramirez and his son were slowly taking the dogs down the line, giving them a chance to sniff at the bags.

Pedro was on edge. *Which?*

*The next man in line. Black leather case.*

Pedro went stiff. *Yes, I smell it. Have to tell—"*

*Not yet. Let me—*

"Now!" Lassiter was suddenly before her in front of the barricade. Navy pants, navy airline bomber jacket, skin tinted dark tan. He was lifting her over the barricade. "Quick, Margaret!"

She sent out the message.

*Do it! Move!*

Pedro howled and jumped on the black leather Vuitton suitcase. Then he set up a piercing barrage of barking that echoed through the hall.

Ricardo stared, stunned for an instant, at Margaret and Lassiter.

Then his hand went to the holster under his jacket as he started toward her.

But Taro had pulled away from his handler and was across the hall and leaping over the barrier. He hit Ricardo at full speed and force and knocked him to the ground. His teeth buried savagely in the hand holding the gun.

A horrified Ramirez was right behind the dog, trying to pull him off.

"Come on." Lassiter had his hand on Margaret's elbow and he was pulling her toward the door to the side of the custom tables.

The entire room was in chaos as security officers tried to calm the passengers, while the dogs' howling and attacks made that virtually impossible.

Then they were out of the room and heading for the door leading to the runways.

Margaret stopped at the door. "Just a minute."

"We don't have a minute. We've got to be on that plane and out of here before Nicos realizes what's happened inside."

"I have to call off those dogs. I won't have them getting shot."

"Then do it. But keep running."

*Off. Stop. Did your duty. Fine work.*

Then she was running at full speed across the tarmac toward the Gulfstream parked in the private-and-commercial area.

The steps were down and the plane was ready for takeoff.

Margaret ran up the steps, with Lassiter immediately behind her. The steps were lifting even as Lassiter headed for the cockpit. "Sit down and buckle up. We're out of here."

"The dogs. I have to be sure—"

"I still have a man on the ground here. I needed a report on what Nicos was doing after we left. I'll make sure no one hurts them. I'll come back with you when we're in the air and safely out of Jamaican airspace." He disappeared into the cockpit.

Margaret collapsed on the cordovan leather seat next to the window.

Was it over?

Not yet.

They were taxiing down the runway, but she wouldn't feel safe until they were actually in the air.

Perhaps not then.

After the tension she had been under since the moment that she'd walked down that pier to Nicos's yacht, it seemed impossible that she had escaped him yet again. He had been her nemesis for so long that it was a miracle that in these few short minutes Lassiter had managed to snatch her away.

No, it had not been totally Lassiter. It had been the two of them together. And she might have escaped Nicos, but that didn't mean that he wasn't out there waiting to go after her again.

And it didn't mean that she'd keep running, because she'd promised herself that Nicos had to be destroyed so that he could never hurt anyone else again.

No, it was not over.

"We're about forty-five minutes south of Jamaica," Lassiter said as he came out of the cockpit. He hadn't had the chance to take off the tan stain, but he'd removed the dark contacts and his green eyes glittered against his dark skin. "We should be okay for the time being. How are you doing?"

"Well enough, considering," she said. "Maybe a little shaky. It's been a rough couple days. Probably not as rough as what you've been going through. Are you going to tell me now how you managed to get Patrick out?"

"Yes." He dropped down in the chair next to her. "But it all came down to your getting that info about Zwecker from Salva. So not nearly as rough as you'd think." He spent the next ten minutes filling her in on Zwecker, Brukman, and the Nalsara Detention Camp.

So much evil, so much pain, she thought. And it had all been caused by one supremely evil individual. Nicos deserved a very special place in hell for what he'd done. "But Patrick is doing better? He's going to be okay?"

"I'd like to say that. But he's still very fragile," he said soberly. "He hasn't turned the corner yet. He could go either way."

"No, I won't believe that," she said sharply. "Not after all he's gone through. Not after what you've gone through. He's going to live. He's going to be fine."

"If you say so." He grimaced. "God knows, I don't want to be anything but positive. I'll move heaven and earth to get him anything he needs to pull him through this. I suppose I'm just afraid to hope too much."

She knew how that felt. All those months when she could see Rosa changing before her eyes, being destroyed, and not able to do anything about it. "It's not going to happen this time. I'm not going to let it. Nicos isn't going to win."

"Hey, stop shaking." He was turning her to face him. "You're not going to have to face Nicos again. I dragged you into this, but you're free now. Patrick is my friend, my responsibility. You're out of this. I told you that I'd be going after Nicos the minute I got Patrick back."

She hadn't realized she was shaking. She tried to control it. "I'm not free. I won't be free as long as Nicos is alive." She wrapped her arms around herself to stop the trembling. "I found that out while I was on the island. I can't bury my head in the sand any longer. I can't tell myself that I should just go on and not remember Rosa. She'll always be here with me." She moistened her lips. "But he has to be . . . gone, Lassiter. He shouldn't live after what he did to her."

"I don't know what you're talking about," he said hoarsely. "But I know it's tearing me up. Whatever you need to do to him, I'll do it for you. I'll do it for both of us."

"It doesn't work that way. You weren't there; you didn't see her. It has to be me."

"No, I wasn't there. I don't know who you're talking about. But I want to know, Margaret." His hands closed on her shoulders. "Stop bottling it up inside you. Share it with me. *Tell* me."

Yes, she wanted to tell him, she realized suddenly. She didn't want to be alone with it any longer. "It was Rosa." She swallowed hard. She mustn't cry. Too many tears . . . "You remember I told you about Rosa Gonzalez? We worked together at the petting zoo in New Orleans. She invited me to live with her family in Guatemala City. I stayed with them for over a year. I'd never really had a friend before I met Rosa. She chattered like a magpie, she was funny and made jokes, and it was so good. She and her mother were very kind to me."

"But it didn't last?"

"Rosa was a couple years older than I was. She liked boys and she met Luis Garcia and went crazy about him. It turned out that Luis was the son of one of Nicos's men on Vadaz Island. He talked to his father about Rosa . . . and me."

"You?"

"I told you that Rosa chattered. Naturally, she talked about me. She didn't mean to hurt me."

"She told him about your communicating with animals?"

"She thought it was funny and interesting and she wanted to impress him." She repeated, "She didn't mean to hurt me."

"But she did hurt you."

"Somehow the story got back to Nicos. He thought I might be useful. He wanted to see me." She paused. "But they thought they might need Rosa to persuade me. So they took both of us from her home in Guatemala to the island. If they'd only taken me, none of it would have happened. I could have done something. . . . But I couldn't do anything, because he kept hurting her."

"That was how they persuaded you?"

"The things they did to her," she whispered. "Sometimes Nicos did it in front of me. Most of the time he just took her back to his house and he'd send her to me the next day to tell me what he'd done. But every time I refused to do something he wanted, I knew that she would be punished. She became only an animal waiting to be hurt or used. She'd beg me to do anything he wanted just to keep away the pain."

"My God."

"And then one night when he thought I'd made a mistake, he shot her in front of me." She stared him in the eye. "So don't tell me I'm out of this. I'm not free. I ran away three years ago because I was too numb to deal with those memories, but I won't run away again. You can't make me, Lassiter."

"I could, you know." He smiled crookedly. "But I'd have to find a deep prison to keep you until it was over. And then you'd probably go after me."

"Count on it. I'm not going to let you hide me away. You're going to take me back with you to that monastery and I'm going to help get Patrick home safe. Then I'm going to be there with you when it's time to take Nicos down." She held his eyes. "Don't you see? That's how it has to be."

He was silent a moment. Then he swore softly and said through his teeth, "I don't know how much more of this I can take." He didn't speak for another moment. "Okay. But I'm warning you, I'll try to keep you as safe as possible. I'm already having massive guilt attacks about sending you back to the island."

"You didn't send me. I told you it was my choice. This is my choice, too." She shook her head. "If you don't realize that, then you didn't listen."

"Oh, I listened." He pulled her into his arms. "And I watched you. Now be still and let me hold you until you stop that shaking."

"You don't have to do that. I'll be fine soon."

"You told me once that contact was good. You even demonstrated. Now be quiet and let me return the favor."

She stiffened and then suddenly relaxed. He was warm and strong and she could feel the corded muscles against her softness. She needed that strength. "I was right: Contact is good." She cuddled closer. "Thank you, Lassiter."

"My pleasure." He held her tighter. "And though I'm

tempted to make you the additional offer you made to me, I'll refrain because you're so vulnerable at the moment. Now hush and relax. When you stop shaking, I'll get you a cup of coffee and then take you up to the cockpit to meet Mandell."

"The man who chose the beach house," she said, remembering the name. "And could hit a target at over a thousand yards."

"Yes, and someone you may get to know very well in the coming days."

"That's good." But she didn't want to meet anyone right now. She wanted to stay here and be held by Lassiter for just a little while. She did feel vulnerable. Sharing that story of Rosa with him had been both painful and cathartic, but it had also been draining. It had left her feeling exposed. But somehow she knew that Lassiter would not take advantage of that vulnerability. Strange, when they had started out light-years from either trust or belief.

But he had saved her today, so accept the comfort and tentatively embrace the trust as she was embracing his arms holding her.

Because his holding her was making her forget Nicos for the moment, and that was indeed an excellent thing.

"You're Margaret Douglas?" Nick Mandell grinned at her as he reached out to where she stood at the cockpit door to shake her hand. "I behold the legend? I've been hearing about you, I've known you were working in the background, I knew that Lassiter was scheduling everything around plucking you away from Nicos, but I admit it made me uneasy that I'd never set eyes on you."

"You've got to be kidding," Margaret said. "I never make anyone uneasy. I don't have the presence for it."

"You could have fooled me when I saw you streaking

across the tarmac toward the plane," Mandell said. "You reminded me of that comic book hero the Flash. You were definitely making a statement." He paused. "And you had enough presence to cause Nicos to fall flat on his face back there. I just got a report from my operative at Montego Airport that there was turmoil galore after you left, and Nicos actually ran into customs to see what the hell went wrong."

"I'm sure he didn't stay long," Margaret said. "Nicos always keeps out of the limelight. But this shipment was important to him and he was probably very angry."

Mandell nodded. "He said something low and venomous to that goon who let you get away and then stalked back out to his car. There was security all over the place and arrests were being made after they found that explosive device in the suitcase. Not safe for a kingpin like Nicos to be hanging around."

"What about the dogs? Taro took Ricardo down when he tried to get to his gun. He wasn't hurt, was he?"

"Are we talking about the dog or your slimeball guard?"

"The dog. I don't care about Ricardo."

"I thought as much. No, the dog was fine and quieted down after his handler got to him with the leash." He grinned. "Though it took a while to make him get his teeth out of this Ricardo. And by that time the police were arresting him for carrying a concealed weapon. Do you think Nicos will bail him out?"

"I think he'll probably have him killed," she said bluntly. "He failed and Nicos won't want him to talk to law enforcement."

"You don't want a report on the other dog?"

"No, Pedro will be fine. He caught the bad guy, retrieved the smuggled shipment, and his only fault was making a ruckus at customs. That's a breach of training. The handlers are supposed to have their dogs be accurate but as unobtrusive as possible."

"But the black Lab didn't care?"

"Taro is smart and dominant and I was able to make him see my point of view." She turned to Lassiter, who was coming down the aisle with two cups of coffee. "But he attacked and hurt someone. Even though the police may consider Ricardo a threat and Taro a hero for disarming him, that's serious stuff. In the end, Ramirez may think Taro too volatile to work at the airport."

"You're worried what will happen to him." He handed her the coffee. "And what do you want me to do?"

"Buy Taro from Ramirez. He won't be happy unless he has work to do. We'll have to find him someplace where he'll have duty *and* a challenge."

Lassiter smiled as he handed Mandell his cup of coffee. "And you have an idea where that somewhere will be?"

"Eventually. It will take time for him to adjust."

Mandell chuckled. "Are we sending him to the K-9 Corps? You warned me the dogs would be her first priority, Lassiter."

"Why not?" Margaret said. "They helped us. Why shouldn't we all care?"

Mandell held up his hand. "I'm not arguing. When I saw Cambry with Juno back at the beach house in Cancún, I understood that we might all have to adjust our viewpoints. K-9?"

"No, they do good work, but Taro needs more challenge."

"Summer Island?" Lassiter asked.

She nodded. "If Devon will take him."

"I believe she will. She's very protective of both you and her dogs." He turned to Mandell. "Get back on the phone and have your man in Montego buy that Lab from

Ramirez. I want him in our hands within twenty-four hours."

"It shall be done." His hand made a gesture of mock obeisance. "I take it price is no object."

"No." He smiled at Margaret. "You heard her. He helped us. We have to return the favor." He turned and started back toward his seat. "Now why don't you come back and stretch out on the couch and take a nap, Margaret? God knows when you'll get another chance."

And she had gotten very little sleep last night, she remembered. Now that the adrenaline was fading, the exhaustion was beginning to set in. She followed him down the aisle. "And what are you going to do?"

"I'll try to nap later. I live on power naps. There are a few calls I have to make. First, I need to phone Cambry and check on Patrick." He pushed her gently down on the couch and took the soft fleece throw and covered her. "You have at least three hours, maybe more. Make the most of them."

"We need to talk." She covered a yawn. "You know that Nicos won't be sitting still. By now he'll know that I didn't do this alone. You have to admit this plane is very recognizable. Even Devon was able to trace it to you."

"We'll worry about that when you wake up." He brushed the hair away from her forehead and dropped a light kiss on the tip of her nose. "Using the dogs might have confused him a bit. They're definitely your signature, Margaret."

"Yes, they are." Her eyes were closing. "I liked doing it that way, Lassiter. He forced me to use them so often. He made Rosa force me. . . . It was good to turn them against him. . . ."

"I can see how it would be." He tucked the throw under her chin. "Go to sleep. Forget about sons of bitches like Nicos and Salva. Soon they won't be around to force anyone to do anything. Think about puppy dogs and tigers and all the things that make you smile."

*He* was making her smile. He was being ridiculous. Tigers didn't make her smile except when they were cubs. They were too sleek and beautiful and dangerous not to take seriously. . . .

# CHAPTER FOURTEEN

"She's sleeping?" Mandell glanced at Lassiter as he dropped down in the copilot's chair next to him. "She looked like she needed it. Ramrod straight, cheeks flushed, but not willing to let go until the last detail was taken care of. Is she always like that?"

"Yes. Sometimes she's worse. She never gives up. Remind me to tell you about the midnight swim we took the first night that I brought her on board my ship." He reached for his phone. "On second thought, don't remind me. It was a bit traumatic for all of us. But then, that's Margaret. I was lucky to get her to take this nap. It may be the last thing I'll be able to persuade her to do until I'm able to hand her Nicos's head on a platter."

"Is that on the agenda?"

"My agenda. She'll have other ideas. Or maybe not." He smiled crookedly. "She told me once that death should be quick and torture no part of it, but after what she told me Nicos did to Margaret and her friend, she could be wavering." He shrugged. "And if she's not, then I'll still give her Nicos as a gift. She deserves it."

"That bad?" Mandell asked quietly. "Then she must have come through it pretty well. She seems tough."

"Yeah, tough. But she's not going to go through anything more. I didn't even know what I was putting her through when I let her go back to Nicos." He shook his head. "Let? I tried to tell myself I had a choice, but we were long past that by the time she got on Nicos's yacht. But I was still responsible."

"Because of Patrick."

He nodded. "And I'm supposed to use him as an excuse? I'm done with it. I just have to keep her safe." He looked at Mandell. "And when I'm not around, you have to keep her safe. Because she'll be going after Nicos and he'll be waiting to gobble her up the first chance he gets."

"You're assigning me as her bodyguard?" he asked warily. "It's not really what I had in mind when I signed up with you, Lassiter. You've kept me very busy and I've been fairly content these last few years. It's certainly not boring. But I don't see myself as—"

"Don't worry about being kept busy," Lassiter said drily. "Margaret is fully capable in that department. I'm just telling you that if I'm not available, nothing must happen to her. You drop everything and concentrate on Margaret."

"As you're doing?" He was studying Lassiter. "Nah, I don't think you'd want me to go that far. You're a possessive bastard."

"Mandell."

"Okay, okay. I'll play the game. As long as she doesn't make me dog-sit like she did Cambry."

"No promises." Lassiter smiled. "Would you prefer tigers?"

"What?"

"Never mind." He was pressing the buttons on his phone. "I just thought it would be less boring for you." Cambry picked up and he told him, "We've got Margaret safe and we're on our way back."

"Hallelujah," Cambry said fervently. "I was getting a little worried. No one was hurt?"

"No. Unfortunately, that also includes Nicos and Salva. But we stirred up the pot pretty thoroughly and there may be repercussions once he finds out I was the one who got Margaret away. It's almost certain Nicos will make a call to the detention camp. Hopefully, he'll make the call directly to Brukman. So keep sharp and call me back and report when he does. And make certain that all the sentries are on alert and there aren't any leaks from Dr. Armando."

"I've asked the doctor not to make any phone calls to his family in Bogotá while he's here."

"There may still be slips."

"He saw what was done to Patrick. He won't want that happening to them."

"Just keep reminding him that it could. How is Patrick?"

"Better. He woke up twice today. Dr. Armando is talking about letting him be moved to the hospital in Bogotá in the next day or so."

"It can't be too soon. We're right on top of that damn detention camp. Then he must be better. Fever?"

"It's not as high." He paused. "Tell Margaret that Juno has been auditioning as a therapy dog. She won't leave Patrick. I think maybe she's helping."

"I'll tell Margaret. Or you may be able to tell her yourself. I don't think I'm going to be able to talk her out of going to the monastery." He added roughly, "Though God knows it's not a good idea. We just got her away from Nicos, and that could mean his goons might be just around the corner."

"Maybe the doctor will let us move Patrick tomorrow."

But a lot could happen in one day, Lassiter thought. Look at what had been accomplished since Margaret had gone to Vadaz Island. All good things that had given them hope and the will to go on. However, that didn't mean that they would keep on being this lucky. Everything could turn sour in a heartbeat, as it had on the night Patrick had been taken by Nicos.

But he'd gotten Patrick back; Margaret was sleeping peacefully in the next cabin. Now all he had to do was keep them safe.

And find a way to fight Nicos off when he came on the attack. There was no question in his mind that would come very soon.

"All we can do is cross our fingers about getting that medical okay to pull out of there," he told Cambry drily. "In the meantime, we'll ask Margaret to have a talk with Juno about increasing the mojo she's using on Patrick. It can't hurt. . . ."

Hyatt Hotel
Montego Bay, Jamaica

"It *was* Lassiter." Nicos's finger savagely punched the disconnect button on the phone. "His private plane landed at Montego at 1:05 P.M. and took off at 7:50 P.M. The son of a bitch spoiled my delivery and then took off with Margaret." His face was flushed with fury. "She had to be working for him. She made a fool of me. I'm going to make her pay, Salva." His mouth twisted as he spat out the words. "She'll be on her knees, begging. I'll stake her out and let—"

"I'm sure you will," Salva said. "But it's a bit late. Do you know how much losing that explosive is costing us?"

"Of course I know. It should never have happened. I had it all planned. It was going to be the biggest score I've ever made in Colombia."

"You might remember I had a good deal to do with

that planning," Salva said drily. "And, if we'd handled it in the usual way, there would have been no trouble. But, no, you had to use Margaret. You gave Lassiter an opening and he took it."

"I thought he was a fool. I thought Patrick meant more to him than getting back at me. How did I know he'd hunt down Margaret just to punish me?" His voice was savage. "Well, he's the one who's going to be punished. They're both going to go through the fires of hell before this is over." He was reaching for his phone again. "And we'll start with Sean Patrick. Did Lassiter actually think I would let him live after this? I'll have Brukman kill him and send Lassiter the pieces."

"That may not be the most profitable way of handling this," Salva said. "We've had a great loss. We need to recoup funds quickly before that terrorist group sends someone to us to get back their money."

"I can handle them."

"But it could mean that we'd have to devote valuable manpower if they decide to attack us. You know how crazy those bastards can be. It would be better just to let them have their money back and offer them another deal. Why not contact Lassiter and offer to give him Patrick for the same money that the terrorists paid us for the bomb?" He smiled. "That way, you'd hurt Lassiter in the wallet and punish him for taking your little voodoo priestess away from you."

"Are you being sarcastic? Whatever made you think that I'd ever take advice from you?"

"Perhaps the fact that you're in trouble and I'm the one who might save your ass?" Salva held up his hand. "Of course I'm not being sarcastic. It was only a suggestion."

"A lousy suggestion. It wouldn't be enough. They both have to hurt."

"You could go after him later."

"And I will, but now I have to show Lassiter I meant what I said and that I'm in control."

Salva shrugged. "Do what you wish. But when the bloodbath is over, remember that I offered you an alternative."

"Screw your alternative." Nicos quickly began entering the number. "And I'm going to tell Brukman that he's to video every moment of the torture on Patrick before he kills him. I want Lassiter to have a permanent memory of what he did to his old friend by yanking Margaret away from me."

"That appears to be in keeping with your usual way of handling your personal affairs." He poured himself a drink at the bar. "Give Brukman my best. I've always admired his skill at what he does. If you recall, I was the one who found him for you when you decided it would amuse you to set up that detention camp."

"He's not answering." Nicos was frowning. "Where the hell is he? I *need* him."

"It's the middle of the night. Perhaps he's busy with one of those whores I send down there to keep him happy. After all, he needs an occasional change of pace from the duties you give him."

"He's supposed to answer my calls. He has orders to be available to me at all times." Nicos hung up and then called again. "Who does he think he is? Whores? I'll cut off his nuts before I slit his throat. This is your fault, Salva."

"I'd like to know how."

"I can't take care of everything. When a man like Brukman thinks he can disobey me and not—" He broke off as the call was answered. "It's about time you answered, Brukman. What did you think you were doing keeping me waiting?"

"Sorry. I was in the can. You know I wouldn't want to make you—"

"But you did, and I'm in no mood to put up with that bullshit. Things are falling apart up here and I'm going to have to put them right. I'm starting with Patrick. Tell me he's still alive."

Silence. "He's still alive. Barely."

"Enough for him to hurt?"

"Maybe. You want me to start on him again?"

"Why else do you think I'm calling you? Are you stupid? What do you mean, 'maybe'?"

"It will take time and skill to make him really suffer. I don't know if he has that time. He'll have to have at least a couple days to recover. Otherwise, he won't last an hour."

"That's not enough. And you'd better make sure he holds on. Lassiter has to see it happening; he has to see what I'm doing to him. Photos, movies . . . no, live."

"I've told you what I thought. I'll do anything you say, sir."

"But you can't promise to give me what I need unless you have two days to get Patrick up to it?" he said in frustration. "I don't want to wait for two days. And it seems I can't trust anyone to do it right. Never mind, I'll do it myself. I'll come down there and Lassiter can watch me cut his old friend to pieces. Just keep the son of a bitch alive." He hung up.

"I'm going to Nalsara." He turned to Salva. "Patrick is barely alive and I'm not going to trust anyone but myself to show Lassiter what happens when anyone tries to make a fool of me. You're going with me."

Salva shook his head. "I should stay here and deal with the fallout from that customs mess. You know how dangerous the situation could be."

Of course I know, Nicos thought savagely. And it was all Lassiter's fault. All the more reason to go down and punish the bastard. "I want you there. I want you to see me do it. You're going with me."

"You persist in wanting an audience. I could much better serve you here." He studied his face. "Oh, very well. But I do hate that detention camp. I've always thought it served no real purpose but your enjoyment." He paused. "And I heard you say that Patrick might not be a satisfactory lesson for Lassiter anyway, unless you allow a couple days for him to heal. Why don't we give Brukman the time to get him in shape while we save you trouble and a good deal of money? What difference will a day or so make?" He started to go through his phone directory. "The least you can do is call Cabalo, the head of that terrorist cell, personally and tell him that you'll meet with him and discuss how to make it right with him in some way. Then I need you to talk to the distributor and let him know that it wasn't a double cross. That might stave off an attack when we do go to Nalsara. By that time, Patrick will be ready for anything you want to do to him."

Nicos hesitated. It was going to be a bother and he didn't want to wait two minutes, much less two days. He wanted to get down there to Nalsara and feel the familiar surge of excitement and power going through him as the blood flowed.

But that bitch Margaret had screwed everything up for him, and Salva could be right. He didn't need an expensive war with those stupid fanatics when a short delay might give him time to find an edge.

He turned away. "I guess I'll do it," he said grudgingly. "I'll call Brukman back and tell him that he can have a little more time. But if Patrick dies while I'm fooling around with this business, you're going to pay for it, Salva."

"Nicos is going down to Nalsara?" Lassiter repeated. "You're certain, Cambry? No mistake?"

"No mistake," Cambry said. "He was foaming at the

mouth and finally decided that Brukman wasn't good enough and that he wanted the pleasure of the kill himself. I believe you pissed him off, Lassiter. This isn't good, is it?"

"Hell no. When?"

"I'd say soon. As I said, he's foaming. He called back ten minutes later and told Brukman that he might have the day or two he wanted but not to count on it. And that he'd kill him if he let Patrick die before he got down there. So what am I supposed to do?"

"The same as you've been doing. But talk to Father Dominic and see if there's any other hiding place we could tap if we have to get Patrick out of the monastery in a hurry. And you'd better have the sentry who's keeping watch on Nalsara be on alert and report any sign that they've been given orders to leave the detention camp and start a search. Just in case Nicos calls anyone at the camp but Brukman. And I'll phone Dr. Armando and see if there's any chance at all we can get Patrick out by helicopter in the next day or so." He hung up and turned to Mandell in the pilot seat next to him. "You heard. Not good. Nicos is not going back to his island; he'll be going to Nalsara. And he's going to be right on top of us if we can't get Patrick out."

"Then you'd better come up with something to take care of it," Mandell said. "Please make it interesting. What do you do first?"

Lassiter got to his feet. "First, I go back in the other cabin and try to convince Margaret to stay in Bogotá when we land and not take that helicopter to Nalsara."

"No way," Margaret said flatly. "I told you I wouldn't let you hide me away, Lassiter."

"We may all be running and hiding if we can't move Patrick before Nicos gets down there. The situation has changed. Stay in Bogotá, Margaret."

"You said we might have one or two days before Nicos is on the move. That might be enough time." She shook her head. "Yes, the situation changed and you'll change with it. It's what you do. I sent you a name on Salva's call directory and you used it to get Patrick free. You got me away from Nicos. You'll find a way to make this work for us. Well, just include me in your planning, because I'm going to be there."

His lips tightened. "Margaret . . ."

"Discussion's over. Start planning, Lassiter."

## San Gabriel's Monastery

The dawn was breaking, but the trees in the rain forest were so dense that it still appeared night as Mandell drove the van through the gates of the monastery and into the courtyard. "Everything seems quiet enough, Lassiter," he said. "No word must have trickled down here yet from Montego. There's been no report of any action at the detention camp. And this place is as peaceful as when we left it."

"That doesn't mean it's going to stay that way. We're going to have to get ready to move fast and hard."

"Fine. That's what I've been waiting for since we came down here." He parked in front of the arched oak doorway, jumped out, and helped Margaret out of the van. "And maybe Cambry actually did a good job of filling in for us. Though I hate to admit that the team could get along without me. I think I'll just go talk to a few of my men and check on progress while you two go see Patrick."

"That seems to be a good plan," Lassiter said drily. "And it would keep you from having to hobnob with Father Dominic or any of these monks who are being so good to Patrick."

He shrugged. "It's just better if I avoid them. I was a little too aggressive with Father Dominic, and that won't make me very welcome. Besides, by now they've probably talked enough to my guys on the team to get a fix on my place in it. They'll know who I am and what I do." His lips twisted. "Though Father Dominic saw right through me from the beginning."

"It didn't help that you were carrying that rifle that looks like it's a part of you."

"It *is* a part of me. And that's what the good father saw. Look, these monks are good people and it's hard for them to know how to deal with someone like me. They don't generally teach it as a course in theology." Mandell strolled across the courtyard toward the gates. "Besides, I need to go back to that detention camp and make sure my guy was right about there not being any activity."

"Be careful," Lassiter said sharply.

He waved a casual hand. "Always."

Margaret frowned as she watched him walk away. "He doesn't like the monks?"

"It's not a question of liking or disliking." He opened the door for her. "As he said, it's the comfort level. I told you that Mandell was a great sniper."

She nodded. "Over a thousand yards."

"But that's a purely clinical assessment. Mandell was the golden boy. Whenever there was a shot to be taken . . . or a man to be killed, the military called on Nick Mandell."

*A man to be killed.* The words came as a shock to Margaret. Lassiter was right: She had been thinking too clinically. A sniper was trained to kill. Mandell had been trained to be the highest form of killer.

"Yes, but it was his duty to his country."

"But somewhere along the way, you can get confused with duty and the sheer excitement of being the best, of taking that next perfect shot." He wasn't looking at her as he led her through the halls. "Particularly if you're as good as Mandell."

Her eyes were narrowed on his face. "You know what that feels like."

"I've had my share of kills," he said. "Yeah, I know how he feels. That's why I hired Mandell when he decided to get out of the service."

"From what I've seen lately, it doesn't seem that different," Margaret said. "Unless you just pay more."

"Oh, I pay more, but it's definitely different," he said grimly. "There's no way that Mandell could quit cold turkey. He's too good. There would always be some agency that would need a killer as skilled as a Renaissance assassin. They'd offer him an impossible kill and he'd do it. When he works for me, he gets a taste now and then, but not enough to feed the addiction."

She thought about it. Mandell's wry humor, his easy, casual manner. "I . . . like him. He doesn't seem like . . ."

"Did you expect him to be all brooding and morose? I don't know what he feels inside. I wouldn't ask him. Mandell made his choice a long time ago. He's lived with that choice, but now he recognizes that the choice is starting to consume him. So he's stepping away from it."

"And from those monks, too? That could be a mistake. Forgiveness is a major part of religion. They might offer comfort and understanding."

"Mandell doesn't think so. These monks are pretty unsophisticated. It would take a good deal of forgiving and understanding." He paused. "Mandell has eighty-two confirmed kills."

"My God." Her eyes widened. "I had no idea."

"If you counted the unconfirmed kills, it would be far higher. And he hasn't been a sniper for all that long.

Give him a few more years and he'd be breaking records. He chose not to do that." He stopped outside Patrick's room to meet her eyes. "You're shocked. I wanted to be honest with you because Mandell is part of my life. But are you going to be able to accept him as he is?"

"Of course I am," she said impatiently. "I told you that I liked him. Animals in the forest hunt for food and kill every day. Only human beings hunt for other reasons and then count their kill. Do you think lions or tigers don't kill more than that over their lifetime? It wasn't Mandell who decided to go on the hunt. He was chosen. And I'd bet he wasn't the one who counted the kills. It seems like some kind of boastful bureaucracy-type thing to—"

"I hear you." He was chuckling. "All I wanted was a yes or no. I didn't know you'd bring in the lions and tigers." His smile faded as he reached for the knob of the door to Patrick's room. "I don't know if you're ready for this. It's one thing to see a photo; it's another to see Patrick in the shape he's in now. I saw what it did to you on the ship and it's already scaring me."

"It's scaring *me*," she said soberly. "All the time we were coming here, I kept thinking of what would happen when I saw him." She moistened her lips. "I've never actually seen him, Lassiter. I've never met him. Yet I feel as if I know him."

"Because you sense how I feel about him?"

She shook her head. "I don't think so. Maybe. I just wanted so badly for him not to be in pain any longer. I wanted him to be strong and well and not . . ." She made a face. "All this talk." She pushed open the door. "I just have to go for it." She stopped for a minute when she saw the white-draped bed, the still figure.

Cambry was sitting in a chair by the bed, looking at his computer, and he glanced up with a smile as they came into the room. "Hi, Margaret. You look much better than the last time I saw you." He got to his feet. "As I recall, you were facedown on that pier and causing me all kinds of guilt and trauma." He came toward her and gave her a quick hug. "Good job," he said gruffly. "I'm sure Patrick would say the same if he could keep awake long enough for us to tell him about you."

"I think I'm better learned from experience, don't you?" She turned away from him to face the bed. Patrick was so pale, his face lined with pain. And he was deeply asleep, as Cambry had said. She drew closer to Patrick's bed, and it was then that she saw Juno lying on the floor beside the bed.

She raised her head as Margaret approached.

*Help him? You might heal?*

She leaned down and touched Juno's head.

*That's what we're trying to do. And you're doing your part too, Juno.*

*He mustn't leave. Too sad. You said she might come back, might still be with me. Not yet. He might not come back, either. Mustn't let him leave.*

She swallowed to ease the sudden tightness of her throat.

*Then don't do it. You're doing all the right things. Just keep on doing them. Let him feel you. Let him feel the love.*

Silence. Those huge dark eyes looked wonderingly into her own.

*You are not her. But you say the things she says. How is that?*

What could she say? Juno needed an answer and sometimes there were no answers.

*I don't know. Maybe it comes from her. Maybe it comes from what you are together.* She bent down and stroked her head again. *Or maybe you're remembering what she would say if she were here. Make up your own mind.*

*I will.* She laid her head on her paws again. *But I'm glad you're back. I feel better when you're here.*

*I feel better when you're here, too.* She straightened and turned to Cambry. "You've taken great care of her. I think that Patrick is healing her as much as she's healing him."

"I had the same idea." He turned to Lassiter. "But now that I have you to take over Patrick's care, could you give me an hour or so's break? Having Mandell's men answering to me and being the one to give them orders wasn't my cup of tea. Plus, keeping an eye on Patrick's vitals and having Juno stare at me accusingly for the past twenty-four hours; all this responsibility is weighing me down."

"You seem to have risen to the challenge," Lassiter said. "Did you talk to Father Dominic about anywhere that might be safe to move Patrick if it becomes necessary?"

"They've come up with a few places. There are a couple villages in the area that might work. I think he was relieved at the idea of getting rid of us. You can talk to him yourself."

"I'll sit with Patrick for a while," Margaret said. "If he wakes up, all the better. I need to get to know him."

Lassiter nodded. "But if he does wake, I need to talk to him." He turned to Cambry. "Unless you managed to get the names of those other prisoners at the camp?"

"Three," Cambry said. "Patrick was trying, but he kept blacking out. Fidel Damos, Diego Estefan, Pierre Gilroy. I ran them by your contact in the CIA and he came up with three missing persons with links to Nicos. Damos is one of Nicos's men who disappeared suddenly after a smuggling deal he was handling fell through. Diego Estefan was the leader of a rebel group that the government was trying to squash. He was considered something of a patriot. He had no direct connection with Nicos, but the government could have paid Nicos to have him disappear. Estefan's group is lethal as hell and was giving the government forces major headaches. Pierre Gilroy appears to be a good guy who owned a coffee plantation near a river that had great access to sea-lanes. He refused to sell to Nicos and was abusive enough about it to piss him off."

"So they all ended up in Nicos's detention camp," Lassiter said grimly. "Plus Patrick and two more."

"But we have Patrick now," Margaret said. "And we'll get the others out. No one deserves the kind of savagery Nicos is handing out."

"You're damn right we will." Lassiter turned and moved toward the door, with Cambry at his heels. "But Mandell is right: We have to make sure we know that camp backward and forward before we make a move. And once we break those prisoners out, we have to find a way to get them safely away. Some of them may be in almost as bad shape as Patrick, and Nicos has guards all over this rain forest. I'll have to work on an exit plan that won't get them killed." He opened the door. "But to do that, I need to know who I've got to deal with in that prison and all the prisoners' conditions. I think I'll stop by and have a talk with Brukman before I do anything else. I'll see you in a few hours, Margaret."

She gazed after them resignedly before she turned back to Patrick. Lassiter was already in high gear, and she envied him. It would have been good to be able to be more active to accomplish something that would bring Nicos down. But she'd offered to stay with Patrick, and she couldn't have everything.

She dropped down in the chair and gazed down at Juno. *I guess it's just you and me. How are your pups doing?*

* * *

Ed Dietrich rose swiftly to his feet when Lassiter walked into the storage room they were using as Brukman's cell. "Everything's going well, sir. Did Cambry tell you? Brukman did exactly what he was supposed to do when he talked to Nicos."

"Yes, did he tell you?" Brukman asked sarcastically. He was sitting in a chair in front of the window overlooking the courtyard with his hands cuffed behind his back. "I was meek and obedient and I saved your ass. All I'd have had to do was tell Nicos that you were stranded down here with Patrick and he would have had this place overrun with his men within a few hours. I was very tempted. You promised me an airline ticket. When do I get out of here?"

"When you're no longer useful. You have to be here in case Nicos calls again," Lassiter said. "And you know what Nicos would do to you if he found you'd betrayed him."

"There might be a way around it." He leaned back in his chair. "And I keep remembering what you did to me in that rain forest. I hate your guts, you know. It might be worth the risk."

"If you even started to go in that direction, Dietrich has orders to make certain you don't even finish the first sentence." His lips twisted. "Quietly. Perhaps a broken neck? All of Mandell's men are very skilled." He glanced at Dietrich, who was standing by the door. "And Mandell's told him what scum he's dealing with now."

Brukman muttered a curse. "Then get me out of here. I'm not going to be caught in this cage like a rat if Nicos finds out what you've done to him. I stalled him, but there's no telling how soon he'll decide that he can't resist coming down to tear Patrick apart. I've watched him for years, and that's possible. Hell, he likes it too much."

"Like you."

"No, with me it's a job."

"And what's worse?" Lassiter made an impatient gesture. "I didn't come here to discuss letting you go. I want to know the names of the other two prisoners you're holding. I have Estefan, Damos, and Gilroy."

"Why do you want to know?"

"Give me the names."

"Screw you." He started to laugh. "My God, you're going to try to get them out? Aren't you in enough trouble? You're certifiable."

"I want the names." He paused. "And what kind of condition they're in."

Brukman shook his head. "I'm not telling you any of their names. I don't have to do it. You believe I'm too valuable because of Patrick to waste time and effort on trying to torture it out of me. Find out for yourself. As for their conditions? A couple of them are close to Patrick's. None that bad. Some of them are a little better." He smiled. "But they're all in very, very poor shape. I do such good work."

Lassiter wanted to kill him on the spot.

Control.

There would be a time and a place. Brukman was right: He couldn't spare the time right now. At least Brukman's ego had prodded him to give him his answer about the prisoners' conditions.

"Oh, I promise I'll remember that." Lassiter turned on his heel and headed for the door.

"Who was the woman?"

Lassiter stopped short and glanced at him over his shoulder. "What?"

Brukman nodded at the window in front of him. "I

saw a woman get out of that van with you and Mandell. You mentioned a Margaret when we were on our way here. Was that Margaret Douglas?"

He stiffened. "What do you know about Margaret Douglas?"

"Only what Nicos told me. We had long chats about the people he intended to send to me for schooling. After she ran away from him, she was tops on his list." He added mockingly, "I can't believe you brought her down here into the lion's den. Do you hate her? Nicos will find her and make her life a living hell. We planned it in detail. Do you want me to tell you about it?"

It took all of Lassiter's restraint to keep himself from leaping across the room and strangling the son of a bitch. "No, I want you to stay alive for a little while longer. That won't happen if I have to listen to you for one more minute." He glanced at Dietrich. "You heard me. He's being a little too cocky, Dietrich. Don't take any chances."

Dietrich shook his head. "Mandell would kick my ass." He settled down in his chair with his automatic weapon on his lap. "Now that would really be taking a chance."

Sean Patrick opened his eyes an hour after Lassiter had left his room. His eyes focused on Margaret. "Who . . . ?"

Juno was immediately on her feet, her head touching Patrick's hand.

"I'm Margaret. You don't know me." She smiled and leaned toward him. "And that's Juno. But I believe you might have met her."

"Yes." His voice was weak, but he turned his hand to touch the retriever. "We're . . . friends."

"She's a good friend to have."

"Nurse?"

She shook her head. "Just a friend of Lassiter." She

added, "Stop talking. You need to rest. But Lassiter wanted the other two names of the prisoners at the camp. Estefan, Damos, Gilroy. Who are the other two?"

"Manual Lucio, Dominic Chico. There used to be a . . . woman. María. Estefan's wife. But she didn't . . . last. Nicos is bad on women."

"I know." She reached out and gently touched his hand. "But Nicos couldn't have been any worse than he was with you. And you lasted, Patrick."

"I couldn't help her." He closed his eyes. "And it was killing . . . Estefan."

The mental and psychological torture must have been almost as terrible as the physical, she thought in an agony of sympathy. "It will be over soon. We're going to get them out."

He nodded and his eyes closed. "Don't let . . . Nicos get hold of you. Bad . . . on women."

Terrible with women. Terrible with Rosa. Terrible with all those tragic little girls he'd used as toys. Terrible with Margaret, with all the torment he'd inflicted over the years.

And it was time a woman stepped up and stopped Nicos from ever doing that again.

"I'll send these other two names and have them run through the CIA database," Lassiter said when he came to pick up Margaret an hour later to take her to her quarters. "It may come in handy to know if they have a power base in the area."

"Why? What difference does it make?" She fell into step with him as they walked down the long corridor. "No matter who they are, there's no question we'll have to go get them. We can't leave them there."

"I didn't say anything about picking and choosing. But everyone in that detention camp has to have someone looking for them. I was searching for Patrick for eighteen months. God knows, I would have been grateful to have had someone call me and tell me that they knew where I could find Patrick."

She slowly shook her head. "That's not what you meant. You said power base."

"I did mean it." He shrugged. "But it wouldn't hurt to gather a little more firepower to help us if we need it. Nicos may bring his men from the island to search the area if he finds out that we've taken Patrick. And we know Nicos has most of the government military forces in the area in his pocket. We could have them to contend with, too, if he decides to turn them loose on us."

"What kind of firepower?"

"Diego Estefan for one. He has a brother, Carlos, who took over the rebel forces when Diego disappeared. I told Mandell to call the CIA and try to locate Carlos's rebel encampment and get me a contact. I want to phone him and let him know where Estefan is being held." He paused. "And now I'll also let them know that Estefan's wife was tortured to death by Nicos's men. I'd think that would give them motivation to help us deal with Nicos." He added, "And I'll go through the rest of the list of prisoners and see if anyone else can be used to block his moves."

She was silent, her eyes narrowed on his face. "You've been thinking about this. Ever since you left me today, you've been plotting and planning, setting up scenarios and then discarding them."

He didn't answer for a moment. Then he shrugged. "Before then, actually. Since the time I found out that Patrick was too ill to chance moving. Everything changed from that moment. That's why I wanted you somewhere safe and out of the line of fire. I knew I'd probably have to forget about going after Nicos later. It was all going to come together now. So I had to have an alternate plan."

She should have known that Lassiter wouldn't just be down here spinning his wheels while he waited for Patrick to heal enough to be moved. From childhood, he'd been involved in cons and intricate manipulations of computers and individuals. It was the natural way for him to go. "What alternate plan?"

"We were going have to go get those other prisoners anyway or else risk having them killed by Nicos. I'm just trying to use the friends and families of those prisoners to help us save them . . . and ourselves, if it comes to that. I'm going to contact them and see if I can persuade them it's the only way to be sure of getting them out alive."

"And how can we protect Patrick?"

He smiled faintly. "I've already started. I just talked to the doctor. He thinks, barring complications, that Patrick will be out of danger by at least the middle of the day tomorrow. We'll try to get him to the helicopter pad by noon and I'll have you and Cambry take him to Bogotá."

Now wasn't the time to argue with him about his trying to get rid of her again. "Noon tomorrow. What if Nicos makes a move before that?"

His smile vanished. "Then I won't be able to get Patrick out of the immediate area. But I'm having Mandell scout for caves or any other places to hide him in an emergency until this is over."

"I thought that Cambry said Father Dominic had told him there would be a couple villages that might be possibilities."

"I decided that I didn't want to place Patrick anywhere that the monks knew about. It could endanger both them and Patrick if they were questioned."

She should have thought of that. So many innocent people threatened by Nicos. "They've been so kind to Patrick. I hate the idea of them being put in danger because he was brought here."

"I know. That's why I've been looking around for caves or any other options in the area."

She made a face. "Caves aren't very sanitary." She held up her hand as he opened his lips. "Look, I lived in the woods for all those years. Sanitary isn't always necessary. We'll make it work as long as Dr. Armando gives Patrick the okay. But it can't be for very long. We have to get him in a hospital as soon as possible."

He raised his brows. " 'We'?"

"What did you think I would do? You're going to set all of this up and I have to find a way to follow through with it. I don't like not having any say in what you've already done, but I'll make sure that I do in what goes forward." She rubbed her temple. "But you hadn't told me nearly everything. I was just concerned about Patrick."

"Perfectly natural. That's where your priority would be."

"No, it shouldn't. I should be worrying about everyone. Those monks . . . and particularly those poor prisoners."

"Look, the prisoners should be safe even if I can't get them out right away. As far as Nicos knows, I don't care anything about anyone in that camp except Patrick. He wouldn't see any advantage in hurting them or using them as pawns. It should be status quo at the camp. There's no reason why we have to move immediately."

"Yes, there is," she said fiercely. "You know there is. Nicos doesn't always think logically or reasonably. When he's angry, he explodes. He lashes out and tries to cut deep. If he doesn't have the target he wants, then he makes do with anyone within range. Those people will be within his range. So don't you dare think coolly or rationally where he's concerned. You work on getting them out now. Understand?"

"I could hardly help understanding," he said gently. "You're very clear. I can't help being logical and rational, but I wasn't going to waste any time. I just want to make sure that we're doing it in the best way to benefit everyone."

"Get them out of there." Her hands clenched into fists. "I *hate* prisons. Nicos had me in one for nine months. I felt helpless. Rosa *was* helpless. Nicos likes to make people feel that way. If he gets frustrated by not finding us, he might strike out at them."

He nodded. "I told you that I was doing everything I could think to do. We'll move as soon as we can." He smiled. "Without being totally unreasonable. Is that all right with you?"

She drew a deep breath. "A little patronizing, but I guess I was a little over the top. It's your fault for hitting me with all this at once." She grimaced. "Of course, I guess I wouldn't have let you do anything else. But you should have told me before this, instead of leaving me in the dark."

"I thought that you should be allowed to relax and get over Montego before you had to face anything more." He added, "And I thought I should be able to get more info and strategies in place before I had to face your wrath over my callousness in not instantly finding a way to get those prisoners out of the detention camp. You surprised me again."

"You still don't get it. How could I think you were callous when I can feel what you're feeling? I felt your pain as you thought about them, just as I felt your pain about Patrick. I can disagree with you sometimes, but I can't not know what— Why are you looking at me like that?"

"I was wondering what it would be like to feel what

you're feeling. It doesn't seem fair that it only goes one way." He was staring into her eyes. "And I was analyzing it in my humble, logical way, and thinking that when you were holding me that night on the beach, I felt part of you." He added softly, "And, if I was still closer, I was wondering if I might just get there."

His eyes, pale green and glittering . . . his body, lean and muscular, which had felt strong and ready against her . . .

Tingling heat.

Her breasts swelling in mindless response.

Her breathing shallow.

She swallowed. "Does that mean you want to have sex with me?"

"Oh, yes. Right this minute." He drew a deep breath. "But I always seem to pick a moment when you're vulnerable or confused or maybe too grateful to me for pulling you out of Montego Bay." He turned on his heel. "And now I think that I'll get the hell out of here and go tell Mandell what I intend to do about those prisoners. Your room is the third down this hall."

"But Patrick comes first," she called after him. "And I want to see where you're going to put him if he has to be moved."

"I believe you can trust me to find him a safe place, Margaret."

"Ordinarily. But this is the rain forest. How much do you know about the animals here?"

"Jaguars, anacondas—"

"The poison dart frog?"

"What?"

"It's one of the most dangerous animals here. It's usually bright blue, but sometimes golden. The golden ones are the deadliest. Only two inches long, but their venom is strong enough to kill ten men. Patrick can't be allowed anywhere near one. You'll have to examine—"

"Okay. Okay. I'll let you look over any place we decide to move him. Heaven forbid that I bring down the wrath of the golden poison dart frog."

"Thank you. I appreciate it."

"You're welcome." He shook his head as he looked at her over his shoulder. "You're a constant amazement. One minute you're demanding that I have to do what you say and the next you're all politeness."

"Politeness is good. Honesty is better. And I had to tell you about the frog so that you could see why—"

"Margaret."

"I'm sorry." She nodded. "I'm talking too much because you said that you wanted to have sex with me. I'm a little off balance and I have to—"

"That makes two of us."

The next minute, he'd disappeared out the arched doorway.

She stared after him for a brief moment, drew a breath, and then hurried down the hall toward the room he'd indicated. It was more a closet than a room, with a single bed and a chest that had an old-fashioned china pitcher and wooden bowl. She closed the door and dropped down on the bed. There were no windows in the room and it was dim and close.

That was fine with Margaret. She needed soothing and she found the darkness comforting after the heat of the last few minutes. Her cheeks were flushed and her nipples were ultrasensitive with every breath she took.

And she could still see Lassiter as if he were standing before her. Broad shoulders, tight buttocks, those pale green eyes . . . Just a few words and he had brought her to this state. No, it was more than that. The chemistry had been there from the beginning. Since their relationship had been stormy and conflicted, it had been incredible that explosive sexual tension could manage to exist.

And now certainly wasn't the time to think about Lassiter or sex. So spend a little time in this welcome dimness and get over it.

Then start to think of Patrick and those prisoners at the detention camp.

And Nicos, who at this very moment might already be on his way toward them.

# CHAPTER FIFTEEN

"How is he doing?" Margaret asked Cambry the minute she walked into Patrick's room four hours later. "Is it my imagination, or does he look less feverish?"

Cambry nodded. "His temp's gone down another degree. He may be on his way back."

"Thank God." She gazed at Patrick for a long moment. He had gone through so much, and still they had almost lost him. It was good to know that he was going to get his chance to live. "Does Lassiter know?"

"Yes, he was here an hour ago. And he had a conference with the doctor. Since then he's been moving at top speed. I saw him talking to Mandell in the courtyard."

"Any news of Nicos?"

"Yes," Lassiter replied for him as he strode into the room. "So far, the news is good. Mandell heard from his operative in Montego who was on watch and he said Nicos was still in Montego and there seemed to be a number of high-powered meetings going on. It appears that we might be getting a reprieve for a little while." He met her eyes. "It could be enough. We'll have to see."

She felt relief rush through her. "At least enough time to get Patrick out of here?"

He shrugged. "No promises."

She knew she couldn't ask for anything other than the tentative hope he'd given her. "Then I'll think positive."

He smiled. "You always do."

"Not always. But I try." She turned to Cambry. "How is Patrick?"

"Breathing steadier. Fever dropping."

"Then could we move him tonight instead of tomorrow?"

"Not unless we want to undo what we've done with him," Lassiter said. "The doctor said we can't rush it."

"Damn."

"I know." He smiled. "But I haven't been standing still, Margaret. I contacted Estefan's rebel group and spoke to Diego's brother, Carlos. He wasn't at all pleased about his brother being imprisoned and tortured and even less when I told him about Diego's wife, María. He was furious. I thought it was going to be an easy fix. Estefan's people know these forests like the back of their hands and would have no trouble taking out sentries. And their numbers are large enough to be able to assault the detention camp if necessary." He shook his head. "But I couldn't get Carlos to commit to making a move toward getting the prisoners out. He didn't trust me. He said he'd lost his brother and his brother's wife and he wouldn't lose anyone else. He couldn't take a chance on my baiting a trap that could snap closed on his entire group."

"So he won't help?"

"He'll help. I just may have to do a little finagling to make him come around." He turned toward Patrick. "But I've set up some insurance just to make sure that Patrick will be safe if everything doesn't go as I think it will."

"What kind of insurance?"

"I found a cave deep in the rain forest, about thirty miles from here. I told Mandell's men to cover the opening with branches. It's completely undiscernible. You'd have to stumble across it."

Margaret frowned. "I want to see it and check it out."

"What a surprise," Cambry murmured.

Lassiter nodded. "I thought you would. I have to take medical supplies and an IV unit up there anyway. As I said, it's just insurance. We wouldn't want to move Patrick until the last minute, so that he'll be comfortable as long as possible." He took her hand and pulled her toward the door. "But I still want everything prepared for him. Let's go."

Lassiter had spoken the truth, Margaret thought as he stopped the van a hundred yards away from the cave beside a small rushing river. It was absolutely hidden from view as it faded into the hillside, which was covered with a jungle of glossy shrubs and trees.

"Satisfied?" Lassiter said as he got out of the van. "It looked pretty good to me."

She nodded as she emerged from the van. "I'd never know there was anything here but all that beautiful foliage." She stood there gazing around her, taking in the exotic orchids and bromeliads, the large twisting vines that wound around the broadleaf evergreen trees that towered high in the sky and formed a canopy that allowed only a hint of sunlight to pierce the secret dimness. She glimpsed a brilliant scarlet-and-cobalt-hued parrot, heard the sounds of unseen life all around her, which were as mysterious as the rest of this shadowed world. "You know, it's wonderful here. I've never spent much time in rain forests. It's so different from the woods where I grew up. I'd like to stay for a while after all this is over." She drew a deep breath of the moist, heady fragrance of earth, ferns, and flowers surrounding them. "Or maybe go down to Monkey Island and then see the pink dolphins. That's supposed to be special."

"Pink dolphins?"

She nodded. "They live in the Amazon River and are sometimes nine feet long. They're either solid pink or pink-gray. I heard about them when I was working at the aquarium in Atlanta."

"You'd rather see dolphins than monkeys?"

"Monkeys are interesting, but dolphins are more of a challenge. Their intelligence is almost alien. They don't really think like we do."

"I see." A smile tugged at his lips. "And we know that you can't resist a challenge."

"Not true. I ran away from one for three years. It's just that the world is full of wonderful and beautiful creatures that should be known and experienced."

He chuckled. "Like your friends the tigers? I'd just as soon not experience them. I admit I'm glad there aren't any big cats hanging around here."

"But there are." She tilted her head, her gaze shifting to the hills far to the north. "Not tigers, of course, but jaguars. There are jaguars living about fifteen miles from here. I don't feel any of them closer, but perhaps I'd better check. . . ."

"By all means," he said drily.

She concentrated, searching the hills to the north, where she'd first sensed the jaguar presence strong and clear. Male. Female. Cub.

She probed the male gently.

He was startled. *Who?*

*No threat. Friend.*

He didn't understand the concept. He was a top-level predator in this rain forest. He did not need friends. But he was intelligent. If she had time, she could make him understand.

She did not have that time.

*Never mind. Later. Others?*

She was getting a flow of thought and pictures from him.

Yes, very intelligent.

She left a memory of friendship, good wishes, and warmth, then gently disengaged.

She turned back to Lassiter. "A male, female, and cub to the north. The closest other jaguar is about twenty miles upriver. She usually doesn't hunt this far south."

"So it would be safe here if we had to move Patrick?"

"Probably. But it's smart to be careful. Jaguars are always dangerous. They have the strongest bite of any of the big cats. Even their name comes from the Native American word for 'he who kills with one leap.' They generally don't hunt human prey, but if they're hungry, they'll eat anything."

"Comforting."

She shrugged. "At least, they don't usually hunt in packs. They're generally solitary. And if Patrick has to be moved, I'd come here with him."

"And try to convince the jaguars to change their spots?"

"You're thinking about that saying about leopards changing their spots. But actually both cats markings are rosette-shaped, though jaguars have spots in the middle of their rosettes."

"I'm glad you cleared that up," he said gravely.

"You're laughing at me."

"No, I'm enjoying you." His eyes were twinkling. "I like to watch your intensity when you talk about your four-footed friends. Though, come to think of it, dolphins don't have feet. So I'd have to encompass an entire—"

"You were wrong." She grinned at him. "And I felt it my duty to try to educate you about jaguars. Though, hopefully, we aren't going to have to worry about them."

"You can never tell. That's why we're here." He

turned and started to unload the equipment from the van. "Grab that other bag and we'll get everything set up for Patrick." He moved toward the cave opening. "We may have to be careful about jaguars, but I promise you there are no golden poison dart frogs. I had Mandell's men go over every inch of the interior and then sweep and clean the area. It's as sanitary as we could make it." He moved the huge branches away from the corner of the opening. "Just to make sure, I'll go in first."

She chuckled. "Stop being defensive. I believe you. I just thought I should check out the animal and insect threat." She looked around as much as she could in the dimness of the cave. "Flashlight?"

He took out his flashlight and handed it to her. "Be my guest."

She shined the beam around the cave. It appeared to be fairly large, with seven-foot ceilings and a ledge that ran across the west wall. There was a little seepage of water coming from the back of the cave, but nothing threatening.

And it was clean, amazingly clean. Lassiter had kept to his word about its being as sanitary as possible considering the circumstances. "You did good. Not that I doubted you would. I knew you'd want the best for Patrick."

"But you had to be certain," he said drily.

"I'm used to having to do things for myself."

"Do you think I don't know that?" he said thickly. "And you're still doing it. Why the hell won't you let me help you?"

She tensed. There was something in his voice, something in the stillness of his body, that was causing a response that was purely erotic. She could barely make him out in the dimness and she wouldn't lift the beam to see his expression.

Because she had an idea what she would find there.

Heat.

The air was crackling with electricity.

"Why should you?" She was trying to keep her voice steady. "I'm responsible for myself. In the end, we're all responsible for ourselves."

"Bullshit. After everything I've done to you, I have a responsibility to keep you safe, to keep everything bad away from you. Not to let anyone touch you or take anything away from you." He laughed harshly. "And the only thing I can think about right now is how much I want to be inside you, have you underneath me. And I can't stop it, Margaret. What the hell kind of hypocrite does that make me?"

There it was, out in the open.

"Thank goodness." She gave a sigh of relief and took a step closer to him. "I thought you'd never say it." She started to unbutton her shirt. "We'll both feel much better once this is over. All of this guilt and angst is silly. Let's just do it."

He went still. "Haven't you been listening to me? This is— Oh shit." She had taken off her bra and was pressing her naked breasts against him. "What are you doing?"

"I'm trying to make you stop thinking of me as this noble self-sacrifice." She unbuttoned his shirt and moved her breasts against the thatch of hair on his chest. She inhaled sharply as it caused her nipples to harden. "Sex is good. Great sex is wonderful. It's part of life. If you want to be responsible for me, just take the responsibility of giving me what we both want. I don't know what's going to happen in the next few days, but there's nothing wrong with taking pleasure now." She buried her head in his chest. She loved the feel of him, the scent of him. "I won't ask anything more from you. I think I feel something for you . . . but you don't have to worry about that. All I want is to be this close to you and have—"

"Be quiet." His mouth was on hers, his tongue playing wildly.

She couldn't breathe. The muscles of her stomach were clenching.

He was tearing the clothes off her. His fingers were between her legs, toying, playing.

She cried and arched toward him. "Lassiter . . ."

"Shh." He was naked, too, pulling her down on the stone floor of the cave. His lips were on her breasts, pulling, tugging—

Then he was inside her.

Driving.

Hard.

Deep.

Wild.

She was trying to help him, but he was too hard, too hungry.

All she could do was take, and take, and take.

Then he was pulling her over him, his hands on her waist as he brought her down and down and . . .

It went on and on, and she could feel the tears run down her cheeks from the sheer pressure and intensity.

How long . . .

Her head was spinning, and her entire body was moving, rubbing, deep . . . deep . . .

"I can't . . . do—"

"Yes, you can." He moved harder. "I know what you are. You can do anything, be anything. . . . Just a little more . . ."

He was right: She could do anything. Because she was part of him and he was inside her, taking, burning, clutching every bit of her. . . .

"Now," he gasped, his fingers buried in her hips.

Faster.

Deeper.

Wilder.

Her back arched. She cried out as sensation after sensation rocked through her.

Then she collapsed against him, her entire body shuddering. She could feel the tears pouring down her face as she tried desperately to get her breath.

She could feel his heart pounding against her, his arms holding her sealed to him as the minutes passed.

"You're crying. Did . . . I hurt you?"

"No. Maybe. I don't know. It doesn't matter." She moved off him and lay down next to him. The rocks were cool against her body, which still felt hot and vibrantly alive. Every inch of her was glowing, flushed with the feel of him against her, in her. "But that wasn't why I was crying. You felt . . . It was beautiful, wasn't it?" She reached over and pressed her lips to his shoulder. "And you're beautiful, too. I've always thought so. You're like one of the big cats. Lean and strong and you move . . . very, very well."

He chuckled. "I'm glad you approve. Which cat? One of your tigers?"

"More like a panther, but I think that your sexual stamina is probably like a tiger's. You were very strong just now." She was trying to catch her breath. "Did you know that when a male and a female tiger come together for the first time, they mate hundreds and hundreds of times in a few days?"

"I wasn't aware of that. But it sounds fantastic. We'll have to—" He stopped. "We may have to postpone that for a while."

She nodded. "No time. It kind of ambushed us, didn't it? But it was beautiful, wasn't it?"

"Yes, it was extraordinary." He reached over and ran the tips of his fingers over her stomach. "*You're* extraordinary. I didn't mean this to happen, you know."

"Sure you did. It's the natural thing when two people want sex. It's instinctive. And if you hadn't been worried about ethics and responsibility, it could have happened before."

"I'm still worried. I'm just ignoring it because I'm damn selfish and I'm needing you again."

"Okay." She beamed up at him. "Now?"

"No, not okay." He sat up and looked down at her. "Why? I know a lot about you, Margaret. You don't come close enough to anyone to have relationships. It's very rare for you. I thought it was just because you were wary."

"You're . . . different. I've always known that. I really don't know the reason." She shrugged. "Because I wanted you, because sex is joy, because every minute of joy is important. Life is too short not to reach out and take it. So stop analyzing, Lassiter. I took as much as I gave. You don't owe me anything." She tilted her head. "So could we do it just once more? I know we can't take much more time, but I'd really like—" She inhaled sharply as his finger moved up between her thighs. "We do have a little time?"

"Oh, yes. You're right: Life is too short," he said thickly as he moved over her. "We have the time."

"It's hard to stop." She was breathing hard, her heart pounding. "Definitely tiger . . . I want it hundreds and hundreds of times. . . ." She looked up at him. She loved those pale green eyes, the sensual curve of his mouth, and the *feel* of him. "I suppose we can't do that." She cuddled closer to him, her hand moving over his shoulders, stroking, her nails digging into his back. "But I think you want it, too."

"No question."

"Maybe later." She suddenly giggled. "Because I think I've finally convinced you that I'm none of the things that you think I am. I'm not vulnerable. I'm not a martyr. I'm not that gladiator wanting to taste life before I go into the arena."

"You told me that you didn't think there were female gladiators."

"I was wrong. I Googled it later. There were female gladiators and they performed by candlelight in the Coliseum. But they were thought to be inferior."

"You would have shown them."

She nodded. "Well, I think I could have convinced the lions not to eat me."

"I think so, too." His voice was husky. "I think you could convince anyone of anything. I was trained as a con man and I wish I was as persuasive." He paused. "I want you to go on that helicopter with Patrick, Margaret."

She was silent. "Let's talk about it tomorrow."

"Because you don't want to argue about it now."

"Yes."

"I believe we have to talk about it now." He moved away from her and sat up. "I'm going to have to leave soon and I want you to give me your word you'll be on that helicopter at noon tomorrow if I'm not back in time to put you on it myself."

She froze, her gaze flying to his face. "Leave? What are you talking about? Where are you going?"

"I'm going to meet with Estefan's brother, Carlos, and persuade him to bring his not-so-merry band back with me to help get those prisoners out of the camp."

A bolt of fear shot through her. "You said he didn't trust you."

"Hey, I'm great at the con. I've just got to see him face-to-face to make it work. It should help that I'm telling the truth." He made a face. "Or maybe not. Sometimes lies do work better. But I'll make sure this isn't one of those times."

"Are you taking anyone with you?"

He shook his head. "That would be a mistake. I have to show Carlos that he's completely in charge of the situation."

"You're leaving right away?"

"As soon as we get back to the monastery. I'm going to borrow the monks' old truck to go as far as I can and then hike the rest of the way to Estefan's base camp. I'll leave the van for you in case you need it for Patrick."

"You have it all planned. What if this con doesn't work?"

"Then I come back, hanging my head."

"If you still have a head," she said unevenly. "You told me that rebel group could be pretty ruthless."

"I'll still have my head intact. I've never had a con that's gone that far south."

"That doesn't mean it couldn't happen." She moistened her lips. "Maybe I should go along. I'm a woman, and it might make you appear less intimidating to them."

He reached out and gently touched her face. "The women in these rebel groups are just as lethal as the men. That argument isn't valid, I'm afraid."

"It should be. Just look at me. I'm not that impressive."

"I am looking at you." He cupped her face in his two hands. "Do you know what I see? You're all golden and true and full of life. That's pretty damn impressive. And I'm not going to risk you."

He was staring into her eyes, and she couldn't look away. There was something there that wasn't passion, wasn't anything that had been between them before. She felt suddenly part of him that had nothing to do with the physical. It was too much. It confused her.

She finally managed to turn her head. "No one has the right to make that decision but me, Lassiter. Not ever."

He muttered a curse and his hands fell away from her face. "No, you have to do everything by yourself. Every decision your own. Total independence." He shook his head. "Well, this time the decision is mine. You came down here to help Patrick; now stay here and do it. He's in your hands until I get back." He got to his feet and started to get dressed. "Which should be before morning."

"You're angry with me."

"Yeah, you could say that. Maybe more about you. I'm angry and frustrated and I want to kill your bastard of a father and Nicos and all the people who made you feel an outsider because of that damn gift. You have to stand alone. You'll come so close and no further."

She got up on her knees and reached for her clothes. "It's who I am." She smiled shakily. "And I came very close to you today. You seemed . . . pleased."

"I was out of my mind. I want to start all over again." He shook his head. "And why should I care if I can have great sex with you? It never mattered to me before." He turned toward the cave opening. "Get dressed. I'll go out and make sure there aren't any tire prints anywhere near the cave."

She stayed there for a minute on her knees, giving herself time to recover. He hadn't meant to hurt her. It had happened because in some way she had hurt him just by being what she was. He was right: She had to stand alone. She didn't want it to be true. Closeness drew her like a bright beacon. So often she had felt that warmth with Lassiter and then had felt herself pushing it away.

And it had happened again today when she'd least expected it.

So accept it and go on.

She finished dressing quickly and then was out of the cave and heading for the van.

\* \* \*

They didn't speak until they were halfway back to the monastery.

"We should talk about the plans I've made," Lassiter said quietly. "Mandell will be in charge while I'm gone. He'll be staying close to the monastery and all you have to do is call him if you have a problem. If Patrick takes a turn for the worse or if we have any word that Nicos is on the move, then call me. I'll turn around and come back at once. Otherwise, I should be back ASAP. It's late afternoon now, so that probably means sometime in the middle of the night."

"Depending on how long it takes you to persuade Carlos and his group to come back with you. And you *will* call me while you're on the road and let me know your progress," she said curtly. "I'll take care of Patrick. I'll do everything right. I won't let anything happen to him."

"I know that." He parked in front of the monastery and sat there staring ahead. "I was an ass. I'm sorry."

"Yes, you were," Margaret said flatly. "I can't be anything but what I am. I don't ask you to be anything else. I like who you are most of the time. And when I don't, I accept it." She opened the van door and jumped out of the vehicle. "And I don't like you going off by yourself. I want to be there for you. But I'm accepting it." She looked back over her shoulder. "What I won't accept is your getting yourself hurt or killed. So don't do it, Lassiter."

She strode away from him into the courtyard before he could answer.

A few minutes later, she was walking down the corridor toward Patrick's room. She knew she probably shouldn't have let her emotions get the better of her. He had apologized and she could have accepted it graciously.

No, she couldn't. She was too emotionally involved with Lassiter, and everything he did or said had an effect

on her. So she was not going to let him think he could
hurt her and walk away. She'd be as open and honest as
she always was and he could take her or leave her.

"So did Lassiter meet with your approval?" Cambry
asked as Margaret strode into Patrick's room. "You were
gone long enough."

She looked at him, startled. "What?"

"The cave. Will it be okay for Patrick?"

At his first words, she'd had an immediate vision of
Lassiter leaning naked above her. "Oh, the cave." She
nodded quickly. "Yes. It's fine. And we weren't gone all
that long. Only a couple hours."

"It seemed longer."

It hadn't seemed long to Margaret. It had been a wild
period of complete erotic pleasure. She could still feel
the sensation of Lassiter moving in her body. Crazy.

And addictive.

She wanted him back again.

Lassiter had been right: Sex had never been that important to her. It had taken a long time to heal from that
rape she'd undergone when she was twelve. She'd been
lucky that she'd still been living in the woods and could
see all aspects of sex in nature around her. Gradually,
she had realized that this was just another wound that
would heal if she didn't hold it close, but released the
pain and not let it poison her. After that she had accepted
the pleasure of sex as she did everything around her that
was full of joy. But she'd had no trouble walking away,
and she would never have risked initiating it if it might
have proved troublesome or a danger.

Yet she'd had trouble walking away today in
circumstances that were definitely troublesome. Lassiter.
It had been because it was Lassiter. And the knowledge
that he was what made it different was an additional
danger to her.

"Margaret?" Cambry was gazing at her, puzzled.

"Problems? It's going to be okay. Everything is in high gear. I guess Lassiter told you that he was heading into the rain forest to try to recruit the Estefan group to help out? Mandell stopped by and told me what was happening and that he'd be sticking close."

"Yes, he told me." She glanced at Patrick. "I told him we'd take care of everything here." She moved over to the bed and stood looking down at Patrick. He did look better. She only prayed he'd stay that way.

*He's not going away. I can keep him here.*

She glanced down at Juno on the floor beside the bed. *I know you can. But it may be hard for a while.*

*He's not like her. She couldn't stay with me. But I can keep him.*

*I'm sure she'll be happy if you do.*

*I know.* Juno laid her head down on her paws again. *So he will not go away.*

Margaret reached out and gently touched Patrick's hand. "Did you hear that?" she whispered. "Juno's trying to tell us something. Now you pay attention to her."

"You're . . . Margaret." Patrick hadn't opened his eyes and his voice was weak. "Don't . . . understand."

"You will." Her hand tightened on his. "You've got all kinds of friends in your corner. All you have to do is hang on and let us do the hard work. I'll be here for you, if it matters."

"It . . . matters." His lids slowly lifted. "Lassiter? Did he get them out of the detention camp? He has to do it. Right away. It . . . can't wait."

"Lassiter knows that's what you want. He's working on it."

"It can't . . . wait. Nicos is—crazy. Don't want my freedom—to be reason for—"

"Shh." He was becoming agitated and his breathing was beginning to be labored. "They'll be safe. Soon. Very soon. First on the list. I'll see to it." She met and held his gaze. "I promise you. I keep my promises, Patrick."

He held her gaze for an instant longer and then his lids fluttered closed. "Then . . . do . . . it."

He was asleep again.

She drew a deep breath and stepped away from the bed.

Cambry gave a low whistle. "I'd say that Lassiter made the right choice to get moving on getting those prisoners out right away."

She nodded. "Patrick's really upset about it. In his present condition, he can't afford that."

"Well, he seemed to believe you when you made that promise."

"Because I was telling the truth. I'll do whatever I can to get them out." She made a face. "With or without Carlos Estefan." She turned toward the door. "But right now I'm going back to that closet they call a bedroom to wash up and change clothes. Then I want to talk to the doctor. Lassiter said he said noon tomorrow, but Patrick's getting better all the time. Maybe he'll let him go sooner. I'll see you later, Cambry."

He glanced at Juno. "Oh, we'll be here. I'm having trouble getting my buddy here to take bathroom breaks."

Because Juno knows that Patrick needs her in a very special way, Margaret thought as she started down the hall. It was one of the beautiful things about life that love could sense and furnish what was needed. Maybe that was why she had heard Juno calling her that night when there was no way she should have been able to do it. Perhaps there was a purpose that had brought her to Patrick at this time when the need was so very crucial.

"Margaret?"

She stopped as she saw Mandell coming down the hall toward her. "I just came from Patrick. He's looking much better, but he went back to sleep, if you're here to check on him."

He shook his head. "I looked in on him earlier. I wanted to see you. I just saw Lassiter off in that rackety truck that belongs to the monastery, and he bent my ear telling me all the precautions I should take with you while he was gone." His lips twisted. "I came to make sure we're on the same page. You keep your phone with you at all times. You let me know if you're going to be anywhere but in your room or with Patrick."

"Where else would I be? I promised that I'd take care of Patrick."

"I'm just making certain that everything's clear. I'm new at this bodyguard crap."

"Bodyguard?" She shook her head. "You're responsible for everything going on here. I should be the least of your worries."

"That's not the impression I got from Lassiter. So keep me informed twenty-four/seven or I'll have to bunk in your room." He grinned. "And I guarantee that the good monks won't like that one bit, since they look askance at me anyway. I have to keep on their good side as much as I can."

She wrinkled her nose. "I don't like it, but I'll do it. I'm not used to this bodyguard crap, either." She looked down at the automatic pistol in the holster at his belt. "But the monks might be better disposed toward you if you didn't wear that inside the monastery."

He shook his head. "I can't buy approval by being something I'm not. You're here; Patrick's here. I'm not going to show up with a prayer book." He turned and moved back toward the front entrance. "If you hear from Lassiter before I do, let me know."

"I will. Though don't count on it."

"Hmm, really? Then I'll let you know. He said he'd try to contact me before he started back and give me the word if we're going to have to go it alone at the detention camp."

"He didn't seem to have any doubts about getting Carlos Estefan on his side," she said drily. "He said it was only a matter of strengthening the force of the con."

"I hope he's right. Sometimes those rebels shoot first and listen later," he said over his shoulder as he went out the door.

She felt a chill go through her at his words. She had been trying not to keep thinking about the danger Lassiter might be facing. She had told him that he shouldn't go alone. She had told him that he was being too confident about confronting Carlos on his own turf. He hadn't listened to her.

And she could do nothing about it now and it made her feel helpless.

But she wouldn't be helpless if she kept busy and let her mind work on the problems she could solve.

Bathe. Get a bite of supper. Then talk to the doctor.

But, dammit, she had to let Lassiter be the one to plan how to stay alive and persuade Carlos Estefan to come and help them.

9:40 P.M.
Rain Forest

Estefan's camp was just ahead.

It was time, Lassiter knew.

Call Margaret now. He might not get a chance later.

For more reasons than one.

He punched in the number quickly. She answered after the first ring. Her voice was tense. "Where are you, Lassiter?"

"Where I should be? In the middle of this damned

rain forest. Hot, muggy, and definitely buggy. Though I don't believe I've run across your dart frog yet."

"You'd know it if you had. That's no answer. Have you made contact with Carlos Estefan?"

"That's next on the agenda. About five minutes, I'd judge. His camp is right ahead of me."

"Then why are you calling me? They have to have sentries all around that camp. Hell, they might even hear you. Get off the phone."

"You told me to check in. I'm checking in. How is Patrick?"

"Better, but the doctor is sticking to his time line. Get off the phone."

"How are you?"

"I'm fine. Why wouldn't I be? Get off the damn phone."

"Just a little longer. Are you still angry with me?"

"Yes. No. What difference does it make?"

"At least you're ambivalent about it. It's complicated, isn't it?"

"Get off the phone. Why are you doing this?"

"Because it's best that the sentries bring me into camp and report to Carlos that I was talking on the phone. That way, they won't shoot me right away, because Carlos will want to know who I was reporting to. It will be a conversation starter."

"Conversation starter? You're crazy, Lassiter."

"Then you should forgive me because I'm not responsible for my actions." He tilted his head, listening. "I'll call you back later." He disconnected and then waited.

Close.

Very close.

He kept the phone to his ear.

He just had to hope that whoever was behind him in those shrubs wasn't trigger-happy.

And then he heard the click of the hammer of a rifle.

\* \* \*

A conversation starter?

Margaret wanted to kill him. He was so confident that he could talk Estefan into doing what he wanted that he was making himself bait for the trap.

She could envision all kinds of scenarios playing out that had nothing to do with conversation and everything to do with being lethal.

And he had hung up too abruptly, which probably meant that the action was about to start. Now all she could do was sit here in her room and wait for him to call her back.

Mandell. She had promised to call Mandell. Though there wasn't much she could tell him. She pressed the number buttons quickly. "I heard from Lassiter. He's reached the camp but hasn't made contact with anyone yet," she said jerkily. "He's setting up a conversation. He said he'd call back later."

"You're a bit upset," Mandell said. "He knows what he's doing, Margaret. It may not be the way you or I would handle it, but he's an expert at what he does. *Silver-tongued* doesn't describe him. He'll get through to Carlos."

"Or he'll get himself shot. You know him better than I do. I hope you're right. If he calls me back, I'll let you know."

"*When* he calls you back," Mandell said quietly. "There's nothing to panic about."

"No, why should I worry if he does something this idiotic?" She hung up and drew a deep breath. Mandell might not think that Lassiter would have problems, but she couldn't be certain of anything except that there were threats all around him.

She sat down on the bed. Nothing to do but wait.

Call, damn you, Lassiter.

# CHAPTER SIXTEEN

10:50 P.M.

Why hadn't he called?

Margaret's nails bit into her palms.

It had been too long.

How long did his "conversations" have to last? Carlos might have been the exception to prove the rule that Lassiter could talk anyone into anything. He could have been shot or held—

"Margaret Douglas?"

Her gaze flew across the room. There had been no knock, but the door was opening.

A tall, broad-shouldered man in khakis was smiling at her. "You *are* Margaret Douglas?"

One of Mandell's men? She stiffened as he entered the room. Intrusion. No, Mandell wouldn't have tolerated that and he would have called her. She jumped to her feet and reached for her phone.

"I don't think so." He was across the room in seconds. His hand knifed down on her forearm and the phone dropped from her hand. "Not after I've run this risk, Margaret. You're my ticket out of here."

She whirled away from him and grabbed the pitcher

on the washstand. She kicked upward between his legs with her foot as she swung the pitcher at his head.

"Bitch." He grunted in pain as he blocked the pitcher from a direct hit. Then he smashed the pitcher to the floor as he grabbed her throat. "Don't fight and I might not break your neck." His hand tightened. "Or then again, I might."

Dizziness.

Intense pain.

Everything was going black. Her legs buckled and she fell to her knees. He released her and she was vaguely aware that he was grabbing the pillowcase off the bed. Was he going to smother her?

Then he was jerking her to her feet.

She could feel the muzzle of a gun in her back as he pushed her toward the door.

"Now be very good and you might have a chance of getting out of here alive. . . ."

He had stopped at the door and was forming the pillowcase into a gag.

"Who . . ."

He didn't answer.

But she was dimly putting all this madness together through the haze of pain and vertigo.

"Brukman," she said hoarsely. "You have to be Brukman. . . ."


12:35 A.M.


Mandell's cell phone was ringing by the time he reached the courtyard after checking the sentries.

Lassiter.

"I admit I'm glad to hear from you," he said when he picked up. "I assured Margaret you knew what you were doing, but it took you long enough to get back to us. I was losing faith in you. What about Carlos? Are you bringing him back with you?"

"No, but he's breaking camp and will be there tomorrow morning," he said curtly. "Where's Margaret?"

"In her room. I talked to her after you called her the last time. That's when I was telling her what a silver-tongued devil you are. What did she say when you told her that you'd managed to—"

"I didn't tell her anything," Lassiter said sharply. "She's not answering her phone. I called twice and she never picked up. Go check her room and see where the hell she is. I'll call Cambry and see if she's with him and Patrick." He cut the connection.

Shit. Mandell was halfway across the courtyard in seconds and was running down the hall toward Margaret's room. It could be nothing. Maybe her phone had no charge. Maybe she was pissed off at Lassiter and had decided—

He knocked on her door.

No answer.

He threw open the door.

Shards of a broken pottery pitcher lay scattered all over the stone floor.

A pillow lying at the bottom of the bed was stripped of its slip.

No sign of Margaret.

He called Lassiter. "Not here. Signs of possible struggle. The pitcher is broken and—"

"*Find her.* She's not with Patrick." He was cursing softly. "I thought you said there was no problem about security. Could it have been someone from the detention camp?"

"No, I swear to you that no one broke into the monastery. The perimeter around it couldn't be tighter." He was running out of Margaret's room and down the hall and across the courtyard. "There's only one way I can think of that—" He threw open the door of the storage room and turned on the light.

Blood.

Ed Dietrich was lying crumpled on the floor beside the window overlooking the courtyard. His eyes were open and staring straight up at the ceiling.

His throat had been cut.

"Dietrich's dead," he told Lassiter as he dropped to his knees beside Dietrich. "That son of a bitch Brukman must have gotten out of his handcuffs, overpowered him from behind, and then grabbed his knife. His throat's been cut." He forced himself to look for more to report. It was hard to get his head straight. Dietrich was only twenty-nine. He had fought with him in Afghanistan and Mandell had always liked him. "Brukman took his weapons, phone, money clip, and credit cards."

"And there's a good chance he also took Margaret," Lassiter said grimly. "The only question is what he intends to do with her." He added, "And what he intends to do, period. Brukman knows it would be a risk letting Nicos know that he helped to free Patrick." He paused. "Unless he thinks he has an ace in the hole. He might try to bargain Margaret for amnesty from Nicos's hit men. He must have figured out that she's a prime target."

"I'll get together a search team and go after him." Mandell added, "I'll get her back, Lassiter."

"Easy to say. Brukman knows this rain forest like the back of his hand. If he had even a couple hours head start, he could lose himself and Margaret with no trouble. And he was a mercenary for seven years before he was chosen by Nicos to head the torture squad at the detention camp. He knows all about manacles, and that was probably how he was able to get out of those handcuffs. You'll have to be careful that he doesn't pick you off with that rifle he stole from Dietrich."

"That won't happen," Mandell said. "God, I'm sorry, Lassiter. I'll find her. I won't let Brukman try to use her."

"You should never have lost her," he said harshly. "I told you that she was first priority. And as for Brukman using her, that could be the best scenario. Brukman hates my guts. He might decide to try his skills on Margaret to punish me for ruining his gig with Nicos."

"Shit."

"I'm on my way back now. Keep in touch with me. But before you leave the monastery, have Cambry move Patrick and the doctor to that cave I told you about. I don't want to take any chances on Brukman getting in touch with Nicos or the detention camp and stirring up all hell. And see if Cambry can persuade Father Dominic and the monks to scatter into the forest or those nearby villages." He hung up.

Lassiter was white-hot angry, and Mandell couldn't blame him. Dietrich had been a good man and he had trusted him. But in the end, the responsibility had been Mandell's. He should have known that Brukman was more savvy and skilled than Dietrich and made certain this couldn't happen. He had blown it, and a good man had died and Margaret Douglas could die, too, if he didn't make it right.

He looked down at Dietrich and reached out and closed those eyes that were staring up at him. How many times had he done this before over the years?

Too many.

Good-bye, buddy.

I promise I'll send him to hell for you.

"Bad news?" Carlos Estefan's gaze was fixed on Lassiter's tense face as he ended the call. "Yes, I can see that it is."

Lassiter nodded jerkily. "Not good." Massive understatement. He was trying to keep the fear under control and his mind working. "And for you, it may mean that you'll have to break camp tonight and get on the move. There's a good chance that Nicos will be heading here very soon. Lars Brukman, the man I told you about, escaped. That means the entire scenario has changed, and not for the better." He met Carlos's eyes. "But the one thing that hasn't changed is that your brother needs you. Will you still go with me?"

Carlos nodded slowly. "I was never afraid of the battle. We're used to that. I was afraid of betrayal, that you might turn my people over to the government forces. You've convinced me that isn't going to happen. If there's a chance of getting my brother out of that camp, then we'll do it." He smiled faintly. "And if we can kill a few of the soldiers of the government that paid Nicos to keep him there and kill his wife, María, that will be a joy beyond imagining." He turned and strode back toward the campfire. "Tell me how to do it and it will be done. We'll be on our way within an hour. I assume you're leaving now?"

"I'm on my way." He was already moving toward the trail that had led him here. "Thank you, Carlos. I'll contact you when I see what the situation is."

"That Brukman," Carlos called after him. "He's a key person? He can hurt you?"

Patrick at risk again.

Cambry and Mandell's entire team threatened.

And Margaret.

He could see her before him, her eyes glittering with humor and defiance and that infinite caring that was such a part of her. He could feel the pain twist inside of him at the thought of her. If she were here, she'd try to stop the pain. It was what she did, what she was.

She was not here. She was somewhere out there in

that rain forest alone with Brukman. And he had seen what agony Brukman was capable of inflicting. Who was going to stop *her* pain?

"Oh, yes, Carlos," he said hoarsely. "He can hurt me."

"You've been very good," Brukman told Margaret mockingly. "Four hours of travel and you managed to stay on your feet. You deserve a reward. Sit down. Suppose I take that gag off you? There's no one to hear you scream out here in this wilderness but the parrots and the jaguars." He untied the makeshift gag. "But you can see how I thought it necessary to be careful when I knew I had to get you across that courtyard and into the forest."

Margaret drew a deep breath as the confining cloth was jerked off her mouth. "You could have taken it off me sooner. You let me go hours with that thing in my mouth."

"I thought you should be aware that I'm the disciplinarian and you're the student. I control your breath and the movements of your body and anything else that I choose. I learned that philosophy from Nicos. But I think you're beginning to understand."

"I understand that you have to be an inhuman monster to do the things you did to Patrick." She tested the leather belt binding her wrists in back of her as she spoke. "Did you enjoy it?"

"Not particularly. It's just a skill I do very well. Of course, I do get a certain satisfaction when a technique works particularly well on a subject. But Nicos is the one who actually enjoys seeing and hearing the details. We've had some long conversations about my work at the detention camp. He's even asked my opinion on the possibility of sending me other people who have annoyed him." He leaned back against the tree. "He was particularly interested in what I could come up with to make the torture of John Lassiter new and different. He was entertained by the mental suffering he was undergoing, but he knew that Lassiter would have to take his turn at the camp." He reached forward and touched her cheek. "And you, Margaret. I've heard about you for a long time. Every time a deal went wrong in the past year or so, Nicos seemed to blame it on you. Some raving about voodoo and punishment and dogs. He was torn between getting you back or sending you to me to punish. He was very excited when I described what we did to María Estefan. I believe he was thinking about you. . . ."

"I'm sure he was. But he's basically a mercenary and he thinks that I'm more profitable alive than dead."

"Either way, you have value for him." He smiled. "And that may have value for me. That's why I took you with me when I escaped. I was tempted to grab Patrick, but he would probably have died before I'd gone even a mile or two. No, there you were, presumably young and strong and the shining evidence of Lassiter's triumph over Nicos. You'd do quite well."

"Do quite well for what?"

"A negotiation tool." He took a swallow of water. "Lassiter must have told you that Nicos is not a forgiving man. Perhaps you've discovered it for yourself?"

"He's insane. And you're catering to a madman."

"But Nicos realizes how valuable I've been to him in the past years. I supply a special need. All I have to do is give him a reason to let him continue indulging that need." He tilted his head, appraising her. "You're a pretty woman. Not as pretty as María Estefan, but you have a certain . . . I don't know . . . something. Would you like me to tell you what she looked like when we finished with her?"

"No."

"Squeamish?"

"You'd enjoy telling me too much. I'm sure you're willing to demonstrate instead."

"Yes, Lassiter must care something for you if he went to all that trouble of taking you from Nicos. It will be a pleasure . . . if Nicos permits. I have to bow down to the son of a bitch if I'm to survive." He finished his water and tossed the bottle aside. "And now it's time I got down to business." He took out his phone. "The first nail's in Lassiter's coffin."

"You're calling Nicos."

"No, I'm calling Salva. Salva originally hired me, and if anyone has influence with Nicos, it's him. He knows how to push his buttons. I'll let him pave the way. Then I'll talk to Nicos." He was dialing as he spoke. "I'm certain he'll want to speak to you to verify that I have you. If you could shed a few tears, I'm sure he'd like it enormously."

"Screw you."

"If I had the time, I could make you weep like a baby, but it's not worth it. All that can come later." He spoke into the phone. "Salva, this is Brukman. I have to talk to Nicos and I know he'll be more receptive if I go through you. I'm going to need you to intercede and keep him from putting a contract out on me. I think you know if you help me, I'll pay you back in any way you choose. Talk to him and then ask him to call me back with orders. Here's what's been happening. . . ."

Margaret felt the tension grip her as the minutes passed after Brukman had ended his call to Salva. If Nicos didn't call him back, Brukman might just cut his losses along with her throat and take off across the rain forest to the nearest airport, where he could go on the run.

"Nervous?" Brukman asked. "Don't be. If you could have heard Nicos talk about you, it would reassure you. He'll probably want you dead later, but you're a lure and temptation right now. And I'll do such a good job on you that he'll be very happy and will tend to forgive me all my so-called transgressions against him."

"You're trying to talk yourself into believing that." Her gaze was narrowed on his face. "You're frightened, Brukman. I can feel it."

"Can you? Maybe some of that voodoo nonsense Nicos told me about in the dead of night? I'll get through this and be fine. I just have to have a little wiggle room. You, on the other hand, won't be able to survive—"

His phone rang.

He laughed and put it on speaker. "Are you ready, Margaret? It's the master of your fate."

"No one is master of my fate but me. I've noticed it's you who are ready to kneel down and kiss Nicos's feet."

His smile faded. "We'll see about that." He accessed the call. "Nicos, I told Salva that the only thing I could do was make the best of a bad situation. I know you're probably angry, but consider that I do have Margaret Douglas. She's right here and I know how—"

"Stop sputtering and let me talk," Nicos said coldly. "Salva is telling me that you may still prove useful to me, but you'll have to prove it. I'm remembering how you lied to me and let Lassiter have everything his own way."

"Everything isn't his own way. I was telling the truth about Patrick being near death. It's Patrick who's trapping Lassiter down here and it's you who caused that to happen. You gave me the orders and I carried them out. Now we just have to spring the trap." Brukman paused. "But we have to hurry, because when Patrick is able to be moved, they'll be out of here." He went on quickly, "Or they would have been if I hadn't taken Margaret Douglas. He went to a lot of trouble to take her away from you. It's possible he cares about her. He might even be fucking her. You could use her to negotiate." He added quickly, "Only a suggestion, sir. Remember those nights when we used to talk about her? I'd be happy to go in that direction. Whatever you decide is fine with me. I took her as a gift to you, an apology. A gesture of good faith to let you know that I'm worth keeping on your payroll."

"And alive?" Nicos added drily. "She's a very persuasive gift, if you're not lying. I want to speak to her. Are you there, Margaret?"

"I'm here. Are you really going to let this weasel back into the fold? He's lied to you before."

"But he's not lying now. I recognize that sweet, barbed voice of yours. And I believe I might enjoy Brukman's presence for the foreseeable future. He has such talent, and he's going to be very busy once Salva and I get down there. I'll see you soon, Margaret."

"You see? I didn't lie to you," Brukman said. "She'll be down here waiting for you. How do you want to handle it?"

"Salva said you're out in the rain forest. You're right: She'll be waiting for me, but I want her in the proper place. Take her to the detention camp."

Margaret felt a chill go through her. That place of death and torture that had been a nightmare of despair for Patrick.

"You're not talking, Margaret," Nicos said mockingly. "Evidently, you were sympathetic about Patrick's time there. Don't you want to taste it for yourself?"

"You'll do what you want. But it wouldn't be smart to surrender what I can give you in pure economic terms just to experience a little sick excitement."

"It wouldn't be little," he said softly. "Not at all. And I'm beginning to think it will be worth it to show Lassiter that he can't have it his way." He raised his voice. "Brukman, our information is that Lassiter's security team has ten or twelve men at any given time and that they're all top-notch. Are they all down there?"

"I can't give you exact numbers, but that sounds right. And they're not all top-notch, at least not better than I am. I took one out to escape."

"However, we have to assume they're very good, and Mandell is supposed to be extraordinary. But we have twenty-two guards at the detention camp and we can call on more help from our military friends who have been paid so well to protect us." Nicos's voice became suddenly harsh. "How Lassiter was able to walk into that camp and take Patrick is beyond my comprehension. You were totally to blame. If you're going to make amends, you'd better show me you're not the fool you appear to be. First, call Stockton at the camp and have him raid that monastery and get Patrick back. And I want Lassiter, Brukman. I don't care how many men Stockton loses; I want Lassiter."

"He wasn't at the monastery when I left. He drove off yesterday afternoon in one of the monastery's old trucks."

Nicos muttered a curse. "Where did he go?"

"I don't know. It's not as if anyone would answer my questions. Everything I learned was from watching and listening. He might be back by now. Or chasing after me, if he's found out I took the woman." He looked at Margaret. "I could ask her a few questions. It would be my pleasure."

"No, I've been looking forward to being the one to teach Margaret everything she needs to know. You'd take the edge off. As long as I have her, Lassiter will come to me. Just get her to the camp and wait for further orders." He hung up.

Brukman smiled as he got to his feet. "It seems that Nicos doesn't wish to share. But he'll change his mind once he gets involved in the process. He knows I'm an expert."

"And he also thinks you're a fool." She was relieved that Brukman had no knowledge of Lassiter's mission when he'd left the monastery. She had no idea if it had been successful, but it was a dim light at the end of a dark tunnel. "Do you actually think you're going to buy your way back into his good graces?"

"I have a good chance, if I work it right. And I'll work it right." He pulled her to her feet. "Now I'll call Stockton and give him Nicos's orders. And then we'll go visit my home away from home. I didn't find it pleasant, and I'm afraid you'll find it even less so."

Smoke.

Lassiter was fifty miles from the monastery when he saw the gray plumes of smoke rising in the distance. Dawn was breaking and he could make out the heavy gray mist that was hanging over the trees and shrubs of the rain forest.

Shit.

He braked and reached for his phone. It rang before he could punch in the number.

Mandell.

"What the hell is happening?" Lassiter asked. "I see smoke up ahead."

"How about worst-case scenario?" Mandell said grimly. "I'm still on the trail, tracking Brukman and Margaret, but I see the smoke, too. And fifteen minutes ago I got a call from the two men I have staking out the detention camp. The gates opened and a truckload of men poured out of the camp and headed in the direction of the monastery. I've been on the phone ever since, giving orders for evacuation. I don't know how many they were able to get out yet. They didn't have much time."

"Patrick?"

"Cambry took care of getting him and the doctor away when you told me to do it hours ago. He's safe."

"Thank God."

"And we tried to persuade the monks to go then, too. Some of them took off, but there were several still there when I left to go after Margaret. I only hope they were able to get out before Brukman's men from the detention camp got there." He paused. "I told my men at the monastery to get them out and then take off themselves. I took half my guys with me and it would have been a suicide mission to try to fight against those odds."

"You were right." Lassiter's gaze went back to the smoke, which seemed to be thickening with every minute that passed. "They have to be burning the monastery."

"That's my take on it, though I haven't been able to reach any of my men yet." He paused. "But right before I got word about the trucks leaving the detention camp, we ran across Brukman's and Margaret's tracks. Brukman had stopped trying to hide them; he was only interested in moving fast."

At least he knew Margaret was still alive. "What direction?"

"He was doubling back south. I think he's taking her to the detention camp. I've got only the two men on watch there, Lassiter. Once he gets close to the camp, he'll call and get an armed escort to take her in through those gates. We can't stop them."

"I know." And once Margaret was behind those walls, she would be totally at Brukman's disposal. He felt the muscles of his stomach twist at the thought. Visions of the photos he'd been sent of Patrick's torture over these last months were flooding back to him.

Block them.

Think.

"If Brukman started north toward the coast and then turned south back to the camp, it probably means he contacted Nicos and it's on his orders. It won't be totally up to Brukman. It may give us a little time."

"But it also means that Nicos will be on his way down here with enough men to give us big trouble," Mandell said. "And you told me how he feels about Margaret. It's not a good idea to leave her there any longer than we have to."

"Do you think I don't know that?" Lassiter asked harshly. "We've got Estefan's group coming, but in case of any large-scale attack, Nicos's first order will be to kill Margaret; his second will be to kill all the other prisoners. There won't be the surprise factor there would have been before. Nicos knows that I'll try to free Margaret."

"Then what the hell do we do?"

It was the question Lassiter was asking himself. "Negotiate. I don't think it will do any good. But it may buy us time to find a way out of this. Call our helicopter pilot and tell him to get it out of there. That's where Nicos will be flying into and he'll make sure that he sends men there to make it safe for him. And we have to try to find out where Brukman will be keeping her in that camp. You said you'd already located where every one of the other prisoners are being held. Will you still be able to get close enough to the camp to pinpoint where Margaret is?"

"Yes. I had my men fall back when those trucks started rolling through the gates. If they search the area, they won't find anyone. Then I'll go in and position myself again. I'll keep out of the trees and go up to the boulders on the hillside and set up."

"Then that's all we can do right now. I'm going to go to the cave and check on Patrick and then we'll arrange to meet." He started the truck. "And I'll have to call Carlos Estefan and tell him to stop where he is and not continue on to the monastery. Get back to me if you hear anything else."

"Right," Mandell said. "I'll be in touch." He hung up.

Lassiter sat there for a moment.

Get control.

Don't think about anything but how to get her back.

Then he started driving toward the gray haze of smoke in the distance.

Detention Camp
7:35 A.M.

"What do you think of it?" Brukman asked as he pushed Margaret through the wire gates ahead of him. "There's a stench to it, isn't there? At times I scarcely notice it anymore, but I'm sure your delicate sensitivity will pick up on it immediately. What do you think it is?"

Pain. Urine. Blood.

And a dozen other foul smells that made her almost ill. "I don't smell anything."

"Liar." He smiled. "Here comes Stockton." He nodded at the man coming toward them. "He'll be disappointed that he won't be able to work on you right away. He really enjoyed María Estefan. Stockton, this is Margaret Douglas. She's a special friend of Nicos."

"Where do you want her? Shall I chain her to the wall?"

"Oh, no. I think we'll tie her to the post in the center of the yard, as we did María. That way, Nicos will see her as soon as he comes in the gate. A kind of welcome present."

"Should I strip her?"

"No, that first humiliation is a pain in itself for a woman. We won't cheat Nicos." His gaze went to the smoke rising above the trees in the distance. "Did they find Patrick?"

"No, Lassiter must have had warning and gotten him out. We're still searching." He was undoing the belt binding Margaret's wrists. He thrust her against a wooden stake in the middle of the yard and fastened her hands to the manacles in back. "The monks were gone, too. But we killed one of his security team." He smiled at Margaret. "There we are." His hand reached out and stroked her breast. "I suppose that's against the rules, too, Brukman?"

"Yes, you'll get your fill later. But Nicos gets all the firsts." He met Margaret's eyes. "He should be here within a few hours. Think about it. I will." He turned and moved toward the bunkhouse. "I'll see you then, Margaret."

Stockman stared at her for a moment, then shrugged and walked away.

Margaret let out the breath she had been holding. She felt terribly vulnerable bound out here in the middle of this dirt yard. It reminded her of someone prepared to be burned at the stake. She was trying to ignore the guards staring at her. How would she have felt if she'd been stripped naked the way that poor María had been?

It might still happen. Prepare for it.

Remember that no one can hurt you but yourself.

She leaned her head back against the post and closed her eyes so that she wouldn't see the smoke from the burning monastery or the guards staring at her.

Those guards were probably not the only ones looking at her, she reminded herself. Mandell had sent men to keep an eye on what went on within this camp. Lassiter had told her how Mandell had climbed a tree in those woods outside the gates and trained his gun on Brukman. If they had found out that she had been brought here, she had no doubt they would send someone to try to find a way to get her out.

But what could they do? They might not even be able to get near those woods now. Brukman would be extra careful now that he had been targeted once.

And she didn't even know if she wanted anyone that close to the detention camp. Her first thought had been a feeling of hope and reassurance that maybe she wasn't alone after all. But now she realized one of the reasons that Brukman had tied her to this stake in full view of the camp and the woods beyond was that she was displayed like a goat to bait the tiger.

And the tiger was Lassiter.

No!

The rejection was instant and violent in its intensity. She had been standing here looking wildly for someone to save her because she was frightened. But if she accepted that role, it would mean that Lassiter might die, because they were using her to trap him.

Tiger. It was bittersweet that she had even laughingly called Lassiter that when they were making love. That time seemed a hundred years from this moment.

And she would make sure she would not be bait for anyone. She had always watched out for herself, and this was no different. So don't expect to be rescued. Work it out. Use your brains and everything you are.

So stay away, Lassiter. You're right. I have to do everything alone. Now let me do it.

Keep calm.

Block out the fear.

Concentrate.

Close out everything.

I'm prey, being hunted. But I'll never make it easy for them.

Find a way to turn it. . . .

\*   \*   \*

"You made good time." Brukman moved quickly forward to greet Nicos and Salva as they entered the gate. "I have her ready for you." He gestured to Margaret bound to the post. "She must be terrified. She's been standing there with her eyes shut for the past few hours. Weird. But I didn't want to do anything to her until you got here."

"Very smart." Nicos moved toward the post. "Since you've done everything wrong since the moment Lassiter got to you, that's refreshing. What do you think, Salva? Do you think our Margaret is terrified at what's going to happen to her?"

"She should be," Salva said. "But she's your toy. You know her better than I do. However, her reactions are always interesting." He stopped a few yards from the post and called, "Tell me, are you playing possum, Margaret?"

"Hello, Salva." Margaret opened her eyes and saw Nicos directly in front of her and Salva just behind him. It came as no shock. She'd been preparing herself for it. "Why should I keep my eyes open when everything here reminds me of you, Nicos? All the filth and the pain and Brukman, who's as ugly and pitiful as you are. I had better things to—"

Her head snapped back against the post as Nicos's hand whipped forward and backhanded her.

Pain.

Don't show him.

Ignore it.

She stared him in the eye. "As I said, I had better things to do."

"Saying your prayers?" Salva asked mockingly.

"Yes," she said calmly. "But perhaps not the way you mean it." Her eyes never left Nicos. "I needed the strength and wisdom to face you and to get you to free me. Who could I count on to give me those things, Nicos?"

Salva chuckled. "Are you giving him that voodoo bullshit again?"

"Am I, Nicos?" Her voice lowered. "Is it bullshit? What happened in that airport in Montego? Did you ever see the dogs go on the attack like that? I told you I was getting stronger. I don't have to use the dogs. Do you want an enemy killed? I can do it for you. Usually with no evidence of foul play. It takes a little time and concentration, but I can do it. You love the idea of having your private slaves. Remember Rosa? Wouldn't I be the ultimate in what you want?"

"She's playing you, Nicos," Salva said.

"Perhaps," Nicos said softly. "But you're not a good judge. You don't believe what I believe. What I've seen with my own eyes. Of course I find what she's telling me is exciting. And it's true that the dogs had never attacked before. That Lab nearly tore off Ricardo's thumb. He had to go to the emergency room to get his hand stitched."

"It could have been his throat," Margaret said.

Nicos laughed. "And served him right, the fool. He should never have let you get away." His smile faded. "You betrayed me."

"Betrayal didn't enter into it. You were threatening me." Her lips tightened. "Lassiter threatened me, too. He wanted to score off you any way he could. Why do you think he forced me to take that risk in Montego Bay? Why do you think he brought me down here when he knew that there was a good chance I'd be killed? He knew I was valuable to you. He doesn't care about anything or anyone but Patrick."

"Bitterness?" Nicos said. "But I've always known that Patrick was Lassiter's Achilles' heel. You couldn't compete."

"I didn't want to compete. I wanted to be left alone by all of you," she said. "But here I am back with you, Nicos. And I'm going to stay alive any way I can. So what do you want from me? Do you want me to take you to where Patrick is hiding?"

"Do you know?"

"Not for sure. But I could probably find him. No, I'm certain I can find him." Her gaze shifted to Salva. "Or perhaps you'd like to test me? I can see how intrigued you are at the idea of lifting your finger and somebody dying. Who shall it be? Salva? He's always annoyed you a bit." Her gaze swung to Brukman. "And you'll never trust Brukman again. It would probably happen anyway. Which one?"

Brukman began swearing, but Salva's expression didn't change.

"Tempting." Nicos smiled. "But you were always tempting in so many ways, Margaret. This one, I admit, is more intriguing than usual."

"Think about it," Margaret said. "I'm at your disposal. No promises. I know you'd never believe them. But do you believe anyone? All you care about is power, and as long as you control me, you'll have the power. Test me. Let me show you."

"I will think about it." He tilted his head. "But what may be more tempting is what Brukman is so good at." He reached out and his hand closed on her breast. "I've been thinking about it all the way down here." His hand tightened with bruising force.

Pain.

Don't stiffen. Don't scream. No expression.

He was waiting for it, watching for it.

And he was clearly disappointed. His hand released her. "But perhaps I can have both."

She shook her head. "Concentration is everything, Nicos. You'd distract me. You'd be cheating yourself."

"I'll take over." Brukman had stepped forward. "Let me do it, Nicos. You'll like it. I promise."

"Are you frightened, Brukman?" Nicos smiled maliciously. "I think you are. I find that amusing. Go ahead and chain her with the others."

"You're believing her lies?" Salva asked.

"You're nervous, too, Salva? When we've been together so long?" Nicos said. "She's eager to prove herself to me. She said she might be able to find Patrick. As for the other, I think that a risk always stimulates competition. It won't hurt to have a threat hanging over both of you until I decide what I'm going to do with her." He turned away. "And it won't hurt to have a threat hanging over her. She may appear cool, but there's always fear."

"Test me," Margaret said again. She looked between Salva and Brukman again. "You know you want to do it, Nicos."

"I'll see you in a little while, Margaret." Nicos glanced at Brukman. "Don't kill her, and tell me if she tries to escape." He smiled slyly as he headed for the bunkhouse with Salva following. "After all, Salva will tell you that she's not really a priestess with black powers, and that her threats mean absolutely nothing, won't you, Salva?"

Margaret could hear Brukman cursing as he undid her manacles. Her legs were feeling weak and she had to make an effort to keep her face without expression. Any show of weakness to any of them would be dangerous right now. They were men who would take advantage of any sign that she could be easily taken down.

She knew Nicos had been swayed by her words, but he was volatile and could waver and turn back at any moment.

"I know it's all bullshit," Brukman said sourly as he pushed her ahead of him. "But it will be worse for you if you don't shut up about me. I don't need Nicos getting any ideas right now that aren't absolutely positive."

"What could be worse for me than what you intend now?" she asked. "And Nicos doesn't think it's bullshit." She looked at him over her shoulder and murmured, "You won't either if he chooses you. . . ."

"Bitch!"

She smothered a cry as Brukman twisted her arm as he fastened her wrists to the manacles next to the other three prisoners chained to the long concrete wall. Then he stepped back and looked down at her. "Do you feel helpless? That's what you are. If Nicos gives me two days with you, you'll be begging me for forgiveness for that twisted tongue." He glanced at the man chained next to her. "Tell her, Estefan."

He turned on his heel and strode away.

Margaret drew a deep breath. She *did* feel helpless. Somehow being chained here to this wall next to these pitifully emaciated prisoners was different from being bound on that stake in the center of the yard.

"Kill . . . yourself."

Her gaze flew to the man chained next to her. He might have been young or old; she couldn't tell his age. Deep lines of suffering were carved on his face under the long shock of dark hair. His skeletal frame was almost naked and the wounds were raw and bleeding over the entire surface of his body. "You're Diego Estefan?"

"Kill . . . yourself," he repeated hoarsely. "I saw Nicos hit you. . . . It's starting . . . again. Find a way."

She could feel his pain, but it was dulled by despair. That, along with the fact that she had never had a chance to get to know him, were the only things that allowed her not to be drawn into his agony. It took her a moment, but she managed to block it. "We're going to help you," she whispered. "I promise you."

He shook his head. "Find . . . a way. My wife was screaming at me to make them kill her before she died. I couldn't . . . do it. I could only watch."

The tears filled her eyes. "I'm so sorry."

He closed his eyes. "Don't be sorry. Just don't let them do . . . that to you."

"I won't. And I won't let them hurt the rest of you, either." She could see he didn't believe her. How could he when she appeared as helpless as the rest of them chained to this damn wall?

So don't think about feeling helpless. Think about being strong.

Concentrate.

Reach out. . . .

# CHAPTER SEVENTEEN

Mandell had Brukman squarely in his sights.

One slight pressure on the hair trigger of his rifle and the son of a bitch's head would blow off his body.

*I've got him, Dietrich.*

Just not right now, he thought regretfully.

He took out his phone and called Lassiter at the cave, where he was still with Patrick. "Nicos and Salva arrived here thirty minutes ago."

"Margaret?"

"She's here. Brukman had her tied to a post in the middle of the yard of the camp. But when Nicos and Salva arrived and talked to her, Brukman took the cuffs off her and then took her away somewhere."

"Dammit, where?"

"I couldn't tell. It was out of my field of vision. But Nicos and Salva went in another direction." He paused. "She might be safe for a while, Lassiter. Brukman didn't allow her to be touched during the time they were waiting for Nicos."

"And when Nicos showed up?"

"Nicos only hit her once when they were talking."

Lassiter swore beneath his breath. "And you still think she might be okay?"

"For a while. It could be a delicate balance."

"What the hell are you talking about?"

"I don't know. I couldn't hear what they were saying. But the body language was an interesting dynamic. Margaret was doing the majority of the talking and Brukman and Salva appeared to be on the defensive. And at the end of the conversation, Nicos must have given the order to take her off that stake. Maybe Margaret talked herself out of something? Or a delay at least. What do you think?"

"That I'm scared shitless." He didn't speak for an instant. "And that Margaret isn't going to wait for us to try for a rescue. She's a loner. She's doesn't really trust anyone but herself, and she's probably already got a plan in place to get herself away from Nicos."

Mandell gave a low whistle. "That's pretty impressive. I applaud the thought, but she could get in our way."

"Or we could get in hers."

"Either way, it might spell disaster." Mandell paused. "I came close to trying to take out Brukman a few minutes ago. It was very tempting. But I'm too far away up here in these boulders. It would take a miracle shot. And I knew, even if I made it, that it would cause the camp to explode and it might get Margaret killed. I can't take out Brukman without taking out Nicos and Salva. If we take out all three, then there's no one to give the orders or pay the salaries. The entire structure of Nicos's world would crumble."

"Exactly. And I'm thinking . . ." Lassiter was silent a moment. "About body language. I'd bet Margaret would have figured that out, too. Brukman and Salva both on the defensive . . ."

"Is she really that good?"

"Oh, yes. What she did in Montego Bay was just the tip of the iceberg." He was silent again, thinking. "Whatever she's planning, she'll probably try to do it by herself. I can't let her do that. I have to get an idea of what she's doing and make sure she knows we're there for her."

"Good thought. Difficult execution. How are you going to do it?"

"Damned if I know. As I said before, we have to start with negotiation. I'll give Nicos a little more time and then give him a call."

"Open your eyes, Margaret. Salva says you're trying to freak me out."

Nicos. She'd been expecting him sooner, but he'd given her at least four hours since he'd had Brukman take her down from that stake.

She opened her lids and straightened away from where she'd been leaning on the wall. She smiled at Salva, who was standing a few yards behind Nicos. "Don't believe him. It takes concentration to gather power. I have to close everything else out to do it. And it seems as if you're the one who's being freaked out, Salva." She looked at Nicos. "Nicos doesn't seem to be frightened." She studied him. "On the contrary, I believe he's excited. Have you been thinking about which one you're going to choose, Nicos?"

"Shut her up," Salva said. "Can't you see she's playing you?"

Nicos chuckled. "Don't worry, I'm not going to have her cast a spell to turn you into an anaconda." He tilted his head. "Could you do that, Margaret?"

"Not yet. I've been devoting my time to the death spells. I thought that would be more beneficial for you and might help me to survive. But we might be able to make him into a zombie."

Nicos laughed again. "Do you hear that, Salva?"

"I heard it," he said sourly. "I'm not amused."

"But I am. Now why would I want you to rid me of a fine, loyal friend like Salva, Margaret?"

She only looked at him.

Nicos shook his head. "She believes I don't appreciate you, Salva. She could be right." His smile faded. "But enough of this. It's Patrick I need to find and take away from Lassiter. You said that you might be able to figure out where Lassiter has hidden Patrick. Where is it?"

"What do I get in return?"

"I don't have to give you anything, Margaret. Your position is vulnerable in the extreme. Brukman is very eager to make you talk. Even more so, since you targeted him earlier."

"And you wouldn't find out anything no matter what he did to me. I've never actually seen the safe haven where Lassiter was going to hide Patrick. It's a cave in the hills someplace and Lassiter didn't trust anyone with the location. Certainly not me." She added bitterly, "Patrick is the only one who's important to him. Lassiter took me as far as the river that runs through the hills and I had to wait there for him. But I could take you that far and, if you give me a chance, I'll track him the rest of the way."

"Or we might be able to find him ourselves."

"I grew up in the woods. I'm a great tracker. I tell you, I can find Patrick." She met Nicos's eyes. "And if Lassiter is with him, you'll get him, too."

"Or be ambushed. We know that Mandell has a small but lethal force."

"Then take a larger force with you." She glanced around the compound. "You seem to have plenty of men. Take Brukman and a dozen or so others along if you're afraid of Lassiter and Mandell."

"Was that supposed to be a taunt?" Nicos's hand

reached down and grasped her throat. "I won't tolerate that kind of behavior, Margaret." His grasp tightened to bruising force. "You're only alive because I'm feeling generous and you made me an offer that intrigued me."

"It wasn't a taunt." Margaret swallowed and could barely get the words out. "I wouldn't . . . be that stupid. I told you, I need to survive. No matter who else you manage to destroy, I'm going to live."

"You don't need her," Salva said. "You're a fool for letting her live this long."

Nicos stiffened. "A fool?"

Salva caught himself. "Just a suggestion. As I said, she's playing you. I didn't mean anything by it."

"No, of course you didn't mean it." Nicos released her throat. "And you wouldn't have been so careless if she hadn't made you nervous. I understand, Salva." He watched Margaret coughing and struggling for breath. "But she's only a woman who wants to live, nothing to scare you. I tend to believe—" His phone rang and he looked down at the ID. "But I may not need her." He smiled. "Let's see what kind of offer I can get from Lassiter himself." He pressed the access and put the phone on speaker. "Hello, Lassiter. Do you want surrender terms? I'm afraid they would involve my turning you over to Brukman, and he's very angry with you at the moment."

"No surrender," Lassiter said curtly. "But I might want to negotiate. You have Margaret Douglas, and I feel bound to offer to ransom her out of this hellish situation. I pulled her into our battle because I knew she was a card I could play against you. Her usefulness is over and I don't want to get her killed."

"A little late, Lassiter," Nicos said. "As you say, her usefulness is over for both of us. Unless I choose to take her up on an offer that I find interesting. But you do have another card to play. Give me back Sean Patrick and I might call my men off and let you live. From what Brukman tells me, Patrick's almost dead anyway."

"Then why do you want him?"

"I don't like to lose. I need to finish him."

"The hell you do. No deal. But the offer is still on the table for Margaret. What's your price?"

"She tells me she has a talent that's beyond price. I might have to explore it."

"Everything has a price. Except my friend Patrick. Think about it. I'd be very generous."

"Was she that good?"

"I owe her. For God's sake, I practically destroyed her life." He paused. "Are you lying? Is she even still alive?"

"She's alive."

"Let me talk to her."

Nicos glanced at Margaret. "He wants to make certain you're still alive. It appears he's more concerned about you than you are about him."

"Why shouldn't he be?" she asked bitterly. "I never did anything to hurt him. He's right: He practically destroyed my life. I was free of you and had friends and a job I loved. Then he decided he could use me to get you, and that was the end of all of it."

"I said that I regretted it, Margaret," Lassiter said quietly. "I'm trying to get you out of there."

"I don't believe you. You forced me to mess up that job in Montego. You didn't care what would happen to me. Then you flew me down here in case you might need to use me against Nicos again." She added passionately, "I begged you to send me back to San Diego. Now you're saying you want to ransom me? Nicos is right: It's too late. You almost got me killed, Lassiter."

She could feel his shock as he digested her words. "That's all true," he said slowly. "But what can I do to make it right?"

"You've already tried to do that. You tossed that

diamond necklace at me after you jerked me on the plane and brought me down here. All you think about is money. Did you think all those sparkling rosettes would be worth the risk to me? I know what Nicos can do. You chose Patrick over me from the beginning, and nothing will make up for that." She added wearily, "Now leave me alone, Lassiter. I'm done with you. I've watched what Nicos does to women who go against him. That's not going to be me."

Nicos laughed. "Satisfied, Lassiter? I believe she's proved she's alive and well . . . so far."

"And I'm tempted to let you keep the ungrateful bitch," Lassiter said. "But I still owe her. The offer still stands. I'll put together a proposition. When you decide you want to talk about it, call me." He hung up.

"I told you he didn't care about anyone but Patrick," she said jerkily. "I thought for a while that he might let me go after I got away in Montego. But he wanted an insurance policy and that's all I was to him."

"How sad . . ."

"Spare me your sarcasm. All I want is for you to let me live and show you how valuable I can be," she said, then added fiercely, "Salva may think you're a fool, but I know better."

"I didn't exactly say that I—" Salva began.

But she interrupted him. "You wouldn't be where you are if you weren't able to pull all the strings, Nicos. Let me help you to do that."

Nicos stared thoughtfully at her.

"I'll think about it. There's a chance that my treatment of Rosa did have an effect on you. I could see you start to weaken when I was doing it. It might have made you more compliant."

She met his eyes. "It had a great effect on me."

He nodded slowly. "As I said, I'll think about it." He smiled. "It would be amusing to have Patrick taken away from Lassiter by the woman he brought in to help save him. I rather like the idea."

He turned on his heel and strode away.

Salva gave Margaret a cold glance before following Nicos across the yard.

Margaret let out her breath and slid down the wall to a sitting position again. A fairly successful several minutes, she thought shakily.

Another encounter with only minor physical pain.

Contact made with Lassiter.

Message given without suspicion.

Progress had been made.

If Lassiter had caught and understood every nuance of what she'd said to him.

"That didn't sound like Margaret." Cambry had come out of the cave and was standing behind Lassiter, with Juno beside him. "Bitter. Very bitter. And not much truth connected to it. What's that son of a bitch doing to her?"

"It may be what she's trying to do to him," Lassiter said grimly. "And, no, not much truth. She practically forced me to bring her down here to help Patrick. Certainly no bribes involved. Everything she said just now was slanted to make both me and Patrick appear to be her enemy."

"Desperation? She knows what Nicos might do to her."

He shook his head. "Mandell said he thought she was more aggressor than victim." He added roughly, "And I don't know what the hell she's doing. I've got to go over that entire phone conversation and see if she was trying to tell me something. I can't just wait and hope that it's not going make Nicos angry enough to cut her throat."

"No, waiting isn't one of your strengths."

And it's nearly impossible when it concerns Margaret, Lassiter thought. "At least I've got Mandell keeping watch on the camp. If the situation changes with her, I'll just have to change with it." He took out his phone and said grimly, "Right now I've got to keep Carlos Estefan from making a few changes of his own. He insisted on moving his rebels into the woods behind the detention camp and he's clamoring to go in and get his brother. If he launches an assault, it could not only get his brother, Diego, killed but Margaret, too."

Cambry gave a low whistle. "Can you keep him under control?"

"I'll do it. I've got to do it. God knows how." He was dialing his phone. "Because I seem to be doing crap in controlling anything else at the moment."

Detention Camp
10:37 P.M.

"Get up, Margaret," Nicos said. "Are you dozing? Or are you doing that concentration thing again?" He knelt down beside her and she could see he was smiling mockingly. "At any rate, you have work to do."

She scrambled to sit up straight. Work. That meant he wasn't going to start the torture and that she had a chance. "I was dozing. I admit I was getting bored. I was hoping you'd make up your mind." She looked beyond his shoulder and saw the camp stirring, the glaring lights coming on, men streaming out of the bunkhouse. "Where's Salva?"

"He's changing to boots and the same camouflage attire I'm wearing. I told him he had to prepare for anything. He was a bit surly. He doesn't really like to hunt. He's much more comfortable behind a computer in his office."

"Hunt?"

"Why, yes. You promised me a Patrick hunt. With perhaps Lassiter thrown in for good measure. I thought all evening about that possibility. I listened to all Salva's and Brukman's arguments." He chuckled. "Both of them had interesting alternate plans for you involving pain and humiliation. But in the end, they couldn't offer me what you did." His eyes were glittering with excitement as he gestured to the noise and activity around them. "Patrick, Lassiter . . ." His voice lowered silkily, "And the victim of my choice. I couldn't get your proposition out of my mind. I thought this would be a wonderful opportunity for your test, Margaret."

"That doesn't surprise me. Murder always intrigues you," she said. "And whom did you choose? Salva or Brukman?"

"Salva. Remember? He called me a fool. He picked the wrong time to do that, didn't he?"

"It seems that he did."

"And you'll use your magic to take care of him." He jerked her to her feet. "No gun. No knife. That would be no test at all." He shoved her toward the truck parked beside the gate. "Prove yourself to me, Margaret. Because only one of you will be coming back here tonight."

"They're on the move, Lassiter," Mandell said sharply as Lassiter answered the phone. "Nicos, Salva, and Margaret just rolled out of here in a truck driven by Herb Stockton, with twelve of Nicos's guards in the back. They left only Brukman to run the show back here at the camp. They have automatic weapons. Traveling fast."

"Toward the monastery?"

"No, they took the road that circles around that area." He paused. "I think they're heading for the hills. You might consider moving Patrick out of there fast. She could be leading them straight to you."

"She wouldn't do that, dammit."

"They're on their way. In twenty minutes, they'll

reach the road leading to the hills. I'll let you know if they turn back." He cut the connection.

"Twenty minutes," Cambry said. "You're sure we shouldn't be getting out of here, Lassiter? I could tell the sentries guarding the cave to start packing up."

"I'm sure. Margaret wouldn't turn Patrick over to Nicos." But Lassiter didn't know what the hell she *was* doing or what was happening. "But Mandell is sure she's definitely heading for the hills." Why would she even get near to a place where Nicos might stumble across Patrick? Had she said anything in that conversation that had anything to do with her bringing Nicos out in these wilds in the middle of the night? Lassiter had gone over her words before and there had been something. . . .

He quickly again went over every word she had spoken. For the most part, it had just been accusations and telling him to leave her—

Untrue accusations.

*Sparkling rosettes . . .*

*You tossed that diamond necklace at me.*

*Rosettes.*

He whirled and stared at the dark hills to the north. "She's not bringing them here. She's taking them to the north hills."

"What?"

"Get our sentries up there right away to welcome Nicos's men when they start crawling all over those hills looking for Patrick. If they position themselves right, they should be able to pick them off."

"Right. Then I'll go with them."

"No, you won't. I'm on my way." He was heading for the van hidden in the bushes. "Someone has to be here to guard Patrick and Dr. Armando. You and Juno are elected."

"No election about it," Cambry grumbled. "How do you know that she's heading for the north hills?"

"Rosettes. She said that diamond necklace had rosettes." He jumped in the driver's seat. "There was no diamond necklace and the only time Margaret ever mentioned rosettes to me was when she was telling me that jaguars don't have spots, they have rosettes." He started the car. "And the only jaguars in the area live in those north hills. She's giving us a chance to take down Nicos and Salva."

And that isn't all she is giving us, he thought suddenly.

He called Mandell. "I know where she's going. It's the north hills area and she's laying a false trail to Patrick. And it's not going to be another twenty minutes; it will be thirty. That means once they've reached there and started the hunt, it would take them at least forty-five minutes to an hour to get back to the detention camp if they get an alert from Brukman." He paused. "Enough time for you?"

"No problem. I have only four of our guys in the area, but you said Carlos Estefan was champing at the bit." Mandell was quickly calculating. "Brukman and eleven of his men still in the camp. You said Estefan's group has thirty-seven. Of course, there's the hostage card that Brukman could play, but I think I can get around it."

"You'll have to get around it. I promised Carlos we'd get his brother out safely. One of the first things Brukman will do is kill the prisoners if he can't negotiate for them." And he didn't know what price Margaret might have to pay if anything went wrong. "Set it up. But don't move until I call and tell you that it will be safe for Margaret. She's going to have to contend with Nicos *and* Salva, and I can see Nicos exploding if he hears about an attack on the camp."

"Then you know the solution," Mandell said softly. "We discussed it before. Remove the threat. Not one. Not two. But all three."

"You don't have to remind me. I'm on my way there now." He hung up.

Yes, he knew the solution. He just hoped he'd get to those hills in time.

"You're very quiet," Salva said. "Not a word since we left the camp, Margaret. Are you having second thoughts about turning over Patrick to us?" He smiled. "I wouldn't suggest that you pay any attention to them. Nicos isn't going to be pleased when he realizes what a fake you are anyway. But to compound it by not giving him Patrick and Lassiter would be truly fatal. Isn't that right, Nicos?"

"Stop baiting her, Salva," Nicos said. "Perhaps she was quiet because she had to focus her attention and power. If so, I understand and approve."

"No second thoughts," Margaret said. "I didn't think I had to chat or amuse either of you." She looked out at the darkness beyond the window of the truck as it bounced over the rutted road. "But I guess I did have to focus my attention on something other than what's waiting at the end of this road. I know neither one of you have any trouble with betrayal, but I've never done it before. I'm not looking forward to turning Patrick over to you again. So if you don't mind, I'll ignore both of you until I have to show you how to get to them."

She thought it sounded plausible and she didn't care if they minded or not. She had only a few more minutes to concentrate, and this was a crucial period.

*Sticks.*

She had to think about the sticks.

She began to focus again.

"Here we are." Stockton stopped the vehicle ten minutes later beside the river, jumped out from behind the wheel, and turned to Nicos. "Your orders, sir?"

"Get the men into the woods," Nicos said. "No noise. Don't use the flashlights unless necessary. We don't know what we're going to find. We're on a hunt, Stockton." He watched Margaret jump down from the truck. "And here's the woman who's going to lead us to Patrick."

"I'll need a flashlight." Margaret said. "I won't be able to track if I can't see."

"Very true." He handed her a flashlight. "Salva, why don't you go with Margaret and help her to get started? I know I can trust you not to let her slip away. I'll be along once I make sure Stockton has the men doing what I need them to do."

"I won't take my eyes off her," Salva said grimly. "And neither should you. This may be a wild-goose chase."

"Then she'll die." Nicos smiled. "But I have to give Margaret her chance. We've known each other so long." He turned and watched Stockton and the men scattering along the river and into the brush. "I'm feeling very sentimental toward her. Just as I am toward you, Salva."

"Come on." Salva grabbed Margaret's elbow and pushed her down the trail. "Let's get this over with. I don't like it when Nicos is in this mood. He's too unpredictable."

"Dammit to hell." Lassiter jumped out of the van, his gaze on the north hills. He could see the gleam of a few flashlights dotting the darkness, and the truck beside the river was unoccupied. He called Mandell back. "I got here too late. Everyone has scattered up into the hills. I was hoping to be here to take out Nicos and Salva when they arrived, but I'll have to go after them."

"Does that mean we have to wait?"

"Not if you move fast. Even if Brukman calls Nicos for help, you'll still have that hour before any reinforcements from here can get back to the camp." He paused. "But I don't want Brukman to make that call before I take down Nicos. You know what Nicos's first order would be."

"Kill all prisoners," Mandell said grimly. "So he won't make the call." He hung up.

Lassiter shoved his phone in his pocket and moved quickly down the riverbank. Mandell had jokingly said that any decent shot from the rocks where he was hiding would be a miracle shot. Now he was going to have to make that shot. Could he do it?

Lassiter couldn't worry about that right now. Margaret was in that forest with two men who wouldn't hesitate to kill her once they discovered that she had lied to them. He had to track them down and get rid of them once and for all.

And that meant he had his own miracle to perform.

Brukman was frowning as he stood talking to one of the guards in the center of the yard.

What a shame the son of a bitch is so unhappy during the last minute of his life, Mandell thought.

He lined up the shot.

Then he adjusted for wind two-thirds down the way to the target, as he always did.

Now clear your mind of anything but the shot itself.

Imagine every step, from pressing the trigger to watching the bullet striking Brukman.

Cool. Precise. Calm.

It would have to be an incredible shot, as he'd told Lassiter, but that didn't mean he couldn't do it. He'd done one almost this difficult five years ago in Afghanistan.

And the motivation had not been nearly this strong.

"Here we go, Dietrich," he murmured. "You might

help a little, if you can. I called Carlos Estefan and told him that he should launch the attack the minute they hear the shot. I'd hate to have egg on my face if I screw up."

Dietrich. Patrick. All those other poor bastards who had been tortured by the man in his sights.

No way was he going to screw up.

He pressed the trigger.

*Yes!*

# CHAPTER EIGHTEEN

"What do you think you're doing?" Salva asked Margaret as he stopped on the trail. "You've been winding in and out of these trails for the last twenty minutes and you've come up with zilch. You tried to convince Nicos that you could track Lassiter. Now do it, or I'll call Nicos and tell him you were bullshitting him."

"And get myself killed?" Margaret stopped on the trail and aimed the beam of her flashlight at Salva's face. "That wouldn't be smart, would it?"

"It's going to end up like that anyway." He smiled. "We both know that you'll be able to fool Nicos for only so long. He's not overly bright, but he has a wonderful sense of self-preservation and a certain cunning. But I admit it was clever of you to try to turn his venom on Brukman and me."

"Try? How do you know I didn't do it?"

"Brukman feeds his bloodlust. And I've made sure that Nicos knows that he needs me to survive." He added mockingly, "Self-preservation, Margaret."

"But you ignored his one characteristic that gives me a chance: ego." She tilted her head, listening. Faint. Very faint. Perhaps . . . "I've noticed you've made that mistake before."

"And when he finds out that you've fooled him, his ego will have him burning you at the stake back at the detention camp. We both know that you have no magic and you're not going to find any tracks."

"There's magic, and then there's magic." She started back down the trail and shifted the beam of her flashlight on the rutted earth before them. "And I know it will disappoint you, but I'm very good at tracking. In fact, I've already found the track I was looking for."

He stepped closer, his gaze on the ground. "You're bluffing. I don't see any—" Then he saw the fresh print Margaret was looking at. "Shit!"

No perhaps this time.

Not faint at all.

He was here.

Now!

*This is my gift?*

*Yes. As I promised you. To seal our friendship. Not worthy, but it should please you.*

A moment of appraisal and assessment.

*It will do.*

The jaguar leaped out of the darkness at the side of the trail!

Salva screamed as the big cat took him down. He struggled desperately to get out his gun.

Margaret warned the jaguar again, as she had when she had linked with him driving here. *The sticks!*

It had been the only term she could think of to describe the danger of a gun to an animal who had never seen one.

But he remembered and acted with lethal ferocity.

The jaguar's strong jaws clamped down on Salva's wrist and shattered it. The gun fell from his useless hand.

Then the jaguar went for his head.

*Crunch!*

Salva went limp.

Margaret was gazing down at that crushed, bloody head. She thought she would feel horror and she did, but it had nothing to do with Salva's death. Salva was a horror in himself and deserved it. Block it. Someone might have heard that scream, and she had to protect the jaguar.

*Go. Take him and go.*

*Of course, I always do.* The jaguar was dragging Salva's body toward the trees. *Too many thieves in the forest to take what's mine. I will take him up high until I finish with him. You will bring me other gifts?*

*I don't know. Only if the gift is true prey.*

*I will be happy to see you. . . .*

And the jaguar was gone.

She knelt there on the trail, shaking. It had been so fast, so violent, that she had barely had a chance to realize what was happening.

No, it had not "happened"; I've done this, Margaret thought. Don't blame fate, when I planned and worked to make this occur. Get over the shock and horror and accept it. Salva had been almost as bad as Nicos. He had killed and made all the evil happen. He had stood by and watched Nicos torture Rosa. How many little girls had he brought to Nicos to curry favor? She reached out and touched a streak of blood on the path. Not much blood. It had all been too quick.

And then Salva was gone.

And she still couldn't stop shaking.

"Very good, Margaret."

Her head jerked up and she saw Nicos standing behind her in the middle of the path. "You saw it?"

He nodded. "I was right behind you. But I would have come running anyway when I heard Salva scream. It was quite bone-chilling." He came toward her. "I gave you the opportunity and you took it. A wonderful demonstration. No guns. No knives. Just pure power . . . The big cats are so much more effective than dogs, aren't they?"

There was something in the way he was looking at her . . . .

She got to her knees, her hands clenching into fists at her sides. "What's wrong?" she asked warily. "I did what you said you wanted."

"What's wrong?" He smiled as he stopped before her. "As I said, a wonderful demonstration. But you can hardly pull a jaguar out of your hat on every occasion. What good would you be if I needed someone eliminated in downtown Miami or Bogotá? What would you do then?"

She met his gaze. "I'd find a way to do what I had to do."

"I believe you." He reached into his jacket and pulled out his gun. "You have power and intelligence, and what you did to Salva was something of an eye-opener. I didn't expect to feel that shocked. You were just a tool. But I watched that jaguar tear into him and it made me realize that it could have been me. Unexpected. Out of the darkness. No warning."

He was going to kill her.

She could see it in his face. It was the same wild, intense expression she'd seen in those moments before he'd shot Rosa.

"But it wasn't you," she said quickly. "I only got rid of the man you told me to kill. You're being unreasonable."

"Am I? Somehow I don't think so. I could keep you as a pet, leash you, think I was safe from you. But you're not like anyone else. And someday there might be a moment like the one Salva just had. A monster attacking out of the darkness." He raised the gun. "So I need to make certain that day never comes."

Think.

Stop him from pulling that trigger.

Keep him talking.

Don't let this end without keeping my promise to Rosa.

Find a way to take him off guard.

"You're right. It could end that way. You're very clever to realize that I'll always be a threat to you." She moistened her lips. "Do you know, I wasn't certain who was going to be the victim tonight. You gave me two possible choices, but you were always in the running. I had several scenarios mapped out and you figured in most of them."

He was listening. Good. Maybe he wouldn't pull that trigger as long as she kept his mind occupied.

"Too bad they'll all go to waste," he said. "You didn't have a chance of taking me down, Margaret. Not from the time I took you and Rosa from her home in Guatemala."

"I had a chance and I took it. I couldn't do anything else. I promised Rosa." She met his eyes. "I brought her spirit back, you know. She was in such torment that it was easy for me. Who do you think helped me to escape you all these years?"

His eyes widened. "You're lying."

"*She* helped me. She's still helping me tonight. She remembers what you did to her." Her glance shifted to a point beyond Nicos's shoulders. "As I got stronger, so did Rosa. Don't you feel her? You should. She's right there behind you. Move a little closer to him, Rosa."

Her gaze shifted back to Nicos. His eyes were glittering with fear, the muscles of his body rigid. "She's going to touch the back of your neck," she said softly. "When I count to three, you'll feel her."

"There's no one there," he said hoarsely, looking straight ahead.

"Why don't you believe me? You know what I can do. *She'll* make you believe me. She's been waiting for this." She started to count. "One. She's moving nearer. . . . Two." She could see the sweat break out on his forehead. She gathered her muscles. "Three!"

He flinched and involuntarily half-turned his head to look behind him.

Margaret picked up the flashlight on the ground in front of her and hurled it at him! She rolled into the shrubs at the side of the trail.

She heard him swear as she jumped to her feet and started running through the forest.

A bullet splintered the wood of the palm tree next to her head.

He was shooting!

She saw the beam of his flashlight bouncing off the glossy foliage in front of her. He had light to see her and she had only darkness.

It would have to be enough. Use her mind and her senses. It was not a forest she knew, but if she opened herself, if she listened, the woods would help her as they'd done before. She started to zigzag through the trees.

Another bullet whistled by her cheek.

Head for the river. The river could save her.

*Pain.*

She stumbled against a tree and held on as the shock wave hit her. She'd felt the agony of the bullet entering her shoulder before she'd heard the sound of the bullet.

"Got you!"

She heard Nicos's triumphant yell and the crashing in the brush beside her.

It jarred her out of the trauma of pain and shock and sent her running again.

She felt the blood running down from the wound in her shoulder.

She could hear the sound of the river now.

Keep moving.

Ignore the pain.

More shots.

She was the prey. But if she could get to the river, that would change.

She was getting weaker.

Another bullet . . . close.

"Stop . . . you bitch," Nicos called. "Give it up. I know I hit you. You're probably bleeding out."

But the river was right ahead.

And she would no longer be prey.

Nicos was very close.

Too close.

Faster.

She had to go faster.

"You're slowing down," Nicos shouted mockingly. "I told you that I—" He screamed in pain. "Son of a bitch!"

"Down!" Lassiter was suddenly beside Margaret. "I only got a glancing shot at him. I was afraid not to take it when he was talking about you bleeding out." His gaze was searching the darkness. "But I hear that bastard still running. Keep down and I'll go back and finish him."

Or Nicos could finish Lassiter.

"No." She shook her head dazedly. "The river. I have to get to the river."

She was running again.

Lassiter muttered an oath and then he was running beside her, his arm around her waist, taking her weight.

The river was only yards away.

Then she broke away from him. She was in the water, wading out in the fast-moving current. Then she started swimming toward the middle of the river. Safe distance. Had to get to safe distance . . .

But where was Lassiter? He had to be safe, too. "Lassiter!"

"Margaret, dammit, you're crazy. You'll drown with that wound." Lassiter had jumped into the water and was swimming out to her. "Or Nicos will be able to pick—"

"Be quiet!" She closed her eyes for an instant. She had to hold on. She had to reach out. But she was so dizzy. . . .

*Here. Safe. River.*

"Margaret!" Nicos burst out of the brush, his eyes blazing, blood flowing from the wound in his side. He stopped short at the edge of the bank. "You thought you'd get away by jumping into the river? You must have been desperate." His face twisted with malicious pleasure. "You, too, Lassiter? My lucky day." He started to raise his gun. "And then I'll go hunt down Patrick. Think about that when I send you both to—"

"I'm not desperate," Margaret called out. "We just had to get in the river because I was afraid there would be confusion." She met Nicos's eyes across the water. "The river was a good meeting place, but I wasn't able to spend as much time with her. She might not have known which was friend and which was gift."

"What are you talking about?" Nicos was scowling. "Meeting place? More bullshit about Rosa? I won't be fooled like that again. You'll have to—" Then he went still as the realization hit him. "Not . . . Rosa?"

"Did I forget to mention that the jaguar who took down Salva has a mate?" Margaret asked. "It didn't seem fair to give him a gift and forget about his mate when she has a cub to feed. She's very hungry. Do you hear her moving through the brush toward you? Remember what you said?" She quoted softly, " 'A monster attacking out of the darkness.' But she's not the monster. *You* are, Nicos. I'm looking at her more as an avenging sword in Rosa's hand."

"You crazy bitch." He swung toward the brush and started firing wildly.

Everything was getting dim, Margaret realized. She had to hold on. It wasn't finished.

"Margaret." Lassiter was there for her, his hand supporting her waist.

He wouldn't let her fall. He would help her get through it.

"Or she might be in the trees above you, Nicos." She kept her voice steady with an effort. "Jaguars are very agile. And they swim very well. There's nowhere you can go that she can't follow."

"You can't *do* this to me." He kept firing and backing toward the river.

Then the word that Margaret had been waiting for came out of the darkness.

*Gift?*

Rosa looking up at Nicos and pleading for her life. Begging for mercy, when there was no mercy in her world.

*Oh, yes. Gift.*

She saw the flash of gold and black as the jaguar streaked in lethal beauty toward Nicos.

She heard him scream in agony before the darkness overwhelmed her.

She opened her eyes as Lassiter was putting her into the van and fastening the seat belt.

She was shivering.

Wet.

"Cold," she muttered. "So cold . . ."

"I know." He took off his jacket and wrapped it around her. Then he ran around to the driver's seat. "You lost a lot of blood and then jumped in that damn river. I think I've got the bleeding stopped, but I've got to get you to the cave and have Dr. Armando take a look at you." He started the van and stomped on the accelerator. The van skittered on the rough ground. "You knew I'd be coming to help you. Why didn't you stall? But you couldn't wait, could you?"

"No." She pulled his jacket closer around her. It was warm from the heat of his body, but the chill wasn't going away. "I couldn't be sure. I'm . . . never sure. I have to be the one. Do you mind if we don't talk? I don't feel so good."

"I do mind. If you pass out again, it will scare me to death." He reached over and took her hand and held it tightly. "Stay with me."

"I'll try." She tried to think of something to say that would make him stop being angry with her. It was too difficult. She would just tell him the truth. "They both had to die, you know. When I was tied to that stake at the detention center, I knew what I had to do. I couldn't wait or depend on anyone else. I was . . . looking at those poor prisoners chained to that wall. I thought of all . . . the misery Nicos and Salva had caused. It couldn't go on. And without them in the world, there would be a much better chance of freeing Estefan and the others. So I had . . . to find a way to do it."

"All by yourself."

"It has to be . . . that way. I tried to let you know what direction I was going." She attempted a smile. "And I wasn't entirely by myself. I just had to cement a couple of friendships."

His lips twisted. "Because those jaguars were the only friends you could trust."

"No, they were just part of who I am." She shuddered. "And I'll have nightmares about this night, but I won't regret it."

"You shouldn't regret one instant." His hand tightened on hers. "And if you need someone beside you to ward off those nightmares, call me and I'll be there."

He was silent a moment. "If it's any help to know that eliminating Nicos and Salva did what you wanted, then you should be happy. Removing them made it safe to attack the detention camp. Before I came after you, Mandell was coordinating the attack with Carlos Estefan to free the prisoners."

Relief.

"It does . . . help." She was so tired. She was barely able to keep her eyes open. "But I'm not happy. Too much pain, too many people hurting. But it's good to know that it will stop. . . ." She drew a deep breath. "Could I please go to sleep now?"

"No. Soon. The cave is right up ahead and we'll see what the doctor says." His voice was soft, urgent. "Stay with me. Hold on to me. We'll get there together."

*Together.* Beautiful word. Beautiful thought.

And perhaps it would be okay to let down the barriers and stay with him for this little while. . . .

Santa Fe de Bogotá Hospital
Bogotá, Colombia

Margaret knew it was a hospital room before she opened her eyes. The scent was familiar and unmistakable from the time she'd kept vigil with her friend Eve in that hospital in San Diego.

Then she felt a soft head nuzzling her hand as it lay on the bed.

Juno?

"You must be awake," Cambry said. "Juno never intrudes if it has a chance of disturbing." She opened her eyes and saw Cambry sitting in a chair by the bed. He smiled at her. "Hi."

"Hi," she said. She looked around the room. Green

walls, brown leather chairs, white blinds at the windows. "Where am I? The last thing I remember is getting to the cave and seeing Lassiter drag the doctor out to the van."

"That was over twenty-four hours ago. You're in Bogotá. We got you and Patrick out by helicopter as soon as we heard that Mandell and Carlos Estefan had secured the detention camp."

"They're all safe?"

Cambry nodded. "Brukman is dead; Stockton was picked up later in the hills. We had a few casualties but no other fatalities."

"Lassiter?"

"He stayed in here with you all last night, but they're operating on Patrick this morning and he's with him now."

She stiffened. "Patrick's not doing well?"

Cambry made a face. "We knew the trip would be rough on him, but I guess we waited long enough, and he seemed to take it pretty well. But Lassiter is moving him to Johns Hopkins tomorrow, and the doctors wanted to reset that bone in his leg before they let him go."

She let out her breath. "Good. You scared me."

"That's nothing compared to what you did to Lassiter. He was a raving basket case when you passed out after he got you to the cave. Dr. Armando said he thought it was just shock and loss of blood, no internal damage, but Lassiter lost it."

"Lassiter never loses it."

"Whatever you say." Cambry shrugged. "Anyway, Lassiter has a common blood type, and the doctor gave you a transfusion before we whisked you and Patrick to the helicopter. You had another one when you reached the hospital. But you still wouldn't wake up." He smiled gently. "And after Lassiter told me what you did in that forest, I can see why you'd want to dig a dark hole to recover. However, Lassiter wanted to yank you out and make sure there wasn't damage we couldn't see."

"No damage." She looked down at her bandaged shoulder. "This feels stiff and sore, but I can move my arm. That must be good. I'll probably be fine soon." She tilted her head and smiled. "And here you are again, taking care of the sick and wounded. You must be tired of it, Cambry."

"I could probably use a change of occupation. A little more activity would be welcome. But, no, I'm not tired of it." He looked down at Juno. "The two of us have kept Patrick alive these last few days. That was worth it." He stood up and took out his phone. "Which reminds me that I promised to call Lassiter the minute you woke. If you'll excuse me, I'll get that out of the way." He was placing the call as he wandered over to the window. "Then I'll see if I can get the nurse to find you something to eat."

Margaret watched him as he began to speak and then closed her eyes again. She felt drained and she had to begin to gather her strength.

*Sad?*

She opened her lids to look down at Juno's huge brown eyes. *No, not sad. Tired. Sad things have happened. But it's better now. And Patrick is better, and you helped to make him that way.*

*Yes, I didn't let him go away. She said that I did good.*

Margaret went still. *She?*

*You're surprised? But you told me she might come back. Suddenly she was just here. Though sometimes I get confused. She's . . . different. But it doesn't matter. She's here.*

Margaret could feel the tears sting her eyes. *No, it doesn't matter. I'm glad you have her again. And when you have the pups, I'm sure she'll be there with you.*

*It's going to happen soon. There are three and they're very eager to be born.* She tilted her head. *It will be good, won't it?*

*Wonderful.*

*And she says I have to pay attention to you and you'll choose what's best for us. You are not her, but you can still be my friend. You don't have to be her. Will you do this?*

*Oh, yes.* Margaret reached out and gently stroked the retriever's silky head. She could feel the boundless love that was Juno reaching out to her, enfolding her. *I will never be her. Why should you need two? I am only myself. But it would be my privilege. . . .*

"You're not supposed to be up yet," Cambry said in disapproval when he came in that evening and saw Margaret, fully dressed, sitting on the edge of the bed. "Lassiter won't like—"

"Lassiter is too busy right now to be a watchdog over anyone. He stuck his head into the room this afternoon to tell me that he was flying back to the detention camp for a few hours to meet with Father Dominic and arrange to have the monks housed until he could build them another monastery. He said that Carlos Estefan had already arranged for medical attention for the prisoners, but he needed to check on that, too." She made a face. "As usual, Lassiter has to be in control."

"Evidently not in control of you," Cambry said drily. "How did you get yourself dressed with that bad shoulder?"

"With great difficulty. I almost went back to bed afterward."

"Which you should have done."

She shook her head. "I want to see Patrick. I checked with the head nurse and she said that he'd be allowed short visits after a few hours' rest following that bone reset."

"Why not wait until tomorrow?"

She shook her head. "It has to be tonight. The only question is whether I can talk you into getting a wheelchair to take me to him. The nurses would have a fit if they saw me trekking through the halls."

"But you'd do it anyway if I don't get you the wheelchair?" He held up his hand. "Wait. I'll be right back."

He was true to his word and a couple minutes later he wheeled the chair into her room. "Okay. Hop in." But he didn't wait. He carefully helped her down from the bed and onto the chair. "Ten minutes and you're back in bed, okay?"

"Okay." She motioned to Juno. *Come on. It's time you were back on duty. I like your company, but he needs you.*

*I know.* Juno trotted down the hall beside Margaret's wheelchair. *I help him heal. I didn't know I could do it, but she showed me. I couldn't heal her, but it's good that I can help him.*

*Very good.* Cambry was wheeling her into Patrick's room and Juno immediately left her and went over to Patrick's bed and laid her chin on Patrick's hand.

Patrick's eyes were closed, but he lifted his hand and stroked Juno's head. "Hello, girl. I missed you." His voice was still weak, but light-years stronger than it had been a few days ago. He had faint color in his cheeks and that was another good sign. He was opening his eyes and saw Margaret being wheeled across his room. "It's good to see you, Margaret. Lassiter told me that you were on the sick list, too." He looked at her bandaged shoulder. "He didn't tell me why. My fault?"

She shook her head. "It started a long time before I met either of you. I'll tell you about it sometime." She reached out and touched his hand. "I wanted to see you. You're looking much better. Now I know you're going to get well."

"I think you may be right." He smiled faintly. "And I'm finding it fairly incredible."

"But it's going to take you a long time. So I'm going to put you to work."

He looked at her warily.

"Juno needs something to do and someone to care about for the next year or so. And then there are her three pups who will need care and training. Pups can be rambunctious and a real headache, but they're worth it. I figure by the time that you get them all straightened out, you'll be straightened out, too." She beamed at him. "Isn't that a good idea?"

"*Four* dogs?"

"You'll like it. And it won't be forever. Your job with Lassiter would take you away from them too much. They'd be lonely. I'll find more permanent work for them once you get well. When you're ready, someday I'll show up on your doorstep and take them away. Though probably by that time you'll want visiting rights."

"I imagine I would," he said drily.

"Then it's settled." Her smile was luminous. "It's the right thing to do, Patrick. I'll send Juno with you when you go to Johns Hopkins tomorrow."

"Send? Lassiter told me that you'd be going with us."

"Did he? But he didn't discuss it with me. Lassiter has this guilt thing about me and he's always trying to find a way to keep me bored and safe." She got to her feet, leaned forward, and kissed him on the forehead. "Good-bye, Patrick. I'll be in touch. Heal fast."

"I will." His eyes closed. "Otherwise, you might wish another dog on me. Four is quite enough."

Cambry was chuckling as he wheeled her out of the room. "If Patrick wasn't sedated, he might have trouble sleeping tonight."

"You know Juno will be good for him. You'll have to stay with him for a while until he's out of bed and on his feet, but then it will work itself out." She was suddenly exhausted. That first burst of adrenaline was gone. "Now I'm ready to go to bed. You may chauffeur me back to my room." She made a grandiose, imperious gesture with her good hand. "Home, Cambry."

3:45 A.M.

Darkness.

But she knew Lassiter was somewhere in the room.

She opened her eyes and saw him standing a few feet from her bed. "Hi," she said drowsily. "When did you get back?"

"Just a few minutes ago. I didn't mean to wake you. I just wanted to be sure you were all right." He took a step closer to the bed. "Are you?"

"I'm fine." She yawned. "So much for being back in a couple of hours."

"It all turned out to be more than I expected."

"Of course it did. That's your life, Lassiter. I've only been with you for a short time and I've learned that."

"The circumstances with us were extraordinary."

"Yes, but so is your life. I understand. I told you: I accept you as you are. Are the monks going to be okay?"

"Of course. It won't be the same for them, but I'll work out things to compensate. I have a few ideas. I'll tell you about them tomorrow. We leave at eleven."

"Go to bed. Good night, Lassiter."

His brows rose. "Am I being dismissed?"

"I'm too tired to talk to you tonight."

He nodded. "I'll get out of here." His eyes narrowed on her face. "But I'm getting very uneasy. You're always honest. If you can't be honest, you evade. I believe you're being evasive, Margaret."

"Yes." She reached up with her good arm and pulled him down to her. "But I want you to kiss me. I'd do it myself, but I'm having trouble with—"

She stopped as his lips covered hers, stopping breath, giving life. She made a sound deep in her throat as her arm pulled him closer.

Joy? Sex? Yes. And something brighter, stronger, deeper . . .

She pushed him away. "I don't suppose you'd have sex with me now?"

"Shit." He looked down at her. "No, I will not. Although it's almost killing me. You're lying there in a hospital bed, you're wounded, you're hurting, and I believe you're trying to distract or substitute. Or do you think you're sensing I'm in pain again and want to help me? What the hell's happening, Margaret?"

She was the one who was in pain, she wanted to tell him. Sex would have been nice, but she really wanted to hold him, feel the strength, let the essence of what he was envelop her. But that was too dangerous. "I didn't think you would. I just thought I'd try." She closed her eyes. She said again, "Good night, Lassiter."

She could feel his gaze on her face and sensed his explosive frustration.

Then she heard him turn and head for the door. "Tomorrow, Margaret." If the door hadn't been cushioned for silence, she knew he would have slammed it.

She could feel the tears sting her eyes as she opened them again to stare into the darkness. It was stupid to feel this weak and sad. It was a beautiful world and Lassiter was only a part of it. She would be fine in a week or a month. She would just work hard, keep moving, and let the sun reach out to her.

She would be fine.

Next Day
9:40 A.M.

This backpack is awkward, Margaret thought with frustration. There was no way she could put it on her shoulders with this bandage and sling. She just had to carry it by the straps. Oh, well, she'd work something out once she got away from the hospital. It was only important she move fast right now.

She stepped off the curb at the front entrance of the hospital and lifted her hand to gesture to one of the cabs at the taxi stand at the bottom of the driveway.

"Going somewhere?"

She stiffened and then turned to see Lassiter coming out of the door behind her.

His lips twisted. "Busted, Margaret."

She tried to smile. "I guess I am. I was hoping I'd be gone before you came to pick up Patrick. Did he tell you I wasn't going with you?"

"No. He was busy with his doctors this morning. But I could read the signs last night." He took the backpack from her and nudged her toward the little park across the street. "I would have had to be blind not to tell that you were trying to skip out on me." His lips tightened. "Would you like to tell me why? You're wounded, alone, and in a foreign country. The sensible thing would be for you to let me take you back to the United States and get you well and strong. Anyone would say that's the least I could do after what you did for me."

"Would they?" She didn't look at him. "Then they would be wrong. I did what I had to do and most of it was for me . . . and Rosa. But I knew you'd feel like this. I even told Patrick you had this guilt thing going where I was concerned."

"I have all kinds of things going where you're concerned," he said roughly. "Lust, gratitude, pity, admiration, amazement are a few to begin with . . . and, yes, guilt. But that's way down on the list these days." They had reached the park and he drew her behind the small graceful fountain. "So stop bullshitting me and tell me the truth. Why won't you let me take you home with me?"

"It wouldn't be a good idea." She moistened her lips. "We're nothing alike, Lassiter." She shook her head ruefully. "Face it, I'm not like anyone. My father called me a freak and so would most of the people on Earth."

"Would you like me to go after all of them with something more lethal than that frying pan that you used on your father? My pleasure."

"It wouldn't change the fact that I'm different. You have trouble with accepting me as I am. Anyone would, but sometimes it still hurts. And you like to pretend you're not kind, but you are. I don't want to look at you someday and see you're only being kind to me." She smiled shakily. "You never said that there might be a someday, but it could happen. So it would be better to walk away."

"Like you've done all your life? Hell, like I've done all my life?" His eyes were blazing in his taut face. "I feel something for you, dammit. And you feel something for me. So come with me and we'll find out what it is and how we're going handle it."

She shook her head. "And you'd try to take care of me. You'd try to control what I do, what I am. You couldn't help yourself."

"Then you help it. You keep me in line." He said recklessly, "You've fought me every step of the way. You've had no trouble so far."

"Yes, I have," she whispered. "That's why I have to leave you. It would be so easy, Lassiter."

He went still. "Margaret?"

"No, it's not going to work."

"The hell it won't." His narrowed gaze was searching her face. "But maybe not now. I can see that you're squaring your jaw and getting ready for battle. But what if there's no battle? Just the greatest con of my life because it's no con?"

"No, Lassiter." She took her backpack from him. "You don't need me. You have to take Patrick to Johns Hopkins and get him well. You have a company to run and that monastery to rebuild that's—"

"And what are you going to be doing?" he interrupted. "Where were you heading after you got into that taxi?"

"Monkey Island."

"What?"

"And I told you that I wanted to see the pink dolphins of the Amazon. I figured this was as good a time as any to do it. I need to get my bearings. It's going to feel strange not to be on the run any longer."

"I could help you to—" He broke off. "Forget it. That was automatic."

"Exactly."

"And what next?"

"I'm going to visit my friend Eve Duncan. I want to meet her new son, Michael."

"Well, that would at least get you back on U.S. soil. Am I allowed to help you get documents?"

"I'll manage."

"Without doubt." He stood looking at her. "You see how civilized and reasonable I'm being?"

"I'm impressed."

"Don't be." He was next to her in less than a second. "That's a true con." His hands were framing her face and he was kissing her. "You'd be such an easy mark, Margaret." He was kissing her again. "You *want* to believe me. Against all the odds."

"Yes." She instinctively moved closer to him. "I always did, even when I thought I couldn't trust you."

"And do you think I'd ever give that up? No one has ever given me a gift like that." He held her eyes. "So go and study your pink dolphins. Go and see your friend Eve. Have an adventure or two and let yourself heal. But don't ever think that I'm going to let you go. I tracked you for over a year and I found you when I didn't even know you. Do you think I won't find you when I have a reason like this?" He kissed her again and then let her go. "No way." He turned her around and gave her a gentle push toward the taxi stand. "Call me if you need me. Otherwise, I'll hold out as long as I can and then come after you. Good-bye, Margaret."

"Good-bye, Lassiter." She walked slowly to the closest taxi. She felt dazed and confused, and something less identifiable that was gradually rising to the surface. Then, as the taxi driver opened the door for her, she realized what it was.

Sunlight. Warmth. Joy.

Filling both her and the world with radiance.

And why was she running away from it, when she had sworn she was through with running?

She turned and looked back at Lassiter. "Hey, you sound like some kind of stalker. All that high drama and mega effort." Her brilliant smile held a touch of mischief. "Don't you know that all you'd really have to do is find out from Patrick when I'm going to come to pick up Juno and the pups?"

**Read on for an excerpt from
Iris Johansen's next book**

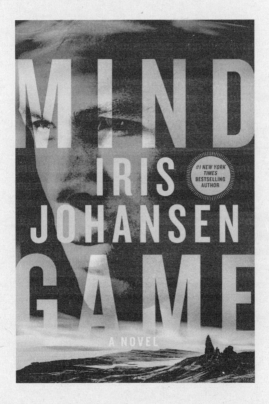

# CHAPTER ONE

Lake Cottage

The woman's face might be beautiful, but it was also the stuff of nightmares.

And Jane MacGuire just wanted it to go *away*!

She jerked upright in bed, her heart pounding.

She closed her eyes, her hands clenched into fists.

She wouldn't do it again. Not again. There wouldn't be any change from the last time. And if there was a change, what could she do about it?

It was only a nightmare. She lay there in the darkness, every muscle of her body stiff and unyielding. Accept it and go back to sleep, she told herself.

But she found herself reaching for her sketch pad on the nightstand even as she gave herself that very excellent advice.

Okay, just *do* it. Get it over with.

She turned on the bedside light and started quickly sketching the woman's face. Same dark flowing hair, high cheekbones, pointed chin, same huge brown eyes, intense, burning eyes, hauntingly familiar eyes, in a face she didn't ever remember seeing before.

Just focus, don't think of anything else but the face

you're drawing. Then it would be over and she would be able to go back to sleep.

Maybe.

Because it wasn't quite the same face. The eyes were still intense, but they held despair.

And this time there was blood.

The lower lip of that beautiful mouth was split as if from a hard blow and a trickle of blood was running from it and down her chin.

It was done!

Now leave me alone, dammit.

Jane threw the sketch pad on the bed and drew a deep, shaky breath.

But there was no question that she wouldn't be going back to sleep anytime soon. She got out of bed and threw on her robe. Okay, get a glass of water and then go out on the porch and get some air.

She padded barefoot to the bathroom and turned on the light. As she drank the glass of water, she noticed her face in the mirror was as strained as that of the woman in the sketch. Her red-brown hair was rumpled and her jaw was taut.

And her stomach was still churning as she remembered the blood running from the lip of the woman in the sketch.

"I don't *need* this. It isn't fair. Find someone else." She turned on her heel and strode through the house to the front porch.

A moment later, she was standing looking out at the lake. If she'd hoped that staring out at those clear, serene depths would soothe her or give her perspective, it wasn't happening.

All she could think about was the blood.

"Problem?" Eve was standing behind her in the doorway. "You should be sleeping. Your flight leaves at eight in the morning."

"I can sleep on the plane." She turned and smiled at Eve. "You're the one who should be asleep. Michael is the most challenging two-year-old on the planet. Between taking care of him and doing your forensic sculpting work, you need all the rest you can get."

"Nonsense. Michael may be a challenge, but he's pure joy." She came out and stood beside Jane and said quietly, "You didn't answer me. Problem?"

It wouldn't do any good to try to lie to her, Jane knew. From the time Eve Duncan and Joe Quinn had adopted her off the streets when she was ten years old, she and Eve had been so close that anything but total honesty was out of the question. Eve was one of the foremost forensic sculptors in the world, but she was also Jane's best friend. They had been through tragedy and joy together, and now that Eve had given birth to a son, Michael, Jane had been privileged to share that with Eve and Joe, too. "Nothing that I can't handle." She made a face. "Maybe I'm a little sad to be going back to Scotland and leaving you and Joe and the baby. Three weeks wasn't long enough."

"Jane."

"It's the truth." She grinned. "But I was getting to the other." She glanced out at the lake. "I grew up here on this lake and I thought the familiarity would be soothing. It appears not to be happening tonight."

"Why not try me? I'm a hell of a lot better than that lake in the soothing department." Her arm slipped around Jane's waist. "I've been told I have excellent credentials."

"Yes, you do." She felt a rush of love as she looked at her. Eve's face was always intelligent and intriguing, but these days she seemed to glow. "But I'm out in the real world with a career as a budding artist these days. I was trying not to bother you with something that's—" She shrugged. "I just feel helpless. I don't know what I—"

"First, you're not a budding artist; you're totally brilliant," Eve said firmly. "Second, you know there's no such thing as bother when it's family. Talk to me. Or we'll be out here all night."

She meant it, Jane knew. Family was everything to all of them. She drew a deep breath. "Dreams. I've had dreams for the past six nights."

Eve went still. "Cira?"

"No." But it was natural that Eve would jump to that conclusion. At seventeen, Jane had experienced a period when she had dreamed constantly of a young actress from ancient Herculaneum. She had even been so obsessed that she had researched and found evidence that the young woman had actually existed. "Not Cira. But it's a woman." She frowned. "Or girl. At first, I thought she was younger, but now she's different. . . ."

"You're not being clear, Jane."

"*She's* not being clear," Jane said in frustration. "At least when I was dreaming about Cira, I had a story. I knew what was happening in her life. The dreams unraveled, telling me her story. I might have believed I was crazy and it was pure fantasy, but I *knew.* I don't know anything about this woman. All I have is a face. I go to sleep and then her face is there before me. Then I wake up and I have to sketch what I've seen. I *have* to do it." She moistened her lips. "And I think she's scaring me."

"Scaring you? Why?"

"Because I think she's afraid. Oh, she's fierce and angry and bold, but I think she's afraid. And this time there was blood." She swallowed. "And I think I know her. She's . . . familiar."

"You sketched her every time you had the dream?"

She nodded. "I *had* to do it. It was compulsive."

"May I take a look at them?"

"Why not?" She turned and went back to her bedroom and snatched the sketchbook from the bed. When she got back to the porch, Eve was curled up on the porch swing. Jane turned on the porch light and handed her the sketchbook. "Here she is." She sat down beside Eve. "She. But I feel as if I should know her name."

"She's that familiar to you?" Eve was slowly going through the sketches one by one. "She's lovely. Full of fire and boldness . . ." She gazed more intently. "And you're right: The first sketches appear to be of a girl who is younger than in the later sketches. But the background is the same. . . ." She raised her eyes to meet Jane's. "You only mentioned the face, but you sketched in an entire background scene. Snowcapped mountains, garden . . ."

"I didn't pay any attention to the background. I was only concerned with her face. Why can't I remember her? Did I know her when I was a teenager? Is she familiar to you at all?"

Eve's gaze narrowed on the sketch in her hand. "Not really. Perhaps a hint . . ." She shook her head. "Nothing is clicking." She turned to the last sketch and froze. "Blood."

"I told you."

"But you didn't tell me that she thinks she's going to die."

Jane inhaled sharply. "Why do you say that?"

"Because you drew it right here, Jane," Eve said soberly. "I told you that you were a brilliant artist. It's here in front of you. Look at it again. That's why you're so frightened."

Jane lost her breath as she looked down at the sketch. The fear was stark and raw on that face. Boldness, defiance . . . and fear. Her hands clenched. "I'm afraid because I don't know anything. I'm afraid because I'm helpless to *do* anything. Why do I keep dreaming about her? Why me?" Her voice was shaking. "For all I know, that woman died centuries ago, just as Cira did."

"Or maybe she didn't and is trying to reach you."

"Why me?" she asked again. "I'm not even sure I've ever met her."

"How do I know? Strange things happen. People are chosen. You know that I believe there's a plan for all of us. At times, the plan seems unbearably painful, like when I lost my little daughter, Bonnie. Like the night Trevor, the man you loved, was shot. But sometimes we get lucky and have the chance to make the plan a little brighter for ourselves or someone else." Eve closed the sketchbook. "Maybe you're the only one this woman could reach. You were sensitive to Cira, but she was gone centuries before you were born and there was nothing you could do for her. Perhaps it's your turn to reach out to someone you *can* help."

"You know I've never been entirely sure that I had any actual connection to Cira. Those dreams could have been figments of my imagination."

"Because you're stubborn and a realist who hates to admit to anything that she can't see and touch." Eve smiled. "But those dreams of Cira have dominated you in so many ways. I believe she's as much alive to you as the rest of us in your life. Even when you fight acknowledging that Cira actually existed and reached out to you, you're still drawn to everything connected to her. You spent months on the Internet and in libraries tracking down references to her. When you discovered she might have fled from that erupting volcano in Herculaneum to Scotland, you tracked her down to a connection with the MacDuff clan." She reached out and touched Jane's cheek affectionately. "And you've been at Gaelkar, Scotland, with the MacDuffs for almost two years, trying to find Cira's treasure. Not because you want the treasure itself; you just want proof that your Cira exists."

"But I don't have that proof yet." She looked at the sketchbook. "And if I don't, then maybe I'm just nuts and I need to see a shrink."

"But what if you don't have time to wait for proof?" Eve asked. "Six nights in a row? And each one of these sketches shows an escalation. Something's happening to make her more afraid every time she comes to you."

Jane moistened her lips. "Maybe it's already happened. Maybe she's not even alive, Eve."

Eve was silent. "It's possible, I suppose. Do you believe that, Jane?"

"No!" The rejection came instantly. "I don't want to believe it. She wants to *live*. She's out there somewhere. But I could be wrong."

"Or you could be right."

"And what am I supposed to do about that? Look in your crystal ball. All I see is her face."

"And the background. She makes sure that she's giving you the background with every sketch. Study them and see if you can come up with something. Research. Go on the Internet, as you did when you were tracking down Cira."

"It was easier to do research on Cira. That was history."

"And this may be a matter of life and death," Eve said quietly. "Stop being stubborn and do your job, Jane. Isn't that what you were going to do anyway? You're out here fretting and giving yourself arguments pro and con when you know you have to see if you can help her." She paused. "So what's your first move?"

"Eve."

"The Internet?"

She sighed. "No, I can start doing that on the plane while heading back to Scotland. I'd like to ask Joe to take one of the sketches to the precinct in the morning and run it through the missing persons database and see if he can come up with anything. She was hurt in that last sketch. Someone struck her. It might be a stranger or a supposed friend or a member of her own family." Her lips twisted.

"Who knows? How many times have you run across the murder of a child caused by people who should have been taking care to keep the child safe, Eve?"

"Too many. But this isn't a helpless child; this is a woman who is fighting back." She got to her feet and handed Jane the sketchbook. "And you're fighting back, too. What's the next step?"

"Identify that mountain range in the background. *National Geo* might help."

Eve chuckled. "Listen to you. This has all been simmering in your mind for how long?"

"I told you: I really didn't notice the background." Or did I? Jane wondered. She wasn't even looking at the sketches, and that mountain range was before her, down to the last detail. "Well, maybe I did."

"Maybe you did," Eve said softly. "Choose the sketch you want to give Joe."

"I will." She made a face. "But he'll probably think it's a waste of time."

"No, you know Joe better than that. He's a realist, too. But he went through that Cira business with you when you were seventeen. And since he's a police detective, he realizes that black and white can sometimes end up gray or even scarlet. He'll get you what you need." Eve leaned forward and kissed her forehead. "And now I'll say good night. If we keep talking, neither of us will be able to function in the morning." She started to turn away and then stopped. "You said you needed to know her name. It's bothering you. So give her one."

"What?"

"Give her a name. Do you remember when I was pregnant with Michael that I felt I had to know his name so that I could be closer to him?"

"I believe this is a little different, Eve," she said drily.

"It doesn't have to be her true name. I give my reconstructions a name before I begin working on them, so that I can form a connection with them."

"I know you do." She had grown up watching Eve work on those pitiful skulls and had known that every one was personal and special to her. "But she may not even exist."

"She'll exist for you if you give her a name. I think she exists for you now anyway." She turned away and headed for the door. "Good night, Jane."

"Good night. Thank you, Eve. I'm sorry to disturb your night. I hope I didn't wake Michael."

"You didn't wake him." Eve turned and smiled at her. "Who do you think sent me out here? He was already restless. I believe Michael was worried about you and sending out vibes. He'll sleep better now that I've done something about you."

"And you'll sleep better," Jane said. The closeness of the bond between Eve and her son was remarkable and far beyond the ordinary. Jane wasn't sure that she knew the full extent of that tie, but she was just grateful that Eve had been given this special child after all the heartache she had gone through after losing seven-year-old Bonnie all those years ago. "Between the two of you, I feel as if I've been railroaded."

Eve's brows rose. "Do you?"

"No, just kidding. As usual, you've managed to cut through all the fog and clarify. You and Michael are a great team."

"With a great deal of help from his father." Eve blew her a kiss. "See you in the morning."

The next moment, the door closed behind her.

Jane gazed after her for a moment before she looked down again at the sketchbook. She'd been telling the truth. She did feel clearer and more focused now that she'd talked to Eve. Yes, she still had doubts that this dream was anything but pure imagination, but Eve was right: She had to explore before she could take a chance on dismissing those dreams. So research, but don't become obsessed. Look upon it as an interesting exercise.

A name. Eve had wanted her to give the woman a name.

Why not?

She opened the sketchbook and looked down at the first sketch. In this one, the woman looked younger than she did in the later sketches. Maybe only eighteen or nineteen. Still intense, still burning and bold, but somehow more youthful.

A name . . .

*Lisa.*

The name came out of nowhere.

Not bad.

She looked at the second sketch.

*Lisa.*

She flipped to the third sketch.

*Lisa.*

Whatever. She wasn't going to sit here all night and try to think of names when her mind seemed to be stuck on that one. It didn't matter anyway.

"Okay. Lisa it is." She closed the sketchbook and got to her feet. "Now either let me go back to sleep or tell me what I'm supposed to do to help you." She moved across the porch and went inside the house. "I'll take a stab at finding you tomorrow, but I can't promise anything. . . ."

But she could still see that drop of blood trickling from Lisa's cut lip.

And she could see those huge dark eyes staring out at her with fear and a knowledge of her own mortality.

"Well, maybe I'll spend more than just tomorrow," she murmured. "But *help* me, dammit."

\* \* \*

Eve was smiling as she passed Michael's nursery. *Satisfied?*

*Satisfied.*

*Jane can really take care of herself, you know. She didn't need us. She would have worked it out for herself.*

*But you would have gone to her anyway.*

*More than likely. Now go to sleep, Michael.*

*I will. Only waiting for you . . .*

He was gone, slipping away into sleep like the healthy toddler he was.

And thank God he is that healthy, she thought as she opened the bedroom door and glided over to the bed where Joe was sleeping. Though no one could call her son exactly normal, he was healthy and caring and possessed a joy, serenity, and an occasional mischievous streak that was wonderful to be around. Okay, so he seemed to sense emotions and disturbance in those around him and could still link with her as he had when she had been pregnant with him. It had been almost as if they were aware of each other's thoughts, as if they were truly one entity. That might fade in time, but for now she cherished that closeness.

She slipped out of her robe and slid into bed beside Joe.

"Everything okay?" He rolled over and took her in his arms. "Michael?"

"In a way." She cuddled closer. "It was really Jane." Her lips brushed his bare shoulder and then she rubbed her cheek on the warmth of it. "She's been dreaming again."

He stiffened. "Cira?"

"That was my first question. No, someone else. A woman, but Jane doesn't have any idea who she is. She's going to ask you to take her sketch to the precinct in the morning and try to identify her."

"Long shot."

"But you'll do it."

"I'll do it." He made a face. "Maybe we'll get lucky and she'll stop dreaming about her."

"That might not be so lucky for that woman Jane is dreaming about. She may be in trouble." She cuddled closer. "It's not as if this happens that often. Cira has always been the main event, and our practical Jane fought tooth and nail against admitting that dream had any basis in fact. She's fighting this one, too." She paused. "But she's disturbed. She thinks she might know her. I don't want her worrying, Joe. It took Jane a long time to come back after Trevor was killed while trying to save her. She loved him so much, and it scared me that I couldn't seem to help her then. I don't want her spiraling down again."

"You did all you could. Jane just had to have time." He gently stroked the hair at her temple. "And I'll do my best to find this mystery woman as quickly as possible. Definitely no dragging of feet."

"I just wanted to explain. I knew you'd do it."

"Of course, there was no question. Jane is family."

"Family," Eve repeated softly. "I've been thinking a lot about that lately."

"No surprise. It's been less than two years since you gave birth to Michael. You'd be likely to be very family-centric."

"No, that's not it. Or maybe it is. I just feel as if I want to make sure that everything is tight and safe for everyone I love. I want everything that touches them to be just right."

"Not entirely possible." He kissed her. "There's a little thing called fate that we have to look out for. But everything that I can do will be done." He lifted himself on one elbow to look down at her. "And I'll wrestle fate if it comes our way and we don't like it. Anything for you, Eve."

"You're joking. I mean this, Joe."

"I'm not joking. I wouldn't dare." But his face was alight with humor. "I'm just having trouble worrying about the future when I'm so damn happy." He buried his face in her throat. "It's good, isn't it, Eve? Better than ever before," he said thickly. "So don't borrow trouble."

Her arms slid around him. "I'm not borrowing trouble. I feel as if we've been given gifts, and I want to protect them."

"Tell me how."

So that he could go out and battle her dragons as he'd always done since the first day she'd met him. "I'm still thinking about it." She kissed him and whispered, "But I promise you'll be the very first to know when I do."

"It's time for you to leave, Jane." Eve opened the door of Michael's nursery and ruefully shook her head as she saw Jane sitting cross-legged on the floor with her son. "You have a plane to catch. Joe's waiting in the car."

"Just one more minute," Jane said absently as her pencil flew over the sketch she was doing of Michael. "I can finish this once I get to Scotland, but I want to catch . . ." Her voice trailed off as she concentrated on getting the curve of Michael's mouth just right.

"Jane."

"Okay. Okay." She reluctantly closed the sketchbook. "But children change so quickly at this age. I just came in to give him a hug good-bye and I saw the sun coming in the window and his hair looked more red than dark chestnut like it usually does. And then he smiled, and I was lost." She knelt beside Michael and held him close for a moment. "See you next time," she said softly. "You take care of your mother and Joe. Do you hear?"

He cuddled closer to her. "I hear." His small hand touched her cheek. "Jane . . ."

She moved her lips and kissed his palm. "And take

care of yourself, too, young man. We can't do without you." She sat back on her heels and looked down at him. So beautiful, with the satin skin that all very young children had. His wide-set eyes were the same tea color as his father's, but his hair was a shade between red and chestnut that seemed to gather light. He was wearing blue jean overalls and a blue shirt this morning. She had to remember how that blue set off his coloring. She'd only had time to draw his face and hair this time.

She gave him another kiss, released him, and stood up. "I'll be thinking about you."

He nodded. "Me, too." His smile lit his face with a special radiance. "See you soon, Jane."

Adorable. She wanted to go back and scoop him up again.

"Jane," Eve said.

"Coming." She turned quickly and left the room, followed by Eve. "It's your fault, you know. You produced that heartbreaker."

"Did I? Joe and I aren't sure how he showed up on the radar. We just thank God for him. When you finish that sketch, I want it."

"If I don't decide to make it a painting instead. Then you'll have to wait until I finish it and put it on exhibition for a few months. I think this one may turn out to be something special. He's looking up at me so inquiringly and yet you'd swear that he had all the wisdom of the ages."

"Maybe he does. Maybe all children do before their vision becomes clouded by life."

"Nah. It's Michael." She grinned at Eve over her shoulder as she reached the porch. "And it's going to make a hell of a portrait. Which will please my agent, since she's not been getting much of anything but landscapes from me for the last year or so. She says that lake in Gaelkar, Scotland, is very picturesque, but she's ready for something different."

"Hasn't she ever heard of Monet's water lilies? I think there're way over two hundred of those. And that lake is mystical. I loved it when I was there."

"I do, too, when I'm not frustrated." She made a face. "I might have given up trying to help MacDuff find the treasure that Cira brought from Herculaneum if that lake itself wasn't such a puzzle. A lake that never loses its mist, that's totally impenetrable?"

"You're the one who had a dream that led MacDuff to think that Cira's gold might be near that lake. You're entirely to blame for MacDuff's being so obsessed."

"MacDuff's been obsessed about finding the treasure for years. He didn't need an excuse. He's been searching all over the world for light systems that could pierce that mist on the north bank, but he hasn't found any yet. The only reason that I was able to come here and spend the last three weeks was that he was going to Perth, Australia, to some lab that's supposed to have had a breakthrough."

"And did it?"

"I'll know when I get back. I figured that it was time that I let you and Joe have Michael to yourselves." She smiled. "I get too comfortable here and I have to remind myself that I have a life and career of my own."

"That's crazy." Eve frowned. "Every moment you spend with us enriches us. We *need* you."

"You also need your space. In a way, you and Joe have started a new life for yourselves. You have Michael and you also took Cara Delaney into your home. I know she's here as often as she can manage to escape from her classes at Juilliard."

"Which isn't that often," Eve said ruefully. "The trouble with bringing a violin prodigy into your life is that everyone wants a piece of her, including her music teachers. We get her for holidays and some weekends when they don't have her doing special concerts. But Cara calls us every other night and that's good."

"Juilliard is in New York. She couldn't study closer to home?"

"She could; she wanted to do that." She shrugged. "But I couldn't let her. It's all about the music with Cara. She had to have the best. You can understand that, Jane. You've heard her play."

"Yes. She's magnificent. I wonder what she'll be like when she's a little older."

"Time flies. She's almost fourteen." She made an impatient gesture. "But that has nothing to do with the fact that you've mentally set me up with a family that doesn't include you. Not going to happen. We're all family and that's the way we're going to stay."

"I wouldn't do that. I'm not that much of a masochist. You're stuck with me. But I *will* give you space, whether you like it or not." She gave Eve a hug and then started down the steps. "I'll call you when I reach Gaelkar. I'll let you know if I have any more dreams about Lisa."

"Lisa?"

"Lisa." Jane glanced over her shoulder. "It seemed right."

"Then it probably is." Changing the subject, Eve said, "You mentioned MacDuff and Jock Gavin several times since you've been here, but not a word about Seth Caleb. Has he dropped by Gaelkar since you went back there after Michael was born?"

"I've seen him once." She tried to make her tone casual. "He and Jock have become good friends. Jock wanted him to look into something for him and he flew in for the day to talk about it." She saw Eve's expression and answered the unspoken question, "Not for me,

Eve. He barely spoke to me. Caleb is very cool to me
these days."

"Caleb is never cool. Particularly not to you," Eve
said drily. "I can see him simmering. I can see him
burning. I can see him plotting. I can see him waiting
for his chance. Never, never cold. You must have really
pissed him off."

Yes, she had, but she didn't want to talk about it with
Eve right now. "You might say that."

"And he might have deserved it. But I'm having trouble condemning him for anything these days. Not since
the night he saved Michael's life." She added quietly,
"I'll always be grateful to him for that, Jane."

"So will I." Her lips twisted. "But you have to be
careful about being grateful to Caleb. He's fairly ruthless about collecting on his debts."

"I haven't found that to be true so far. I just thank God
that Caleb has that weird ability to control the flow of
blood in everyone around him. It saved Michael." She
met Jane's eyes. "It even saved you once, Jane. That's
two people I love he gave back to me. So until he proves
me wrong, I'm going to consider I owe Seth Caleb big-
time." She smiled. "Now go get on that plane. I can see
Joe is beginning to fret. You'll be lucky if you don't
miss it."

"Right." She ran the rest of the way down the steps.
"I'll try to get back here for Michael's birthday."

"Oh, I think I might see you before that," Eve said.
"You heard Michael. He said he'd see you soon. Michael
is usually fairly accurate."

"From the mouths of babes?"

"I've never thought of Michael as a baby except for
maybe that first week. He's just . . . Michael." Eve called
to Joe as Jane opened the car door. "Stop and bring
home Chinese for lunch, Joe."

"Right," Joe said. "And Jane may join us if she doesn't get in the damn car. Stop talking to her, Eve."

"Sorry," Eve said. "She said it was Michael's fault she was late and then I had to ask about—"

"Bye, Eve." Jane was in the car and swinging the door shut. "Love you."

Eve nodded and waved as the car pulled out of the driveway.

Jane watched her as long as she could see her. "She's so happy, Joe. She glows. I've never seen her like this before."

"Neither have I. I believe it's her turn. I just pray it lasts. Because then it's everyone's turn who loves her." He covered her hand with his own and changed the subject. "Dreams, Jane?"

She grimaced. "Yeah, but I'd rather think about Eve. I don't believe that woman I've been dreaming about is anywhere near as happy. I don't even know if she's a real person. Eve thinks I have to treat her as if she is." She handed him the sketch she'd put into a large envelope. "Thanks for the help, Joe."

"What's family for? Now sit back, relax, and take a deep breath. I'll get you to the airport on time. I just want to take one quick look at the mystery woman." He took the sketch out of the envelope and glanced at it. "Very pretty, but I'm not seeing—" He broke off, his eyes narrowing. "What the hell? Maybe you're right. Familiar. Damn familiar . . ."